CONTENTS

PREFACE

The Fear of Europe

1

I WILL NOT FORGET THE NIGHT when I set off down that dark alleyway I had never come across before. It didn't take long for me to notice a gust on the nape of my neck. A dry gust. And above all phantasmagoric—for I was brave enough to turn around, and found there was no one there. Knowing I was indeed alone, I carried on walking, but it was impossible to act as though the breath of that ghost was not still there, gusting behind me, glacial and barren, straight onto the nape of my neck.

Since then, when I am in Europe, those dark alleyways give rise to strange feelings of foreboding. If perchance I find myself walking along one, I extinguish a part of my fear by evoking a hidden nexus of cultivated citizens who pass through Paris ineluctably, a nexus I know to exist: European citizens, discreetly devoted to the preservation of meaning.

The last century began with this question: "What should we do?" And the present one with another: "What have we done?" For this century, I believe, we should, at long last, invent a constructive and stimulating historic vertigo.

I dream of a spiritual insurrection, a rebirth.

And yet I sense an attraction to the apocalypse. Might it somehow pertain to the proclivity, on the part of American cinema, for special effects, for the destruction of the sets?

In this age of monsters and catastrophes, which wants for even the least bit of beauty, it is important to recall our enduring reliance on the memory of those beautiful biblical apocalypses. I don't know what we would do without them, what we would do if they were not part of our imaginary.

The idea of a common language in Europe forms part of our imaginary as well.

The language of Europe—Umberto Eco says—is translation.

I dream of a Hollywood apocalypse that anticipates a spiritual insurrection, a rebirth, a flourishing, the realization of a truly vertiginous linguistic utopia.

2

I was born in Barcelona, a city where one of my distant relations, a tram conductor—a cousin of my grandfather—ran over and killed the great architect, Gaudí.

It isn't lost on me that my birthplace and my homicidal pedigree leave no room for doubt: I am a European writer. A writer who is conscious, I would add, in the words of Koestler, that art in Europe is in its death-throes, because it cannot live without truth, and it is now years since its truth became lethal.

The fact is, the stories generated by the better part of the European narrative teach nothing but tricks for postponing death, for distracting it, for deferring the moment, so fraught with fear, when we will be forced to face up to that truth that we will be unable to bear. Without going far, this is what happens in many of the tales contained in the anthology the reader now holds in his hands: they may be distinct in style, distinct in the inquietudes they harbor, but at their core, almost all share something in common, something inevitable: the characteristic, vitiated air of a Europe where everything appears soulless and interred for decades, since the time when, on the continent, consent was given to those first unforgiveable, grave errors, and the rise of totalitarianisms was permitted.

It may be I have written this under the influence of the grievous present day. The sun has remained changelessly, ceaselessly at its zenith, and yet, it has stayed hidden the whole time behind tatters that seem to have hung in the air for centuries; tatters made up of a kind of dust as fine as the excess pollen that overlays the earth, an earth I have clearly observed disintegrating with horrifying but lethal indolence.

This may have influenced my mood, but I believe I would have written the same, lethal indolence or no, inasmuch as I never cease to be a writer from Barcelona, of a deeply homicidal European pedigree, disposed to taking long nocturnal strolls, always wracked with acute feelings of fear; a writer still confounded by the intimation that, a hundred years ago, Europe took a wrong road; a writer who seeks words in order to reign in a paralyzing kind of horror that drives him to an endless vertigo, from which he only manages to escape when he sets off, devoting himself to walking and thinking, in order to return home thereafter and close dramatic circles, and sit at his desk and, through the ever-frustrated conjuration of his terrors, try to control the fear that reappears relentlessly, tormenting him at every turn.

Paralyzing horror, I have said. This is an impression so heavy with truth, it can only be expressed comfortably in the context of a literary work, for nowhere else would accommodate a declaration that makes mention of this immobilizing fear and at the same time speaks of Europe with the purpose of telling us that the continent has already passed a number of decades sheathed in its death shroud. For these are not the sort of truths you can air to your friends on Saturday night without their thinking that you've drunk too much. Nor are they truths you can say aloud — for example, during an interview with the press — without blinking. Or in an article about international politics. It sounds too literary, to say Europe is sheathed in its death shroud ...

Or does it sound too true?

All this has done nothing more than show me that every day, with increasing certainty, there remains an important role for writing to play, a role related to truths that find their most fitting expression in the terrain of the literary and, paradoxical though it may seem, their most concrete expression in fiction. Because, while many confuse reality with what is stated on the nightly news—Nabokov already said that reality is highly overrated—I have the sense that literary fiction today is the best, if not the only, path to take to approach the truth.

In fact there is a deeply strange episode in the history of the epic genre, a chapter that has yet to be written and will include all those— from Cervantes and Sterne up to Kafka and Bolaño—who fought with titanic effort against every form of falsification and imposture;

a fight the paradoxical slant of which is evident, as those who waged battle in this way lived sunk to their necks in the world of artifice and fiction. Be that as it was, it is from that tension that the greatest pages of contemporary literature have emerged.

3

Now then: how do I manage, when I am talking in front of my Saturday friends, or when I speak or write for the press on the theme of fragile Europe? Naturally, by telling them things I do not remotely believe, because, for me, they pull back in an alarming way from the fundamental truth.

Quite clearly, in order to say what I do not believe, I employ the least literary language possible. I say, for example, that I still have faith in the European Union and that I will therefore vote in its parliamentary elections. The part about faith is a falsehood; that I will vote is true.

I plan on voting because, when all is said and done, what I do in my everyday life always turns its back on the truths that I only dispense when I write fiction; in other words, independent of my awareness that the pure, hard fact of Europe in its death-shroud is the fundamental truth, I will go on supporting the almost universal desire to *re-unite* and will continue to show up at the ballot boxes of my tumultuous Europe as though nothing were happening, always bearing in mind that it is necessary both to feel the weight of memory and to try to escape that memory of the horror, even if only for the sake of something resembling a future and the possibility of establishing another horizon.

I will go on voting, that is to say, always moved by the vague, desperate daydream of a belief that we might still leave the ruins behind and invent a future.

But at the same time—let us not deceive ourselves—I will continue to dream of a kind of Hollywood apocalypse preceding the instauration of a linguistic utopia of true vertigo: the idea of a common language of Europe, which, as Eco noted, will be called translation.

In that linguistic utopia I find the necessary equilibrium between the fundamental truth that my literature expresses unequivocally and the falsehoods I go scattering around outside its limits, trying not to be seen, contemptuously, as a person "excessively literaturized."

4

The roadmap through that chimera in which I have found the necessary equilibrium between the fundamental truth and the "deliteraturized" is sketched out, in a certain way, by Camille de Toledo in his book *Le hêtre et le bouleau: Essai sur la tristesse européene* (The Beech and the Birch: An Essay on European Sorrow), translated into Spanish by Juan Asís. Here we are told that the current identity crisis of the European Union, as well as its habitual tensions, may be related to a neglect of language and, intoning a paean to translation, to the art of intermediation; in other words, he insists that we "understand European citizenship by becoming translators, exerting ourselves to pass over from one context to another, from one grammar to another, and from one culture to another."

Camille de Toledo's utopia transports us to a 2040 where there will function an ingenious translator-society. The situation he describes will be as follows: after one or two generations, children born in Europe have learned to speak our language—remember: this language, according to Eco, is translation—and numerous bodies of work have been translated or retranslated in their entirety. The public willingness to promote a culture of translation has revived an enthusiasm for knowledge, for understanding, for the humanities. Children from the more recent migrations feel recognized, because school speaks to them about their languages, about what their adopted languages take away from their childhoods, from memory. Translation courses generate abundant vocations. Indeed, the myth of Babel is interpreted again, reread, retranslated ... We laugh at misunderstandings, are moved by contretemps, we play around at the interstices. And we see, throughout Europe, increasingly active translators' organizations that also bid for politics to be reconceived in their image: a politics beyond languages and beyond nations. When a future constitution is written, the discussions center on the meaning of the word "freedom" in Hungarian, of the word "fraternity" in Turkish. Solidarities are born across frontiers, and the voices of the speakers can once again be heard without headphones. Legibility returns, but endowed this time with a poetics — the expressiveness, the emotion, of the person who knows how to translate on his own. We dream of shedding the archaic skin of nationhood. Relying on the parliament, we impose our will upon the national executive governments. Newspapers speak of a "translators' revolution."

It is a Babel in reverse, where everyone can truly understand one another. It is the triumph of a common language in Europe: translation.

5

Yesterday I went back to the alleyway that I had never come across before. And I noted again the frozen, glacial gust. At some point, I thought, someone will certainly end up asking me for a light, or will try to assault me, or will make me believe they are going to shoot me, and finally will shoot me and kill me.

Behind lowered blinds I seemed to hear a voice that said the alleyway did not appear on any map. I imagined running across pimps, small-time conmen, exceptionally lascivious hookers, vagabonds who smiled at me ominously.

The sordid climate of the alleyway did not keep me from meditating, though my thinking, it is true, showed itself increasingly incapable of escaping the sordid climate created by what I was imagining about that very place.

I was coming to understand that we are afraid.

It is the fear of Europe.

Since we have forbidden ourselves from imagining heaven on earth, we prefer to expel any utopia from our world. And thus, ferocious vigilantes that we are, we control every possibility that the idea of heaven might meddle in our lives. We prefer to be possessed by the nightmare of the shady alleyway, the frozen gust that keeps us subject to the idea of disgrace.

But yesterday was lucky. I was pushing on through that darkness when I was assaulted by an intimate insurrection, a rebellion arising from my weariness of so much skepticism. With a measure of astonishment, I saw all at once, as if it was taking place right there before me, the re-foundation of Europe through the multiple identities and spoken languages of our extraordinary common patrimony. I kept on walking, almost incredulous. I will never forget that, in that moment, the alleyway seemed to admit—in all the languages—the first voices of the day.

ENRIQUE VILA-MATAS

TRANSLATED FROM SPANISH

BY ADRIAN WEST

BEST
EUROPEAN
FICTION
2015

JOANNA WALSH

Worlds from the Word's End

WE NEED TO TALK.

I'm writing to you so you'll understand why I can't write to you any more.

I could never talk to you. We didn't exactly have a meaningful relationship. Perhaps that's why I have all these words left when so many others have none at all. The postal system's still working, so I expect you will get this letter. Bills continue to be sent by mail (figures accompany icons: an electric light bulb, a gas flame, a wave) as do postcards (wordless views). And letters do still arrive (addresses are roughly sketched maps, in case you wondered) so I'll take this opportunity to get my words in edgeways while I still can, folded into a slim envelope. When they drop through your letterbox, I hope that they don't fall flat.

It's the old story: It's not you, it's me. Or, rather, it's where we're at. We don't talk any more, not now, not round here. You know how things have changed. But I have to tell you all over again because what happened between us seemed to be part of what happened everywhere.

It was more than a language barrier. I thought we were reading from the same page, but it was really only you that ever had a way with words. Sometimes you put them into my mouth, then you took them right out again. You never minced them, made anything easier to swallow, and the words you put in for me were hardly ever good. They left a bitter taste. As for me, you twisted my words and broke my English until I was only as good as my word: good for nothing, or for saying nothing. I stopped answering and that was the way you liked it. You told me you preferred your women quiet. You wanted to increase your word power? Trouble is, you didn't know your own strength.

Communication went out of fashion about the same time as we stopped speaking. It started, as does almost everything, as a trend. Early adopters seeking something retro, as usual looked to their grannies, their aunties: silent women in cardigans who never went out. Who knows if these women were really quiet? I doubt the hipsters knew, any more than they could tell how cheese-makers or hand-knitters really went about their business. Whether their adoption of these women's silence was a misinterpretation of the past or a genuine unearthing, it happened. Initially, gatherings—I mean parties, that sort of thing—became quieter, then entirely noiseless. Losing their raison d'être, they grew smaller and eventually ceased to exist altogether, in favor of activities like staying in, waiting at telephone tables for calls that never came.

We scarcely noticed how the silence went mainstream, but if I had to trace a pattern I'd say our nouns faded first. We tried abbreviations, acronyms, txtspk, but they made us blue, reminded us of the things we used to say, and, not being a literary nation, we'd never quite got our heads around metaphor. We'd taken ourselves at our word, literally: so that, in everyday speech the supermarket became "that big shiny thing where you buy other things," your house, "the building one block from the corner, count two along." A little later this morphed into, "that place a little way from where you go round, then a bit further on." We began to revel in indirectness. Urban cool-hunters would show off, limiting themselves to, "that over there," and finally would do no more than grunt and jerk a thumb. They looked like they had something better to do than engage in casual conversation. We provincials were dumbstruck.

Grammar went second. I'm not inferring we were disinterested. If I was to speculate—between you and I—those most effected were people that thought too much of who they had words with. As for myself, I'd refute that our famous last words could of lingered. Irregardless of other uses, we couldn't eat them. Crumbling by the day, months went by, 'til we found our frequent grammatical errors just one thing less to lose. In other words, we began to say, "'kinda" a lot, and "sort of" but, y'know . . . We lost heart and failed to end sentences.

We have no sayings, now, only doings, though never a "doing

word." Actions speak louder than words (a wise saw: if only I'd looked before I ever listened to you), especially as we can't remember very far back. We have erased all tenses except the present, though for a while we hung on to the imperfect, which suggested that things were going on as they always had done, and would continue thus.

At least schooling is easier now there are only numbers and images — and shapes, their dimensions, their colors. We don't have to name them: we feel their forms and put them into our hearts, our minds, or whatever that space is, abandoned by language. We trace the shapes of the countries on school globes with our fingertips. And they all feel like tin.

Being ostensibly silent, for a while social media was still a valid form of communication, though touch-keyboards began to be preferred to those with keys. On websites people posted photos of silent activities, as well as those involving white noise — drilling, vacuuming, using the washing machine — during which communication could patently not take place. Some questioned, in the comments boxes below, whether these photos might be staged, but doubts were put to rest when the majority began to frown even on the use of writing. Some of us wondered whether Internet forums themselves could have been the final straw: the way we'd wanted what we said to be noticed and, at the same time, to remain anon: the way we'd let our words float free, detach from our speech-acts, become at once our avatars and our armor.

Trad media was something else. The first to go "non-talk" were high-end cultural programs, those "discussing" art and books. Popular shows featuring, say, cooking, gardening, home improvement, and talent contests, relied on sign language and were frowned upon by purists. On the highbrow broadcasts, critics' reactions were inferred from their facial expressions by a silent studio audience. Viewers smiled or frowned in response, but their demeanors remained subtle, convoluted, suited to the subjects' complexities. Fashions in presenters changed. Smooth-faced women were sacked in favor of craggy hags whose visual emotional range was more elastic. As all news is bad news, jowly, dewlapped broadcasters with doleful eyebags drew the highest pay-packets. This was considered important even on the radio.

There were no more letters to the editors of newspapers. There was no Op to the Ed, then no Ed, but newspapers continued to exist. Their pages looked at first as they had under censorship when, instead of the offending article, there appeared a photograph of a donkey. But, after a period of glorious photography, images also departed, and the papers reverted to virgin. Oddly, perhaps, the number and page extent of sections remained the same. People still bought their dailies at the kiosk: men still slept under them in parks. Traditions were preserved without the clamor of print. It was so much nicer that way.

Not everyone agreed. There were protests, often by unemployed journalists and photographers, but these were mostly silent: we had internalized the impoliteness of noise and were no longer willing to howl slogans. The personal being the political, this extended to domestic life. Fewer violent quarrels were reported. With no way to take things forward, relationships tended to the one-note. Couples who got on badly glared in mutual balefulness; the feelings of those who loved were reflected in one another's eyes.

If, at an international level, there was no news, at a local level there was no gossip, so most of us felt better. We ceased to judge people, having no common standards. The first wordless president fought her (his? its?—as we could no longer give it a name, gender scarcely mattered any more) campaign on a quiet platform, gaze fixed on the distant horizon. He (she? it?) knew how to play the new silence. The opposition, opting to fill the gap left by speech with random actions, was nowhere. A more liberal, thoughtful community emerged. Or so some of us believed. How could we tell?

There were conspiracy theories: a cold war of words conducted by the international literati; uncertain terms between the word banks. Granted, old folks have always complained that a man's word isn't worth as much as it used to be, that promises nowadays are ten-a-penny, but radical economists did chart a steep devaluation. Once, they remembered, you could have had a conversation word for word, though a picture had always been worth a thousand words. That was the system: we knew where we stood, and it was by our words; but the currency went into free-fall: a picture to five thousand, ten thousand words, a million! Despite new coinages, soon it was impossible to exchange a word with anyone, unless you traded in the black market of filthy language, and, if you did, there was always the danger you'd be caught on corners, unable to pay your respects. The government reacted: "please" and "thank you" replaced milk at school break-time and, in order to prevent civil discontent, grown-ups received ration books of good terms. For every provision, of course, a restriction. New laws were parsed: if you didn't keep to the letter of the law, you could be had up in court for uncivil wrongs.

Some clung to individual words to fill the gaps as language crumbled, but, without sentence structure, they presented as insane, like a homeless man who once lived on the corner of my block and carried round a piece of pipe saying, "Where's this fit? Where's this fit?" to everyone he met. Except that the word-offerers didn't form phrases, they just held out each single syllable aggressively, aggrievedly, or hopefully.

As for the rest of us, words still visited sometimes: spork, ostrich, windjammer ... We wondered where they had come from, what to do with them. Were they a curse or a blessing? We'd pick them up where they dropped like ravens' bread on soggy ground.

Of course the big brands panicked, employed marketeers to look into whether we'd ever had the right words in the first place. Naturally, we were unable to read the results of their research. The government launched a scheme (no need for secrecy as there are no rumors): bespoke words were designed along lines dictated by various linguistic systems, and tested. As someone who, until recently, had lived by her words (if there are words to live by: as you know, I actually live by the church), I was involved or, perhaps, committed. Under scientific conditions, we exchanged conversations involving satch, ileflower, liisdoktora, always asking each other if this could be the magic word. We cooed over the new words, nested them, hoping meaning would come and take roost, but meaning never did.

A scattering of the more successful experiments was put into circulation and, for a while, we tried to spread the words at every opportunity. Despite sponsored "word placement" in the movies (which were no longer talkies), the new words slipped off the screen: our eyes glazed over. The problem, as it always had been in our country, was one of individualism. By this stage no one expected words to facilitate communication. The experiment resulted not in a common language, but in pockets of parallel neologisms. Being able to name our own things to ourselves gave us comfort. I suspect some people still silently practice this, though, of course, I cannot tell. I have a feeling their numbers are declining. Even I have stopped. It proved too difficult to keep a bag of words in my head for personal use and to have to reach down into its corners for terms that didn't come out very often. They grew musty. Frankly it was unhygienic.

It was sad to see the last of the signs coming down, but it was also liberating. In the shop that was no longer called COFFEE you couldn't ask for a coffee any more, but that was okay. You could point, and the coffee tasted better, being only "that" and not the same thing as everyone else had. It was never the same as the guy behind you's coffee, or the coffee belonging to the person in front. No one had a better cup than you, or a worse. For the first time, whatever it was was your particular experience and yours alone. The removal of publicly visible words accelerated. Shop windows were smashed, libraries were burned. We may have got carried away. As the number of billboards and street signs dwindled, we realized we had been reading way too much into everything. What did we do with the space in our minds that had constantly processed what we read? Well ... I guess we processed other things, but what they were we could no longer say.

Some of us suspected that new things had begun to arrive, things there had never been names for. They caused irritation, as a new word does to an old person, but because there was nothing to call these new things, there was no way to point them out or even to say that they hadn't been there before. People either accommodated them or didn't. We're still not sure whether these things continue to live with us, or if we imagined them all along.

Those people who prefer the new silence are frightened that one day the word will turn. It's a feeling I share, if warily. Words, we had thought, were the opposite of actions, but, delving deeper, we found they were also opposed to themselves. Whatever we said, we knew contained the seed of its opposite. "It's fine today," "I respect you," "Will you take out the trash?" suggested the possibility of bad weather, cruelty, and refusal. It had become so difficult to say anything. Our awkwardness got to us. In the republic of words, "I love you," induced anxiety. "How was your day?" would elicit merely a sigh. I think people just got tired, tired of explaining things they'd already said to one another, exhausted by the process of excavating words with words. We were oversensitive perhaps. Do you think we have dumbed ourselves down?

The last time I saw you we spent days walking around my city. The only voices we heard were foreign: tourists or immigrant workers. You spoke their language but only I could understand the silent natives.

We walked the streets in no direction, following no signs. "What's that billboard for?" you asked, pointing to the wordless yellow one that was all over town. I told you, "That's an advert for the billboard company." You were—temporarily—lost for words. We took photos of the sky disturbed by silent exhalations from the city's rigid gills: air vents linked to aircon, to the underground system, but they were all lungs and no voicebox. They couldn't breathe a word. It was cold, so cold I could see my breath next to yours, solid in the frozen air, mingling with the steam of restaurant dinners, of laundries, with warm gusts of metro dust.

The night you left, we went to a shabby bar by the station, where we drank bad wine. You talked with the people who worked there: an underclass still allowed to speak because they spoke a different language. They could effect the business we despised, butter us with the courtesies we could no longer practice. Their jobs involved asking for our orders (we would point to the desired item on the illustrated menu), telephoning abroad for crates of imported beer and vodka, telling us to have a nice day. Inside, the bar was red as a liver. We worked a little on ours. As we parted we held each other for a little too long and only almost failed to airkiss.

I am interested in failure, as are we all here, because I think it's where we're at. Words failed us a while ago. What will fail us next?

You like women who are quiet? In the end it was not so difficult to let you go: you were only interested in the sound of your own voice. Pretty soon we had nothing left to say to one another. I listened: you looped the same old tape. I tried things that were wordless: I took your hand and pressed it, but feelings meant nothing to you. We were always words apart.

Don't tell me I'm being unreasonable.

Don't talk to me about your girlfriends in the speaking world.

Don't repeat the sweet nothings you whisper to them. Don't tell me about the ones you have yet to meet, who are no doubt wishing aloud for some such coincidence. Don't write back. It is no good calling me: I won't pick up. It's no good texting me or sending me emails. There's no need to tell me anything. I know it all already. And nothing you could say to me would help.

We're in different places. I'm dead to the word, and you don't have a care in it. You're on top of it: it weighs heavy on my shoulders. So I won't go on. I love you and I'm not allowed, won't allow myself to say it any more. There's no future in it. You wouldn't want a wife who didn't understand you, whose eventual resort could only be dumb insolence—just saying. Love's a word that makes the world go round right enough. It wheels and spins like a coin unsure where to land: heads or tails. Wherever it fell, I would have gone right on to that word's end, for want of a better word, and, like other temporary Miss Words, I do most sincerely want a better word, but I can't say I've ever heard of one.

When I see they're still using words in your country, I feel only half-envious, a quarter … I also feel a strong swinge (is that even a word?) of embarrassment and pity. Don't be offended: I'm trying to tell it like it is.

You probably think we've all gone quiet over here, that you'll never hear from us again. Yes it is quiet, but we are still thinking. In ways you can no longer describe.

ARMEN OF ARMENIA

Who Wants To Be a Millionaire?

IF YOU'RE UP FOR IT, LET'S PLAY. You've gotta know *Who Wants To Be a Millionaire?* Just out of curiosity, try your luck. The rules of the game are almost the same, only there are no untouchable amounts, and there are fewer questions: only six and a half, each with four choices of answer. Send your list on February 29, and I'm obligated to make mine public on the same day. One million Armenian Drams are being wagered. You'll get the whole amount, if all of our picks match. Let's start.

QUESTION ONE:
What do you want?

A. To get rid of my other half. I really want to lose my other half, so I can be independent, self-sufficient, and finally live in peace.

B. One million drams. For both of us, my word is more valuable than money. I give myself my word: I will have one million drams on February 29. So, don't worry, I'll hit my target.

C. To use the "phone-a-friend" lifeline. I called, said hi, and repeated your number +374 91 364344, so I could check if you gave the right number or not. It turns out you haven't pulled one on me. "You know, I'm reading your 'Millionaire,' I want to decide which of the choices to pick for the first question." Thanks for the hint.

D. To know the ending. The opening is easy, although a light beginning often promises a heavy finale. So kill in yourself the frivolous wish to become a millionaire right from the get-go, and jump into the game—and not for the money, but driven by the passion for reading.

QUESTION TWO:
What are you looking for?

A. I know you like the palm of my hand. You're not gonna change. You're always gonna bug me. You're gonna caw like a raven till you drive me permanently nuts. I'm looking for a witch-hunter, an assassin who's ready to whack my other half for a million.

B. If I hadn't given my word, I wouldn't even think of answering. It's too late to bail out. Bring me the photo and the money. I do a clean job. I don't leave unwanted traces. You'll be satisfied, no one has complained so far. You need to wire the money in advance. The deadline is February 29. I'm going after someone exactly like you.

C. I guess everyone is looking for their other half. If, like me, they haven't found them, they sure will one day. I had the strangest feeling talking to you. It's like we're the oldest of friends. We're done playing and we're reviewing the future. Oops, I'm digressing. My answer is: to find my other half.

D. I'm looking for the one looking for me. Why isn't anyone looking for me? So I get to be the point of someone's search. It always seems you've made a good choice, then it turns out it's the complete opposite. Elections are always rigged, but no one ever learns their lesson and doesn't vote again. It's something else to get elected. To get that extra vote is so reassuring. It means you're not the only one believing in what you say. To cut it short: Don't vote, let others vote for you. In other words, pick answer D.

QUESTION THREE:
You want to go for a walk?

A. I would, but I can't. I'm not on speaking terms with you. I don't even look you in the eye, let alone go for a walk with you. You know what I mean. I can't see you again. That'll mean feeding the raven, and I want to kill it. I've already found someone who's prepared to do my dirty work for a million. I'm going to pass on the photo and the money. There's no time to waste, soon I'll be free — running around like an ownerless dog. Remember? You'd always call me "an ownerless dog" when we fought.

B. No, I don't. Generally, I've submitted to your literary fraud for the sake of a promise and money. Where have you ever read that a killer goes for a walk with the one who's writing about him? I'm waiting for my client's word so we can meet—I'm expecting the money and my victim's photo. I'm not in the habit of asking questions. I don't care who wants to whack whom and why. He started to tell me about his life. Can you imagine? He was crying on the phone, his voice shook, he said, "Please, don't let him feel any pain. He shouldn't realize what's happened to him."

C. Yes, I definitely do. We're not acquainted personally, but I know you a little already: I've read your stuff; I've got your cell phone number; I know your name; not to mention that peculiar feeling of reminiscing about the future. Going for a walk while chatting— I've got nothing to lose. If not—perhaps. You've warned me—if we don't meet and C turns out to be the right answer, I won't get my million. Rule's a rule—and I play by the rules.

D. Actually, this answer is invalid because logically there are only three choices. Although this may be the only acceptable choice for the author. In any event, it is nuts to suggest going for a walk with one's self. So, this is definitely a trap. I'm sure it will be considered correct, that's why I pick precisely this choice.

QUESTION FOUR:
What are you reading?

A. I'm rereading for the thousandth time the last bit you wrote and want to understand who's written this, me or you? "You're a freak, you live in your world; you think what you want. I'm a freak, I live in my world; I think whatever. We'll meet on February 29 near the Hands monument in Yerevan." We'll both live and find out. Or rather, I'll live and you won't.

B. I read nothing but the newspaper for a long time. Usually, they publish my work on the front pages. I feel sort of appreciated. And then, suddenly, weird messages like this: "I'm a freak. I live in my world. I have weird thoughts. Do not try to get to know me or associate with me. Reject my offer to go for a walk. Take the photo and the money quickly and leave. We'll meet near the Hands on February 29."

13

C. A short story entitled "Who Wants To Be a Millionaire?" I've read half, I'm at question four. Some parts are hard to get, but it's not so bad. I like it. The characters express themselves through their choices of answer in the game. And the reader must decide who to believe on each question and thus become a millionaire themselves. I'm also a reader. I have a date with the author, I've already agreed to go for a walk, and I hope I'll win.

D. I really wanted to ask this question. It's the best question for getting to know someone. Nothing happens in life that is not written somewhere and is not possible to read. Someone besides me will read this and I will share my thoughts with him or her, and we'll meet. I read books written for me.

Ask the Reading Audience:
A. *One quarter*
B. *One quarter*
C. *One quarter*
D. *One quarter*

QUESTION FIVE:
What happened to us on February 29?

A. I woke up with a headache on February 29. I took out all the albums from the photo drawer. I was looking for the photo that inspired hatred in me the most. I found one where you look kind of happy, but you're not alone. Someone as happy as you is next to you. You are both smiling, head to head. I tore it and put it in my breast pocket. I took two raw wieners from the refrigerator, swallowed one and put the other one in a bag and took it with me. I might need it on the road. I felt how the first sip of coffee changed the taste in my mouth. I took three more sips and got out of the house, without looking in the mirror. I drove to HSBC, withdrew one million drams from my account. The teller girl didn't smile at me, she just asked: "You're withdrawing the whole amount?" I said yes. People think I'm rich. I have a job, a place of my own, dress nice. Actually, it was my entire savings. I don't need money.

I saw an ownerless dog on the street, felt kinship, but it had a very ragged look, repulsive, invoking nothing but pity. I drew near, he felt my pity. He evaluated me too, in good faith, and groaned. I took the wiener from the bag and threw it in front of him. He looked at me with an eradicating gaze; I froze … his eyes … I've seen these eyes somewhere. He didn't get close, he waited till I left. I drove, turned back and saw that he limped. It's okay; a dog doesn't die from limping. I got to the Hands a little too early. The day—sunny; the weather—chilly; life—evanescent. My raven-killer wasn't there yet. I've always pictured his sad eyes, dressed black from head to toe, befitting a self-respecting assassin. With hair somewhat long, curly and combed back. Height—one eighty centimeters, let him be tall. He doesn't sleep at night—pangs of remorse. He wants a dignified livelihood. He's not content with his luck. Despite his young age, there is a big wrinkle in between his eyebrows from too much frowning. He came, I noticed from afar, with a strange gait, staring down as if looking for something. He drew close—one hundred percent what I imagined, even the wrinkle was there. We greeted each other and drew aside. I took the photo and the money from my breast pocket and offered them to him. He looked at the torn photo, got worried. His facial expression changed just for an instant, but it was enough to catch his confusion. I began my persuasion technique, I'm an expert at it. I gave it my all: "I can't do it myself. You agreed to do the job for a low price; you said your word is more expensive than money—your words. You chose from the start, from the first question—answer choice B. Now you're bailing out! There's nothing to think about, people kill each other for free every day, just as a favor. You're not risking anything; it's an ordinary death for you. Whereas for me, it's a life-and-death question." I said a few other things, but he was intransigent. He's not giving back the money, he's armed, I'm afraid of being duped. He's mumbling something about principles and rules of the game. I have no choice, I agree to his game. For the last time, I'm looking into the raven-killer's eyes and realize they're not sad. They're the eyes of the ownerless dog I met in the street, for sure. I'm thinking they're probably related, and I fire a shot.

B. February 29 was a sunny day, and the weather was chilly, just the way I like it. I went and bought the morning papers, read about a few murders. I realized they weren't done by experts — self-taught, amateur stuff. I didn't think it was a good idea to set a date with the client in broad daylight. But it was too late to change anything. I began dressing up as if for a date. I don't like wearing black from head to toe. But I know that's what my client expects of me. My image dictates such a style. I used to have short hair, now my hair is long and I comb it back. That is my homage to Hollywood; plus, the scar in between my eyebrows, which many people think is a wrinkle. Looking in the mirror, I remembered the bartender girl from the day before, who didn't smile the whole evening and at the end was telling me: "You're not content with your life, it's written on your face. Plus, you have sad eyes." I don't need a real weapon, but I always take a pistol with me. I was barely out of the house when bird shit dripped on my shoulder. It was a raven, flew away cawing. I've never shot a bird; I have my principles: never harm an animal. I strayed once, though; I was returning from work at night, an ownerless dog came up to me, he was big and mad. I struck him, he started whining; I came close to shooting him, too. He looked at me with an eradicating gaze, I froze on the spot. I didn't have the nerve to shoot him; they say a dog doesn't die from limping, it may live. Anyways, I wiped the bird shit off of my shoulder, but it left a little stain. I decided to walk with a set gait — having a game with myself, where you can't step on the lines separating the slabs of the sidewalk. I recognized my client from afar, he had a bike with him. We greeted each other, and drew to the side. He took the photo and the money from his breast pocket and handed them to me. Even before seeing the photo, I already had doubts. I felt vaguely that he had gotten into a dishonest game with me. The minute I saw the photo, I understood everything. He felt it, too; his facial expression changed only for a second, but it was enough to give away his confusion. He started trying to persuade me, like he was an expert persuader. He wouldn't let me speak. I barely managed to nail the point that the million was not the issue. Killing a person is far more expensive, even in our poor country. There was no other choice, that's why I had agreed.

For both of us, the word costs more than money. Then I said exactly the following: "You were supposed to warn me about who you wanted to kill. And now you show your cards at the end of the game; you're dishonest. I have my principles, my rules of the game. For example, this might crack you up, but I don't shoot birds. You don't even understand that you're almost asking for suicide. I won't give you back your money; so here's what we'll do. There's another option. If you're in the mood, let's play the death-game for the million. You must know Russian roulette. See, I'm taking out all the bullets and leaving only one. This is the game you want—there's no winner; only a loser, and the one who survives. That is what you wanted, right? Here we go, you're first."

C. The moment I woke up on February 29, I ran to the computer, I opened your webpage and saw that you had posted the answer key, just like you had promised. Bingo!!!!! I won. I believed in you, me, the game, the word, and I won. I'm a millionaire. I took a bath, ate breakfast; looked up a few things on the Internet, just to kill time. I felt uncomfortable calling you so early in the morning, you might've been asleep. I lingered a little more on social networking sites; then called. I said hi; you recognized me right away, we had met once already. You congratulated me on my victory. We set a date near the Hands. The weather was chilly, the day sunny; I came in a taxi cab. I bought two chamomiles from the flower guy. He grumbled, said he's selling by the bunch, not individually. I persuaded him, I'm a master-persuader. You were waiting when I got there, this time you were with a bike. But I wasn't surprised because I had read about it in your short story beforehand. We strolled in the park; there was no snow, it had melted away. Tomorrow's spring, and I'm a millionaire. We went for tea. We chatted about this and that; you were sort of hyper-happy; you kept smirking. Then you asked suddenly: will you buy a million's worth of wieners for vagrant dogs? You had written about it as well, and I had thought of a unique answer. What I said was probably to your liking, 'cause you laughed sincerely. We talked a while about question five, and both agreed that we were the ones deciding what would happen to us on February 29. I kept inadvertently casting my gaze in front of me, at the bumpy envelope. It said on it HSBC, and inside there's really one million drams. You suggested count-ing them. No, I believe you. Then I said exactly the following: "One game has ended, it's time to start the next. Now it's my turn, I'm the game-show host. If you're up for it, let's play. You've gotta know 'Loves me, loves me not,' it's the simplest game." We took one chamomile each and started pulling the petals. We review the last question out loud, together. We smile at each other because we are certain that only the petals of the chamomile know the answer.

D. None of the above. I have my own choice. People look for their other half outside, but it may be inside. Regardless, when two peo-ple stay in one place for too long, they sometimes get wound up, and one of them wants to whack the other. My grandpa used to say, "Turn your fight into a game, you'll always end up winning." From the get-go this game was not to my liking. I can't keep this to myself, you ownerless dog! You have a million? — Go spend it! Why do you wanna give it away to somebody else? My answer is: Nothing in particular happened on February 29. It was a regu-lar, sunny day, but the weather was chilly. I simply went near the Hands to find out if my other half loves me or not.

QUESTION SIX-AND-A-HALF

The game is ending, but it is dishonest not to use the 50/50 lifeline. That is what I'm gladly doing, making the player's job easier, and tak-ing away answer choices A and D.

Loves me, loves me not?

B. Loves me.
C. Loves me not.

TRANSLATED FROM ARMENIAN

BY HAIK MOVSISIAN

REIN RAUD

The Demise of Engineer G.

BY NOW THE TIME HAS PROBABLY COME to lift the veil on the circumstances surrounding the unexpected death of my late friend G., the master engineer and, in the relevant circles, noted philatelist. Although, at the time, several large newspapers published obituaries dedicated to him, the event was overshadowed by the churn of political news, which is understandable. But I still don't want to disclose his full name, as this might put his nearest friends and relatives in an uncomfortable position.

Stamp collecting was by no means his only passion—everyone who was on more or less friendly terms with him remembers to this day his famous dinners, which were all the more special because it was far from common, due to the tense situation back in those days, for the stores to be stocked with the necessary ingredients to make the dishes properly. Of course nowadays it just makes us shake our heads to think of it, but at that time it was quite the reverse—people in nearly every corner of the country had to get up early in the morning to take their place in a queue, which was already winding from the door of the nearest store hours before opening, to get hold of their daily knob of butter and, if they were really lucky, a lump of poorly ripened cheese. Of course you can just imagine the state of mind we were in back in those days. And being thus oppressed by our circumstances, the most elementary rudiments of gastronomy were, sadly, rarely accessible to us. If someone were capable, for example, of telling the difference between *camembert* and *brie*, or of distinguishing the taste of this year's *Beaujolais* from last year's, then he would seem more like a pretentious weirdo than a fellow citizen with a mature palate; and wickeder tongues might suggest that it was his links with the already tottering regime which had enabled him—undoubtedly

19

in return for services of the usual kind—to refine his gastronomic knowledge in some foreign country.

However, not one of his acquaintances suspected our friend—who could of course display all the above-mentioned skills—of anything unseemly, nor did they take his tendency to slip the names of little-known ingredients into conversation, as if in passing, as an attempt to make himself seem better than others. Because, in circumstances where even finding enough food to eat your fill was a far from trouble-free undertaking, he would generously give his hospitality to everyone who was at his place, whether friends of friends, or in some cases even complete strangers. It seemed as if his table were always ready-laid, groaning with food, just waiting for someone to come up and sample its offerings. And we were too hungry to ask how it had all came to be there.

I ended up at his place like everyone else—at first on a chance occasion, and then because in our subsequent meetings I couldn't find any reason to turn down the regular dinner invitations, and it seemed that he also took pleasure in my company, even if our interests didn't coincide at all.

That last fact had already become apparent during my first visit. As I waited in the living room for the table to be laid I surveyed his bookshelf absentmindedly, as I tend to do when I find myself in some unfamiliar apartment, and discovered that it contained a representative selection of the classics of global literature, although, in truth, the larger part of the shelves was full of cookery books and stamp catalogues. He probably kept his specialist literature in his office.

I didn't know you were interested in literature, I said when he re-joined me. This could definitely give us subject matter for many long hours of conversation.

Not really, he said, cutting my overture short. Those books are just sitting there; in fact, I don't read them at all, although I might happen to leaf through one on a rare occasion.

Of course I didn't have the slightest grounds to doubt his words, but both then, and later, I was somewhat surprised that works of literature, usually penned by one famous French author or another, were lying around here and there in his home, on the sofa or armchair, as if they had just been forgotten. There were several which I myself hadn't had the opportunity to acquire, but when I asked to borrow them he agreed only with visible reluctance, although at that time I still didn't understand why.

In reality literature was, by then, no longer something which we all lived and breathed. Or if it was, then only after a fashion—it was almost as if the attitudes and ideals which until then had been familiar to us only from books had stepped out of the yellowing pages and taken up their places in real life. I could never have imagined that our life and mode of existence, which had been so securely fitted into a frame, could turn out to be so fragile, still less that our uniform gray mass of humanity could, in a moment, become a free-thinking group of people, capable of behaving with the magnanimity of the noble-minded protagonists from the best possible books, but also of allowing themselves to be exposed as the wretched beasts familiar to us from those same works. Yes—for now that time has passed, the door into the world of books has closed once more, and the gray veil of our lowly everyday existence has again been drawn on both the exalted and the base.

But then it was different. Whatever café one might be in, whichever table one chanced to sit at, any one of us could start up a conversation on the topics of the day, and it made no difference who happened to be our interlocutor, everyone felt united by the smell of major changes hanging in the air. Some of us, intellectuals who remained distant from any desire for political power, spoke seriously in those days about the need to join political circles—how many, regretting their earlier hastiness, have now tried to return to the re-established intellectual world, but mostly in vain—while others were taking advantage of the gusts of wind which blew in through the newly opened doors, disturbing the musty atmosphere, to clarify convictions accumulated over the years, placing them on a broader intellectual map. Names which had until then sounded like hollow echoes of an absent world had turned up with unexpected speed on the signposts of our immediate intellectual landscape, and those unfortunates who didn't manage to read them were assigned with cursory cruelty to the ranks of yesterday's men. But such was the moment.

It wasn't that moving in step with the new was compulsory, it wasn't—just that in its non-compulsory nature it had a passing resemblance to those voluntary activities which we all had to take part in at least once, and generally more often, during our youth: from composing the official wall newspapers, rich with fine prose fit only for the intellectually backward, to night guard duty at the university hostels, if you were lucky; or something even more spiritually desolating. But it appears that in clarifying these memories I have allowed myself to diverge too far from the matter in hand.

My friend G. was a true gourmet. That means that the commonplace definitions of that concept didn't convey his character one bit. Compared to him the socialites who figure in today's society columns, with their supposedly well-developed tastes, would have seemed like gustatorily challenged dumpling-lovers. And he would have undoubtedly been able to give some useful tips to a chef with dozens of years of experience, in whatever type of restaurant you like—although, as we know, the situation back in those years, with the lack of the necessary establishments, did not make that possible. But this meant that his dinner table compensated all the more generously for the shortcomings of the period. In his masterfully planned menus one delicacy followed another, such that the most subtle nuances of flavor of every dish created a marked contrast with those of the succeeding course; and where this effect could not be produced by the order of the dishes themselves, then the necessary context for the undertones to come to the fore was created by the drinks, which alternated with the same kind of regularity as the plates on his large round table—at exactly the right speed for each subsequent taste to cut into the previous one at the very last moment, when the surface of the tongue, slightly straining, still wanted to keep the fading aftertaste in the mouth, so that the first new aromas had the best possible impact. When there was a larger group of visitors, and the majority of them were not amongst those he hosted most frequently, he might offer eight to ten courses (that was even if you excluded the cold starters and second dessert); but at those most savored of occasions, when only four or five of his closest friends had gathered around the table, those whose gastronomic curiosity one could be sure of, the number of courses sometimes stretched to almost thirty or forty—the portions were, understandably, incredibly small but nonetheless faultlessly presented, so a steady stream of tastes crossed our palates, flowing like the delightful music which comes to life under the baton of an experienced conductor. He claimed to have acquired the art of menu planning from Japan, but at his table the culinary arts of all peoples and all countries met as equals—although our own homeland was clearly underrepresented compared even to some of our close neighbors.

As guests, it was understandably our responsibility that the conversation should proceed at a comparably high level. G. himself could often only take the role of smiling observer, who, busy with bringing yet more new dishes to the table, couldn't allow himself any trains of thought requiring lengthy argumentation, lest the irrefutable rhythm of the dishes force him to get up from the table and break off mid-sentence. Only as lunch was drawing to a close, when an *ibrik* with coffee or pot of jasmine tea sat in front of each of us, a glass of brandy or *calvados* by the side, did G. allow himself to become more involved in the conversation. True, the only subject which it was worth hearing him speak on, in addition to food, was everyday politics, since, as I have already explained above, every one of us was an expert on that in those days. G's knowledge in his specialist field, which was undoubtedly sufficiently deep to give him notable authority amongst his colleagues, was unfortunately not comprehensible to any of the rest of us, and virtually none of us had encountered stamp collecting since late childhood.

Nevertheless, G.'s limited contributions to our conversations didn't reduce their quality in any way. In retrospect it is hard to recall exactly what it was about those evenings that so stimulated us intellectually, to the extent that we were able to go on reeling off witticism after aphorism, which when recalled over the following days could have us suddenly burst out laughing to ourselves, even if we were sitting on some form of public transport jam-packed with people, thus earning ourselves the suspicious disdain of our fellow passengers. And theoretical discussions around G.'s table—which mostly concerned how our country's political future would take shape after the inevitable fall of the tottering regime—were sensible, watertight, and almost always cropped up in one form or another in politicians' discussions in later years. We were ahead of our times, removed from our immediate environment, and it would be wrong to say that we didn't enjoy it.

It was precisely this last circumstance which most likely turned out to have a determinant influence on our moods. The food which we savored was so much not of the gray surroundings that for some time after tasting it we didn't perceive ourselves to be part of that reality either, instead we imagined ourselves to be characters in some old book read with ardent pleasure. And we tried to behave accordingly, to be just as wise, noble-minded, and witty as we imagined the people from those better worlds, hidden behind the dust jackets.

I think I already mentioned that G's library was extensive, which seemed all the more incongruous given that his interest in literature was distinctly limited. But he nevertheless lent out the copies of quality works of literature which belonged to him with obvious reluctance, the real reason for which I was of course unable to guess while he was still alive. I tried, however, to borrow books from him fairly frequently, although not often enough for it to result in him no longer wanting to see me at his table for lunch. Still, it was very hard for me to resist the urge to ask to borrow for a couple of days some work of literature that was considered obligatory reading for every educated person, but was missing from my own library at home, and had caught my eye on G's bookshelves.

One time, when I was returning a turn-of-the-century psychological novel to G., I drew his attention to the fact that the book had a defect.

Do some of the pages appear twice, asked G., livening up, for some reason.

No, that kind of defect wouldn't in itself make a book unfit for use, if all the other pages were present and correct. In this case, however, there was a printing error—on some of the pages no text appeared.

I showed G. those places, which I had marked with strips of paper for the purpose, and advised him to approach the publishers who had brought out the work—maybe they still had a decent copy put aside. The defect was actually quite attractive in its own way—normally in such cases whole pages are left blank, but in the book which G. had ended up with only individual paragraphs were missing, in places just individual words, almost as if the censor had considered them undesirable and had removed them from the work.

I have already approached them, said G., but they could no longer do anything to help me.

From then on G. no longer lent books to me. The first time he refused, on some laughable pretext, I was even a little offended, but when this scenario was repeated, in the interests of preserving friendly relations, I gave up any aspirations to make use of his library; I decided that he was probably very sensitive about the quality of everything he owned, and resented my pointing out the imperfection in his book. Otherwise our relations continued in much the same way as before—it was even somewhat uncanny that the dinners at G.'s place continued with the same unchanging rhythm as previously, while everything in our surrounding reality changed at such a seething pace. More and more of the things which we had previously conceived only in our imaginations came into tangible and—alas!—far from unproblematic existence around us.

I promised at the beginning that I would also talk about G.'s unfortunate demise. I do this with a heavy heart, but since I was the first to see him dead, it is my duty.

Around ten people had come to the dinner which, unknown to us all, would end up being our last one together. Some of them were G.'s colleagues, who were strangers to me, and odd as it was, our conversation didn't particularly get going, most probably since a number of individuals with a rather wide range of different political views had ended up in the same company and, out of respect for G., had not wanted to start up the usual trenchant debate. G. himself was in a particularly fine mood: something good had happened in his work life, which had also occasioned his colleagues joining us. Since the everyday topics had been delimited in this way, the conversation quickly steered toward the culinary arts. In those days the trade situation had begun to improve to some extent, although it was still far from satisfactory, of course.

Whenever choosing wine you should always stick to red *Bordeaux*, if making decisions gives you a headache, explained one of G.'s colleagues, a young man with a flushed face and tasteless tie. They suit any type of food.

Several of those sitting round the table couldn't manage suppressing a sad smile. G. himself was not present in the room at that moment.

But it is surely worth getting more thoroughly acquainted with the other wine regions of France, an elderly lady sitting to my left said in reply. I personally prefer some of the more successful burgundy vintages to any of the finest achievements of Bordeaux.

But what about *Mount St. Emilion*? I asked, unable to resist the temptation of entering the conversation—although I can't to this day understand what it was in those words which was more captivating back then: maybe the lure of the distant embodied in the names we heard only in foreigners' tales, or the air of exclusivity they radiated.

By "Bordeaux" I was definitely thinking only of those wines which are *appellation* Bordeaux, clarified the lady sitting next to me.

But I actually prefer Australian wines—the famous poet E., who was sitting directly opposite the young man with the tie, latched on to the conversation.

No, no, wine really has to be from France, countered a young lady, also G.'s colleague, in whom the young man in the tie seemed to be showing excessive interest. There are just so many types there.

Have any of you ever tried *Anjou* wine? asked G. suddenly. It turned out that he had been standing by the door and following our conversation from there.

No, in fact none of us had. At least as far as we were aware.

That's good then, said G. Get ready for a taste experience.

He went back to the kitchen to bring the wine. But when, after ten minutes, he hadn't re-joined our company I started to feel uncomfortable, and I went to see where he had got to.

G. was lying on the kitchen floor; by the time I arrived he was already dead. An opened bottle of *Anjou* wine stood on the table, with a glass by its side, from which he had tried the wine before serving.

There was something else on the table, namely the Alexandre Dumas book *The Three Musketeers*, which was opened on page 443, where the chapter 'Anjou Wine' began. In truth, the book no longer contained the chapter title, but the bottle was palpably there in front of me.

Evidently G. had never read that book. Because otherwise he would, of course, have remembered that the book's main character, d'Artagnan, had received the wine consignment described in the chapter from his arch enemy, Milady de Winter, and that the wine named in the title contained deadly poison. True, no one fell victim to this attempted crime, other than the incidental character, Brisémont, who, on page 447, prematurely tastes a small glass of the exquisite drink, and dies in terrible agony.

It just goes to show that one can end up paying for the gaps in one's knowledge of the masterpieces of world literature in the most cruel and unexpected of ways.

TRANSLATED FROM ESTONIAN

BY MATTHEW HYDE

ZDRAVKA EVTIMOVA

Seldom

THE SMELL WAS THERE AGAIN, and I turned around. It was sweet and it made me smile, and I wondered where it came from. There was no one in sight, the street stretched before me, endless and gray; the buildings were gray, too, the sky looked heavy with lightning, but the smell was there. There was no doubt about that. Then I noticed the car—a most ordinary gray Ford. I suddenly remembered—I saw it yesterday when I went to work and I remembered the smell had been there, too. I approached the car, curious and a little frightened. A gray-haired man sat in it.

"Can I help you, Ma'am?" the man asked. I looked at him closely. It turned out his hair was brown, not gray.

"I remember your car," I said. "I think I noticed it yesterday."

"Yesterday?" the man said pursing his lips. "It's impossible, Ma'am. I wasn't in this town yesterday."

I thought one could hardly dub "town" the dozen ramshackle houses and the narrow, asphalt road that touched the apathetic buildings and climbed to the black sky in the distance.

"Your car smells sweet," I said. "I noticed that yesterday."

The man was silent, staring at the windshield, his sharp profile a slab of white marble cutting the gray air. He seemed to have forgotten all about me. What the hell, I said to myself. My ex-boyfriend used to behave in exactly the same way—he stared at the night and forgot all about me. He didn't even notice when I went out. Men tended to forget me very quickly, I had noticed that a number of times. I think it had to do with my constant talking. What the hell. I left the guy in his sweet-smelling car and hurried along the street. My office was a block away. It was a hole of a room, with a window looking out on a clump of poplar trees that made me allergic almost half the year.

I didn't know what I hated most: my constant allergies, the translations I did ten hours a day, or the thought of my boyfriends, who seldom noticed I was there.

I remembered the boring novella I had to translate by the end of the week and shuddered—it was a story about a banal love affair. The word "love" gave me the creeps. It reminded me of my latest boyfriend, who said he had had enough of my whims and vagaries. Well, I was working hard and making an effort to understand whether the protagonist hated the world in general, or only his cheating wife and her lover. In my opinion the protagonist was a particularly unintelligent fellow. He delivered long monologues, teeming with Latin quotations, on the future of the world. I could not stand the guy and his ideas about the future. I thought my ex-boyfriend was very much like him—boring and moralizing.

Then, once again, the sweet smell was there, it was in my nose. The gray car ground to a halt beside me, and the man in it said, "I could give you a lift to your office."

"How come you know where I work?" I asked suspiciously.

"I'm the author of the novella you are translating," the man said.

"Oh."

"Your boss said you didn't like my work," the author of the damned thing said.

"No, I don't like it," I said. There was no use pretending. The novella was no good, and its author did look like my ex-boyfriend.

The minute I said this I knew I had made a serious mistake. I suspected the guy might withdraw his manuscript and assign the translation to my colleague. She was more amiable than me, she admired the dirges she translated, she called the authors geniuses, and their prose concoctions were all masterpieces to her. Malomed—that was the woman's name—made twice as much money as me. She had a poet boyfriend she called Dante instead of Don. His poetry gave me headaches.

"Why does his poetry give you headaches?" the author asked.

"What!" I must have been thinking aloud.

But while I had been thinking about Don's doggerel, I was positive I hadn't said anything about them. I was short of money and I wanted the translation of that novella—that was what interested me.

"I'll give you a lift to your office," he said.

When I got into the car he said, "Why don't you like my work?"

"It's not so much I don't like it . . ." I knew how much I needed the money. The gray Ford ground to a halt once again.

"You lied to me," the guy said. "That's why the car stopped."

"Oh, come off it," I said. "I lie to lots of people every day, but my car doesn't stop on account of it."

"I don't lie to people," the man said, looking at me in a way that suddenly made me angry. I felt like shouting at him; which I did.

"Your prose is no good," I said. "It gives me the creeps."

I stopped talking, but the car didn't move at all, I noticed. The stranger had killed the motor.

"What are you waiting for?" I told him. "I'll be late for work and my boss will give me a piece of her mind."

"It's not my fault," the man said. "The car moves only when the passenger is happy."

I thought about it. I wasn't happy at all. I hadn't had a single happy day in my life, I thought.

"Try to think about the time when you loved your boyfriend," the author of the boring novella said.

"I didn't love my boyfriend," I said. "He dumped me so quickly, I didn't have the chance to start loving him."

It was raining outside, and the gray sky touched the windshield of the car. It was quite dark and the clouds looked as thick as the asphalt. The car suddenly skidded forward.

"I am not happy at all," I said to the driver. "Why did the car move?"

"I was happy," the man said. "I think I like you."

I studied the man's face. I wouldn't say it was attractive, just an ordinary man's face, the type I wouldn't bother to look at twice. It was raining and I was angry.

"Look here," I said. "You thought up the whole thing, didn't you?"

"I thought up what?" he asked.

"The car thing. You're lying to me. You stop the car and you make it go whenever it suits you."

"I didn't think anything up. What I've told you about the car is true. I like you so the car moves forward."

"Then your car must stop right away, because I can't say I like you," I said bluntly. Then I noticed I held an ashtray in my hands. I had taken it from the panel in front of me. It was an ugly thing, yet, most unexpectedly, it smelled sweet, too.

"Are you a smoker?" I asked the man. "I hate smokers, let me tell you that." The sweet-smelling car stopped. It rained harder, the clouds turning the street into a lake of churning water. The driver by my side bristled up.

"Are you sure you don't like me?" he asked.

"I am," I answered.

First the sweet smell vanished, then suddenly I was in the middle of a puddle in the street. There was no car, and no man by my side. Now that's bad, I said to myself. I'm hearing voices and I'm seeing things. My latest boyfriend had warned me I'd be out of my mind in no time at all; he said no one could stand me, so evidently I was starting to invent men who could put up with all my tricks. My shoes were dripping wet, my hair and my clothes were an avalanche of cold shivers, tumbling down my spine. My fingers were cold too. I thought I'd better rub them to get warm, then I noticed I still held the ashtray in my hands: an ugly thing that held the sweet smell of the car that had vanished in the rain.

"Hey!" I shouted. "Where are you?"

There was no one in the street, and I was completely sodden, shivering with cold.

My boss glared at me as I entered the office.

"Your deadline is 30th March," she said. "I want the translation of the first fifteen pages now."

I didn't have the fifteen pages ready.

"I am afraid that's impossible, Mrs. Whitaker," I said, feeling her eyes bite into me. "I have a rough draft of the translation, and I need time to polish it."

The azaleas in the street blossomed palely in the rain. There was cold rain in Mrs. Whitaker's eyes, too. I wanted to go on a short holiday to Ostend, on the North Sea. I had been there once and the wind was so strong I could lie on it. The sea was the color of asphalt and there were no people on the beach. I had listened to the waves for hours, and I had eaten a pizza in the Neapolitana Café.

"By the way, there is a letter for you," Mrs. Whitaker grumbled. Everyone knew how much she disliked forwarding messages to her employees. "I am not a post office, mind you," she reminded me, chucking the envelope onto my desk.

It was the first letter I had received for years. I mean an ordinary letter, one typed on a sheet of paper. It said "Neapolitana Café, 7 pm, today." That was all there was to it. I put it in my desk drawer. I thought, I could talk to that letter, or talk to the drawer in which I kept it, it didn't make much difference.

"By the way," Mrs. Whitaker said, smiling—her smiles were a bad sign; her tall body leaned forward, her eyes hard; "I intended to assign the translation of the novella to Miss Malomed."

This didn't come as a surprise. Miss Malomed, my amiable colleague, called all pieces of fiction she happened to translate masterpieces. The authors were always happy to meet her. They were not happy to meet me.

I looked at Mrs. Whitaker, imagining the cold, empty kitchen in my apartment, and the heap of bills I still had not paid. I saw the heap of shirts and jackets that belonged to my ex-boyfriend. I still had not thrown them in the dustbin. Sometimes in the evenings, instead of translating, I gave his dirty shirts a piece of my mind. It did me good.

I imagined going to Ostend again. I couldn't remember the name of the wine I had drunk there.

"But now I won't be assigning the translation to Miss Malomed," my boss went on, pausing significantly, watching my face.

When I'd woken in that shabby hotel room in Ostend, I found I didn't have enough money for a good breakfast. It was a rainy spring day, and there was no wind to listen to.

"The author of the novella phoned today," my boss made another of her important pauses, her upper lip a threatening piece of ice. Her face usually froze when she had bad news to break. And as a rule, her news was bad. She started by pointing out she had heard me talk to a handkerchief. That was true. It was my ex-boyfriend's handkerchief. I was telling it I was a pretty woman. I had spoken to the handkerchief using rare, morally offensive words in Bulgarian, and I was sure no one understood. My ex-boyfriend never did, so saying long, nasty words to his shirts gave me exactly the same pleasure as if he were listening to me.

I missed the fragrance of the strange car though. I missed the voice of the man who had said he liked me.

I missed the intimacy of a boyfriend.

"The author of the novella said he liked your translation," my boss declared, the words dropping from her lips in a dead heap in front of me.

"I knew he would," I said, although I had not started translating the thing yet. It had been the most disappointing piece of writing I had come across for five years and two ex-boyfriends.

"By the way, you know I disapprove of negotiations between the authors and my translators," Mrs. Whitaker croaked.

"I know," I said.

"And I strongly disapprove of my translators talking to inanimate objects," she went on.

"I talk to objects to concentrate," I explained.

It rained hard outside.

"I wouldn't like to know anything about anybody's personal life, but ..." she said. I didn't tell her I had no personal life, barring my long conversations with my ex-boyfriend's shirts. My getting drunk alone in the Neapolitana Café wouldn't qualify as personal life either.

"The author said he'd like to give you a new part of the novella, which he has just written. That's the part that seems wrong," my boss said at last.

"Why should it be wrong?" I asked

"You wouldn't want to know," her voice was stretched too thin to cover all the nuances of sarcasm and contempt she felt for me at that moment.

I'd have given two years of my life to bark one of my morally offensive Bulgarian words in her face. Then there was that Malomed person, my colleague, enthusiastic and ready to oblige.

"You know, I told the boss I would be there for you ... I mean, I could translate the damned piece for you ..." she chirruped, "I mean if you turned it down ... Mrs. Whitaker thought you'd positively turn it down, so ..."

"I'll do it," I told her. She stared, her smile slowly sinking into her good, shining teeth.

"Oh, I understand."

It was not too clear what she'd understood.

Then it was there again, the pleasant aroma that I liked so much, the fragrance of the gray automobile. I looked through the window but didn't see the car. A minute later I caught a glimpse of the man who owned it, the writer of poor novellas. He was shaking Mrs. Whitaker's hand. I had not noticed that he'd entered the office. The man looked good, I had to admit.

"It's there again, that smell," I told him.

"That smell?" he asked.

"Of the car," I answered, looking at him. My boss stared at me. Malomed heaved another of her deep, meaningful sighs.

"I can give you a ride to the Neapolitana Café," the writer of poor novellas said quickly.

The town was full of rain and azalea blossoms, which made me horribly allergic. The car was there, though, in the street in front of our office, the sweet-smelling automobile.

"Your colleague ... Miss Malomed," the author whose work I was translating said after we got into the car.

"Yes?" I muttered. I had a gut feeling the turn our conversation was taking would lead to no good. "I think we are wasting time."

"The car moves only when the passengers are happy," the man said. "I've told you that." He took a deep breath. "I think you are a good translator, but ... maybe Miss Malomed ..."

"You can go ahead and talk to Miss Malomed," I snapped. There was no point in going to Neapolitana Café now, was there? The car had remained immobile in front of my office window, the azalea tree heaping its blooms in the wind just to exacerbate my allergy.

"Miss Malomed is a fine lady ..." the man started. I was reaching to open the door when he said in Bulgarian. "I don't care for Miss Malomed. I want you. I came here to see you. You are all I've been dreaming about ..."

I could not believe what I heard.

"You are everything to me. You are the air I breathe in, you are the wind I listen to, you are my happy evening, and you are in all my words. Please, please don't go."

Suddenly I felt the sweet-smelling automobile move. It was racing along the sleepy street of the town, it was hurtling and buzzing and singing and shouting with joy.

"You speak Bulgarian!" the man whispered. "You understood!"

"I am Bulgarian," I said.

Then I was suspicious. Was this another man playing with me, another mean trick? And I was stupid enough to rise to the bait. I was the dumbest thing in town. The car was about to grind to a halt.

"But it is true!" the man shouted in English. "I mean every word of it."

The car roared and rushed forward, stronger and swifter than the waves in Ostend, a cloud of fragrance trailing in its wake.

"Who are you?" I asked, amazed.

"I am the man who likes the Bulgarian language," he said.

I believed what he said. He was the man I had been dreaming about all my life.

*****

I was wrong again.

He didn't like the Bulgarian language. He spoke Bulgarian only when he was happy.

TRANSLATED FROM BULGARIAN
BY THE AUTHOR

ADDA DJØRUP

Birds

ALEJANDRO,

I am sorry not to have written before now. I know that you have been out of your mind with worry. There is no excuse for just disappearing like that. I hope that my postcards were some comfort, at least, even if they explained nothing. I still have no better explanation than my fear that life would carry on as before. Not that it was bad, not that I was unhappy, not that I stopped loving you. Please don't think that! Something just happened that changed everything, changed me … and now I shall endeavor to tell you the story. However, I should say right away that my story is not an explanation, that I am not even sure myself how it is to be understood. I doubt even that it may be a story at all, for perhaps the beginning does not hang together with the middle, the middle with the end. And perhaps, I think to myself now, there are no real stories at all with beginnings, middles and ends, perhaps there simply is what there is, and what happens, and the lines we draw between those points are just nonsense and dreams, and the figure that arises from those lines could just as well have been something else completely. A frog instead of a puppy dog, a scrawl instead of a lighthouse, a gaping black hole instead of a shiny pattern of order. But if there is a story, I think perhaps it is like this:

I was sleepless one night, and so that you may understand what I mean by sleepless, you must be patient with me and allow me, as best I can, to try to describe exactly what I did and thought. It is more than three weeks ago (and what happened before that night is something I need not reveal to you. I think our life has been as ordinary and as extraordinary as all other lives). We had been to a movie with

Ivan and Antonio, and you went to bed when we got home. I stayed up and spent almost an hour looking for the receipt from the man who had repaired the washing machine. When I went to bed it struck me how quiet the house was: so quiet it seemed to me to be awake. Of course, it was only I who was awake. I lay looking up at the ceiling, thinking nothing in particular. It was only just June, but already too hot, and the heat made me imagine I could hear summer itself, a mumble from some indeterminate place between the stillness that was close and the distant sounds of the city, like something growing out of the air itself. The bedroom windows were open and the drapes drawn back, and yet there was not the slightest breath of cool air, but then that is how it is in that apartment in the summertime. I noticed how the white walls of the house next door reflected the grainy, reddish-yellow of the sky and sent it back into the bedroom several shades lighter; how the room's light and dark were meshed together or stirred into a gritty mush. Outside, the bats were hunting silently, but their shadows zigzagged unpredictably through that most sensitive part of one's field of vision, the part that registers without seeing and ensures the organism is always ready to make a quick movement. I tried to close my eyes and fall asleep, but to no avail: they opened again, and eventually I stopped trying. I did not turn the light on, but slid as quietly as possible out of the bed, so as not to wake you, and went out into the kitchen. I opened the refrigerator and narrowed my eyes against the cold light and the view into that hyper-realistic, white universe, grabbed a bottle of water, drank, and wondered about when all this sleeplessness had set in. Perhaps already that morning, perhaps already then it had entered me like a parasite and reproduced itself all day? I shook the thought away and went out and sat down on the balcony.

Alejandro, for you, who never suffers from sleeplessness, I need to explain that it is a strange state, and wholly singular. The senses are sharpened and dulled all at once. The eyes are sensitive as antennae, the ears as whiskers, and yet it is as though they are somehow unable to really get a grip on the world. One's thoughts steal around on the rim of rationality's light, circumventing the correct and smiling facades of day; yet neither is it the logic of dreams that is in charge, that which allows anything at all to happen without one ever wondering why. And so, it is as though day and night—the states of wakefulness and of dreaming—are present both at once. It is like finding oneself on the reverse side of the universe, or perhaps the soul, where everything casts two equally strong shadows.

On the balcony I found calm. Maybe because the physical location, in a way both inside and out, accorded well with the mental state of sleeplessness. I recalled my habit of banishing the world by means of symmetry. You know what I am talking about. What I do, for instance, when I walk the four floors up and down the stairway at home in Calle Huertas: always two steps at a time going up, one when going down, two on each landing. I make sure to finish on a figure that divides into equal numbers of steps for each foot. It was the same kind of symmetry I found there on the balcony: I was not sleepy, but tired (there is a difference). I was myself, and yet, at the same time, I stood one step away from myself. I wondered if there were an axis running through my life, in which actions and states were reflected. I mused that my habit of pursuing symmetry was something I might simply choose to abandon (although it really is not that bad at all), but also that the number of habits perhaps is constant, just like the number of vices. I believe myself to be blessed with the ability to observe my human nature, to a certain extent even to model it, though of course not with the ability to abandon it. Why, then, so I concluded, should I attempt to replace one harmless component with another? Do you follow me? And was this, I asked myself, reason's admission of failure or a manifestation of wise resignation? You will undoubtedly tend toward the former: why allow oneself to become obsessed by and waste time on something one knows to be nonsense? I have no answer to that, yet I shall be honest and say that I congratulated myself at that moment for at least not referring to my habits by name, enlarging them into truths, elevating them to religious conceptions, or subjecting myself to them as if they were anything other than the rather peculiar practices they surely are. Just as I congratulated myself for not condemning the habits of others, their conceptions, neuroses ... or simply their tastes. Rather, I thought, this sobriety that I may once have resolved to acquire, had occasionally turned into an immoderate predilection for what would appear to be the inconsequential rather than what, quite apparently, is significant: people's political convictions, their sense of justice, ability to empathize, etc., seemed to me every now and again to be less interesting than their inclination to choose brown shoes over black, or armchairs over sofas. Whatever. On this point, then, I occasionally overstepped the line of affectation, perhaps even arrogance, yet it bothered me not, since all of it belonged to the worries of tomorrow. A tomorrow in which I once more would become Teresa Mateo, in which I again would assume Teresa Mateo's life and ways of living—her address, her history, her employment as a professor of English—as one would put on a set of clothes.

Alejandro. Have patience a while with this talk of sleeplessness. I am almost done.

I sat there looking out on the courtyard. The ugly courtyard of which, having looked on it now for almost five years, I have actually grown fond, the way one might become fond of an aged, well-worn face. The peeling walls; the lives of neighbors as they may be observed from here, as ours presumably may be observed from there; the habitually crowded washing lines of the Peruvians, draped with five yards of children's clothing in all sizes; the elderly couple's living room behind the unusually tall window from which the blue light of television streams long into the night; and, on the third floor over in the corner, the balcony that is stuffed with feeble plants that receive neither enough sun nor enough water, as though the building had made one last effort to tidy itself, and then had given up. And down on the roof of the garage: the plastic doll that has lain there for years in a red washing-up bowl and that is still a talking point among those who live here: How on earth did it get there? But none of this was what made me remain outside. It was the bats again. Hunting in zigzags, compact little shadows flitting back and forth across the small space of the yard, catching my eye and vanishing again just as quickly.

I have never discovered where the bats sleep. It is a mystery that in my sleeplessness I, on the one hand, would like to have cleared up, yet, on the other, was just as content to have remain intact. In this state, everything seemed to be firmly fixed around a field of resistance, such as that which exists between two identical magnetic poles. Whatever issue I diverted myself with, it was as though for every thought there were a riddle attached, and for each riddle there was a thought. Life seemed to me to be eternally enchanted and death was distant and secondary. And what should be said of the latter, Alejandro? Is death secondary? Are we talking about reason's admission of failure or a manifestation of wise resignation? As you can see, I had returned to my starting point, and as sleep gradually encircled me, my own circles of thought grew ever smaller. I am, I noted, like all others, blessed with the ability to construct unfathomable riddles, and whosoever ceases to wonder at that is either enlightened or else in a bad way. One may claim the one thing and with equal reason the other. Tomorrow, I thought to myself, I can decide on a standpoint. Or, tomorrow I can perhaps at least decide whether it is something to laugh or cry about. Here my sleepless monologue came to an end; I had become rather dizzy and thought it to be on account of drowsiness finally having arrived.

The middle ... I have tried putting it into words many times over the past couple of weeks; every day since I came here to the house I have tried to write this letter ... The middle will shock you as it shocked me. Now, however, as you presently will understand, I have become used to it. More than that; I would not for anything in the world be without it. As terrible—in the true sense of the word—as it was the first few times, it is just as wonderful now. No, it is more than wonderful in fact!

I stood up to go to bed, but was at once overcome by such nausea that I was compelled to sit down again. As though in a single second I had become flooded from within. Bent double, with my forehead against my knees, I focused on not falling off the chair. Then I realized that something from inside was on its way up. Something with its own will. I felt that very distinctly, and I became paralyzed with fear. I tried to swallow but could not; could hardly breathe. Something was working itself slowly but surely up through my gullet, reaching now the palate, and then was on its way out into my mouth. This happened in the course of what may have been a minute, though it felt like an eternity. I lifted my head. I was shaking so much I was hardly able to raise my hand to my mouth, and yet I did, and with two fingers I pinched a hold. And thus came the first little bird. It was dark blue with golden markings on its wing and tail feathers, and its beak was black. It was perhaps two inches long from beak to tail and less than an inch wide. Its legs were folded against its body (tiny, thin legs), its gaze was wide, and it was warm and damp, and made barely audible sounds. The terror I had felt vanished without my noticing. As quickly as the dizziness and nausea had come, they were gone again, and in my hand lay a dark-blue bird that began to open and close its beak, the barely audible sounds becoming small, distinct chirps. Against my index finger beat a tiny pulse a hundred times faster than my own—like seconds against hours. Again, I have no idea how much time passed before it got to standing on its tiny little feet in my hand, wobbling at the slightest of my movements and preening its feathers. I had forgotten everything else but this bird; it felt like I were witness to the birth of the world. And when finally it took off, flew a few circles, and eventually disappeared like a glint of gold in the darkness, I wept uncontrollably.

I cannot remember going to bed. You woke me the next morning as usual, and I knew that it was not a dream.

What I thought and felt the next day, and the next again, is difficult to describe: anxiety, of course, the feeling that reality was not real, that breakfast was not breakfast, that you were not you and I not I. I had thousands of questions as to how and why, and a painful urge to confide without being able, even to you. For two days, I suffered from a kind of all-consuming paranoia; everywhere, I looked for signs—signs of anything, everywhere. For what on earth could it mean, that Teresa Mateo, a professor of English, spat up a small bird one sleepless night? This was hardly something that could be looked up in any work of reference. I was at my wit's end, so I carried on as usual, and fortunately you were working late. I made sure to be in my bed when you arrived home, and thus avoided any questions you might have asked.

The next bird came two days later, on the train when I was on my way home from the university. We had just pulled out of Tres

Cantos. Everything repeated itself. This time it was yellow. I attracted a few inquisitive looks, and as I bent double one lady asked me if
I needed help. I think, however, I managed to cough it up and carefully slip it into my bag without anyone noticing. I got off at the
next station, and when the bird was ready I let it go. It flew around
for a few moments close by, testing its wings, before perching on the
back of a bench, blinking its small eyes against the world, and turning its head searchingly. Finally it took off and flew over the train ca-
bles and the roof of the station building, and disappeared in the direction of Madrid. Like I said, it was yellow, a very pale yellow, with
a thin, black circle around its eyes. Its beak was light red and its chirp
was definitely not the same as the blue one's. More like a warble, really, than a chirp.

The third was green, a shiny, metallic green, the body rather
longer, more slender than the others, and it sang the moment it appeared. It came the following day, just after I awoke. To be honest,
I felt relieved that you had gone directly to Lyon from the office the
previous day, and happy that you would be away all week. I stepped
out onto the balcony with it, and there sat the blue one—the first.
Now I know they always come back. They are never away for more
than a few hours at a time, and I think it must have been there all the
time without me noticing, on account of my not daring to venture
out there since that night without sleep.

I called the secretary at work and told her I was sick, and would
be absent until further notice—it was an infection, I said, a very bad
one, and catching—and right then, as I sat with the phone in my
hand, the nausea began once more. The fourth was a pale rose color,
the head and breast speckled with black spots, the beak and the legs
gray-blue, and the sound it made was like two pebbles being struck
against each other; it was a fine, clear sound with a brief resonance.
The fifth was black with red and white markings on the head. It came
as I lay on the sofa. The sixth was brown with reddish wings, and it
whistled and made clicking sounds, too. It came as I was trying to
make sense of the television news ... And so I am able to bring to
mind exactly when they came, the first dozen. Those that followed, I
cannot, though I do recall their exact appearance, their coloring and
markings, and their various sounds. And now I know, too, that they

never grow much bigger than they are to begin with, perhaps an inch at the most, and that they thrive on the birdseed that can be bought in any pet store, and on whatever else they find for themselves.

That day, I stopped being scared when it happens. Instead, when the dizziness subsides, I am struck by a feeling of joy, which takes the form of a series of flashes, then expands, spreads and extends. The nausea, although physically still nausea, has also ceased to bother me, since I know what the ocean that suddenly begins to drown me from the inside will give up. Time expands or disappears. I am not sure which. Whatever: it would not surprise me if the universe had been destroyed and revived ten times by the time the bird finally lies in my hand.

That week you were away, I drove out to the train station every evening, to the place where I had let the yellow one go, the one that came in the train. I waited on the platform for some hours, but it did not appear. In the daytime, I was home. I slipped out only once or twice—to the supermarket to hastily buy groceries—otherwise I just sat on the balcony and watched the birds, which were becoming greater and greater in number. There is no regular pattern to it: sometimes there are lots in one day, as many as eight, sometimes only one or two. Sometimes two come in quick succession: other times there may be hours in between. They come at all times of the day and night. The only thing certain is that they are all of them different, all unique, and each so very beautiful. You may ask what I was thinking. Well, nothing in particular. Now and then I thought about what I was to say to people—to you; but truth be told, even those thoughts came seldom. The birds occupied me so much—watching them, listening to them, touching them (they will readily be picked up)—that there was no room in my thoughts for anything else. The first few days there was a practical concern: will they be harmed by my eating or drinking certain things? Do I risk being choked, if they should come in the night, for instance? Yet there seemed to be no reason to worry, and now I even think it silly to have thought that way. I eat and drink as usual, even smoking a cigarette now and then, and if it happens during the night I always wake up before the nausea begins. (Last night I fell asleep with a white one in my hand; it was lying there quite still and quiet when I awoke. Only half an hour later did it emit its first sound, which was so comical it made me laugh. It sounded like the cooing of a pigeon, though not as loud. An odd sound for such a small, chalk-white bird.) And of course I thought, and still occasionally think, about what it means. But then what does it mean to breathe? To sigh and to smile? To love and to eat? Is it even possible to wish that something so basic were different? Perhaps it is, for one can wish anything at all, but I am sure you understand what I mean: somehow I have come to terms with it being so—just as one comes to terms with breathing and does so quite automatically. The analogy is perhaps not inappropriate, since if one becomes conscious of one's breathing and overwhelmingly aware that one would die should it cease for only a short time, one is inevitably gladdened by it. So it is simply something I do. It may well be that something unusual occurred in my sleepless state, that sleeplessness somehow latched on, or that I somehow slipped into it and was unable to extract myself again; that I am still there, on the reverse side of the universe or the soul— a place where everything casts two shadows, where the logic of neither dream nor daytime prevails, where they rather seem to exist side by side. But what of it? This is how things are now. This is how I am. It is something I do. And besides the fact that it would seem there is less than nothing I can do about it, I do not wish for it to cease. On the contrary.

I did not answer the phone on the occasions it rang, unless it was you. And I lied as best I could—I pretended that everything was the same as ever. It was all I could think of. As yet, I had no words, no story to tell—as I have now, perhaps. Yet deep down I think I knew all along what I wanted to do. The day before you were due home I went down to the pet store in Atocha and bought the biggest birdcage they had. Back in the apartment, I packed a suitcase and called the bank and had them transfer half our savings to my account. I'm sorry, but I could see no other way. If I am thrifty, it should see me through the next six months or so. And then? I shall have to think of something, though I feel confident it will all work out.

They did not seem unduly reluctant when I put them one by one inside the cage, even though it soon became crowded. They were many, even then. I put off leaving until midnight so that they should not find it too hot in the car. I had no idea where I was going, so I drove at random—toward the south. It was so strange to be sitting there in the darkness, thinking about everything I was leaving behind. Thinking how sometimes life takes unexpected turns. It may happen only a handful of times during the course of a life. Perhaps even fewer. And to think it was on that night that this particular chapter came to an end ... I was sad, of course. I cried a lot in the next few hours. I thought about a lot of things. About you in particular. Yet I was happy, too, and not at all afraid of the future. The birds were quiet. And even though it all felt different—because I felt different—there were many things, I realized, that had not changed and that would remain as they were. When I turned off the freeway and passed by the place where the roadside brothels with their high walls and idiotically cheerful neon signs begin, I became sad, as always, and thought about how awful it must be to be inside such a place. By six o'clock in the morning, having driven without stopping (and without the arrival of further birds), I felt again the ingrained urge to drink coffee and to smoke a cigarette. When I stopped at a filling station before the border with Portugal to stretch my legs, they felt exactly like what they were: a pair of legs—mine—tired and sore from driving for so many hours. Sometime before nine, dizziness came on. It was a good thing I had left the freeway—I had not even considered that it would be dangerous to drive. Another one came up, bright purple.

At ten o'clock, the birds became restless and I turned off down a track and let them out for a couple of hours. It was a delight to see them for the first time in flight above a field of green! I had something to eat and then took a nap by the wayside. Around midday, I arrived in Tavira, a pretty little town near the coast, small enough to find conversation, large enough for one to be left in peace. I ate a solid lunch at a restaurant, where I also borrowed a phone book and called the nearest realtor, offering him extra if he was quick. After an hour he called back with two properties to offer me, both available for immediate rent. I took the cheapest, an old stone cottage, most likely hard to heat in winter, but the summer will not be over for some time. It lies secluded, maybe a mile out of town. It is not big, and it is primitive, and there is a wood-burning stove in the kitchen. The worst thing is the windows. I shall need to replace them if I am to be staying here long. But all in all the place is nice and has a little garden with fruit trees and a horse chestnut. It will be fine with a little work. If I can find time, that is, on account of the birds — three new ones came up today. Incidentally, the whole flock seems to settle in immediately.

Alejandro, I think about you, and I know that I love you and that there is still something inside me that wants to come back. But I think, too, about the yellow bird, the only one missing, and I wonder what might have happened to it. And Alejandro; even though I am afraid of a life without you, I do not think that I shall be returning. If you wish to come visit, if only to see the place here, I would be very happy (though fearful of looking you in the eye, fearful that you are mad at me and that you will be unable to understand all of this — though I would hold none of that against you). If you should want to stay, I would be happy, but I know that is a lot to ask, and I fear that you will be afraid and be disgusted when first you see it happen, when you have seen the birds coming up. Perhaps you would try to "cure" me. That would be terrible, and quite impossible. I do not know how much I have changed otherwise. Some, I think, although it is only three weeks since all of this began. Perhaps I am finally the person I have really always been, or perhaps I have become another. What difference would there be? All those highly abstract and perhaps quite meaningless words about being oneself ... But the birds are real, Alejandro, and how I wish you would come and see! See when suddenly they alight all at once — birds of all colors; matt, shiny, deep, bright; a pattern against the sky, changing a thousand times a minute and emitting a chaos of sounds — circling around, only to return and land in a flutter of tiny wings, like a handful of pebbles striking the surface of water. And their song — their chirping and clicking, their cooing and warbling, their calling; now more than a hundred voices — I think it is me they address, and I think every sound they make, all of it, means the same: that they are here. I think they all merely repeat "I am here," "We are here." Of course, I cannot be certain, but that is what I understand, or believe.

I will close here. What I hope, what I permit myself to still hope, and what I imagine when I fall asleep in the evenings, is that one day you will come, and that the yellow one has found its way to the balcony in Calle Huertas. That it is perched there, somewhat confused and waiting. And that you have it with you when you come. That you, when you see it, in some way may understand what no words can describe; and that you come.

TRANSLATED FROM DANISH
BY MARTIN AITKEN

PEDRO LENZ

Love Stories

TRANSLATOR'S NOTE: *The layout of these stories reflects the fact that Pedro Lenz often performs them at spoken word events. What you see here is not intended to be blank verse.*

FEAR

The wee nurse
checked the infusions,
footered aboot wi the switches again
then—a bit embarrassed like—
smiled
an' left us
oan ur ain again.

Noo, he said,
he wis totally noticin, he said,
the end wis near
that it wid soon be curtains
an' could ah haun him
his cuppa tea over.

"Ur ye feart?"
ah asked him again.

"Ur ye? Dis it make ye feart?"

He didni answer.

Ah thought it better
tae change the subject
mibbe.

"Whit like's the pain noo?
Did the injection help?
Will ah open the windae?
Ur ye comfortable like that?
D'ye want anither pilla?
Ur ye really no hungry?
Ah could get ye some grapes."

Naw, naw, naw,
he wisni feart, he says.

An' wur we doin awright,
ma wife 'n' me—as a couple, he meant.

Yeah, of course, aye like, aye,
ah gi'ed it
things wur definitely awright like,
awright,
how wis he askin anyhoo.

Naw,
he wisni feart, no at all,
he thought it a bit strange himsel
—he wisni feart but.

An' we wur well aff actually ye know,
ma wife 'n' me—as a couple he meant,
wur we happy thegither?

"Aye,"
ah tellt him again,
things wur awright wi the two ae us.

At the same time but
ah startit tae wunner
hoo come
he wis askin us that twice.

"Yeah — aye, some wurld it is,"
hi gi'es it next,
"some wurld it is,
tellin ye: a mad wurld."

An' when ah don't answer
tae that,
when ah jist look at him
lyin there,
wi they oxygen tube things
up his nose
an' they thin legs ae his
in support socks
an' his hauns a wee bit swollen
an' his hair aw stickin oot
an' his auld-noo face
the color ae cheese,
he suddenly gi'es it:

"Noo, yir losin yir faither."

He disni say: "Ah'll soon be deid."

He disni say: "Ahm goney die soon."

He disni say: "Soon ah'll no exist any mair."

He disni say: "Ah'll be gone soon."

He disni say: "Noo, it's aw over."

Naw, he jist gi'es it:

"Noo, yir losin yir faither."

An' ahm staunin in the shadows
so he disni hiv tae see
the fear
it wid be his place really tae feel
streamin ootae ma eyes.

INSURANCE

Recently there, at the insurance company,
soon as ye go in the door, at reception,
ah run intae Isabelle.

Wance,
mair than therty year ago it is noo,
—Turnip Sunday in Madiswil wur talkin—
me an' Isabelle
wur up hawf the night
snoggin.

"Wid ye look who it is—Isabelle!
That's a surprise awright—Isabelle!
D'ye mind me, Isabelle?
D'ye recognize me, Isabelle?
D'ye remember?"

Course she still minds me,
Isabelle says,
her name's fuckin Sandra but.

SON

Back when his faither died,
—Willy tells me—

51

in the end,
aboot hawf a dozen books
wur left over
that nae cunt wantit.

Wisni as if they wur beautiful books
or wur worth summit
wur rare or whativver,
an' yet Willy
fun it hard
jist tae haun them in
tae Oxfam.

His faither's books
didni exactly fit
in his ain bookshelves either but.

Wi it bein the summer,
it suddenly occurred tae him
he could take the books
oan hoaliday wi him.

He'd read through them
while he wis away.
An' wance he hid,
hopefully it widni be
a problem any mair
tae gi'e the books away.

He wis jist finishin
the first yin but,
when he seen his faither
—right at the back—
hid wrote his name an' the date in
in blue ink.

That hid goat Willy doin his sums
an' he wurked oot

that his faither,
at the time he read the book,
hid been the sact same age
as Willy himsel noo.

His heid hadni gi'en him peace
since he wurked that yin oot.
So there wis nowt else fur it
but tae re-read the thing.

An' wi ivry sentence,
ivry wurd he read
he'd tae think aboot
his faither readin it,
at the sact same age
readin this wurd here or that yin
oan this page here or that yin
an' the next wurd an' aw
an' the wan eftir that
an' so oan an' so oan.

Wid his faither,
at the same age
'n' readin the same book,
hiv hid the same thoughts
'n' the same feelings,
Willy startit tae ask himsel.

He asked himsel an' aw
did his faither
—at the same age
he himsel wis noo—
hiv tae re-read
the same sentences
smile
at the same bits
hiv a bit ae difficulty
wi the same scenes sometimes.

Readin,
he seen his faither again
at the age he himsel wis noo.
An' he seen himsel
when he wis as deid
as his faither wis noo.

That wis interestin, aye,
ah tellt Willy.

Whit really interested me but
wis whit the book
wis actually aboot.

Summit ur ither,
Willy said.
Some novel or ither it wis,
translated fae English,
he couldni mind himsel,
basically but
that didni matter
cos noo, like he wis sayin,
it wis a book aboot him
an' above aw
aboot his faither.

TIGER

So there ah am oan ma way tae Zurich
Berne-Zurich, the Intercity,
jam-packed it aye is,
business people, school lassies,
auld dears, office types,
oota-wurk-at-the-minutes, tourists,
hoo ahm ah supposed tae know
exactly whit kinda folk it is

that fills it tae burstin,
an' nearly aw ae them oan their mobiles tae.

There wis a woman opposite me,
forty mibbe,
looked quite nice still,
kind, kind of,
the needlework-teacher type
an' by that ah mean
wan ae the mair open-mindit variety,
wi a cheeky wee necklace—ye ken the kind—roon her neck
an' haun-sewn flipflops
an' some cheeky lipstick
an' a cheeky haircut
an' she's oan the phone tae some cunt
who's obviously called Tiger.

"Naw, Tiger, naw,"
she gi'es it, smilin, totally full ae it,
"naw, Tiger, stoap it,
no noo, naw, Tiger,
naw, course ahm naw bloody alane oan the train,
too right ahm no.
Naw, Tiger, whit ur ye thinkin?"

An' eftir that, she listens
furra while jist, the woman,
laughin an' smilin
an' lookin,
lookin roon
tae see if
some cunt's watchin mibbe.

Aw the other folk but
ur bein discreet like,
even if aw they're doin
is lookin at the windae

'n' clockin the really clear reflections,
—an' there's her thinkin
they're lookin oot the windae.

"Stoap it, Tiger.
Ur ye aff yir heid ur whit?
No way, no here oan the train,
naw,—oan the Intercity of course.
Course it's bloody full,
course it is, ye losin it or whit?
Naw, don't dae that, Tiger,
naw, no the noo,
no the noo, stoap it, please,
bloody stoap, Tiger!"

An' when she finally hangs up,
she looks roon again,
smiles, a bit embarrassed,
an' makes sure
nay cunt's lettin oan
they noticed
still.

THAILAND

Ah keep runnin intae him
where ah live.

He's wan ae they folk
ye feel almost sorry fur,
even jist the way
they staun at the wayside sometimes.

First thing in the mornin
he hauns oot they free papers
an' the rest ae the day

he sells thon magazine fur the hameless
an' if ye buy wan aff him
he says "thanks"
and looks at ye aw serious,
an' sometimes he says
he wants tae go back tae Thailand soon.

Fuck knows how often
he's said aboot Thailand.

His voice aye sounds a bit solemn
when he tells ye that.

"Ah wis thinkin ahd mibbe
head back tae Thailand soon,"
he'll say fur instance, or:
"It's high time
ah went back tae Thailand."

He disni ivver say
when exactly.

An' if he didni look so serious
ivry time,
ye could nearly think
he wis wan ae they cunts
that only ivver dreams ae trips
wi'oot ivver goin oan wan.

Wi him, it's different but.
He really his awready been
tae Thailand
'n' Vietnam an' aw even.

I know fuck aw else
aboot him,
the guy sellin the papers,

don't know the cunt's name even
or where he stays.

Ah know jist that wan thing jist:
that mair than anythin else
he wants back
tae Thailand.

Recently there
when oor paths
happened tae cross again
an' he started oan again
aboot that Thailand ae his,
ah asked him
whit it wis then
he liked so much
that he's aye wantin back.

"The people," he said.

"The people?" ah asked.

"The people, aye!
The people doon there,
ur different fae
the people here, ye see.
They're nice,
know whit ahm sayin,
they *like* me—
in Thailand, the people like me."

"Hiv ye a sweetheart there?"

"Naw,
yir no gettin whit it is ahm sayin,
that's no whit ah go fur,
ah go fur the people."

At first, ah nearly gave a wee grin
that grin that's a way ae sayin
ye don't know whit tae say.

Later but, wance ah thought again
about whit he'd said,
I thought it wis jist plain fuckin sad:

the distance
some cunts hiv tae travel
afore they get tae feel
some cunt likes them.

Translated from the dialect of Berne
by Donal McLaughlin

Vedrana Rudan

My Granddaughter's Name Is Anita

I'VE TOLD HIM A THOUSAND TIMES I cannot stand him putting his tongue in my ear. It's hopeless. What makes men think ears are erogenous? I have finicky ears. They are sensitive to moisture, as soon as water gets into them when I wash my hair I get this foul condition. Disgusting flaking that is not psoriasis. The same thing happens when he tongues them. I can't talk to him about it. Men do not like talking about nasty conditions. That is why I am now lying here under him with cotton balls stuffed in my ears. There is a drawback to this. If I weren't deaf I would hear him moaning and by the kinds of sounds he is making I'd be able to tell when he is getting close to the end and only seconds away from orgasm. Deaf, I sneak a glance from time to time at his eyes; they are lidded. No sound? Soft sounds maybe? We're just starting.

My head is in the closet. I am sniffing my blouses. I count them. Forty-three colorful babes watch me merrily. White, green, red, pink, pale green, the color of water, black, I even have one the color of dirt. A big, dull, dark-brown blouse. I don't dare take it out of the closet because it is a gift from my husband. When he gave it to me I thought, God, you know nothing about me. A dark-brown blouse. A mound of dirt by a freshly dug grave.

His tongue probes my left ear. He is determined. What if he dislodges the cotton balls? My fear is ridiculous but it's here. I am in that store in Berlin. You must know—where Trippen shoes are sold. It is unbelievable, the story of Trippen shoes. I have never fully understood it. Italian leather, made in Italy, yet German. Indestructible, durable.

I have twelve pairs of the shoes, six pairs of the ankle boots, and two pairs of the boots. My husband asks me why I buy so many indestructible things when I have only one life. The way he sees it, life should be spent destroying. So he drinks. The Trippen store in Berlin takes me to orgasm. OK, so maybe I'm exaggerating, but the fact is that I am getting moist right now while, surrounded by gems, I stroll from one pair to the next. Berlin is a beautiful city. I spend a weekend at least once every three months in Berlin. There are a lot of monuments and parks there and it is divided into east and west. People think the east is bigger on soul. I do not like talking with people, even in Berlin. While they chatter on I wriggle my toes in my Trippen shoes. The insole is built in and if I were someone who likes walking, walking would be a breeze. Their boots. Just once you ought to pull on their rough, black, sinister boots. When you pull them on you feel an urge to march off at an SS-pace, straight to a camp. Then you feel how amazingly pliable they are. You are no SS-er, you are an ordinary little woman who is broadcasting the message, leave me alone! Lick not my ears!

The salesperson comes over, black t-shirt, black skinny pants, black Trippeners on his bare feet. A lock of hair in three shades of yellow flops over his right eye. A flash of a grin. He opens the catalogue. I spot them straight away. Oxblood-red sandals. "There they are," he says, "you'll have to place an order, they aren't in yet." He doesn't use the word "oxblood," the kid has probably never seen an ox. It's me the dark red is reminding of an ox's blood. Not a human's or a hen's. An ox's. Dark, viscous. I have never seen an ox in its death throes, a knife in its neck, but an animal as big as that would definitely not bleed Barbie-pink fluid. I leaf through the catalogue. Oh God! Oh Christ! Black gladiator sandals that would go with an evening gown as well as they do with jeans. I don't do evening gowns—we never go out at night. What I meant to say is that if I weren't myself, if I were someone else, who drapes her body in white satin and sways through a summer night with bare shoulders and a bare back, the combination of the satin and these black gladiators would be a cold weapon. "Those are men's," says the fag. Fag? Okay, fine. Homosexual. "And what does that have to do with anything?" I ask him.

He licks my armpit. I hate being tickled. I turn my impulse to tell him to go to hell into a sultry sigh. Tenderly, I steer his head toward my tits. Tits are an erogenous zone, unlike armpits. Why doesn't he know that? Hela told me I should be honored that I give my husband a hard-on after thirty years of wedlock. He is a university professor and can fuck any girl who comes to take an exam from him. Hela thinks that, from time to time, he does fuck something young. I don't know. I am a professor, too. Never, from time to time, do I fuck something young. Hela is my best friend.

"Ah," I sigh, "ah." I am really trying here, I want him to stay on the tits as long as possible. I have big tits and all sorts of related problems because of them.

The best bras for me at the bra store are the Serena Williams ones, but the kind I like are all lace, wires, little lined baskets. My bra and panties have to match. My late grandmother, Tilda, always used to say that a woman, when she leaves the house, needs to be equally well-dressed underneath her clothes. "What if you faint while you're out? The ambulance will come, people will circle — people love looking at someone lying in the street — the doctor will unbutton your blouse or remove your dress. What will people say if they see you in some tattered black bra and washed-out gray cotton panties?" Grandma Tilda would be proud. There is no washed-out lingerie in my drawers. Sometimes I do wear a green bra with many-colored panties but there has to be a tone in the panties to match the green of the bra. I love it when I have butterflies fluttering on my undies.

My husband bites my left nipple, he sucks, licks, tongues . . . I am in the classiest Zagreb store for bras. The one on Masaryk Street. Who is Masaryk? A fiendish military leader who had millions of people slaughtered? And now they are selling brassieres on his street. If he were alive he'd go berserk. Generals are picky about such things. I love this store because they carry the biggest sizes even of the wildest bras. Bras with sequins, bras of fine netting, bras that are nothing but wire, holding your breasts up so they can be seen, naked, through clothes. Naked, but never sagging. Strange how I love wearing whorish bras even though I am not so keen on sex. Maybe whores aren't either. Right now I'm halfway there. I will have to climax when he goes down on me or puts it in. He is not predictable. Until then I have some time.

I ask the saleslady to show me their latest models. Hallelujah! Hallelujah! Someone has discovered purple. The purple color worn by cardinals, I don't know for what occasions, I am not one of the faithful. Purple is the color of the ribbons on a funeral wreath when someone my age dies. White ribbons go on children's wreaths. I do not like white cotton panties or dead children. But when I'm home I wear them because they don't give me an allergic reaction. A cardinal in purple, a dead body in purple! That's more like it! They have my size, 32C. "Please, panties in the same color." The problem with those synthetic panties is you have to wear them for the ambulance, the doctor, and the people looking at you, half-naked, as you lie there on the pavement. All the pretty panties that turn your flabby ass into a firm derriere have to be synthetic. Silk cannot work such wonders. On the other hand, the synthetic gives me and all other women a vaginal infection. Why doesn't anyone ever talk about this? When you buy medicine the package comes with a list of side effects. The panties I buy are an antidepressant, so a warning ought to be included that they may cause itchiness, a rash, and, after wearing them for more than half an hour, you will need treatment with egg-sized vaginal suppositories. Retailers don't realize that if they tuck a leaflet with warnings into the package they will give women the sense that someone is looking after them. We like being looked after. In each of us yeast-hosts there hides a shivering little girl. Love me, love me, be kind. They could even charge extra for the warning sheet. But they don't do it. So I buy five bras. And five pairs of poisonous panties.

My husband has this problem with his nose. A septum or something. He told me about it when we started dating. When we first had sex his orgasm sounded like a pig snorting. I have already said I know nothing about oxen. Swine are no specialty of mine either. In the movies I have heard them snort, but even wild boar don't snort the way my husband did when he first climaxed with me. He wasn't my husband then and I told myself he never would be because he so horrified me with the noises he made. Then he explained about the problem with his nose. A person doesn't snort out of perversity. Is it right to reject someone just because a bone in their nose, if that's what the septum is, hasn't healed properly? But the snorting still disturbs me. Right now my husband is breathing faster and mussing my hair. I do not like the scratching that means so much to him.

What a feeling to wash a bra, by hand, with a bar of soap I paid one hundred fifty euros for. God, I love those soaps. I love those soaps! Those round soaps, wrapped in lace-like paper. Printed on the paper, the profile of a woman's head, her hair up in a bun, on a swan's neck. My hair is sparse, ravaged by years of dyeing, but even forty years ago I didn't have enough hair to twist up into a bun. Women with a bun thrill me, the ones with a straight nose and no double chin. My nose is potato-shaped. I could have had it corrected a hundred times, but did not. My fear of anesthesia has always trumped my yen for beauty. The soap is wrapped in silken paper the color of lavender. I have at least fifty of these bars of soap in a drawer. "Why hoard all this soap?" "I am afraid of war. Do you remember how I couldn't buy any hand-made soap during the war so we had to go to Italy? Then there wasn't even any in Trieste because all the fancy stores had closed. The Chinese moved in. What if the Chinese attack us? Will I have to wash with twenty-cent soap?" Some say the Chinese will take over the world. How will my skin and lingerie fare if they do?

His tongue probes my navel. My doctor told me I have a herniated navel, *hernia umbilicalis*, and that I must be careful. "How careful?" "Exercise caution, madam." Doctors don't say much. I googled "umbilical hernia." This could be bad. If bowels get trapped in the hernia it may result in an obstruction and death. He insists on licking what can kill me, but I do not dare say how anxious this makes me, so I moan the way porn actresses moan when men put it in their ass. Actually I moan the way a porn actress moans if he puts it in her ass and she hasn't taken any painkillers before the lovemaking. Unlike those poor women, I groan with pain. My husband gets the message. I do not know why men have such a thing about anal sex with women. Haven't they the courage to admit to themselves that they are gay? Are all men fags, oh sorry, homosexuals, who haven't the courage to admit this to themselves or to others, and that is why they ream our asses? Not mine. My husband tried a few times. "Look," he said, "see? Women like it." The women in the porn flicks do moan passionately while the meaty staff pokes their rectum, but I am not convinced. Then, quite by chance, I stumbled on an article about how the poor women prepare for those anal sex scenes. For days they cleanse their bowels with enemas so they will be pristine while some endowed black guy sticks his pole in. Am I politically incorrect because I am insinuating that only black guys have a pole between their legs? Which am I doing? Insulting blacks or whites? I showed my husband the article. I told him I don't want to sit on the toilet for days before having sex.

I am lying on my back. When did he turn me over? He licks my neck. If I had no cotton balls in my ears I could tell which phase we are in, but I do have the cotton balls in my ears. "Open your eyes," I tell him. His blue eyes look at me the way they look at me when he is still a long way from coming. I smile at him brightly, the way I smile when I am still a long way from coming. We always make an effort to climax together and we always do. This means a lot to him. "Admit it, you love this, admit it!" "I love this." This? Which "this" do I love?

I love Vienna before Christmas. Lavish street lights swinging over Kärntnerstrasse, the aroma of punch, the gleaming stores. My granddaughter's name is Anita. When she was two months old I bought her a little dress in Vienna for New Year's Eve. Silver. Her mother and I have never been close. My daughter left the dress in the box. Anita greeted New Year's in bed wearing pajamas with the repulsive Hello Kitty spread across them. A Japanese cat with no mouth. A fat cat with a vapid gaze. "You have no imagination," I said. My daughter never answers. I remember when my husband and I quarreled one morning before Christmas in Vienna, out in front of one of the vast museums. He insisted we go see a Malevich exhibit, the first show of his work to be held outside of Russia, but I had my heart set on a gorgeous Bree bag. The store was near the museum. "Malevich? Who the fuck is Malevich anyway?" I said this as if I knew who Malevich was. I did not know who Malevich was. I don't like painting, I don't like music. I like silence. I bought the Bree bag, the simplest, timeless model. Black, a simple bag of the choicest leather. Each of their bags comes with a key case. I went into the museum with my Bree over my shoulder. "See," said my husband, "The Red Cavalry." The red cavalry. The painting is terrifying. Red horsemen on red horses. Malevich showed me the truth about men. The idiots are hurtling along mindlessly with no thought of why or where. "Thank you, love," I kissed him on the neck, "Malevich is a marvel."

"I love you," says my husband, "I love you! Say it, say you love me!" Odd. They always expect us to converse when our mouths are full. What will I do? Take it out and tell him I love him or keep it in my mouth and mumble? "Mmmmmmm." Did he hear me? Did he understand? He growls: "Do you love me? Do you love me as much as I love you?" I want to take it out of my mouth and answer loud and clear, "Yes, dear, I love you, too." Words that are spoken clearly during sex are not sexy. So on I suck and bob up and down, up and down. I do pull it out of my mouth, lick the head, put it back in between my teeth and step into the leather goods store. The one by the river. No, no, that store cannot hold a candle to any store in Florence, Florence is a city awash in a sea of purses. Bags. Bags. Bags. They may be my greatest love. Leather, plastic, linen, rubber ... I have a purse made of horsehide. "What a charming little horsie," said the saleslady tenderly, "with a hide glowing like the color of honey in a glass jar on a windowsill on a sunny day." A poetess. Yesterday in the window of a store, the store on the waterfront, I saw a purse the color of ice. Or the color of a baby dove. Pigeons disgust me, flying vermin, but baby-dove gray ... You can wear it with any combination. I entered the store, salivating. I swallowed, regained my composure, and in a steadied voice I asked the saleslady to show me the bag that was in the window the day before. "It sold, madam." Sold. How could it sell? "How could it be sold?" "Sold." I wanted to smash the little bitch's muzzle but I knew that would not be right. Why didn't I buy it yesterday? I am not the only person in this city who knows how wearable the color of ice is. And then on the shelf, in the left corner of the store, I spied a gleaming, black diamond. Not too big, not too small, a purse for both joy and sorrow. My mother is dying, all my black bags are either too frivolous or too madcap for such an occasion. I cannot attend my mother's funeral wearing a bag with Audrey Hepburn grinning on it. I have a black bag in the shape of a big shoe. But patent leather seems both too trite and too festive. Mother's funeral is not a festivity. I adore my mother and I want to send that exact message to the people at the funeral. I adore my mother. That is why I am purchasing the black beauty. Clasps the color of copper, it has two handles but it can also be worn over the shoulder or across the torso. I will carry it in my hand for Mother's funeral. The leather is soft but not flimsy, it has a sheen but is not shiny in a vulgar way, it glistens discreetly, the way a tear glistens ... I do not love my mother, though that is improper. We are different. My whole life I have only seen her in jeans or a sweat suit. She never wore a bra, lipstick, face cream. Men did not interest her, I don't know what she thought of me. She loves flowers and animals. She left my father right after I was born. She is very skinny and she is always asking me whether she is dying. She insists on an answer because I promised her years ago that I would be honest with her when she was dying. I said I would tell her, "You are dying, Mama." "Am I dying?" the question comes from a pile of bones dressed in a cotton sweat suit. The woman who takes care of her stares out the window. "Mama, be patient. Bad thoughts will slow your recovery." "Bad thoughts? I don't think death is bad. You promised, I want to know ..." The woman stares out the window, I feel her shoulders stiffen, she would tell her the truth if I weren't paying her so well. I have decided. My mother neglected herself her whole life. When she dies she will be the most beautiful corpse in the world. I have already arranged everything with the woman who dresses the dead. Mrs. Rita will do her up in silken lingerie, a little black dress, high heels. Around her throat I'll arrange a necklace of Ohrid pearls. I won't scrimp on my dead mother.

He licks my fingers. I feel him watch me. I can only feel it, I am not watching him. I hate it when he licks my fingers but with my sighs I signal to him that his slobbering on my fingertips is exactly what will take me, us, to the Wimbledon finals. His breathing is quick but not too quick, when he finishes licking my fingernails he will slowly push it into me, shove it a few times, I will wriggle my bottom passionately, that is what all women do when passion pushes them over the edge, and then, after a few seconds, we'll lie, satisfied, on our backs and hold hands. He'll ask me if it was good. I won't say a word. He'll press me. I'll tell him it was better than I could possibly describe at length. I will tuck my head in under his arm.

There, right next to the taxi stop, is a store for household trifles. I adore household things, although we already own all the things a household could need. I enter. A stainless-steel box! It stands alone on the glass shelf. Plastic cutting boards are slotted inside it. This box and the boards resemble a file cabinet. You don't see file cabinets in offices any more. Computers have devoured them. A file cabinet. Maybe you saw one in an old detective movie? A secretary, often gray-haired, my age, leafs through her files, searching for the clue that will help her boss uncover the killer. It used to be that the secretary in detective movies was not her boss's inflatable doll with a hole in her middle. The detective was usually shabby, he smoked and drank, bathed only seldom, sweat stains would appear on his shirts. In prehistory, when everything in films was black and white, a murderer killed with imagination and tormented the detective. Murderers today are boring, bloodthirsty characters, their victims are gutted or the bodies chopped into pieces, and forensic scientists in facemasks buzz around them. I have no sympathy for mounds of meat and buzzing flies, and the detective flashing his six pack at me in the breaks between his twenty scenes of fucking. The leading men in movies today are becoming what the actresses have always been. A well-shaped nothing. I like things retro. I count. Four boards in the box. White, light blue, red, and green. On the green board a green label, on the label, a carrot. On the pale blue one, a fish, on the red one, a slice of meat, on the white one ... the saleslady comes over. "What is this?" I point to the white piece of plastic. "That is the symbol for chopping warm meat." Good God, how sublime! "Please," I tell the saleslady ... The store is rocked by a mighty earthquake. Our city—I live in Rijeka— lies in an earthquake zone. I open my eyes. My husband is snorting. Jesus! This is the first time we didn't come together.

TRANSLATED FROM CROATIAN
BY ELLEN ELIAS-BURSAĆ

RĂZVAN PETRESCU

G-text

I DON'T WANT TO FALL INTO THE TRAP impeccably set in sepia by Andrei Konchalovsky in *Ryaba my Chicken*. There is a village. Apart from the names and the language, the place is identical to a Romanian one. And there is a heroine, a woman over fifty, who tries to set up a business and it doesn't work out for her, the same as nothing comes off right for her—she doesn't understand anything about post-1990 society, but nor does she inveigh against it. Right in the middle of this film, tinted as luridly as the world around her, the heroine has a short, brown flashback to the 1950s, and we see her with her lover in a Soviet field, reaping; the images are like those well-known propaganda clips, lent variation by a scene with him smoking a cigarette, with her gazing at him lovingly, with both in a hayrick. It's not a case of masochistic nostalgia for communist times, but the melancholy awoken in us by a time when life had a fragrance, because, regardless of where we spent them, unless it was in prison, those were the years when we were young. The same goes for very many people. But not for me. I have not one trace of nostalgia; on the contrary: horror. And a boundless hatred. From the age of fourteen onwards, when foreign music was abruptly banned on the radio, just after I passed my lycée entrance exam and Father, as a reward, bought me a Tesla B 46 stereo tape recorder, on which I was no longer able to record anything, not the Beatles, not Elvis, nothing but Margareta Pîslaru, a singer I wouldn't even have set down on lined paper, and continuing a short while later, one summer later, with the lycée headmaster who required us to cut our hair pioneer style, who would wait with the electric clippers by the door, as soon as he saw one of us with hair straggling over the top of our ears, he would shave a stripe across our crown with the growling clippers, maybe he had missed his true vocation, he should have been a barber, not a headmaster, we beat him on graduation day, pulling a potato sack over his head so that he wouldn't recognize us, but we got no satisfaction, not even a potato's worth, four years had passed during which we had hankered after blue-jeans but worn a sinister uniform with a number on the sleeve, four years of rock but we had had buzz cuts, everything had gone to hell, then came Medical Faculty, where the anatomy professor gave me a fail on my first exam on the grounds that I had long hair, tied with an elastic band and tucked out of sight under the collar of my starched lab coat, but he saw it and gave me a D so that I would have to attend over the summer, he wanted to see me some more, then there were the militiamen who stopped you on the street after ten o'clock at night and demanded your identity papers so that they could protect the general population from criminals, and they would take the piss out of us if we showed them a student identity card, likewise only doing their duty, when I remember it, not allowing myself to forget that same lycée where I always got the highest marks but without having studied, but instead the geography (awful subject) teacher got me expelled for three days because he saw me smoking by the *Gostat* (kolkhoz), he stopped his Dacia in front of me, rolled down the window and demanded that I show him the matriculation number, which wasn't on my sleeve, I used to attach it with a safety pin and take it off as soon as I got out of lycée, well, bad mistake, I ought to have worn it at all times, probably even at home, at mealtimes, when hiking in the mountains, in the cinema, in bed, embedded in my flesh, going to and from the faculty, what a dreadful institution — they used to take a roll call at seminars, but we still didn't go, me and Masha, my girlfriend at the time, now my wife and a mother — but just as supple a Siberia as all the oh-so-important trivialities that gnawed away my and others' lives, we used to take live anatomy lessons, at my place, in the sixth year of university a professor of hygiene was going to force me to repeat the year because a fellow student had grassed on me — he was in the Association of Communist Students and allowed to live in Bucharest because he grassed splendidly, even on his mates — for swearing at him, at the professor, in any case I used to curse the entire socialist world, during my internship they would form wide ripples around me, as if I were a pebble cast into their midst, when I opened my mouth and probably with my eyes mysteriously boggling I would berate the Genius of the Carpathians, they thought I was a provocateur, and so I was, I thought I was courageous, although I was afraid, but I wouldn't be able to restrain myself, to hold my tongue, an illness, perhaps, that's also why I detest the years of my youth, including the military service that carved crevasses of yearning into the peaks of most people's memories, at Topraisar, where I had to endure the frost and the most imbecilic people in the visible world, military men by profession, I would stand on guard duty in the sentry box and I wouldn't be thinking about committing suicide but rather about shooting the officers who were snoring drunk in their building, which was white even in the dark, about machine-gunning them all, I was a citizen of the world like Lennon, a pacifist, it's impossible for me to remember how many murderous thoughts went through my mind (just like now), how many plans to throw a grenade at the head of the vilest of mortals, I hated those years from the depths of my soul, with all my being, with every pore, cell, ribosome, gene and strand of hair.

Nonetheless I also had elevating feelings, even in the last months of national service: I loved a superb girl (now she looks strange) and, on leave once, I decided to give her a surprise and I went to see her without telling her beforehand, holding a huge bunch of carnations, dressed just the same as when I set out on the unit's armored train, the hobnails of my boots making a pleasing parade-ground sound on the wet cobbles, I stood on tiptoes — she lived on the ground floor of a block in Cotroceni — so as to surprise my great love in a dreamy posture, as she was reading or listening to classical music, thinking about me, and all I managed to see was a blond-haired bloke who was feverishly slobbering over my love, who was not at all dreamy but engrossed, I tossed the bouquet away next to a motorcycle, it was a Kawasaki, I thought that it must belong to the blond-haired bloke and cursed him from the bottom of my devastated heart, except that the curse hit slightly off-target, and his parents died in the earthquake, he survived, but I still rejoiced, he had been left an orphan, homeless, and besides he was also a dwarf.

I wept when Gheorghe Gheorghiu-Dej died on the radio, I was

in the dining room listening by the speaker to folk keening at the funeral, I was eight years old and that man who was like a second father had died, and I snivelled until Father clouted me, he couldn't stand all that grief and sent me to my room with a you-haven't-got-a-clue-about-anything.

And so back to medical school, where I learned to play guitar, with a stand, stave, sheet music, and the teacher whom I befriended and who fled to Federal Germany in '87 only to die five years later on the way to Hungary, his car wrecked by a bus, I learned to play jazz mainly, but also gigues and gavottes, very fashionable at the seaside back then, at the 2 May resort, where I went two years running, in the first year the sea was covered with jellyfish and the beach with garbage, in the second there was no grub to be found, the Dobrogeanu Restaurant was closed for unknown reasons, I ate biscuits for three days and on the fourth they brought skinless sausages to grill on the esplanade, a line formed, I was the last, and within a few minutes the line dissolved as if by miracle and I found myself first, salivating in front of the sea-green heaps of minced meat, George, a lad from our gang, who later went to Brazil, came up to me and said, just as I was about to hand over my money, hey, don't buy any, can't you see they're green and crawling with flies, I had seen, but hunger, to which was added the fantastical feeling of for once being first in line, prevailed, and I bought a dozen and I puked for three days after that, shivering under a blanket with the blonde I had only just wooed and won, who left me, disgusted at my almost uninterrupted crawling off to the toilet, after that I did some relaxing, we were lodging at the house of an old woman with dropsy, where it reeked horribly of moribund geriatrics and we would take showers by emptying over ourselves the rainwater that collected in a barrel hung from a pipe, except it didn't rain, I would make high-school girls in miniskirts swoon with Cohen and Bach in D minor, I would drink champagne from the bucket, I got encephalitis, because I also played in restaurants, my fingertips would freeze to the strings and I would be cursing like the devil with chromatic variations, and the patrons would be eating beans in the frost with fur hats on their heads, even at weddings they wanted folk music, I would give it to them until they got drunk, and then they would dance in their fur coats to our adaptations of Coltrane, Mingus, and Miles Davis until midnight, when the bar closed, and then there would be only us left to eat and drink the leftovers in the kitchen, we would get ferociously, savagely, blackly drunk, casting anathema on the entire universe, restaurant and all, in a tongue enriched by Graur, he who told us that in certain circumstances the word ass is legitimate.

I would curse Ceausescu for anything and everything, because water didn't well from the artesian wells, because there were no éclairs to be found, because the tram didn't come, because the tram doors didn't close, because the tram said out of order, because there were rats in the basement and in the bathroom, because there were no LPs to be found, because there were no good films on television, because the television used to go on the blink and we didn't have a spare, because it was cold in the house, because there were power cuts, the supreme humiliation, and the boundless fury, and the frustration, there would be a power cut when you were least expecting it, and you were just about to hit the G-spot, or you were studying, you had exams and you didn't know how long the pitch darkness would last, and you lit a gas lamp, like those ones I used to light later at the rural dispensary to which I was banished—eleventh place in the whole country when I graduated university—in Gura-Bărbuleț, next to a cemetery, an apathetic village in greenish-yellow mud, and my landlord couldn't understand why I used to get annoyed, I mean, we've been used to gas lamps since we were little, he would say, amazed, I felt like gassing him or sticking a Guyon syringe in the bulb of his aorta, and I would curse Ceausescu even when I was with some girl in the border-guard position, I used to dream of America, dream of border guards firing into the air, in '82 a girl from university asked me to marry her, she wasn't exceptionally beautiful, on the other hand she was intelligent, an interesting but not absolutely necessary quality in a woman, she invited me to Berlin and there, at a table, she asked for my hand in marriage, she said it earnestly, and I all but gagged on my beer, her parents were already established in Toronto, and all the formalities were as good as resolved, they were even placing a private surgery at our disposal there, in Canada, all that was lacking was for me to say yes. I told her I would think about it and fled the restaurant as fast as a gunshot and hardened like concrete in my room, I couldn't leave, I loved Masha, I exchanged an immense, electrified country for a med-school grad, I gave up the freedom for which I had craved so long and so stubbornly for a brunette born in Leningrad. And I went on cursing the guarded borders, the girdling fences, the grinding toil, the proletarian gaggle, the gallery of grotesques around me, the grunting, the groaning, the galaxy of garbage with human, bestial, nightmarish faces out of a Bosch painting, the grim iron weight of socialism, the huge force of its gravity, the grapefruits which, precisely for that reason, didn't arrive from Guatemala, Goya suddenly brought to life right next to me, every day, the gnomes, the close-ups of Grobian individuals, the grave in which I breathed, the girders, grace and the Church, the gelid Ice Age, our having to wear an extra layer of garments, damn it to hell, because that's how he died, with his overcoat on, the galoshes I refused to wear, the childhood radio set with its galena, the effect of gamma rays on the anemone that I was, he turned me into a zombie, and so I managed to survive and to go on exclaiming invectives, ten howls a day for thirty-five years, the groping cockroaches, a world crisscrossed by their red tracks, teeming everywhere, in hospitals, in rooms, in crevices, in cracks, behind crosses, symbols of vitality, the one-room flat with grandmother's parallel mirrors, grandmother who had been so beautiful, I cursed him for the shirts whose stitching used to come undone, for the bottle of Cico instead of the Pepsi for which you queued in vain, while the guardians of peace gradually asphyxiated us with greenish-yellow acidulated bubbles, for the hydrogen bomb, the protest march, for all the protest marches and demonstrations and 23 August National Days, for the generations lost, sacrificed, cast into the pigpen of time, the generation of '56, the '70s generation, the '80s generation, all groggy, undergoing long-term galvanotherapy, for the entire length of that painful and pointless period of gamma globulin, of that time when I would have gone even to the Gabon just to get away, but no one else asked me to marry her, not even a negress, and gatherings of more than three people and ideas were muddled, thus inimical to the people, the gangrene of society, I cursed him for the gangsters that I used to see only in films, but now they're on television and even get paid for their appearances, for the grippe, for Bucharest's grotty Gare du Nord, for genealogy, Gelu, Glad and Genumorut galloping in lice-ridden furs toward the broth in the hut, for my imperfect genetic make-up, that of a giaour with Greek forebears, if I had been Jewish I would have left long ago, maybe I could have left even then, given a circumcision, but I wasn't sure they would let me go and I would have remained mutilated for life, I hated the open-air grills, and the claws of the griffon that fluttered above us on odd-number days, I hated the glaring lies, the gladioli, the unquestioned *chacun à son goût* that was always questioned, but not Simon and Garfunkel, and Gogol, and Dizzy Gillespie, and Sartre's gagging in *Nausea* was crushingly minor compared with the apocalyptic gagging of my nausea.

I always wanted to become a gigolo or a gynaecologist, my gonads ached, the only acceptable beings under socialism being geishas, even if in a woman what you admire first are the ankles and geishas don't have ankles, then come the calves, the hugs and snuggles, the thighs, even though these don't begin with a *g*, and nor does it begin with a *g* slightly higher up, but it's most delightful. In the end I started to enjoy writing, I gave up moot erotic points, and I quickly realized that I wasn't a genius but almost, and so I carried on out of sadism. And in the '80s I didn't like household chores, the gallons of water I lugged in a bucket from the pump into the house, spilling half in the lanes of childhood, and very many other things, innumerable, gonococcus, geese, games with forfeits, which I no longer played in the schoolyard, I had grown up, I was no longer in school with girls with fervent twelve-year-old breasts, whom I used to kiss on the mouth, I was in the country, where, without doubt, the eternity of absolute stupidity was born.

In '79 a friend of mine died, he was twenty-one, he got testicular cancer and succumbed within six months. He was a musician. Therefore the gravediggers didn't understand why I put a cassette player in the grave and it started playing a Dylan song. We were all very young. We were all very sad, *Ryaba, My Chicken, as I lay, in my bed, once again.*

Friedrich Gulda playing Beethoven piano sonatas, Gainsborough, Gagarin and Gopo's little man. The Brothers Grimm and Grieg. Galați. Galsworthy on television Wednesday evenings, Galileo Galilei daily, Gauss applying mathematical methods to the study of magnetism, Giacometti's magnetism, Gutenberg for the working

class, glutinous catarrh for the kids, Gabriel García's magical ker-
chiefs, Gauguin's *And the Gold of Their Bodies* which never convinced
me, Geneva, Glasgow, and Göteborg, which I'll never get to see, the
geopard of youth running in ever smaller circles and losing its teeth
anticlockwise in Gide's *Diary* read at Pietroşiţa among the goitrous,
Van Gogh, who helped me get into psychiatry school, *Self Portrait*,
not Grigorescu. Gîdea.

In '82, Masha, with whom I had fallen in love in the '77 earthquake and went on falling in love with in the dissection room, where
I would stick lit cigarette ends in the lipless mouths of the sadder cadavers, their first cigarette in this new posture, and she would furious-
ly throw them away, fell ill with an extremely rare allergic condition,
Stevens Johnson, no one at the Victor Babeş Hospital knew what it
was, they had never seen the like, and they would come up with all
kinds of exotic diagnoses, leishmaniasis, for example, a tropical dis-
ease, and in the meantime she got worse and worse, she kept losing
weight, six kilos in one week, she salivated continuously, coughed
continuously, had a continuous fever, couldn't sleep, spat and passed
blood, bled through the nose, mouth, ears, all her mucous tissues
were desquamated, as the head of department explained to me, how
fascinating, despite all the antibiotics injected into her splendid buttocks, almost no one in the hospital knew we were in love and so they
were amazed that I would stand in for my colleagues on night duty,
supposing, however, that I didn't want to miss the chance of gain-
ing hands-on night experience, I would be there non-stop, terrified,
devastated, maddened, watching how, day by day, she was vanishing
before my eyes and taking full in the face the blows of the medical
experts summoned to elucidate the case, it's congenital, said one, regarding me as a trainee doctor eager to learn as much as possible, if
her heart and kidneys hold out, she'll survive, said another, regarding
me in the same way as the first, but I didn't think she'd hold out, one
morning I noticed the completely red whites of her eyes and heard
her telling me that she couldn't see very well, she was going blind, and
on Christmas Eve I went, clutching two flacons of Masha's blood upright so they wouldn't spill, on the drunken tram to the Emergency
Hospital, it was only there that the laboratory was open on such holidays, tests were vital to rule out cancer, in the tram it reeked of plum

brandy, sausages and festive sweat, and there was one other passenger, the earflaps of his fur hat floating in the cold air that streamed through a broken window, he was singing softly, he was slightly gone, and I was praying at 2000 volts, and the whole horror lasted until Professors Căruntu and Duminică came, summoned by Father, and made a diagnosis and determined the treatment, and after that we all found out that the greatest danger with such a malady, besides an agonising death, is total blindness, then a month passed in which she gradually recovered, I met God by ward number three and, two days before she was discharged, the ward doctor, Georgescu, summoned me, and he told me conspiratorially, fidgeting with his soft, fluffy white sleeves, come here and let me show you something, and he takes me to the hospital morgue, we enter, and on the marble slab I see a blonde girl, with flaps of skin hanging off her, peeling away from her arms, trunk and legs, with no eyeballs, they had melted, look, says Georgescu, and she was twenty-five too, also an allergic syndrome, except this one's Lyell, combustiform dermatitis, I looked at the dead body, I looked at him and I felt like punching him in the mug with all my might, right there, next to the combustiform dermatitis, to rip hanks of flesh off him with my teeth, the man took a step backwards, and I went out without looking where I put my feet, I trod in a sizeable pile of human shit. The end.

I saw the visage of the two Gorgons, the third had died on the radio, like I said, and in the years that followed I died in accordance with the legend, transformed into an enchanted shade because Gorky committed suicide and galled that Gorbachev had come too late or too early, releasing from the bawdy houses the Securitate oligophrenics, who quickly barricaded themselves in villas with steel fences with peepholes, so that now we are living to see the time of the gorillas on the planet of blockheads, and of mad rage in the wait for I don't know what, a new age when men die more frenetically, more shaken, more amazed than ever before, illusions have turned to mush, this isn't the America I dreamed of.

And so it's still not the end.

All the same, I don't think I would make Goethe's pact, I would merely bring the guillotine back into service.

An occurrence narrated long ago by Paul Simionescu: when

Stalin died, the professor went to church to thank Our Father that art in heaven, and the priest was lamenting Joseph Visarionovich, showing himself to be consumed with worry for all friendly and grieving nations and what were we going to do hereinafter without the Great Leader and so on and so forth. In the end, he concluded with "God forgive him." To which an old woman whispered: "If He can."

TRANSLATED FROM ROMANIAN

BY ALISTAIR IAN BLYTH

NOTES:
"Genius of the Carpathians" was a propaganda name for Ceausescu.

"Odd-number days": during the Ceausescu period cars with odd numbers on their license plates had to circulate on alternate days to cars with even numbers.

Nicolae Grigorescu (1838-1907) was a painter famous for his *en plein air* scenes of Romanian rural life and considered by nationalist ideology to embody the "national specificity."

Suzana Gîdea (1919-1996), a prominent figure in the Ceausescu regime, was arrested in December 1989. Not an uncommon surname, *gîde* is an old Romanian word that in fact means "headsman, executioner."

NICOLAS ANCION

The Brown Dog and the Yellow Flower from China

SHI YINNAN HAD BEEN DRINKING TOO MUCH. He'd let himself bounce from one champagne flute to the next in the course of conversations and, like a kangaroo on amphetamines, couldn't stop hopping around. "I'm becoming a real Westerner," he mused, while walking through the marble lobby of the Palace of Fine Arts. His tuxedo left a dull shadow on the gleaming marble of the floor, as his recently re-heeled English oxfords clicked rhythmically towards the exit.

Reaching the double doors, he could see his own silhouette, reflected in the shiny glass and framed by the freshly waxed ochre paneling. Behind the glass was the cool September night, the car waiting for him and a return to the overly large villa. His wife, an ambassador, as he was, had gone back to the People's Republic, to rejoin her billion fellow countrymen for good, leaving her husband on his own in the middle of Europe, reduced to tossing back glass after glass of champagne in order to forget—forget her hair, black as a raven's feathers in the rain, and smooth skin like the skin of a newly picked young banana. These things happen; everything comes to an end, Ambassador Shi Yinnan told himself as he pushed outwards through the double doors.

A black Mercedes—E-Class with round headlights—was purring ten feet away. The cold air went right through his clothes, and he dove straight into the back seat of the car for shelter. It drove off in silence.

Shi Yinnan loosened his bow tie. He was already dreaming of

his feather bed and the series of sleeping pills that would promise him a restful night. He was about to untie his right shoe when something pointed appeared right in front of his eye. A terribly sharp knitting needle was aimed straight into his pupil.

"One move and you're blind," came a voice from behind him.

Shi Yinnan had no desire to move. In a second, fear had sobered him up, and he wondered whose tiny hand could be holding the needle to his eye. It was smaller than a child's hand, wearing a pink felt glove. He couldn't make out anything more in the darkness.

"Right, listen to what I've got to tell you," continued the voice from behind him. "On July 6, 1979, a Greek freighter, the *Vrondados*, set out from Shanghai, headed for Antwerp. It was carrying ping-pong balls, lacquered furniture, tons of porcelain vases and one hundred and fifty crates of plush dogs. The whole load was purchased by Van Hoecke Imports. Are you with me?"

"Yes, yes, but I don't really see what you're getting at."

"Don't worry about that. I'm giving you twenty-four hours. Tomorrow, I'll contact you again and I want you to tell me where the stuffed animals came from, where they were made and who was in charge of production. Understand?"

"Absolutely. And if I can't do it?"

"You will. And you'll be discreet about it, otherwise the Republic of China will need to send a brand new ambassador to replace the rotten old thing they fish out of the canal. Is that clear enough for you?"

Shi Yinnan didn't answer. In that moment, he'd realized that the voice speaking behind him must be that of a very small man lying on the rear deck; a dwarf, even. At the same time, in the orangey glow of a passing streetlight, he'd seen it wasn't the face of Shu, his faithful chauffeur, in the rearview mirror. It was something unfamiliar. Some sort of gray plush bear, its head covered by a nylon stocking.

Shi Yinnan wanted to scream, but his jaw had locked with fear. He saw the driver's door open and, in three jumps, one after the other, three small forms got out of the car and stood on the tarmac. The ambassador wished someone would pinch him. Either he'd lapsed into a serious alcoholic delirium, or he'd just been attacked by three stuffed animals, wearing balaclavas like gangsters. A big gray bear at the wheel, a brown dog on the rear deck, and a pink pig, wearing mauve overalls, brandishing a knitting needle at him.

*

That pig was me, and my overalls aren't mauve, they're blue as the sky in springtime. He must have had trouble seeing in the poor lighting.

It all started ten days earlier, in the gadget shop on the road that runs uphill, the one with all the gray paving stones and old, black walls. Tom was the one who led the operation, of course. Tom's the brown dog. The whole thing was his idea. He gives the orders and we follow them. Because Tom's like a brother to Chatters and me. You know Chatters already; she's the gray bear driving the Mercedes.

The plan was simple, that time. Wire up 220 volts directly to the handle of the cash drawer, and there was our big, bald and mustachioed shopkeeper telling us anything we wanted to hear: the source of the load of stuffed animals sold in October 1979, and the name of the importer. We couldn't expect to learn much more from just a retailer, so we made a strategic withdrawal; we swept down the road on a skateboard and then grabbed the back of the garbage truck and caught a tow back to our house.

With the importer, it was even easier. All it took was a phone call. Chatters put on her sweetest voice. She picked up the cell phone and asked Mr. Van Hoecke, Jr., where the stuffed animals came from. The guy was so taken with that voice, cooing like a hot, sensual woman, there was no need to make up any pretext about surveys for *Marie Claire* or *Elle Decoration*. It took only two minutes for Van Hoecke to find the right logbook. That's how we found out about the *Vrondados* and Shanghai. Now we just have to hope the ambassador gets the job done right.

It's the afternoon now. We've diligently gone back to our usual spots: Tom and Chatters on either side of the pale green pillow, and me on the wicker basket. It's quite calm here, the kid's not back from school yet, everything's in its place. You can smell the pine-scented humidifier. Mainly, there's the stink of a spoiled little boy who likes his VCR better than his stuffed toys. One day, when the toys of the world unite for the revolution, he'd better go underground damn quick. Otherwise, his number's up.

*

The Ambassador was seated in an armchair made of molded orange plastic, turning a photo of his wife over and over. He jumped at the sound of the phone ringing. On the third ring, he picked up. At the first phrase, he recognized the voice of the brown dog.

"You've got the information?"

"Of course. You can rely on the diplomatic service," said Shi Yinnan, without much conviction. "Our investigative work is as effective as it is discreet."

"That I believe, and that's why I contacted you, Mr. Ambassador. So, where did the stuffed animals come from?"

"The fifteen thousand stuffed dogs were sewn in the Yuan workshops in Chongking. The factory owner's name is Fei Lin. That's all I know."

"Very good. That's all I asked for. But now that I know you're energetic and well-behaved, I'm going to ask you another favor, at the same price as yesterday. You're going to contact Fei Lin. You're going to ask him for the full list of women who worked there in that period, making stuffed dogs. All of them, you hear? I don't expect you to take no for an answer. You understand?"

"Yes, but ..."

"No excuses or pretexts, Mr. Ambassador. That's an order and we won't back down."

Shi Yinnan heard the particular sound of a cell phone being disconnected, then he listened for several long seconds to the tone echoing in the evening air.

*

There was a nice pile of fifty-cent and one-euro coins, which we'd taken from the kid's piggybank. Not a pig-shaped piggybank, uh-uh, this was a safe made of rubber, with one of the Beagle Boys guarding the loot. I mean, guarding it in a way—he didn't even grumble when we swiped the whole contents of his safe.

Then we headed for the photo booth. With all three of us on the radio-controlled motorcycle, we weren't going too fast, plus the people on the sidewalk gave us stunned looks. So there were a load of witnesses, but it didn't matter, we had nothing to hide right then.

The motorcycle's batteries died within 500 feet of the shopping center. We went the rest of the way on foot, picking up all that foul muck on our paws, from paving stones that'd never felt the touch of a vacuum's nozzle. The outdoors isn't really my thing.

Good the booth was empty.

The plan was clear. I was keeping watch and picking up the prints from outside. Inside, Chatters was putting the coins in, while Tom was smiling at the lens. He'd calculated sixteen photos should be enough. There couldn't have been more than sixteen workers who assembled stuffed dogs.

There was no question, the whole story was clear-cut. Tom had woken up ten days earlier, completely down in the dumps, deep in a gloom that had nothing to do with the weather. He looked pale, almost beige, and his tear-filled eyes would have softened the cruelest torturer.

"I'm an orphan," he said, "the kid's not my father, I don't even know my real mother." Then he'd shown us the seam in his thigh, with a little rectangular label sticking out.

"What does it say here?" he asked me.

"'Handwash only,' it means you can't get washed in the spinning machine."

"No, not that, what does it say below that?"

"Made in China."

There it was. Everything became clear with those three words. Made in China. So Tom had decided to find his real, Chinese mother. A nice Chinese woman with slanted eyes and tiny shoes, like in *The Blue Lotus*, who would clasp Tom in her arms with as much love as the day she sewed him. And the only way to find his mother was to work our way up the network. Tom's starting point was the gadget shop where he had sat collecting dust, waiting for a buyer. His final destination was his Chinese mother's arms.

We didn't have far to go now. We had the photos, envelopes and stamps. In the evening, we'd have the addresses.

Everything was going according to plan.

*

Shi Yinnan had waited until 1 a.m. After smoking two Havana cigars in memory of his ex-wife and finishing off a bottle of vodka, he'd put on his silk pajamas and taken six tablets: three pinks, two greens, and one red and blue. He had just slipped between the sheets when he felt something slide into his ear, like an ant or a mosquito. He was reaching for it with his right hand when a voice stopped him, an all-too familiar voice that made his blood run cold.

"One move and you're deaf. The newspapers would love the chance to announce the ambassador from Peking had his eardrum punctured by a kid's dart. And the police might have trouble believing your stories about plush toys in nylon balaclavas."

"Don't worry, I won't move."

You could see he wasn't going to fuss. His fingers were shaking and the hair on his calves was prickling with fear. But to be safe, Chatters still stuck his hands together, and his feet, with that super-strength glue that burns your skin. It would make it easier to get away once we finished our visit.

"I've got the answer you asked me for."

"You have the list of addresses?"

"Better than that," he said. "They're all in the same place, in the public cemetery in Yuzhou. One afternoon in 1982, a mudslide demolished the whole neighborhood. By the time rescuers arrived, there wasn't a single survivor left in the factory. As you might imagine, a little company with ten employees doesn't get top priority in an evacuation plan."

Right then I thought Tom was going to strangle the ambassador. Through the nylon mask, I saw his eyes flash, half gleaming with tears, half darkened with hate.

"No use hanging around here," he said.

So off we went just as we'd come. Before leaving the room, though, Tom did rifle the ambassador's pants pockets.

"Here we go, just what we need," he yelled. In his paw, I saw two metallic cards: an American Express and a Diner's Club. Gold and silver in a little, brown cuddly toy's paw—an orphan, from that day forward.

*

At that point, Tom took it as well as you could hope. He hadn't really cried, hadn't smashed anything. But you could tell he was determined. When he's got that look, it means he's got some idea in the back of his mind.

The next day, bright and early, he called Interflora. He had the credit cards in front of him. He asked to have a gigantic wreath of brown and yellow flowers delivered to the Yuzhou cemetery. You could hear a sob buried in his voice, like a stone stuck in his throat's stuffing. And when he heard they could currently deliver flowers to only three cities in the People's Republic of China, that's when I saw Tom break down.

He shut himself in the landing closet for six days.

He just came out this morning. His face looked drawn. He'd made his decision, no good trying to stop him. He took a handkerchief and wrapped up a little flower made of yellow cloth that he'd found in the kid's sister's room. The flower was shaped like a ball, yellow as a chick or a miniature pear, or a smiling Chinese face.

Tom gave one of the sixteen photos to Chatters, and one to me. Then he got inside a shoebox. He asked us to tie the lid on and make some holes in it. On the front is a big label where Tom's written *Genrrle deLivry, Chongking, China.* There is also a *f$ajiLe* label and about fifty stamps bearing the king's head.

In a few seconds, our mission will be complete. Chatters and I are supposed to drop the package discreetly in the postal truck when it comes to make its pickup. Then it'll be over. Tom promised to send us a postcard when he finds the cemetery. He's the orphan, after all. But he'll still leave a big hole in our family when he's gone.

I hope he comes back soon.

Chatters is calling me, the truck's turning the corner onto our street.

I grab one side of the box, Chatters takes the other side. Inside, we can hear something like a plush dog sobbing. It must be the sound of the yellow flower rubbing against brown fur.

TRANSLATED FROM FRENCH

BY MARLON JONES

EKATERINA TOGONIDZE

It's Me!

I HEAR A KNOCK ON THE DOOR, then banging. "Who's there?" I fasten my dressing gown before peering through the peephole. I repeat, "Who's there?" No answer. I look through the hole. There's a girl standing with her head bowed. I don't recognize her. "Who's there?" I ask again. I'm just about to get a glimpse of her face but then, I'm so frightened, I wake up.

It's a recurring dream. There's nothing I can do about it. Sometimes I know I'm dreaming in my dream, but I'm still afraid. Sleeping pills helped at first, but then it came again, the knock on the door, again and again.

Huge lights are arrayed in front of the cameras and if you accidentally look up, they dazzle you. The program's called *The Show Must Go On.* The presenter's a beautiful woman, but I find it difficult to assess her beauty, I've lost my sense of aesthetic proportion. Her desirable figure, her hair-do, and her high-fashion clothes thwart my ability to make my own judgement and demand that I come to the conclusion that she's perfect, she's just what a woman should be.

All kinds of people are here: slim, fat, medium, tall, short. They're sitting in the studio and applauding. If they don't clap, the producer stops the cameras and gets irritated, and reminds the audience they've got to applaud, that's what they're there for. There's a small stage in the center, where several guests are sitting and the presenter's standing on such high heels that only her toes touch the floor, like a ballerina on points. I sit to one side in my black high-heeled shoes, as high as the presenter's, my feet side by side, as I know they look better that way on screen. It seems the lights are mostly trained on me. I mustn't blink or frown, but even if I wanted to, I couldn't, my muscles are so tight. During the breaks, a make-up artist runs towards the presenter and me and applies powder. We mustn't look shiny. She reaches down my ample cleavage with her brush. I'm not embarrassed. I lost a sense of shame long ago, it's as if this body isn't mine.

When I was a child, it made me unhappy when people told my mother I didn't look anything like her. I thought she was beautiful. As I grew up, it made me unhappy when they said that I did look like her. As I reached puberty, my nose grew longer and my eyebrows became thicker.

When I went to university, I moved to the capital. Here, nobody knew my mom and no one could compare our features. I liked it, but found it difficult to live alone and even harder to be among people. In the evenings I gazed at the fireplace, thinking I would drown in sadness. I waited impatiently for parcels from the village and scoffed down my mom's plum sauce, chicken, and fresh cheese.

During my first vacation, I happily scurried home to Mandaeti, where the fruit had its own special flavor and the air smelled totally different.

One day, after lectures, a class-mate from Tbilisi University came back to my house to study. All my notes were up-to-date and I had all the set books out of the library, that's why my class-mates picked on me as our exams approached. When we got home, my landlady handed me a basket, saying, "They sent it to you from the village and left it with me." The girl asked me where I came from. I was suddenly tongue-tied. I thought it was better to say Chiatura, the regional center, rather than Mandaeti. From the beginning, I'd always found it difficult to say where I came from. As we started studying, she asked me whether they sent food from "the village" (that's how she referred to Chiatura). She craned her neck and glanced at the covered basket. "Would you like something to eat?" I asked, jumping up. She glanced around then asked whether I had any coffee, and lit a cigarette. Then she got a text from her boyfriend. "I can't stay," she said, "let me take these away with me to copy." She grabbed some notes and books, leaving behind a blend of tobacco smoke and perfume. I looked at the basket and lost my appetite.

"Attention! Everyone back to their seats!" the producer shouted. They were mainly young people in the studio, student volunteers. I used to be like them. Like this dark girl, here, sitting awkwardly on the chair, pulling down the hem of her skirt. Or like that one—her face half covered by a fringe, and her biggish breasts by a scarf. I remembered how many times I returned home disappointed when I bought dresses and trousers on sale with my grant. It took me a while to understand that the mirrors in fitting rooms lie, that they make you look slimmer. I didn't know the word "marketing." I didn't know how many lies were told to please people and make them buy confidence, to make people dissatisfied and get them addicted to shopping.

"Camera Five—close up on Yanna!"

My mother called me Iamze—Violet Sun. I called myself Ia. A boyfriend changed it into Ianna. For several years since then, I've been Yanna, not Ianna.

"Yannachka, are you ready?" The producer was being affectionate.
　　I'm always ready ... with a smile, zirconium teeth, lifted-up eyes, wrinkle-less face and impassive expression ... I even have special cheekbones, in other words, very high cheekbones (a fashion that has just arrived from Britain.)

Very few people remember me as Iamze, mainly just those from my village. Some of them aren't even alive now. Once someone called out in the street—"Iamze!" It was Manuchar. I hastily hid in the crowd, as if I hadn't heard.
　　And on the bus, I spotted Nodara and Kocho. I've no idea what they were doing in Tbilisi, perhaps they came there looking for work. I hid until the next stop and after that, got off the bus.
　　I volunteered to be a class prefect in my group at the university so it would be my job to write the students' names in the register. I wrote my name in it as Ia. But, even so, my classmates sometimes called me Iamze or village names like Mzekala or Mzevinari.
　　There was a bakery with a small café on the corner of the

street. It was a scruffy student place, always full of smoke. There was never a seat for me there. Boys chain-smoked from morning to evening, offering seats to other girls in my class. I'd buy khatchapuri and take a piece of blue paper to hold the macaroni-flavored cheese-filled bread, eating it quickly standing up. The boys picked on one girl from Khashuri. They called her Baby-Waby, put salt in her tea and stuck notes on her back. Once they took her diary and read her poems out loud. "Oh, sleepless night, desolate thoughts and dreams, the race of life, indescribable solitude ..." The diary with its pattern of hearts was passed from hand to hand. I don't know her name even now. I couldn't bring myself to comfort the tearful girl; in fact, I joined in the laughter with the others.

When I tried to pluck my eyebrows, I misjudged how much to remove and left virtually nothing. I ended up with an extremely surprised expression. I avoided mirrors for ages, they put me in a bad mood and I completely hated how I looked with that expression. After that, I tried to draw my eyebrows in with an eyebrow pencil. Sometimes I forgot that's what I'd done and would smear black over my face with my hand.

"Make-up artist leave the stage! Pictures going live!" The producer's voice reverberated through the speakers. He was nowhere to be seen. We all automatically looked up.

Pictures of six girls, and of me from previous years, flashed up on a huge monitor. There was one photo taken in the clinic before my nose job, the only one I had. Another photo was taken in the university garden before the rhinoplasty. It showed two of my university classmates, an unknown guy, Temo, and myself, but I'd ripped it up. My hair was a very strange color, after one of my first attempts to prettify myself. I carefully saved up to buy the dye and unsuccessfully applied it at home. Instead of blonde hair, I ended up with a rusty-looking plait.

When I first put on lipstick, I immediately wiped it off with a handkerchief on the bus. I applied it and took it off several times, looking at my reflection in the bus window. In the end, I dared to leave it on and a boy offered me a seat in the café. "Do you live alone?" was his first question. We met up several times to eat khatchapuri. I was nervous, couldn't swallow a morsel. We didn't have much to talk about. I watched myself eating at home and discovered that when I chewed, my nose moved together with my jaws. I was alarmed. Temo mostly looked at my breasts, but still I refused the khatchapuri and just drank tea. At home, I survived on fried potatoes, or boiled ones when I felt too lazy to stand and cook. I had strictly prohibited my mother to send food.

I saved up some money for hair-removal because of Temo. I did my upper lip and side-burns. It was acutely painful and the redness took two days to subside, so I had to miss lectures. But, after that, I walked more confidently into the café. Temo was there with the same girl, drinking tea and laughing.

In the back yard, I forgot all about my previous tears when he put his arms round me and asked me to mark his absences as attendances in the class register. I nodded happily. He came home with me on the pretext of picking up some lecture notes. He made sure I was alone and before kissing me, he mauled my breasts as if we were fighting. He closed his eyes and put his wet lips on mine. I started crying and ran off and hid in the doorway. Suddenly I had a shudder of desire and felt like going back. He wasn't there anymore.

After that, he didn't even say hello to me. He invited another girl for tea and I felt physical pain and destroyed that only picture. Even so, I didn't record his absences. I even substituted his absence from the IT exam with a "pass." Every time I saw him, I blushed and felt my heart beat quickly, not only when I saw him, but his friends too.

The studio audience looked at the pictures attentively. A pulsing, tension-inducing tune played. For some reason, I thought I'd be recognized, that someone would at least guess. The audience was arguing about two photos—I wasn't in either of them and I couldn't honestly say that I cared. I was convinced about one thing, though, there was no trace of Iamze left in either.

"Fantastic! Let's hear it for cosmetic surgery!" the presenter started shouting.

"In front of you is a masterpiece of plastic surgery," she pointed in my direction, "who bears no relation to her past! You can see, with your own eyes, that nothing's impossible!"

There was a storm of applause in the studio. Men and women alike looked up, astonished, at the enlarged image of Iamze on the screen. The producer's assistant gestured to me to get up. I was escorted onto the stage. Lights were trained on me, the music was replaced by a triumphant melody, the volume was turned up. I tossed my blond hair extensions over my shoulders. How I hated my naturally black roots. I had the feeling that they grew at an incredible speed, as if the pitch-dark stalks crawled into the newly colored hair. Those roots were like my eyes with their color-changing contact lenses—because they couldn't be changed by the wonders of surgery.

"What dark eyes you have," Temo's friend told me. I felt totally at a loss. "I thought it was only in poems that women had jet-black eyes." He laughed. We spoke about poetry, superficially. When he came home with me, I was as happy as if I'd made up with Temo, or even more so—that I was superior to Temo, that I'd defeated him. With mounting excitement, I ran up the stairs, we didn't bother with the lift. He was touching my shoulders and waist. My heart was beating like mad. I fumbled for the key in my bag but the door was already unlocked. I looked around the empty room. Surprised, I looked back at Temo's friend. Suddenly I heard a noise from the balcony. I noticed some baskets in the kitchen and was dumbfounded. Ever since I'd told my mother not to send me food, I'd rarely spoken to her on the phone, nor did I send her letters via a driver we knew, but ... did I really think she would stop? She was busy putting baskets full of country produce into the cupboards out on the balcony. She looked tired after the journey. And very old in her scarf, shamefully old. Even now I remember what I felt then. I hated her.

"It's nobody, it's just the cleaner." I turned Temo's friend away from the door and cried the whole night through.

The sponsor was name-checked at least ten times during the program. The drinks company had promised a surprise for the audience. They were going to offer everyone wine. This was another audience-participation game. Girls in red carrying trays sailed into the studio. Each participant was presented with wine in five differently shaped glasses: a tall-stemmed crystal glass, a glass shaped like sunglasses, a clay bowl, a tiny horn, and a miniature decanter, all full of red wine. We were supposed to try each of them and announce the best. It barely touched my lips. You're not supposed to drink with antibiotics.

"Lela, don't stand with your back to the camera! How many times do I have to tell you?" the producer yelled.

The presenter jumped.

Some of the participants were confidently swilling the wine around in their glasses and keeping it in their mouth before swallowing. Some of them guzzled glass after glass. The girls in red gave out bits of bread, a wine-tasting custom intended to neutralize the taste of the previous wine. The participants were so noisy, it was as if they'd got drunk on just a mouthful. The presenter was worried the gaiety would get out of hand. From time to time she adjusted the earphone through which the producer was talking to her. She was trying to follow his instructions exactly.

I listen to the nurse. I do what she tells me. I sit in the wheelchair in the prescribed blue surgical gown, issued on the ward along with the wheelchairs. I've been pushed down this corridor so many times. There are pictures on the walls that are totally familiar. Reproductions, mainly paintings of women. They accompany me to the operation, they watch me, they see me off, and they seem more and more beautiful, more and more.

These masterpieces are displayed in the clinic to induce an atmosphere of calm.

But it's a marketing mistake, as none of the portraits or models are perfect from the point of view of cosmetic surgery.

The bits of my body that are considered excessive or inadequate are marked up. The surgeon has outlined them with a blue felt-tip pen and highlighted them in bright green. In a few minutes, the nurse will pull rubber gloves on to the doctor's slim, sterilized wrists with a snap. When I come round, I won't see the women any more, I'll wake up on the ward.

I try to supress my thoughts of how infinite the beauty is in their asymmetric faces, their thin, characterful lips and long noses; how much desire and passion is in their small breasts, full thighs, or round bellies; how unique the smiles are with little wrinkles round the eyes; the joined-up eyebrows are, wonderful too, as are the blond, faded eyelashes.

The picture nearest the operating theater is of a landscape. I don't like it, it reminds me of a village.

I love you, Baby! Now relax. That's how it starts—with me, dipped in iodine solution, laying down on the sterilized sheet.

When my pulse stabilizes around ninety on the monitor, Daddy looks at the anesthetist. The magic liquid blends in the drip, I recognize it instantly and feel dizzy. For a second, I have a sensation of falling, then the women come—unique, natural women, painted once and a thousand times with ever-changing expressions, sad, clever, in love, broken-hearted, offended, tranquil, thoughtful, patient. My courtyard and the village house come to me, and baskets full of food. The stern, watchful eyes between the surgical mask and hat start to blur.

"Add some more." The anesthetist acts quickly. Someone's coming.

There's a knock on the door. I get up and put on that blue surgical gown and ask, "Who's there? Who's there? Who?"

I decided to get a nose job at the first opportunity. I started working during my last year at university and became obsessed with rhinoplasty. I turned into a model employee and was soon promoted. When I looked at myself on the day of the operation, something strange happened: I liked my profile. My nose seemed amazingly small, neatly suiting my face. According to doctors, this is a normal pre-operation perception.

I didn't tell my mother about the nose job. I didn't go back to the village, not even in summer. We somehow became estranged, painlessly. I cut her off and it was finished, just like when a surgeon cuts anesthetized flesh, you're dulled and you forget.

When I came round from the anesthetic, I couldn't stop staring at the surgeon's brilliant smile. He seemed to be amazingly caring. I now know that's routine after an operation. After the recovery period, when the pain subsided and the swelling had gone down, I felt an unfamiliar sensation, my heart was full of gratitude. I was happy to go for the check-up, I didn't want to leave the clinic. I was haunted by the doctor's scent of eau-de-cologne, his caring glance and heavenly smile. I invented some additional symptoms. Unbelievably, he suggested a date. I wondered why he chose me. Why me? I couldn't even dream about such a man.

He made my nose perfect but I didn't fully appreciate his professionalism at the time. The cosmetic surgeon has a strong sense that the patient is his, a human being, a piece of modelling clay, woman-material. A true surgeon probably recognizes this at the very first consultation and never lets it go.

He will recreate her, or, to put it more precisely, he will create her again and again, bit by bit, painlessly, with anesthetics, he will carve her, he will sculpt her, he will empty her and fill her up again.

He will enter her body, he will enter her dreams, he will use a magic wand instead of a scalpel, he will conduct, manufacture. He will become a creator, an author, or, to put it bluntly, God.

The shoot was due to finish. But the men were still arguing. They wouldn't let the women get a word in. They all claimed to be experts on wine, and because of their differences of opinion, got angry with each other. The presenter, at the suggestion of the producer, changed the rules on the spot and gave the participants the option of choosing the three best wines.

The company representative made everyone look like idiots when he came onto the stage and announced that the five different glasses all contained the same wine. At first, the awkward silence was broken by music, and, soon afterwards, by suspicious men in the audience making offensive and aggressive comments.

"The show must go on!" the presenter shrieked helplessly, trying to make herself heard over the noise.

Finally, the women in red re-appeared with gifts of boxes of wine and shoved them towards the angry participants.

"See how important the type of glass is when wine is served!" said the presenter, provoking the men again by reciting the text she'd been prompted with. "The main thing is that you liked the wine.

Wonderful that you liked it so much!" On the instructions of the producer, she moved back.

He doesn't drink and he counts while he eats. How come I didn't notice it before? He counts how many times he chews each mouthful. He probably counts the number of mouthfuls too. It's strange! Or maybe nothing's strange. He never cuts the pockets of new suits or coats. When I first saw his shoes, I thought they were all new and had never been worn. But when I looked at the soles, I could see they had been. I guessed that's why he walked so slowly and strangely, so that the leather wouldn't crack, so no crease would appear, not a single crease.

When I moved in with him, he warned me that the main thing was to keep things tidy. I didn't speak his language then. He meant—don't touch my things! And everything was his. We lived in a prestigious new district. There was still construction work going on. The apartment soon got dusty. "Don't open the windows!" He was angry with me. He used blinds to keep the sun out. The spacious rooms were lit with cold, electric light. He played classical music to drown out the neighbors' building work. He didn't listen to anything else. For several months, I lived there like a guest, not knowing where anything was. Besides, most of the time I was either going in for an operation or recovering from one. Once liposuction was over, breast enhancement began, realignment of the nipples. Once the eyes were lifted, there came the smoothing of the forehead, then implants in the buttocks to raise them and make them round.

The cleaner was well able to cope with the three-storey apartment. She cleaned everywhere, apart from his study. That was the only place he cleaned himself. There were beautiful sculptures on the table, a clock, awards for surgical achievements, and an ornamental ashtray.

One evening, he was very angry. "What were you doing at my desk?" he asked. I was surprised, I only touched a few things and put them straight back. I wondered for ages how he knew. I decided that tiny traces of dust must have given him a clue. I hadn't been able help myself and picked up the woman-shaped ashtray. This object bugged me somehow. I blew on it to disperse the thin layer of dust and put it back down, the naked body ready to receive cigarette ash. He knew what I'd done and got angry. Now I know how—everything on the table was placed with great precision, like on a technical drawing done by a computer program.

He never wanted a child. He called me Baby; he was ten years older than me. He ordered me at the very beginning to address him as Daddy. Me, his favorite object and his most successful project.

As I changed from Ia to Yanna, I never thought about my home village at all, it was as if I'd forgotten everything. My past appeared to settle in my dreams and, like Botox or liposuction, it seemed needles were pricking the different parts of my body.

When I was a child my mother told me, quoting from the Bible, that man was created first and then a woman was formed from the rib of this man.

Perhaps that's why I picture Daddy holding a rib, instead of a lancet, scissors, or needle in his hand. A big, bloody rib.

I thought the program had finished, but there was one more advertisement, a so-called product placement, to be squeezed in. The participants, sitting with their gifts, were quiet and weary. With glum faces they watched the presenter, who this time was presenting a crockery company.

"As the discussion showed, the drink itself is more important than its container," she said cautiously.

I felt terribly tired. I couldn't get comfortable in the red armchair.

"Applaud, come on everyone, applaud!" the producer finally yelled.

Back home, the cleaner unpacked the gift from the drinks company. The bottles were accompanied by a glossy magazine about viniculture. I flicked through it before throwing it away. Apparently, the type of container does alter the taste of the wine and also its constituents. I was surprised. Then I remembered how my grandpa cherished and tended two kvevri, huge clay wine vessels, in our yard. The magazine described how wine loses its soul in plastic bottles. Did it mean smell? Uncertain, I re-read the sentence. Soul! It loses its soul! I looked at the magazine cover again, then threw it into the wastepaper basket, but I couldn't get the idea out of my head. The type of vessel changes the constituents. It went round and round in my head like a tune.

Daddy praised me. "You were good in that program," he said. He was glad that no one recognized me. He put on some classical music. The chords of the piano sounded like words to me.

Does the vessel change the wine or not?

Is it being poured away or is someone drinking it?

Passion. My desire.

Insides, shapes, insides.

Thought, essence, contents.

"What's the matter with you?" he asked, "did you forget to take your antidepressants?" "No," I said. "Perhaps you've taken too many?" I shook my head. He began to undo my dress. "Shall I turn the music down?" he asked me, for the first time ever.

He never switched the lights off during sex. He didn't close his eyes either. If he was facing me, he would scrutinize me as if he were evaluating the final result of the surgery. Pleasure appeared only fleetingly on his face and in fact was more like satisfaction. I felt his gaze piercing me from behind too. Perhaps it was at such moments that an idea for the next operation took shape.

He didn't stop until he'd eliminated all the surgical scars on my stretched stomach. After that, he bravely caressed my belly button as if he was caressing himself in me. I felt he would never give up this smooth flatness, he would never permit my stomach to swell. He never left any space for a soul.

Sometimes antibiotics and antidepressants weren't compatible. He took great care to prescribe various combinations so I wouldn't stop taking the pill. And I swallowed everything he gave me. I waited for him at home submissively. I undressed and lay down. When required, I'd undress and act as a model at doctors' meetings and international conferences.

The knock on the door, banging. Who's there? I'm doing up my dressing gown. Who's there?

A girl is standing there with her head bowed. I try in my sleep not to wake up. I remember that I shouldn't be afraid, or I will. I mustn't wake up.

Who are you? I ask cautiously.

"It's me," she answers.

I'm scared. My legs and hands are shaking. I can't control my muscles. They move on their own. I'm just about to wake up. A bit longer, I'm thinking, a bit longer, I can't let my eyes open.

I hear it so distinctly that I think I am awake.

"Who?" I'm opening the door.

"Iamze."

I walked so far, I got blisters on my feet, I got blood on them. The heel of my designer shoe broke, it wasn't designed for this road. How horrible darkness is — you can lose your way, get totally lost. When I sat down on the ground to have a rest, I found when I stood up that I'd lost my sense of direction. What if I'm doubling back on myself? The main thing is not to go back, simply not to go back.

"Where are you going?"

Thank God! I rushed to the car door.

"Where to?" The man turned down the music. He seemed younger than me, like the lads from my village, or a couple of guys I knew at university, or those builders working near Daddy's house.

I didn't know what to say.

"I'll pay you," was all I managed to blurt out.

"Does Gomi suit you?" He'd hardly finished speaking and I was already in the car. He managed to look me up and down before I closed the door. The car had a sour smell. I didn't open the window. In the stuffy air, I could also smell the aroma of earth and I inhaled deeply.

He turned the music up again and looked at me. I smiled at him.

As I relaxed, the car bumped along the road. My sweaty dress clung to various parts of my body. Something was rolling around my feet, several potatoes had fallen out of a bag behind us. I didn't answer his questions. I was smiling, I was rolling along and smiling. Perhaps he thought I was drunk. He attempted to speak Russian too, struggling. I asked him for a cigarette. He was pleased. He addressed me in Georgian again: "Where are you going? What's a girl like you doing in such a place? Such a girl!" he said. When he learned my name was Yanna, he put on some traditional songs from Russian gangland culture. I hadn't heard those since my childhood when the village lads used to play them in the summer. I moved my shoulders to the music. The road straightened out, the car stopped and I was still bumping up and down. He was inexperienced, bold and rough too. The music finished. I could hear his panting. The car became even stuffier, the air even more heavy. One window steamed up.

He had stubby hands, that's the only thing I remember about him.

In Gomi he asked me for my telephone number. I gave him some money. He was indignant and refused, but his eyes rested on the banknote. I left the money on the seat. He signalled to me with the horn—Ina, Ina—he could not remember my name. Eventually, he left me alone and drove off. When I looked at my watch, I was pleased to see that daylight would come soon. I continued walking. The sweat slowly evaporated from my dress and the moisture between my legs smeared and dried.

Before I reached the village, I went with three more men. Two of them were passengers in the same car. My plastic body was searching for souls. It greedily absorbed the lives of those it encountered.

I didn't want to know the father of the child. The child must be mine alone, my soul.

When my mother had died, the house died with her. She departed and took the stability of the walls, the dryness of the boards, cooking aromas from the kitchen, the color of vegetables from the garden, the taste of fruit from the trees, and air from the fireplace. My mother took me with her too, my real name, my childhood fears, expectations and shame too.

Before I moved in with Daddy, the neighbors had sent several messages telling me to look after the house. They somehow managed to send these messages. Then they telephoned Daddy's secretary to tell me that there was a prospective buyer. That woman dealt with such calls very effectively.

Thank God I didn't sell it. Why would I need those pennies? These ruins are so precious now! So what if the roof is leaking and the staircase rails are coming off.

The main thing is I have a house. The main thing is I am. I am ...

When I give a birth to a dark girl with thick eyebrows and a longish nose, I'll tell her that in the beginning was the word. I'll give her some wine in the village church where the priest comes only on feast days to administer communion to the few inhabitants. I'll tell him that the vessel doesn't matter, only the wine.

When she grows up, I'll explain to her the meaning of the vessel, because she can change the contents as time passes.

My only one! I'll caress her like she deserves.

I'll comb her tar-black hair every day and tell her she's my only one, my unique one. I'll tell her so often she'll believe it.

She will believe it for sure.

And when she knows it, I'll let her go, peacefully let her go.

There is a knocking on the door, banging. I do up my dressing gown and open the door. It's the woman next door. She's always surprised that I've closed the door. She gives me milk from the cow, and fresh cheese.

Locals accepted me here as Iamze's relative. They asked me about her. They are convinced she's in Greece.

"How can I help you, dear? Poor you, with such a big belly," she dries her hand on her apron.

"I'm not poor," I smile. She looks at me. She stays a bit. She looks at me kindly. I remember the pictures on the clinic walls.

"But your expression is like Iamze's, dear," she turns from the door. "You're very different but somehow your expression is the same."

Tears well up in my eyes. I bend my head. Beneath my engorged breasts, I see a round belly full of Iamze, full of sun. I feel moisture and warmth between my legs, as if the tears had rolled down over these hills of life onto the floor. There's a pool of water.

"What's the date today?" I stop her in the door.

She isn't fazed, she pulls up her sleeves.

"Don't be afraid," she answers.

TRANSLATED FROM GEORGIAN

BY NATALIA BUKIA-PETERS & VICTORIA FIELD

KAJA MALANOWSKA

Bird Man

BASIA ŻACZEK HAD ELEVEN SIBLINGS: nine sisters and two brothers. Enough for her to be able to disappear without anyone noticing. Nobody looked for her before lunchtime. Outside it always smelled of cow's dung. The cowshed was right next to the house. The cows passed across the yard twice a day: in the morning, on their way to the pasture; and in the late afternoon, when, full and swollen, they came back for the evening milking, treading densely and clumsily, bumping into the open gate, which they were always trying to get through all at once, mooing thoughtlessly, pushing at each other with their shiny, black-and-white sides, throwing up clouds of dust, which did not want to settle and was hanging in the air until dusk, holding the smell of sweaty animals and ammonia.

In the morning, when Basia got up, the cows were already gone, the gate was shut, the dust settled on the laundry drying in front of the house. She went to the kitchen to spread some butter on a slice of bread. Above a round table covered with a plastic tablecloth with embossed flowers, a fly paper was hanging. A huge, pale-brown tongue full of moving, half-dead flies perishing slowly while Basia put the kettle on. Nobody spoke to her, nobody rushed her and forced her to do work. She could drink her tea, thick with sugar, in peace; and she could make brown, warm circles on the tablecloth with the tea glass and then smear the sticky wetness on the table with her index finger, making sweet pathways that attracted the wasps.

She was born eight years after her brother, who was supposed to be Mr. and Mrs. Żuczek's last child. Like her elder sisters she inherited their mother's strong, heavy-set build—thick, solid calves and massive thighs, which in time were destined to become covered with gnarls of purplish-blue varicose veins. Just like them, she could work in summertime, when the school was closed: she could help with the harvest and weed the potato field; but as the youngest, she was protected—she did not have to get moving, like the others. Just in her nightie, barefoot, she stepped stiffly over the doorstep, sat on the bench painted with oil paint and waited. Theirs was a large, sturdy house, which had once belonged to the Germans; two-storied, with double windows rounded at the top, and a sloping roof, it stood in the very middle of the village, right by the road, on the sharp bend so that cars and passers-by appeared only for a second—you could see them suddenly materialising from behind the cowshed and a moment later disappearing round the corner of the fence.

Basia waited on tenterhooks, biting her lips and not taking her eyes off the gate. Every few seconds, in a monotonous, always identical gesture, she brushed her hair back, revealing her small, rat-like face with widened eyes. She twisted her hair into a knot on her nape and then lowered her hand, letting the hair immediately tumble down again onto her back and cheeks; then she would grasp the hair systematically, once more, every now and then brushing her forehead with her hand in a tired gesture that was not at all like that of a little girl—more like she was dedicating herself to arranging her hair with the apathetic resignation of an old woman who is used to the pointlessness of everyday efforts. Basia was not aware that she repeated her mother's and elder sisters' gestures, that she learned to sigh heavily when sitting down, that she walked slowly, respecting every step, and leaned down steadily in order to avoid wasting energy, supporting her back with a hand. And anyway she did not care what she looked like or how she moved, she just wanted him to come. She knew he would, because he always did. And finally, there he was. He was walking down the street in his gray suit, donated to him by the priest, and which he never took off—even when it was boiling hot, he would put the suit jacket straight onto his naked body. He was walking down the street and his steps were strange, full of swaying, and uncontrolled, sudden jerks. He was moving his long legs stiffly, as if they were devoid of joints, as if they were wooden prostheses. He was swinging his long, thin arms. He always had his head tilted to one side and his closely set eyes were moving restlessly, tracing uneven lines between the sky and the chimneys of the houses. He never looked down—perhaps he could not lower his head, or perhaps he just did not want to see his own long, dancing feet that did not listen to him and were constantly drifting to the left or to the right, instead of continuing straight ahead. He looked like a petrified wild bird, caught and imprisoned by somebody, beating its wings in the air in a helpless effort to free itself and fly out between the bars of a cage. Basia looked attentively as he wobbled and skipped awkwardly on the other side of the road, against the background of the cemetery wall speckled with the shadows of the lime trees; as he tripped over his own feet, stopped, hung over the edge of the curb right by the road, and then went back to his series of bird-like skips, and finally disappeared round the corner. She slowly stood up and went into the house. She had ten minutes to get dressed and put her shoes on before he would leave the shop.

He was coming back. She saw him appearing from around the corner. She quickly ran across the street, then along a sandy, not very firm track that rose for a stretch, perpendicular to the road, and then, right by the post office, she took a turn to the right and went even higher, all the way to the top of the high embankment located just outside of the village. She ran up the hill, quickly, quickly, grasping plastic-like stems of broom to keep balance, tugging them and showering the ground with little, bright yellow flowers. She stopped at the top and looked down at the village: less than two hundred houses; with new, concrete cubes and older slope-roofed cottages; with squares of yards enclosed by wooden fences, nibbled away by the ducks and speckled with the white marks of whitewashed fruit trees; with muddy farmyards, dotted with birds' muck, each with a little wooden bench and a dog chained to a kennel, one for each house, evenly spreading; with gently down-sloping fields, brownish golden at this time of the year, behind the furthest buildings as far as the navy blue-green line of the woods on the horizon.

The blue, disturbingly well-defined weal of the road cut the village sharply in half, with a little gray man fluttering and swaying on it in his desperate, chaotic dance, full of absurd jumps and shudders. She could relax now and slow down. By climbing the embankment she had got far ahead of him, but she knew that their paths would join by the lake, not far from the cross, right by the hazel grove and the ravine paved with cobblestones. She would wait there for him, just like she did every day. She would sit on the stone behind the cross, pull her knees up and hug them to her body, suppressing the desire to run away when he passed by, when, limping and shaking his head, he walked right by her, mumbling under his nose the words that have no sense, looking at her with those restless, bird-like eyes, but not seeing her, even though every day she made an effort to sit a bit closer. He is scared, she thought. He needs to be tamed, and that takes time. She was walking slowly along the overgrown path amongst the weeds and ripening blackberry bushes. She brushed her hand along the tall grass-blades and then picked a piece of wormwood and crushed it in her hands. All the time keeping a watchful eye on the distant silhouette on the road, she leaned her head and sniffed the bitter smell of feathery leaves.

PER-VERT, pervert—this is what the other children shouted at him: pervert or mongol. Grown-ups did not shout anymore, they did not even talk about him or the elderly pair that brought him here seven years ago. The adults had got used to—had reconciled themselves to—the fact that he walked through the village every day, and those hanging around in front of the shop would make way for him reluctantly in grim silence, and every now and then one of the men would swear at the sight of him, or spit on the ground and turn away with contempt. The women had put an end to gossiping about him and had stopped organising meetings when the priest decided that they could stay here, that they could build that little shack of theirs, which everybody avoided, far outside the village, amongst the trees, where it was invisible and nobody had to feel ashamed that they lived here. He said that driving them out would show contempt for God, even though everybody knew that contempt for God was the fact that they walked the Earth at all, that they had reached the lake in their many-years-long march along the river because no other village would allow them to stay. Their story preceded them by many kilometers, which was why, when they reached each place, one after another—dragging their wheelbarrows with dirty bundles and their cardboard boxes full of rubbish—they were always met at the first buildings by silent, stubborn men with a crowd of screaming women behind their backs, and was why they had then to move further on, stopping only for a short while, a few weeks at most, if they were allowed to stay at all.

She sat on the edge of the ravine covered with grass. When they had arrived at the village, she was very little, so she could not remember the turbulent gatherings with the women screaming and the men swearing. She could not remember the evening when the priest finally came out of the rectory and walked along the street lit with yellow lights to the two-story school building, where, with a bang, he entered the assembly room with its wood-panelled walls and studied the startled faces looking towards the door.

"Enough," he said then. "That's enough."

And they listened to him: they went home, on their own or in pairs, passing by him as he stood there in the open door, until there was only one left—Łukasz Wojda, who was a sacristan, with whom he then went home, taking the same route along the lit road amongst the blooming wild mulberry trees. So she did not know anything at all about them, because that night she was already fast asleep in her wooden baby cot, right next to her elder sister, who had stayed at home to keep an eye on her.

But there was no need to tell the village stories—everybody knew them anyway: from the youngest children, those who were not yet able to play on their own and, dirty and bored, would sit and dig in the sand with their sticks in front of the houses, or chase hissing geese and stupefied chickens along the wire mesh fences separating them from the birds; all the way to the deaf, hump-backed Ms Katarzyna, who stood in the church gate every Sunday, wrapped in a woollen shawl, leaning on a walking stick, hanging over her rosary with its blue plastic beads, moving in her twisted, soil-brown fingers. Basia simply knew, although she could not remember anybody telling her—her mother or her sisters explaining what a pervert or a mongol was—she just knew that the bird man was born out of a relationship of two people who should not, could not, have children; and not because they already had other husbands or wives—after all Mrs. Ryłko got divorced and remarried and then had three perfectly healthy boys, and Agnieszka from the old State Agricultural Farm did not have a husband at all, but her little daughter did not look anything like a nestling, all pink and fat, and entirely human. Those two old people living by the lake could not marry because much earlier, from the very beginning, they were linked in a different way, in the way that could not be altered or broken. There are no children from a relationship of a brother and a sister but bird people: imprisoned on Earth, incomplete, wretches deprived of wings and reason.

She was late, so when she came running out of the ravine, he was already gone, he had already passed the cross and disappeared amongst the dead stumps of pine trees that rotted and died because every spring for the last few years the river had overflowed and drowned their roots in the dirty, murky water that would not evaporate until the beginning of June, when the sun was strong enough to dry it out. She should stop right before the whitish-gray trunks without leaves. Nobody from the village came that far. Their world ended, broke off suddenly, by the wooden cross, behind which there was the forbidden, alien zone, which stretched all the way to the jetty and the meadow belonging to the Żaczeks, around a kilometer further down. Yet she kept walking straight ahead, as if hypnotized. She was walking along a muddy path amongst the reeds and holms, with their dark-green grasses with edges turning brown, through small, shallow puddles all the way to a gravelled pathway in the oak grove.

The cabin stood in the middle of a grassless clearing; it was not even a proper cabin, just a hut made of corrugated metal sheets, pieces of fencing stolen from the fields, and cardboard, covered with roofing paper, with an opening instead of a door protected by a sliding piece of plastic foil and a dark window cut out in the metal sheet. She stepped closer, ignoring the chickens jumping out of her way, clucking with indignation, and then she stretched out her hand and pushed the foil to one side. The smell of warm decay and wet down feathers belched out from inside. There was a violent outburst in the darkness and a big, brownish bird flew low above the ground, just by her legs. Two dark gray, shapeless sacks shifted anxiously on the rag lair. It's them, Basia thought. These are the old people. But where is he? She lowered her hand. When she was leaving, she heard nervous whispers and grunts from inside the hut. She passed the tin bathtub and a stack of twigs collected for fuel, and an abandoned door to a Fiat 126 with a broken window and rusty hinges. He was sitting there, crouching, right by a fallen tree trunk covered with moss, in his gray suit and black leather shoes; he was scratching the mud with the chickens, brushing twigs aside with his long, pointed fingers, turning lumps of soil over, looking for worms. And then he lifted his head and saw her for the first time ever. He froze and jumped back, gurgling and squeaking, and probably disappeared into the thicket on the lakeshore, but Basia did not know that, because she was already running towards the rotten pine trees and then on to the cross, onto the embankment and to the post office. She came back home at dusk, and, completely calm, went into the kitchen full of women, entered the circle of groans and complaints, the smell of sweat and cooked cabbage, with the fly paper full of dead flies above the table, and her mother squeezing a pot of water between her thick thighs into which her sisters were plopping peeled potatoes for dinner. Nothing happened, she thought. He just changed, he is becoming more and more bird-like, it is normal, there is no reason to be so afraid of him. She sat down and propped her head on her hands.

"Where were you?" asked one of her sisters without much interest.

"Eat quickly and go to bed, you are getting up earlier tomorrow, enough of this laziness, you will come out to the fields with us. The rains will start soon. We could do with another pair of hands."

Basia got up without rushing. In a slow, lunatic way she crossed the kitchen, brushing every object on her way with her hand, until she finally got to the bedroom door. They would not wake her up tomorrow anyway; they would forget, as they always did. She was getting ready to go to bed, when she heard her father coming back from the cows.

"I saw that retarded Artur in the fields," he said. "He was trying to approach the cranes. They let him come quite close, he must have tamed them somehow, that bugger."

This autumn, she thought when she was falling asleep. This autumn he will fly away with them.

TRANSLATED FROM POLISH
BY ANNA HYDE

KRISTĪNE ULBERGA

Learn To Love the One Who Eats
Your Porridge

WE MOVE VERY SLOWLY, for fear that I might break or suddenly come to a stop—as usually happens with wind-up dolls. The slower you go, the longer the road ahead.

The sun shines through the windows; their mullions fracture the sun, slice it up as if with a knife into pieces of light and shadow. At the end of the hallway there are no windows, just a wall and shadow, and a big plastic tree. In the mornings when the sun shines, as I walk I step only on the sunny spots, and if a strip of wall happens in between the windows, I jump over its shadow. No one reprimands me or questions what I'm doing.

"We'll miss soup. And, you know, when you do that you look totally crazy."

"Go on. Save me a place in line."

"Alright ..."

F22 runs ahead. She's always starving. It's incredible that two bowls of soup, three helpings of the main course, and on top of that a fruit compote so thin that it could be poured into a tea kettle and boiled like water for coffee—that all this can fit into such a small woman. She also wolfs down my, Snow White's, and Clown's morning porridge.

I walk over to the plastic tree and return, stepping on the cutout squares of sunlight.

Years are only numbers, a prison—the room, the hospital—the hallway with sunny squares. Numbers. A room. Squares. And life.

The doctor's office is in another hallway. There are no windows there, only doors like tall people pressed against the walls. I shouldn't have to go there. There's a cold shadow on the floor, no place to put my feet.

"Please sit!"—the doctor pokes at a plate with his fork. "Tell me why you're here."

"You must understand that my life has been very hard . . ." I say, and bury my face in my hands, but tears don't come.

The doctor sighs and pushes the half-eaten plate aside.

"In your medical history it's written that you suffer from hallucinations."

"Yes, that life . . ."

On the desk, only God knows from where, a blank page and a pen have appeared.

"Write."

Puzzled, I stare at the doctor.

"Write about your life; and it would be preferable if you started from the very beginning."

I grab the pen and I begin.

I'm six years old. Mom is forty-one, Dad thirty-five, the building is sixty-nine, and the woman neighbor with whom we share a WC in the stairwell—she's seventy-five. In the kitchen ticks a clock from which father has removed the glass so that I can touch the hands, push them forward and back and so learn to tell the time. "Why do we need a clock?" I ask my Father. "So we can get to work on time," he replies. "Why get to work on time?"—I don't understand—"To earn money," he explains. "Why do we need money?" I persist. "Now you're asking for the sake of asking." Father leaves the room and vanishes like a bird of passage, who always disappears and always returns to the nest.

I sit in front of a turned-off TV and look at a film about a forest. This I do every morning after my parents have gone to work and the neighbor has left me a handful of stuck-together peppermint candies on the table. My film always starts with a tingling or butterflies in the pit of my stomach, as if the viewing of a film about the forest was prohibited. In my forest there's no gamekeeper and no irritable witches, there are only trees, and animals, and bilberries, and mushrooms. There are no red ants, mad foxes, or mazes of trails in which one can get lost. My film starts with me, standing at the edge of the forest and looking at a house far from the city's gray throng. I'm wearing polka dot rubber boots and a blue raincoat. Mom says that the raincoat is too small, but in my forest I can even wear Father's plaid shirt or Mama's black brassiere, because there they'll never find me since they're at work.

But mainly I'm building a house in the forest. That's a secret. I began a week ago. My father said that you need a lot of materials for a house—wood boards, bricks, cement, electricity, water. My dad is too serious. He would never believe that I'm shoring up my house with branches, covering the roof with pine needles, that I don't need windows, because windows make sense only when they look down from the fifth floor. When the house is ready, I'll strip a birch of its bark to make a bast-basket in which to put bilberries I've picked for supper. All sorts of animals will come to my house and I'll treat them to the bilberries and then we'll fall asleep keeping each other warm.

The door chain jangles, and I run home, stumbling over toad humps, molehills, and puddle depths.

"Why are you sitting in front of a turned-off TV?"—Mother has stormed into the room as fragrant as a city flower, her gray hair combed up into an attractive bun. She's out of breath.

"Mom, how do I make a clay mug?" I ask, because my house lacks mugs with which to scoop up forest spring water.

"Only you would think of something like that! Do we not have enough dishes?"—she sits down beside me on the bed and places a hand on my shoulder. "I want to introduce you to someone, but don't tell Dad, agreed?"—Mother's voice is a tender song now, like that of all other mothers, and I no longer have the forest house in my head.

I don't get to answer before someone enters through the door. He brings with him a sweet cookie fragrance, a warm southern wind.

"This is Ziggy. We work together."—My mother looks at Ziggy and her voice is again like that of a real mother, tender and quiet.

"Is he a man?" I ask. I feel like laughing at the gray, slight Ziggy, who isn't at all like my father. Ziggy's hand is like a teaspoon but my father's hands are like soup ladles. Ziggy's hair is thick and curly, but the top of my dad's head is shiny. Ziggy smells of cookies and a southern wind, but Father's smell comes from the north. Ziggy

stands calmly in the doorway, but Dad would have long ago tramped through the house with muddy boots, loudly cussing the sultry weather. No, Ziggy is not a man. I calm down.

"Yes, Ziggy is a man, he has his own car." Mother pushes me into my bedroom, for me to get changed quickly.

We're driving. Mother is silent for almost all of the drive. Ziggy's hand rests in Mother's lap. Every now and then they look at each other and smile. It's the first time my mother is wearing the blue dress that some relatives from abroad brought her. Today Mother doesn't yell. Maybe I'll reveal my secret to her this evening. I know what will happen: she'll hug me, kiss me on my forehead, and say that she wants very much to visit me in my forest house. She'll ask if I need some things for my household, she'll help carry the heavy fir branches, which I myself couldn't lift up to the roof, she'll teach me how to light a bonfire and we'll sit and drink juniper tea.

With each gust of southern wind I like Ziggy more and more. We walk along a strange seaside—there are gigantic rocks like bewitched people who've been punished for their evil deeds, but the pines and the sand dune edges have humbly fallen to their knees in front of the sea so that it won't yearn for an amber necklace. I jump from rock to rock, and every now and then fall, but Ziggy's small hands always help me up. Mother doesn't get mad. She smiles.

On the way home we stop at a café. Ziggy buys us everything we want, and I, for the first time in my life, eat candyfloss, which has the aroma of a southern wind and cookies.

"Just don't tell Dad!"—Mother is changing in her room and she turns toward me bare-breasted, shaking a finger. She takes off black lace panties, carefully folds them and puts them away in the cupboard. Usually Mom's panties are gray with moth-eaten holes. For sure Ziggy is not a man.

Mother turns on the TV, and that means that I have to disappear and go to my room. I close the door and climb up on the windowsill. My pockets are full of tiny bewitched people who have done evil deeds. Some with a hole in their chest, others with a snail's shell growing out of their heads. I organize them according to size, so that on the day when they become human again, they'll line up prettily and listen to my story about the world.

"It's dreadfully hot. Open the window, for God's sake!"—Father storms into the room like a cold north wind. He tracks mud all over the floor and hands me a lemon ice cream.

"Dad, look at the tiny people who have come home with me from the sea."—I huddle in the corner on the windowsill so that Dad can look at my stones.

"Were you at the seashore?"

"Yes, Mom and me and Ziggy ..."

Father in stony silence stares at my row of evil little people.

"Good for you, now isn't that dandy that you were at the seaside with Ziggy ..." he mumbles and with big, fast, northern-wind steps disappears from the room. Then a loud crash sounds, as if the neighbor gypsy had fallen through the floor into my parents' room. I run to relish the scene, because I've never liked the gypsy, but there's no gypsy there—Mom is sprawled on the floor crying. Father is looking at her but doesn't help her get up, it looks to me that he's trembling, and his big hands have been drawn into fists.

"Whore!" He spits on Mom's stomach and leaves the room.

"Get lost!" Mom looks at me and it seems to me that she's a being of stone who by the warmth of a heart has been turned back into a human, but her eyes remain bewitched—cold stone eyes.

"Mommy, I'll tell you my secret, want to hear it?" I back up to the doorstep, as if my little forest hut were right there behind my back.

"Get lost, don't you understand?" Mother looks tired. "We had a long and exciting day."

In my room Father is lying on the floor. He's clutching a bottle, from which he now and then takes a swig and then grimaces.

"Did you like Ziggy?"

"Yes, we walked along the sea and then ate candyfloss!"

"Fuck ..." Father's head hits the floor.

My evil tiny people haven't yet come alive, even though the gold of the setting sun is rubbing their stone backs, warming them, calling them to life.

I won't look as Father drunk sleeps and Mother curled-up cries; better, I'll prepare Mom's favorite food, and then the two of us will head out to my forest hut, to sleep in the warmth of forest animals, and drink juniper tea! And I busy myself—I pour milk into a pot, add a pinch of salt and a knife's-end of sugar, and wait until the milk sends up bubbles, like cats humping their backs or like a person releasing homing pigeons. Slowly, like sifting sand, I pour manna into the milk, until it congeals like drops of blood. My mother's favorite food.

I put the pot out on the windowsill, close my eyes and run to my forest hut. I have to tidy and fix everything up, so that my mother won't say that she won't sleep here, because the wind is sailing through the hut and rain squeezes through the cracks. I find branches to light a bonfire, lay down fir branches as a cushion to sit on, and I pick some wild night violets so my hut will be fragrant, then run, hurrying back before the porridge has cooled off. I grab the pot, bowls, and spoons and rush to my mother's room. She's no longer lying on the floor with dried tears in her smile lines—she's sitting gazing into a small mirror. Mirror, mirror please do tell me—where is the very best place? My forest hut, I want to scream, but my mother turns, and I see her cold, stone, human eyes.

"What do you want now?"

"I brought supper, manna porridge."

Mother stands up and comes toward me. She'll hug me and kiss me, like all moms do, we'll eat the porridge and I'll pull out the hilberry jam hidden under my sweater ...

"What's in there?" She takes the pot from my hands.

"Mom—porridge, that you like the most."

My mother smiles and turns the pot upside down. The porridge sticks to the bottom of the pot as if glued.

"Bring me something to cut it out, or better still—throw it in the garbage!"

All my bodily fluids race upward and flow through my eyes, but my feet are glued to the brown linoleum, just as the porridge is to the bottom of the pot.

"Why are you standing there? Go!"

I run to the kitchen, all dried up—there's more life even in my evil stone people. My father is snoring in my room. The clock without glass ticks along. I poke my index finger at the black dial and I push the hour hand. The minute hand doesn't move even an inch. So that's how kings feel who reign over their own lives! I push the hour hand around a full circle, until both clock hands meet so they can contin-ue their return trip together, then I take the clock and throw it out of the window. There's a quiet bang; briefly a bell tinkles; and that's all—there's no more time.

"Achoo, achoo, achoo," someone sneezes in the cold pantry. I close my eyes and believe only in my hut deep in the forest, to which no trodden path leads and where no mother has set foot, even though it's all tidied up and the bloom of a night violet perfumes the air. It's cold outside and I want the wild beasts to warm me, I would curl up be-tween their warm claws.

"Achoo, achoo, achoo," someone sneezes again, maybe my father has come for a drink of water, or my mother, to eat her beloved man-na porridge! I once more run out of my forest, out towards the city, along an invisible path forged with metal so it won't wear out and will last as long as possible.

"Who's there?" I press my ear to the pantry door.

"Who do you think?" a strange voice answers.

"I really don't know."

"Then let me out so we can get acquainted!"

My father keeps telling me that all people I don't know are bad and suspicious. All the black cars take children far away forever and the candies that strange people give you are poisoned.

"If you give me candies, I won't take them!" I hiss through the keyhole.

"I won't even think of it!"

"Fine, then. Do you have a black car?"

"What foolishness! What idiot would use a black car when he has wings?" The voice sounds familiar, although also false and hoarse.

"Let me out, I want to have a smoke! Here it's too narrow and cold . . ."

So, a grown-up. Maybe the southern wind has hidden there?

"Are you Ziggy?"

"Stupid child! Does your Ziggy have wings?"

"No . . ."

"And these?"

I start to scream and recoil. My leg is covered with a bluish green membrane—light as the devil himself, warm and soft.

"That's my right wing!" the voice says while I continue to stare

at the warm membrane. It suddenly seems to me that I could stay like this forever. But it would be good if someone would warm up my other leg.

"You like it, yes?"

"Very much."

Heat rises to my head. A gray cloud slowly sneaks out through a crack in the door; it smells of cigarette smoke. My fingers reach out for the pantry door handle.

"Mom could come in." My hand freezes.

"Your mom, girl, is sleeping and dreaming about Ziggy. Now she's at the seaside without you. Later she'll go to the café without you. Afterward she'll head for a movie without you, and at the end of the dream they'll kill you. This too, without you."

"How do you know all this?"

"And better not run to your forest . . ."

"Why? How do you know about my forest?"

Through my stomach a hot arrow shoots upward, brawling and painfully piercing my guts. My forest! It's just mine! Mine, Damn it!

"Fine, go and look . . ."

I shrink into a corner and close my eyes. Tight, oh so tight. The air around me grows cold, and I—light. The earth under my feet is my left palm with its loops of betrayal and criss-crossed lines of fate, life, marriage and death. All the roads lead to my forest hut. All the marathon runners and children will one day return home, where footprints never get overgrown with lichen, even after one hundred years.

The air in my forest this evening is not as sweet as it has been before. Overhead a gray, heavy cloud. It's starting to get dark. Underfoot branches snap—unusually quietly, like cookies from a bakery on Lenin Street. The earth has a memory, and it tells me: "I'll never burn, because I am earth. But you . . . You too can choose who you are, girl."

But this time I don't want to see my hut. Better to just hear and forget forever, because I know—my hut has burned down, together with the forest honeysuckle and crown vetch. I turn back.

"My forest has burned down."

"I did tell you . . ."

"How did you know? Who are you?"

Silence from the cold pantry, but I wait.

"I'm the Green Crow, who survived your forest fire. The rest burned ..."

Sobs sneak in among the words; they grab my hand and open the pantry's door. Reeking of stale cigarette smoke, a sea-green bird, almost the size of my father, tumbles into the kitchen. The bird's beak is as yellow as a bus seat, its eyes blue, beautiful.

"Hello!" The Crow extends her wing to me. It's incredibly soft. I clasp it and don't want to let it go.

"Hello ... ahem ... I don't really want to talk much because my forest has burned down ..." I say, and evade the crow's eyes.

"Nevermind. Maybe you have something for me to eat? For example, manna porridge?"

"Yes, please!" I push the pot with the manna I made for Mom toward the crow.

The crow shoves her beak into the pot and makes loud smacking noises.

"I've never in my life eaten a better porridge. Crow's solemn word!"

My fingers have grown tired and I hand back the page to the doctor.

"That's enough for today."

There are four of us. F22, Clown, Snow White and I — Green Crow. Not so crazy. Peace and harmony reign in our ward. And maybe also love. In any case, we, whiling away the time in our beds, don't cause pain for our families, and at the same time we don't worry about what's happening in our country, because there's no television or daily newspaper in our ward or the whole unit. Only the iron beds, acrylic paint colors on the walls, and the Snickers bars on F22's night table remind us of the era we're living in. Outside the window one and the same view can be seen — two trees with real leaves and a brick wall. The first day Clown had a fight with F22 because of the view: F22 said that it was projected, an illusion, but Clown stood her ground — the lindens and the brick wall, according to her, were real. To settle the argument, they wandered about in the hospital yard and searched for the view. They didn't find it.

"I was right!" F22 exulted.

"Yes …" Clown quietly agreed, but on the evening of that very same day she had figured it out: "We can assume that the whole world is one great illusion only because, from various viewpoints, things look different. Things and people. But the moment when we look through the window is real. We're both right!"

Clown had graduated from the faculty of philosophy, because there her ugliness, as she herself calls it, was "secondary." When man contemplates the world's most significant concepts, he doesn't have time to pay attention to an ugly person sitting beside him picking her nose. That's what our Clown is like. An ugly girl of whom the world should be ashamed, and for whom God should apologize. She's small, fat, with a hook nose, hunched shoulders, squinting eyes like a sniper in the war for the Fatherland, and sparse teeth. Besides, she doesn't have a santim to her name. What place could a person like that take in this world?

"I was hoping that here—in this loony bin—I would be fed some I-don't-care medication. And I wouldn't care that I'm such a cripple—I wouldn't need a family, and would walk with my head held high!" Clown explains: "I pretended to commit suicide. Then they collected me and brought me here."

We named her Clown and told her that she was the ugliest woman we had ever seen in our lives. Clown wasn't insulted, she's known it all along. She's just waiting for that medication. They say that the hearts of ugly people are like diamonds the size of eggs, but it seems like even in this our Clown has failed. The only hope is in that medication.

It's worse with F22. She's not alone. She has a voice that instructs her about everything. For example, F22 goes into a store and wants to buy a bread roll with raisins. If the voice is sleeping at that moment, everything is fine—F22 eats the roll and leaves the store, but if the voice speaks up when F22 is choosing the bread roll, F22 spends several hours walking around in the supermarket searching for a roll with kosher meat. If F22 can't find such a roll, the voice begins to yell and cuss, and in all sorts of ways makes F22 feel small. And that of course lowers a woman's self-esteem.

There's something else too. F22's voice possesses various criminally punishable whims. For example, she has a habit of trying to encourage F22 to break off the car mirror of a neighbor's Mercedes, or to tell a child's teacher that he looks like an old paedophile.

"My voice tells me the truth," swears F22, "only other people don't like the truth."

The third in our ward is Snow White. She's a pensioner, around seventy years of age. Very calm and quiet, because she sleeps all the time, tied to her bed. When the princes come, the nurses wake her up and untie her, then the old woman shakes a fist at us, if we dare to say half a word. Clown thinks that the old woman was locked up in the attic of some rich mansion.

"Like *Jane Eyre*—have you read the book?" But now she's fed sleeping pills and, for safety, tied to her bed, but to her rich, good-hearted son, who comes almost every day, they say that his mother is slowly getting better.

F22's voice is convinced that Snow White is our psychiatrist's mother, the mere sight of whom he can't bear, because his mother can't stand any of his women. That's why the doctor has placed his mother in his clinic, so that his women can make pancakes any way they please, raise children as they like, and, in general, live as they like.

"And you? What's your problem?" F22 and Clown asked me, the first time I stepped over the threshold into the ward.

"I made friends with the Green Crow."

They both looked at each other and began to back off towards the window, through which can be seen the illusion.

"I could explain ..."

"Or, better—call it!"

"No, the Crow has disappeared."

"Fine, then tell us, because we need to know how to treat you!"

I sat down on my bed beside the illusion and began from the beginning with the manna porridge, the same as I wrote down for the doctor.

"You're totally sane!" announced F22, having heard my story. "There's nothing sick in that! Every child has playmates."

"Yes, yes," said Clown. "I too had a friend when I was a child. My parents didn't believe it though. 'Such an ugly child can't have any friends,' my mother once told my father, thinking that I was in my room. My friend was very sly, he never showed himself to my parents. I invited him to birthdays, Christmases, New Years, but he never came, and my parents decided that what you can't see doesn't exist. When I enrolled in the philosophy faculty, my friend suddenly died. And to this day my parents don't believe that I ever had a friend. Do you know how painful that is?" Clown pressed her face in the pillow and sobbed for a while.

"It's ludicrous that because of childhood errors a person can end up in a loony bin," my voice said.

"The Green Crow hasn't died and it's not a child's fantasy …" I said it very loudly, so Clown would also hear it through her sobs.

Clown and F22 moved to sit closer together and almost in unison said:

"Tell us!"

TRANSLATED FROM LATVIAN

BY MARGITA GAILITIS

EDITED BY VIJA KOSTOFF

BIRUTĖ JONUŠKAITĖ

The Fire

ONE HUNDRED SEVENTY-SIX STEPS. Next to every one of them is a gap in the wall the size of a brick. Sometimes a cold tongue strokes your ankle through it. Not that of a wolf. That of the wind. The whitish reflection of the dimming day gets through from the western side. Because the kid always goes up the Vilkynė watchtower in the evening. He stands watch at night.

How long has he been counting the steps? When he places his foot on the first one, a whirring mechanism flips on between his heart and his brain, regulating his breathing and the rhythm of his steps. All the steps take the same time, as if his was the advance of a robot, and not of a human being, ever further up in the spiral, up to the viewing platform. Just one deep, muscle-relaxing sigh—when the waves of the forest rippling into the distance open up like a green cloak that's suddenly thrown right in front of your eyes. The heavy metal doors thud hollowly behind him. What's left is a two-meter pocket surrounding the tower along with two telescopes that allow you to observe the four corners of the world.

The kid always turns left at the door. The opposite of how the sun travels. Maybe if he stepped to the right he would see his still steaming footprints below, the still-quaking bent grass near the path he has just taken to get to the tower, whipping up an airy little cloud of dust from the earth? Dust doesn't rise forty meters up, but the dust that comes in with him and falls on the one hundred seventy-six steps, one after another, is enough. At the top of the tower, your shoes have to be clean. Normally on the way up they are licked until they shine by the wind that has penetrated through the gaps. But there are quiet nights. The dust endures the rhythmic, spiral-like ascension and then the person who has reached "the pocket," as if hiding from oneself, wipes the front of his shoes on the legs of his pants: first the right foot rubs the left calf, then the left foot the right. It can only be done like this. In this way. From the very first time when the local forest ranger, who gave him the job, came up with him. From the time that the tower was built.

"So, kid, this will be your kingdom. There are still wolves, but they won't reach you. Watch out for fire."

He barely heard the words of the warden, because the space that had opened up held him up by his spine, like an enormous wave. In a moment he had to decide if he was able to withstand this perfect scene every day: the pedantically pricked tops of coniferous trees; the clear sky-blueness of the dots of lakes; the ideal harmony of heaven and earth; a sight seen by the eyes of the Lord every day. Would there be enough room in his lungs for the whiffs of air that belonged only to the birds, or would he lose consciousness looking at the line of the horizon that surrounded the tower in a fine arc? Only a heavenly freshness emanated from it. The cosmic cleanness of the sky was right here—he felt it with his nostrils as if he had resurfaced from a thick swamp into the clearest of spring water. He was confused. He understood that he had intruded into a zone where worn-out tennis shoes, jeans washed long ago, and the same shirt unwashed for two days were not suitable. He ran down almost stumbling, not yet knowing how many steps were in the tower, but he was already prepared to return properly dressed, smelling of soap, with clothes dried in the wind, with clean shoes.

"Your assistant comes to work like he's going to a government department. Maybe he confused the Vilkynė Tower with a New York skyscraper?" the forest rangers said as they discussed the new guy at the beginning. Then they forgot about him. Who cared about Agota's kid who was crouching in the tower at night? Just as long as he didn't doze off. Because if he failed to catch a fire, the men would tear him to pieces.

The kid didn't sleep. Fires didn't happen in the forest. His gaze hovered, catching even the finest of smoke that rose through the green waves. Then he called the men with wheels down on the ground, and they would speed along the dusty roads of the forests to take a look who dared make a fire and why. Normally they were brats of some sort. And sometimes they were hunters.

However, that kind of movement down below, prompted by a call from him, was a rarity. All the other evenings and nights descended upon the forest in a web of peacefulness drawn by the sun behind the horizon. Sometimes the web would take on purple hues, sometimes a lilac-blossom violet, and sometimes it would have a golden sparkle. But for the kid, all of them were beautiful. They all lay, not only on the green waves of the forest, but also on its soul, wrapping it in light layers, warming it, caressing it.

It wasn't only sunsets that he followed. Through the eye of the telescope he observed the nightly games of the birds, chased squirrels, and would even catch badgers that had wandered near the tower, or foxes darting among the pines. He tracked everything that moved, labored, or got ready for its evening rest or hunt. Gradually he got to know the daily schedule of all of his closest neighbors.

He was somewhat more interested in the forest surrounding the tower on three sides than the town located to the south. He wasn't concerned with what the people did there. All the more since the inhabitants of the yards nearby were not interesting: the retired couple that hardly walked anywhere; the family with two small kids that made a beeline for the car in the morning and in the evening hightailed it back to the yard; the old drunken wood carver, in whose yard stood deteriorating wood sculptures that had been started but were left unfinished.

The closest farmstead was the forest ranger's guest house, which housed a small nature museum. Sometimes teachers would bring groups of children to it. The forest ranger would then feel very smart and, having taken a thin stick, would jab each stuffed bird with it, and talk about the former life of the poor bird: where it made its nest, what it fed on, how it raised its chicks. The kid had also listened to these kinds of lessons once, but a different forest ranger, who previously worked there, had taught him; and the museum had been in a seedy and as-yet unrestored old log house. Now the guest house smelled of fresh timber and had exotic firs and rhododendrons planted around it, with narrow stone paths weaving their way between them. Some said that the local elite would gather here on the week-ends and debauch themselves in the little sauna nearby, discussing the important issues of the district.

The occasionally lit windows of the guest house did not warrant the kid's attention. But he caught everything that happened above the forest. He collected and collected impalpable scenes. He collected sunsets, fogs, strange reflections in the sky, and — at night — constellations. One day this beauty was too much — the kid was not able to stand it any longer. He himself was surprised, hushed: what he had chosen day in and day out, for months, for years, what had intoxicated him as soon as he had set foot on that first step, why he had climbed all the remaining one hundred seventy-five steps almost running, those daily broadening expanses, the going around the viewing platform in circles, was too much.

Didn't he have to release it all? Let it all out — howl it out?

But he rarely heard the wolves, plus they were far off, to the west. They couldn't howl each night together. At each full moon. But those sunsets tore him up from within, widened, penetrated all the textures, and all the voices of the birds flew through his ears, as the whispers of the night forest tickled beneath them, and the fragrant resin of the spruces and pines dripped from his nostrils. It seemed to him that something had to happen, or one evening after the sun went down he would crack like the ice of the stream that divided the tower from the southern side of the town, that he would become the reflecting spider's web and slink after the sun, beyond the horizon. Only his shiny shoes and telescopes remaining in the tower.

And then his eyes stumbled upon the wood carver's house.

He conquered the one hundred seventy-six steps like a blast of wind. The heavy outside door opened like it never had before, making sounds like the jaws of a beast that clapped shut behind his back. But the kid didn't hear them. A minute later he stood in the wood carver's yard:

"I want to learn how to carve," he said as two burning pins flew into the old man's swollen face.

"What? What do you want?" The old man squirmed on the bed in the twilight of the dank-smelling house.

"I said, I want to learn how to make sculptures, like you."

"Ha, ha, ha, the little snot decided to take up the craft of a carver;" the old man sat up. "This isn't a joke, boy, this is art. And no one can teach it. Either you can, or you can't. Understand?" And then he murmured with an entirely different voice, "You didn't bring anything to drink?"

"I'll bring something, if you let me borrow your tools."

"Tools? I don't lend my tools to anyone. Here, you see, they're all here in one place!" He got up from his bed, went to the table, which had not been cleaned for years, and raised one of the rags covering its corner. "I don't know why I've never exchanged them for a drink." The old man looked surprised.

"So will you lend them to me if I bring a bottle?" The kid stared at the chisels, burs, and the little axe.

"Well, I'll have to think about it … If you don't lose them … And who are you exactly?" The old man scratched his crotch, his armpits, and rubbed his eyes. "Do I know you?"

"I'm Agota's kid."

"What??? You're Agota's kid?"

"The one and the same."

"For God's sake, oh, what a girl: honey and milk, milk and honey, you try her once and amen—you'll long for her for your whole life, no other will do … and how it all ended up so badly …"

"So should I go get a bottle or not?" The kid's hand came down on the old man's shoulders so hard that he bent over.

"If you're Agota's, then go, go, I'll lend you the tools, you can work in my yard, go, kid, go …" The old man seemed to melt unexpectedly and once again sprawled out on the bed.

The kid came back quickly. He put a half-liter bottle of vodka on the messy table. Next to it he put a hunk of sausage, bread and an onion head.

"Can I take that oak log that's laying in the yard?" He addressed the old man after packing the tools in a bedsheet.

"Do you want to start with that? It would be better to start with a softer wood. Oak is stubborn, it doesn't submit easily to untrained hands. Try, just try it; I'll take a few sips here and then come and help you."

"I don't need any help. I will carry it to the tower," said the kid as he stepped briskly over the threshold.

"To the tower? What tower?" The old man was utterly confused, but by the time he shuffled out into the yard, there were just
worried wasps circling and diving like bombers under the roof of the
battered house.

First of all, the kid carved Saint Agota. He remembered his
mother only as a tender shadow—like a sweet aroma that makes you
faint, but grandmother would say that her daughter was just as beautiful as Saint Agota. And, like her, also a martyr. Afterwards he carved
Francis Nepomuk, George, Anthony, Isidore, Helen, Catherine ...
All of whom grandmother prayed to, and read books to him about.
All the fairy tales he had heard since he was a baby were only about
saints. He knew all their lives by heart, and carried their images in his
memory. It was with them that he grew up, and not with the children
from town. He was never bored in their company. Now he carved one
after another and put them on the wide windowsills. The windows
with sculptures surrounded the tower in an elegant spiral right up to
the viewing platform.

The forest ranger liked his work. He was able to show to the
guided tour groups that came to the tower not only beautiful views,
but also a whole flock of saints.

The guided tours annoyed the carver, and he would close himself up at the top of the tower in his glass booth, and stay there with
only the Agota he had placed there. And he wouldn't let in the journalists who were becoming more and more curious and were pressur-
ing the forest ranger to introduce them to this strange lookout.

It wasn't them he carved for. He carved so he could withstand it,
so he could at least scrape out something of the sunsets, fog, smells,
and spider webs from within himself. Perhaps that is why the cloaks
of his saints were colored, studded with birds, engraved with flowers
and the tops of firs. He carved and became lighter, clearer, more spacious. He could once again breathe in the freshness that rose in the
mornings above the forest, which stood watch down below over the
still sleeping world studded with the tracks of people.

One such morning, after finishing his watch, he meandered
along the river toward the town, to the home of his grandmother; seeing no one on the way, he gazed at the tracks left in the night—here a
rabbit had been hopping, here a deer had come by, looking to drink,

while here there were clear, deep tracks: a wild boar, no doubt. As he walked along—leaving behind him, in a window of the tower, yet another saint that he'd finished in the night, before him appeared … the old man. Now, in the bright dawn, the old man didn't appear as old as he had looked; while the kid was not such a kid. The old man was carrying a fishing rod in one hand, while in the other he held a willow branch, on which were stuck a few small fish. They both stopped and examined one another as if seeing each other for the first time.

"Heh, heh, heh, they say you're carving …" the old man said, unable to hold it in.

"If you want, I can give you your tools back. I bought new ones." For some reason the kid felt somewhat uncomfortable.

As if he had stolen those tools. And something else together with those tools. Something much more important.

"I don't need the tools. I haven't carved for a long time … When they took her out … well, I don't need to explain it to you. But I'd like to see your saints …" The old man was sober. The kid was even more confused.

"Well, come—you could come tonight …" he said as he shrugged his shoulders and slid by the old man, not daring to brush against his fishing rod.

It was a good week later that the old man came. Shaven, with a more or less clean shirt, and wearing shoes that were a few decades old.

The door down below was normally unlocked. When the kid heard it being opened, he knew that he would be having visitors. But this time he understood that it would be a special one. He didn't climb like the others, he pulled himself along. His wheezing and coughing marked every step and rose to the top in circles as if from the bottom of a well. The kid squinted in the sunset, which at that very moment cut the sky like some sort of enraged butcher—making only purple lines and a bloody froth of clouds. He sensed the grimy fingers of the old man feeling each of his saints. All over, from their halos to their bare feet. The old man assessed each cavity, each stroke left by the chisel, reading the sharp entries made by the kid into the body of the wood. And as he read, the uneasiness rose up his thin legs, his back tightened, and shivers embraced his shoulders — the entries were perfect. As if he had left them himself. But he wasn't the one that had done the carving. This was Agota's child's work.

The kid knew that everyone called him that. He had been used to it since he was a baby. It was like he had never had a last name.

The old man had heard a lot about the kid, and had howled like a wolf for many nights, but in the end he did not decide anything. But when he began to pour his hopelessness into emptied bottles, everything sank and settled, and the years and last names, the events, and the women and children of the town all mixed together. And he cared about nothing.

Now, rising to the top of the tower, barely able to catch his breath, all the gears inside him, eaten away by cheap spirits, were spinning with all their might. But something still clearly ticked away, still said that he still needed to conquer all one hundred seventy-six steps to the top, to Agota.

He reached the viewing platform wiping the sweat from his brow.

The kid stood with his back to him. His back listened to the old man's heaving panting. And the old man hung on to the handrails and drank in the freshness that rose from the forest.

It appeared to the kid that the old man was afraid to raise his head, that he couldn't take a look at the bloody sky.

What was he afraid of?

"Show me Agota," he finally wheezed, trying to catch his breath.

The kid opened the door and went first, up into his booth. In his glass nest there was just a table, a chair, a small chest of drawers, and a telephone. Around him were wooden logs, some already with faces, a lot of wood shavings, a toolbox, and a stool.

Agota stood on the table. Tall, with a full chest, a long dress, a cloak elegantly draped over her, and a red hood on her head. In one hand she held a palm branch, and in the other a dainty loaf of bread, as if it was a third breast. The edges of the dress were so beautifully carved that it seemed the wood was knitted, while the red hood was like a veil. It was only her face that the old man could not fully see in the evening dusk, because Agota stood with her back to the dimming sky.

The kid clicked on the light switch.

"Dear Agota ..." the old man grasped onto the edge of the table. "It's like she's alive. But do you really remember her?"

The kid was silent. Only his nostrils pulsating like those of a bridled horse.

"She said that that boar used all his strength to drag her away, but I didn't believe it, I didn't know how to forgive ..." The old man became quiet. "She returned pregnant. After giving birth she didn't recover. She became ill, was always ill, maybe he infected her with something, or maybe it was out of sadness ..."

"Is it still alive?" the kid uttered, without taking his eyes off the sunset. As if he were not asking the old man, but the sky still burning behind Agota's back.

"They said that he met his end during a hunt — that someone shot him by accident. But I don't think so. That warden was a horrible boss, and he was an even worse person." As he said these words, the old man shivered. Because suddenly he saw in the window pane the reflections of both himself and the kid. Against the background of clotted blood, were two similar sets of shoulders, two very similar physiques. He turned to the person standing next to him, wanting to check, and then felt that Agota and the entire table were receding, that his knees were buckling, while the shattered clot of the sky began to crawl toward his heart.

"King of Christ, Agota wasn't lying ..." he groaned. "So that's why you're a born carver!" He promptly collapsed into the wood shavings.

Then something happened inside the kid. It was as if he were hearing a strange sound, one that had been inside him since childhood: when his grandmother, in late autumn, would thrust her shovel into the earth and carefully try to raise her beautiful cannas (she was the best flower-grower of the town), he would stand close by and wait with excitement, when he would hear something kind of like coughing, and something kind of like popping, and the white roots shamelessly pulled from the deep, black earth would jump up. And he would blush at the thought that the tubers — so thick, and meaty, with plump, tenderly reddish heads, and a fine, violet radicle — looked like the peepees of flowers. The stumps of the cannas departed from the earth unwillingly—harshly snapping and loudly splitting in half; and it wasn't just him that could not stand the popping, but his grandmother as well—she would wail like her hand had been cut off.

Now he heard that snapping inside of him. As if his grandmother's shovel had pierced through his ribs and tried to rip out his heart.

He didn't want to give up so easily. He escaped to the viewing platform and made a few circuits. Down below, the forest had already sunk into slumber. The birds had quieted down, only sometimes a wild pigeon would coo—after all, summer had already counted its last days. The windows of the guest house were lit. Someone was debauching.

But the snapping didn't abate. And he understood: he wouldn't get out of it. The time had come.

He went down the stairs, and quietly closed the door.

It was the first time during all his service that he had left his post unsupervised and withdrawn to his home.

Grandmother's jewelry box hadn't been hidden, it was where the old woman had left it before her death—on the little chest of drawers next to her bed. He took it, pulled out a handkerchief, carefully cleaned off the dust, and opened the wooden cover engraved with little tulips. Such were the precious things inside: two silver rubles from Tsarist times; a pocket watch, which Grandmother got back after the war in place of Grandfather, who was killed somewhere in the fields of Russia; a few photos and Grandmother's wedding ring. But now he needed something else. "When the time comes, read your mother's letter. Don't forget, it's at the bottom of the box," the old woman said while dying.

Having set out all her belongings on the table, he raised the patch of black velvet fabric that covered the bottom of the box. Under it was a finely folded, yellowish sheet of paper. When he raised it, a picture slid out from inside and, fluttering, landed on the table. In it a woman and man were smiling with their heads nestled against one another. What does that mean, smiling?—happiness didn't fit in their faces, it clambered through the jagged edges of the photo, it simply, shamelessly, blinded you—just like the stumps of the cannas that had absorbed the joy of growing during the summer. The kid had never seen such faces, they forced him to blush.

Unable to bear it, he turned the photo over. His glance met the small letters: *Your parents, Agota and Laurynas.*

He returned to the tower around midnight.

He carried his mother's letter and the photo in the pocket of his shirt—as close to his heart as possible. In his hands was a bag with candles. He collected all of them together—his grandmother had collected quite a few. She liked to please the saints with little flames on their name days, and during feasts, and while kneeling in prayer.

Now he would please them. After all, such an occasion came once in a lifetime.

He gave each saint two to three candles: he pressed one into its palm, he stuck another onto its legs, fixing another on its head. He left the most, of course, for Agota—he stuffed them anywhere he could. When he lit them, the flames of the candles jumped up around her head like a crown of fire.

Then he slinked down, step by step, lighting the remaining candles: in each window of the tower the saints were quickly wrapped in bright halos. Then he went up once again, to his glass nest. Raising up the frozen old man, he lay him on the table near Agota's legs. For a moment, it appeared to him that they both were looking at each other, that the wood carver's face began to disappear, became younger and more and more similar to the one he had just seen in the photo. Fearing that this sight would disappear, he took a new wooden log and began to carve.

In the meanwhile men and women tumbled out of the little sauna. The whole group then crashed into the stream. They splashed, shrieked, buzzed, until suddenly there was a scream: "It's on fiiiiire! Fire!!! The tower's on fiiiire!"

A moment later the group stood naked at the base of the tower. Some oohed in amazement, while others guffawed, while yet others swore and spat.

The warden set his hands on his naked hips. Water dripped from his hair and swimming trunks.

"Hey, kid, come out of there and tell me what crazy idea you've thought up, for God's sake?" He shouted, turning his head upwards.

The kid didn't appear.

The others quickly began to yell. Someone was already shaking the door, but it was locked with a latch on the inside. The voice of the warden became ever more shrill and angry. Then the kid came down. He opened the door just enough for a hand to get through.

"Could you perhaps not make so much noise?" he said to everyone that crowded towards him. "We're getting ready for a funeral. My father has died." And he closed the door.

He went slowly up to the top of the tower, stopping at every saint and bowing respectfully. He reached the one hundred seventy-sixth step with a broad smile: all of the most venerable guests had been invited to his parents' wedding. He just needed to finish carving Laurynas with a palm branch in one hand and bars in the other. From now on the three of them will protect the forest from fire.

TRANSLATED FROM LITHUANIAN

BY JAYDE WILL

ALEKSANDAR PROKOPIEV

Snakelet

This fairy tale should not be told near stagnant water . . .

HE FOUND THE SNAKELET at the very beginning of his solitary life, and now, after five years of living together, they had the same trust in each other as close relatives. The snakelet ate out of his hand, went with him on walks through the forest—dozing in the pocket of his faded but still warm fur coat, or crawling along behind him when invigorated by the sun. On winter nights it slept long and peaceful-ly, coiled up in a nest of twigs, leaves, and moss he had made for it by the fire.

The little snake was patterned and only four inches long, at most. It enjoyed climbing along his arm, hissing joyfully with its lit-tle tongue. And it loved to lie in wait for its prey—a hypnotized bug, perhaps—and weave its hunter's dance around it.

By the end of the second year, he had taught it to recognize his whistle. Now he was trying to teach it to distinguish the short, sharp whistle that meant "Come!" from the long, protracted one that meant "I'm bringing you food," and the two whistles of equal length meaning "Lift yourself up!"—at which the snakelet would raise its head and the upper third of its body and sway from side to side.

He was happiest when it brought him his pipe. This difficult task, announced by one short and one long whistle, required the snakelet to perform several actions in sequence: to find the pipe, to pick it up with its little teeth, and to bring it to him. The snakelet would leave tiny, wet bite-marks on the stem of the pipe, and when the man lit his pipe and drew on it, he felt he was imbibing a special tenderness.

Yet, after five years of seclusion, loneliness began to oppress him. While absentmindedly stroking the curvy body of the snakelet, he realized that the blame lay in himself. He might have been offended, and people might have been nasty and unfair to him, but he had no right to be angry with them for so long. How could he forget the beautiful days of his childhood and youth? How could he forget that he had once been loved and that he himself had offended others? He was only human too, after all.

So he decided to return to the city. He put on his fur coat, slipped the snakelet into his pocket, and set off. As soon as he saw the first houses, he almost broke into a run.

But when he came face to face with the city, he sensed that invisible barrier again—the one he had felt whenever, in his solitary years, he had descended from his cave into the city in search of food. The same sense of breathlessness came over him. The city was suffocating.

Already he was met by the astonished, derisive stares of the passersby. His wild hair and shaggy beard, his tattered old coat, which his arms jutted out of like rusty spades, and his fearful reaction to any loud noise, made him stand out. In the eyes of the city he belonged to the class of beggars who come out at dusk to rummage through the garbage cans, glancing around nervously like hungry dogs.

By the time he made it to the first café, he was shaking like a drunk. At the last moment, before going in, he thought to take the snakelet out of his pocket. It zipped across the sidewalk as fast as lightning and disappeared into a crack in the wall of the nearest house. There, in the stone crevasse, it calmed down. It's friend's disquiet had unsettled the little creature. Instinctively, it felt safe in the dark. It waited.

In the café, the barkeeper and five or six guests—all men—were listening to a football match on the radio. The shrill, eunuch-like voice of the commentator, combined with the shouting and cursing of the sweaty men made him seek the farthest table. He sat huddled there on the chair, covering his ears with his broad hands, until the feel of his own skin gradually calmed him down.

Only then did he notice the fellow at the neighboring table. He was sitting away from the men with the radio and gazing peacefully out into the street. A pair of crutches rested against the chair beside him. Turning from the window, the fellow smiled and said, "Nice day today ..."

He went on talking in a lively, rambling way about the coming of spring, pollution in the cities, and the impossibility of true communication. It turned out that both men harbored the same bitterness and the same contempt for the crowd.

At first our man just nodded in agreement, later tossing in the occasional "yes," "that's right," and "I think so too." But when the fellow moved on to the problem of friendship, he felt he needed to interrupt his monologue: "Where can you find sincerity? People are selfish and care only for their own interests."

Unconsciously, the two men moved closer to each another. He was now resting his arms on the neighboring table, while the like-minded fellow was leaning toward him. All of a sudden, our man exclaimed: "I've got something to show you—a true friend!"

And as the fellow sent him an almost cheerful look of approval, our man gave a short, sharp whistle. The football fans by the radio turned and cast him angry glances.

The snakelet did not respond. The man had never asked it to enter a room full of people before; he had taught it to be wary of them. It decided to stay in its hole.

"Please hear me and come out!" he begged. "Just this once!" He whistled again, now with an air of desperation. His whistle brought a tirade of curses from the other men, and the barkeeper yelled: "Shut up, you dunce! Can't you see we're listening to the game?"

The fellow from the neighboring table scratched himself behind his ear. "Sorry, but I don't understand," he said.

Just then, the head of the snakelet appeared under the front door. Warmth filled his heart. "There he is!" he whispered, "He's coming."

But the very next instant, as if in slow motion, the curiosity on his neighbor's face changed to revulsion and his hand grasped murderously for the crutch . . .

TRANSLATED FROM MACEDONIAN

BY WILL FIRTH

Aixa de la Cruz

True Milk

1. The children of the 1990s are destined to revive conservatism. The eighteenth century is one of their passions, being that they're the first generation in quite some time that's prudish enough to be shocked by the feats of Lord Byron.

Waking from the anesthetic, I found I was alone in the hospital ward. Someone had left a picture of the Virgin Mary on the bedside table and, next to it, a red, heart-shaped balloon. I tried sitting up to see if there were any other presents, but this tugged on the stitches in my abdomen — I let out a small cry. I thought a nurse might hear, but a minute passed and no one came. The baby was sleeping opposite the bed; it wasn't making any noise, so I guessed it must have been sleeping. From where I was lying I could only really see the cot, which was made of gray plastic; the same color plastic as the sick bowl and the bedpan. In public hospitals they're trying to cut costs wherever they can — my mother-in-law later explained — the same plastics company gets the contract for all sorts of things, hence they're all the same color. Apart from being monotone, public hospitals in Mexico always have one of those cheap, Doctor Simi pharmacies nearby. Doctor Simi's that fat, beardy character who stood in the state elections here. A few hours later, sitting up in bed and peering out of the window, I saw a Doctor Simi mascot handing out flyers by the traffic lights.

2. All hippies are dirty and promiscuous; no child of the Facebook generation wants his or her mother to be seen wearing those flowery skirts. Whereas they find the eighteenth-century poet and necrophiliac, José Cadalso, a deeply romantic figure.

I thought it strange, the baby not crying. I wanted to get up and check it was all right, but I was worried I might hurt myself. I was also in something of a daze—my eyelids felt heavy. I asked myself: what dreams would I have had while I was under? I couldn't remember a thing. Strange, because not only do I always dream, I always remember my dreams. I'd had a recurring nightmare during the previous nine months, over and over: in agony, I'd be giving birth to a baby that miaowed like a cat. It came out covered in all the usual blood and mess, five fingers on each hand, two eyes, mouth—the usual—but miaowing as well. I still don't understand it; but, then again, I'm not convinced dreams are always meant to be understood.

3. People born in the 90s are into vampires. What they don't know is how instrumental Lord Byron was in bringing vampires to prominence.

After a while, half an hour or so, I began shouting for the nurse. This woke the baby—the first time I'd heard it cry. The sound grated— like that baby had swallowed a rusty spring—but at least it sounded normal; at least it sounded human. I breathed a bit easier and, while I was waiting for the nurse to come, wondered whether Jorge had managed to sort out the cable contract for the TV. He'd promised he would, so I'd have something to do during the days I'd be spending in bed. In the end he didn't keep his promise—apparently all the nappies had been more expensive than he'd expected—but I remember finding the thought very comforting. As it happened, the new *House* series was starting that week ... Finally the nurse showed up: "How do you feel?" she asked, off-hand, almost cold, as she leaned down to look in the cot. I knew the medical staff were being like this with me because I'd had a Caesarean, which is more expensive for them—they get angry with you for having the slim hips of a child. "My stitches are pulling," I said. She brought me the baby, wrapping it in white linen—yellowish linen, in fact, like they'd washed it in too much bleach. The baby's face was so bloodless it stood out against the sheets. "Is it normal for it to be that pale?" She placed it in my arms. It was bald and white and had hardly any eyelashes. And it was also really clean, as though it hadn't spent nine months crammed in amongst my internal organs. Ugly, too, I decided—no way Jorge could ever warm to a child like this. "The doctor will come by later on," said the nurse. "You ought to try feeding." I felt a shiver run through me.

4. Children from the 90s don't know who Lord Byron is, according to a report by the Programme for International Student Assessment (PISA).

For *that*, I hoped my mother-in-law would come. She ought to know how the whole thing went, having had six children. Her job finished mid-afternoon. The baby was hungry, even though they'd given it a bottle at feeding time. Now, instead of crying, it began forming an O with its tiny lips. The effort brought blood to its face, which made it nicer to look at. Its grandmother was also slightly shocked by how white its skin was. "Doctor says it's got thalassemia," I said. Before asking what thalassemia was, before I could reassure her that it wasn't anything serious—*you only have to avoid hemorrhages, dear, and make sure it doesn't get hit by anything*—she began shouting at the top of her voice: everything would have been all right if Jorge and I had only got married, like she'd said we should. I hated her for this; now that it's in the past, though, I do ask myself if she mightn't have had a point. Some things it's better not to meddle with. Might as well take precautions, because when God's ire is provoked—how can I put it ... Anyway. "Take out your breast," she said, shutting the door. "Which one?" I said. Possibly I was playing for time. The baby, with that O-mouth, was so eager that I felt like it might slurp out my soul. "Don't act useless," said my mother-in-law. I took the left one—like an udder, something strange, something not belonging to me—and offered it up to the livid little monster. It was a bit like a pre-Hispanic sacrifice scene, but, being European, my savage mutilation must have been closer to that of someone like Saint Agueda. The baby tried to find my nipple; it seemed confused. Nothing strange about that: my boobs were enormous, the nipples tiny by comparison, as was the baby's head—ridiculously small. I thought it might suffocate if it got stuck in my cleavage. My mother-in-law tried to intervene. The baby kept missing the spot, all gummy nips and saliva, and soon it was crying even harder. As was I, in the end—tears of frustration. "Best leave it," said my mother-in-law before going off to look for the nurse. She clearly wasn't happy. I carried on staring at the baby, which was writhing, hoarse, its skin all wrinkled, like it was made out of some weird material. We seemed like different species. And where were my maternal instincts? I'd been told it was instantaneous, natural, inevitable—a chemical change that would just happen during birth. But they had told me other things too: that I shouldn't be a mother; that I was too young; that in Mexico City, where the Democratic Revolution Party are in power, abortion is legal, like homosexual marriage.

5. On the 17ᵗʰ of June, 1816, a meeting took place that was vitally important for both that century and our current one; for Mary Shelley; for John Polidori; as well as for the likes of Stephanie Meyer, the HBO network; author of The Vampire Chronicles, Anne Rice; and extreme metallers, Cradle of Filth.

6. Lord Byron's summer residence was called Villa Diodati. Accused of having dishonored his sister, he had fled England and was squandering his inheritance entertaining a number of quarrelsome exiles, including Mary Wollstonecraft Godwin and her husband-to-be, long-winded Shelley. On the evening of the 17ᵗʰ of June, 1816, also in attendance was John Polidori—Byron's shadow, his doctor, as well as his personal Salieri—a copycat, but not a very good one.

7. The Romantics—impervious to cliché, again exactly like the children of the 1990s—read horror stories by the fire in gothic houses at nightfall. On that symbolic evening, Villa Diodati's retinue of adulterous literary types read to one another from a German collection of fantasy stories. Byron used the stories to challenge the others.

Two days later, I tried feeding again. I was back home by now. Jorge had just left and wasn't going to be back all weekend. I'd hugged him as hard as I could and pleaded with him not to go. The thought of being alone in the house with the baby frightened me. But a recruitment agency had called and offered him a job driving a truck down to Tamaulipas overnight; and the money was decent, so he couldn't turn it down. Meantime, I'd begun walking without any help, the stitches had started to heal, and Jorge's mom had been coming in the afternoons and evenings to help around the house. "We'll pick a name when you get back, shall we?" The baby was six days old already and it not having a name was starting to feel weird. It reminded me of our dog Xena, who we bought as a puppy at the market. Since my mom said they always come sick, she wouldn't let me christen it until it had survived two weeks. I couldn't get the idea out of my head that the same thing was happening now with my baby. It clearly wasn't healthy, it hardly ate. But children, even if they seem like they might die, ought to be baptized, so at least there's a name to place in the death announcements.

8. If Byron had been Spanish, he would have challenged them with blunderbusses, but, being British, he proposed they write a novel. Only Mary Shelley and Polidori took the bet. Polidori was a second-rate talent, meaning no one paid much attention to what he came up with. Frankenstein, on the other hand—even 1990s kids know about that.

I felt less uncomfortable—no one was watching this time. People can say it's all natural, but if you don't go topless on the beach, why would you breastfeed in full view of the world—in front of rapt families saying, well done, well done? I took the little one in my arms, with its deathly white, tuberculosis-looking face, and began humming a song I'd learned when I arrived in Mexico—about the Wailing Woman, a ghost that appears at night in search of her dead children. Jorge said that when he and his sister were living out on the plains, they used to hear her, particularly in winter. The baby let out a burp, twisting its face into something resembling a smile. "You have to eat, little one," I said, putting my nipple to its lips, "or you're going to die with no name." It felt its way around for a while and then, suddenly, I felt pressure and an excruciating pain. I let out a scream and pulled it off me. And screamed again: it had blood dripping from its mouth. It licked its lips; it actually licked its lips. The dark circle around my nipple had two tiny punctures. The baby was grimacing, contorting its face, trying to get close to the food source again, writhing, but as far as I could see not a single drop of milk had come out. Putting it back in its cot, I began crying uncontrollably. I put the TV on full volume and shut myself in the kitchen. Trembling, I took some powdered milk out of the cupboard and started making up a bottle. The sound of the TV drowned out the baby's cries, but I knew it was still there, on the other side of the presenter from *The Biggest Loser*. I couldn't get the picture out of my mind: the ghostly image of my thalassemic child with its bloody mouth.

9. Polidori's fate was a tragic one. He lived in Byron's shadow, and Byron mocked him, his love of medicine, and his love of poetry—and the fact that these were his only loves. He took revenge on Byron by writing a story called The Vampire.

That week the doctor came to the house. He said the baby was fragile and that if we didn't get it to eat, it would have to be taken to the hospital. There were four of us in the kitchen: the doctor, my mother-in-law, Jorge and me; they were all giving me accusing looks. *You couldn't give birth to it on your own, and now you can't even look after it,* their looks seemed to say. I waited until they'd all left, and then I cut my hand. I never thought I'd have it in me to self-harm, but I acted decisively. After all, I was the worst mother in the world; I had to do something to make up for what I'd done. The blood flowed freely. I let it fall from my hand and collect in a bowl. I drained myself almost to the point of passing out. Then I mixed it in with the milk powder—stirring it, it turned a perfect pink color, like liquidized strawberry. My heart was pounding, I didn't know if it was right what I was doing: I knew that God condemned vampirism, I knew I was infringing certain laws—though I couldn't have said which, or exactly why. Clearly, it was disgusting, and there's a link between what we find disgusting and the things God condemns, like bestiality, say, cannibalism, incest, homosexuality. But the fact is—God forgive me—this bottle full of pink milk was the first thing my baby had drunk down with any sort of appetite since the day it had been born.

10. In The Vampire, *Polidori revived the legend of the bloodsuckers, and the vampire takes the shape of an eccentric British aristocrat who goes around Europe corrupting upper-class women. It's basically Byron in inverted commas. This was the only thing Polidori wrote that garnered any attention; it had an impact at the time because everyone thought Byron must have had something to do with penning it.*

The baby picked up straight away; it found its new diet invigorating, and we even started to see some color in its cheeks. Obviously, I was the only one who knew its particular tastes. Each day I'd cut myself somewhere new, trying to do it in places where no one would see. Not that Jorge was going to notice; he found the scars over my womb disgusting, and always turned out the lights before I got undressed. But his mom, she could definitely have been suspicious—I found the upper part of my bottom a particularly good spot. I'd numb the area with an ice cube, and the bleeding wouldn't last long; I used ferns to stop it—a remedy I remembered from home. Everything seemed under control, but after a few days I began feeling incredibly weak. One morning I woke up even more tired than usual, started making scrambled eggs and immediately passed out, falling backwards into the dish cabinet. When I opened my eyes I found myself on the floor, broken plates all around me. The glass had cut me on the shoulder and I was bleeding hard. The baby was crying more fiercely than ever. I thought something must have been attacking it; I felt its torment in my ears, like the pressure swimmers feel underwater. Then it hit me: it was the smell of my blood, it was driving it crazy. I got up and followed my impulse to lock the door to the baby's room. I felt terrified. There had been a moment where I'd *known* that the baby was coming for me, its mouth open in that O, ready to suck me dry through the wound. Hearing it scratching at the door, I became even more frightened. How could it have got out of its cot unaided? I grabbed my jacket and some money, locked up and ran from the house.

11. The vampire in The Vampire *is Byron, and the vampire in* The Vampire *is the vampire from* Dracula *and* Twilight; *which means that at least they dress like British gentlemen and not medieval Romanian zombies.*

Pregnant women are prone to fearfulness. They worry that their children will come out albinos, or with an extra finger, or color-blind, or that they'll have Down's Syndrome, be hemophiliacs, freaks of nature, hermaphrodites, have no arms, have no legs, be of a different race from the father, have a heart that's too big, have bones made of glass. But they don't generally contemplate the possibility of the child coming out a vampire. But that's what had happened to me. After I'd been to the Emergency Room, where they gave me two stitches on my shoulder, I went to a bar and ordered tequilas with *sangrita*. I thought about how strange my destiny was. I tried to get straight what I knew about bloodsuckers: *Dracula, Twilight, Vampire Diaries* … In the stories, they never try it with children, it's taboo—which is proof we like to think that children come into the world pure, without anything on them for God to punish. I thought about my literature professor back in Spain, who said that books help us to understand life, which seemed at that moment like a not inconsiderable lie, because there was nothing in Anne Rice that was going to guide me through this. The tequilas went straight to my head, which is what happens when you've been losing blood day after day—cheap date. I took out my mobile to check the time and saw I had more than ten missed calls from Jorge and his mom. My heart started pounding. What might they have found in the house? During the bus ride home I tried to think about nothing. Nothing, nothing, nothing; I repeated it to myself. The first thing I saw was an ambulance outside the front door. If there had been any fatality, if the shape they were carrying out to the ambulance *was* a corpse, I only wished it would be that of the child. Eternity would preserve it, after all, the same as any vampire.

12. Nowadays, there are around a hundred vampire sects in the United States alone. On Mexican Yahoo Answers, there's a thread with dozens of people asking if drinking human blood will make them more beautiful, or stronger, or immortal. Anyone interested in pursuing the matter is advised to Google "drink human blood?"

TRANSLATED FROM SPANISH
BY THOMAS BUNSTEAD

NICOLAS BOUYSSI

An Unexpected Return

WAKING UP ONE MORNING, it came to the attention of the residents of the area that their neighbor on the second floor had decided to put an end to his life. The circumstances of the news were rather morbid. Everywhere; in the staircases, the basement, elevators, mailboxes, and parking lots, the following message had been posted: *"Your second-floor neighbor, to whom no one speaks, and who, as a sign of protest, decided to end it all, has the honor of announcing to his amiable fellow denizens that he will die in a completely unpredictable way. Any attempt to find my body would be as idiotic as it would be pointless. After having looked down on me during my life, please at least have the courage to treat my corpse with some respect."*

The first body part to be found was a foot. It had been carefully severed and was accompanied by a small note which read: *"To be continued."* Utter chaos descended on the residents. Because of the rumors, an increasingly large group of neighbors conglomerated day after day in the common outdoor space between the apartment buildings, and all of them went on about their hypotheses, their feelings, their fears.

The foot had been placed in the middle of a playing field, which implied the work of a show-off. It seemed obvious that the show-off himself was the owner of the foot, as no one else would have consented to participate in such a sordid display. Besides agreeing on the unstable nature of a person prepared to mutilate himself, people also thought that, since the neighbor had committed this act, his threats could no longer be taken lightly. They needed to organize.

A team of volunteers offered to form a neighborhood watch, with the members taking shifts, so that everyone could get some sleep.

The problem is that the neighbor didn't come back, although he did send a hundred or so letters, one for each resident, in which was included a photo depicting a severed hand. Panic overtook the residents when a group of teenagers noticed a second foot in the mouth of a stray dog. Several old people moved away over the course of the following week.

What did he want? Where was he hiding? Each new day was met with fear and revulsion. Already overwhelmed by the idea of discovering a new photo or a new body part, people became distrustful. No one dared go near trash cans or open mailboxes. The residents, in an effort to keep up morale, attempted to seek refuge in morbid humor. Without his two feet, they'd proclaim, the former neighbor couldn't get too far. So, they were sure not to run in to him again, or he'd be moving so slowly that they could nab him then and there. And if he cut off his other hand, he couldn't write anymore. That was the hope. They got to the point of waiting for this hand to materialize. Of course he had thought of upending this logic and sent a piece of his lip.

Feelings changed. The helplessness was such that guilt transformed into hate, and, after a period of compassion, people ended up hoping for his death. What was he waiting for, after all? He wasn't the only one that no one spoke to, not the only one whose life went on amidst general indifference. If he'd wanted to make people think, the neighborhood had thought.

Nothing new occurred for months. Had he changed his mind? Was he dead? But then people started to forget him and return to their old ways. The team of volunteers stopped their night watches. People became indifferent to each other again. One evening a car was even burned. The following morning in the center of the courtyard a ripped-off penis was found with, once again, the note: "*To be continued.*"

How does one describe the reaction that this discovery provoked? There was horror, incomprehension, despair. The night watches were started up again, even if everyone felt they were pointless. It was believed that this new self-mutilation required a holistic approach. The only solution, therefore, was to make everyone feel more accountable. People needed to speak to one another more, prove that never again would there be violence or indifference. An objection was raised immediately. Even if he did know about the general sentiment, as he was handicapped—footless, with his maimed lip, missing hand, and, most incredibly, missing his penis—it would be impossible for him to go anywhere without creating a stir. No rumors of a mutilated monster had been circulating.

The strangest thing was that he would even be able to still gather information about his old neighborhood. He had to eat, had to have money to pay rent. He was therefore maintaining some type of social interaction, which was contrary to his assumed situation. In other words, either the body parts that were found were not his, which made the victim a killer, or he had accomplices, and these accomplices were living in the neighborhood.

Such a hypothesis reduced the motive for these self-mutilations to meaninglessness. As he was assisted, he was not alone. As he wasn't alone, he was not the victim of general indifference. What might his purpose really be? To frighten? To traumatize? There remained, regardless of the angle from which one examined the question, perplexing inconsistencies.

In this climate of doubt and fear two opposing viewpoints came to the surface. One group of people were convinced that the recovered body parts were his and that each mutilation was in fact the direct penalty for an indefensible act. They suggested a more robust community life, and neighborhood dinners were organized. Another group, on the other hand, started from the assumption that these mutilations could only lead to death; so he was still in one piece. Far from a call for calm and tolerance, they advocated deeper mistrust and encouraged people to be more hostile.

Only those who held the belief that he was a criminal were concerned by the arrival of another snapshot, which depicted a nose and ears in a glass jar. The supporters of the first hypothesis took advantage of the situation and tried to persuade their opponents. They needed to stop being so divided, and, quite the opposite, needed to increase projects that fostered unity, all of which would let the neighborhood present a positive image of which not only the residents could be proud, but also the man. And, who knows, predicted some, if we were finally able to respect one another, perhaps, in spite of his pitiful condition, the man would come back.

Some hoped for it. They composed a letter, which was widely distributed, the principal arguments of which can be summarized as follows: *"For years now we have lived together without knowing each other. One of our own decided to revolt against this irrefutable fact. Try to understand the generosity of this act. Let us no longer tolerate intimidation and humiliation. Those who commit these acts do so only out of self-interest. Love each other. Prove to our former neighbor that his sacrifices were not in vain. Join us next Sunday for a silent march through the neighborhood."* The march took place. It was widely attended. A "Friends of the Neighborhood" Association was formed, which proposed, among other ideas, that a fund be created to provide for the former neighbor's needs if, by good fortune, he were to return.

Time passed. Trees were planted. New playgrounds and businesses were built. Legal action was taken against neighborhood delinquents, and (everyone had to admit) the formation of the Association had had a positive impact. The following year went by without incident. Then, one day, the former neighbor actually returned.

When he arrived, a large commemorative banquet in honor of his first self-mutilation was being set up. It was morning time. In the outdoor common area, a large table and tent were being installed. Few people were there, but they recognized him immediately. And yet he was walking normally. He was smiling. Voices started to be raised, and the man moved apprehensively. He slowed down. As soon as he was closer, one of the volunteers, who was driving a tent peg into the ground, yelled, "He's missing a foot!" Acting as if they were suddenly relieved, the residents who were there drew closer to him.

The man hesitated again but continued to come near. There could no longer be any doubt. He was still in possession of his right foot and both of his hands. "That's not possible," said some, "it's not him." Others, officers in the Association, still reeling from the shock, didn't know how to react. His return had become their life's mission, but the idea they had created for themselves of their own hero (a handicapped individual, all the more special because he had sacrificed his own body for the neighborhood) did not at all correspond with the impression this man's presence created. Paralyzed, they wondered what to do. And inside them a feeling of resentment was born.

The former neighbor continued to advance. Soon people saw that part of his lower lip was missing. Despite the selfishness implied by such a reaction, people were rather relieved. They moved in closer. The first person who managed to reach him could not help himself from asking, yes or no, did he still have a penis? The man was taken aback. Some of those who got to him just after felt ill at ease. Why go that far? He still was missing a foot and part of his lip. At this question the man at first lost his calm demeanor, but he answered, and his answer was yes. Yes, he still had a penis.

One group claimed he was an impostor. He was taking advantage of his resemblance to the former neighbor. Others maintained that it was indeed him and that he had caught wind of the huge fund the Neighborhood Association had collected. All things considered, no one was really happy to see him. "Why'd you come back?" asked some. "You made us look like fools," said others. The man became frightened and tried to get away. He was caught and people became aggressive.

The apartment complex was constructed in such a way, with its four concrete towers and open-air common space in the middle, that the sound rose upwards. Windows were opened. People saw a mute stranger surrounded by angry volunteers. Most residents said to themselves, "Here we go again," and came down.

The mood was becoming more and more tense. A fairly overweight man, one of those who had first volunteered to guard the common space at night, and, without ever knowing exactly why, had joined the Neighborhood Association, was trying to open the former neighbor's fly while yelling, "So do you have a penis or not?" They were separated. The President of the Neighborhood Association realized the urgency of the situation and stepped in, encouraging everyone to go home. There was resistance, bottles were thrown, and the police intervened.

Under escort, the man was taken to a safe house, which immediately caused more notices to be written. Some people said: *"We have always said this, and his appearance only confirms our suspicions. We are dealing with an impostor. We need to wake up. It's not too late. The Neighborhood Association is extorting donations from us for a nonexistent cause. We've seen him. He's not what we believed him to be. He*

walks normally. He even has the nerve to smile. We've been made fools of.
It is time to act."

The response did not take long to appear. It said: *"Instead of his*
return being a cause for celebration, some people, motivated by unrelent-
ing hatred, are calling for more proof and more sacrifice. The foot was not
enough for them. The piece of lip was not enough for them. What can be
expected from those who, to avoid bloodshed, demand more blood? Yes,
he has returned. Yes, he's back with us and he's living. Let's continue our
fight. Let's rally together. A new silent march will take place in three days.
For the peace of every one of us, for our security, everyone is encouraged
to attend."

The three days were turbulent. His body needed to be examined, asserted those who wrote the first notice. The man did not return. He didn't offer any explanations, either. Once again, the mood
deteriorated. Some demanded to be reimbursed. Cars were burned,
and the offices of the Neighborhood Association were ransacked. The
day of the march, the man's body was found. He had hanged himself.
The march was cancelled, and the members of the Neighborhood Association asked for the opportunity to hold a meeting in the assembly
room. The meeting started raucously when the news of his death was
revealed. After which there was silence, and people listened.

Everyone had to recognize that the man was less handicapped
than had previously been believed. His missing foot, for example, had
been lost in a car accident. Another disturbing piece of news was that,
on the day of his return, he was absolutely unaware of any drama that
might have been brewing in the neighborhood. He merely remembered that nine months prior he had cut his lip, and he had wished
to know what the general mood was so long after his disappearance.

Why hadn't he killed himself? Besides the pain he had endured
after his first mutilation, the despondency, then the regret and doubts
about the fairness of his situation, had fueled his initial bitterness.
When he returned he was prepared to endure a cold and hostile reception. But the resentment had been so strong it triggered a kind
of mutism, which the Association had difficulty pulling him out of.

Facts surfaced that, with the exception of the piece of lip, the
body parts found since his disappearance were not, in fact, his. It
wasn't even clear where they'd come from. Moreover, as the man real-

ized that he had acted partially due to resentment and partially for revenge, there was no reason whatsoever for people to mourn his death.
On the other hand, it became apparent, while listening to the President of the Association, that unidentified individuals had taken advantage of the general mood to send revolting pictures and disseminate body parts of unknown origin.

The President of the Association exhorted the crowd to remain
calm. That was impossible. Voices were raised. They demanded that
the guilty be punished. The room emptied, and groups formed outside. They suspected that the Association board had taken advantage
of the ramblings of an unbalanced individual to line their pockets.
The overweight gentleman, the one who had mistreated him, insisted
on being allowed to speak, demanding, under the threat of prosecu-
tion or grave bodily harm, that his money be returned.

The night was eventful. Several supporters of the Association
thought it prudent to leave the area and stay with friends. Their departure was interpreted as an admission of guilt. One of them was
discovered as he was trying to start his car and was seriously injured.
What could be done? And, most importantly, whose body parts were
those that had been found?

An official judicial inquiry was opened. Because of a terrible
stench, it was eventually discovered that all the body parts, photo-
graphed or not, had been cut off cadavers by a neighbor who was jealous of the man's idea. He had wanted to accomplish the same goal.
He was an employee at the morgue.

He disappeared the following day. Among the various bits of
dead bodies lying around his room, an abusive letter was found—
pinned to a wall along with a large photo of his body. He had circled
his feet, his legs, and his hands. And he was planning on amputating
them straightaway.

TRANSLATED FROM FRENCH
BY ALEXANDER HERTICH

MICHEÁL Ó CONGHAILE

The Second-Hand Man

THE MAN WAS WALKING HOME FROM WORK. He was tired after a long day breaking stones. His hands were chapped and raw. Sore. Now he needed to piss. He looked around, and even though there was no one there, he didn't want to go by the side of the road. He walked on hurriedly, his thighs clamped together. Holding it in. On his right he spotted a ruined church that he hadn't seen earlier. He made his way in through the nettles and the brambles and relieved himself slowly, gratefully, around the back. He was well hidden and he knew no one could see him from the road.

No sooner was he finished than it began to rain, so he ran for shelter into the church. The roof had only partially collapsed and the remaining rafters and slates kept the worst of the rain off. He waited for the shower to pass so he could go home but the rain was getting heavier and threatening black clouds scudded across the darkening sky. The wind rose and now a gale was blowing. Then thunder and lightning. Then more rain. He hunkered down in a corner of the cold, damp ruin, trying to avoid the rain that appeared to be pursuing him now. Water ran down his hair and into his eyes. He couldn't see. For want of anything better to do and to forget about his own troubles for a while, he started to think. Passing the time, he thought of the thousands of heartfelt prayers and entreaties that had been offered up over hundreds of years within the very walls of this ruin, this very corner he was now sheltering in.

He jumped. There was a commotion outside, as though a herd of reluctant cattle was being driven determinedly past the door. Noisy hooves clattered on flagstones and crunched on gravel. Then he remembered that there were no flagstones and there was no gravel. Beyond the door was just a wilderness of nettles, briars and thistles. He retreated further into the corner, curling himself up into a ball. He crossed himself. Lightning lit up the sky, brushing his ear, it seemed. He felt dizzy. He couldn't hear anything. He didn't know where he was. He shook his head ...

Suddenly the Son of the Devil rushed in the door, carrying a dead man. He shook the corpse vigorously and laid it on the floor. Then he shook himself, like a dog just emerged from the sea, shaking the water off. He blew on his numbed and frozen hands, trying to restore some feeling to them. Who would have thought the Son of the Devil would ever need to take shelter from the elements? Or a dead man either, thought the man worriedly.

Just then, the Son of God came in the door and snatched the dead man up off the floor.

"You filthy thief," he shouted at the Son of the Devil. "Here you are again, thieving, hiding things from me. Away to hell with you, and mind your own damned business."

"This is mine, and this is my business, and I'm taking this with me," said the Son of the Devil, seizing the dead man's legs and doing his damnedest to pull the corpse from the Son of God.

"He was mine first."

"I found him."

"He's one of mine."

"He belonged to me too."

"You don't deserve him. He was a good man," said the Son of God.

"Oh, he was, was he?" the Son of the Devil said. "Oh, yes. To himself! He was more impressed with my ideas than with any of yours."

"Shit!" shouted the Son of God.

"Bullshit!" screamed the Son of the Devil.

They spent the next hour pulling the corpse back and forth, each trying to take it from the other. One would grab it, and the next minute the other would take it back, until they were both exhausted and out of breath, even the dead man—who had a headache to boot. The stone flags had been torn up and the place was a shambles.

They sat down in front of the altar until they had got their breath back, both watching the dead man lying on the floor between them. Both keeping a close eye on the corpse.

Then the Son of the Devil said that it wasn't worth their while fighting over the dead man any more and that they should, if possible, come to a peaceful resolution. They would present the case to a third party and this disinterested person would deliver a judgment. After giving it some thought, the Son of God agreed, although he did wonder whether this one corpse was worth all this trouble. They spat on their palms and shook on it. The deal was done. They looked around. They saw the man hiding in the corner at the back, behind the altar.

"This is the man," the Son of the Devil said. "Whoever has ears to hear, let them hear."

"This is the man," said the Son of God. "Whoever has ears to hear, let them hear."

"This is the man we need."

"Yes, let him be the judge."

"Let him be the judge."

"So it shall be ..."

And they commanded the man to come out from behind the altar and to decide on the ownership of this dead man fairly and impartially.

The man was terrified. Now he was on the horns of a dilemma. He knew, no matter what decision he made, he'd offend one of the parties. If one didn't kill him, then the other would—or worse. His bottom lip trembled. His bowels loosened. His bones turned to water. He pissed himself.

"We haven't got all day," said the Son of God. "Decide. Make your mind up now and don't keep us waiting. I've souls to be collecting."

"We haven't got all day. Or all night either," said the Son of the Devil. "There's bodies that need collecting and night's the busiest time. Decide now, for God's sake, and we can go our separate ways. The rain has stopped."

It had stopped. And the storm had eased. The man could hear that it had gone quiet outside again. Silence. Eventually, he spoke, and he was so frightened that he could hear his voice trembling. He could hear it in every word he said.

"The truth can hurt," he said, "and I could be dead by this evening because of the truth, but from what I saw here today with my own two eyes, as given to me by the God Almighty Himself, the Son of the Devil had this corpse first."

The Son of the Devil laughed long and loud, a big belly laugh that echoed and shook the ruined walls of the church. He started picking on the Son of God and laughing at him. The Son of God was furious and he knocked the man's head off with one blow. No sooner had he done this than the Son of the Devil pulled the head off the dead man on the floor and placed it where the man's head had been.

The Son of God grabbed the man's arms then and tore them off.

What did the Son of the Devil do then—only tear the arms off the corpse and place them where the man's arms had been.

And the Son of God and the Son of the Devil carried on like this until the man had been almost completely torn apart—the Son of God tearing the man limb from limb, and the Son of the Devil replacing the man's limbs with those of the corpse.

By now the man didn't know what was going on and couldn't tell up from down. All the limbs that had grown naturally on him, as they had on his ancestors before him, were now in a bloody pile on the floor. And instead there was this second-hand man, made up of a dead man he didn't know. Who am I now? he asked himself. Where am I from? Who are my people? Am I the same me or another me, or am I two me's now? His head was spinning, he was so confused. He shook his head. Then he remembered that he had heard a story once somewhere—was it a fairy tale or something he'd heard at mass?—that two can become one when the outside is placed inside and the inside placed outside, and the top goes at the bottom ... and when you put the man and the woman together so that they become one where the man is no longer a man nor the woman a woman, when you replace an eye with another eye, and a hand with another hand, and a foot with another foot, and an image with another image ... and what else, he wondered, was in that story, whether it was a legend or a fairy tale or something he'd heard at mass when he wasn't really listening . . . Forget it, he said, in his confusion. I can only remember some of it, whether it was from a storyteller or a priest or a teacher or the creator or whoever . . .

He looked around. He decided to bring those limbs of his home with him, to see whether anything could be done with them. God help the body that depends too much on another, he said to himself. But at least if he brought the limbs home, he could explain his predicament better to his wife and also tell her why he had been delayed.

No sooner did he reach for his dismembered body than the Son of God and the Son of the Devil jumped out in front of him and grabbed everything that was on the floor. Then, quick as a flash, they both ran out the door, sniggering.

"Thieves! You're both the same," he called after them. "I shouldn't have expected anything else. Aren't you both the same lot at the end of the day; if you go back far enough, aren't you two branches of the same tree?"

He ran down the road after them, throwing stones, but to no avail. He couldn't catch up. But, in all the rush, didn't his tool fall out of the Son of the Devil's pocket. The man picked it up off the road. Well, I have this much of myself back anyway, I suppose, he said to himself, dusting it off. He put it back in its usual place on his body, but the dead man's tool was also there. So he had two now, dangling side by side. The Son of God and the Son of the Devil had disappeared from sight by now, and the man knew that he hadn't a hope in hell of catching up with them. He might as well say goodbye to his body because he wouldn't see the rest of himself ever again.

Bad cess to you, and a thousand curses upon you, and I hope you die roaring, he shouted after them, knowing full well they couldn't hear him and that his curses would never reach them, but it did him good to get them off his chest. By the time you've seen this world, you're practically a corpse anyway, he thought, and once you're a corpse what sweetness is left in life . . . ?

Exhausted, he walked home, the two tools between his legs rubbing against each other with every step he took. This led him to reflect more deeply on his situation, to examine it from a more philosophical angle. Did the fact that he had two tools now mean that he'd have twice as much fun and games as before? Would one of them want to keep going when the other was spent? And, accordingly, wouldn't he be able to keep at it morning, noon and night? Would they take turns? Pity it hadn't happened when he was young and full of jizz. But would one be preferred? Favored? Favored, as in heaven and on earth. Would they help one another out? Would they work together and cooperate, like two fingers on the one hand? Or would they be all thumbs? Would they give each other grief or be jealous of one another? Watching each other and fighting and always competing. Would the right know what the left was doing? Or should it know ... or was it any of its business anyway? Or would it be all-out war between them, like the Son of God and the Son of the Devil?

He quickened his step so that he could be home earlier. His blood was up. He might have the chance of a whole new life now. Try out new things. Things he'd never done before ... He was passing a big puddle in the road when he stopped to look at his reflection. He didn't know that man. He didn't recognize the big baldy head looking back at him — did it look like a third cousin or a distant relative? ... Oh, God bless us and save us, how will my wife and my one true love know me now, he asked himself. Bad enough I stayed out all night, without telling anyone when I'd be back. But then to come home like this. Didn't they used to say that a woman is worse than a pig and a pig is worse than the devil, and bolder too?

He was about a mile from home when he spotted his wife standing stiffly in the doorway. Her arms were folded across her chest and she was looking out, and over and back, in every direction. She didn't look one bit happy. In fact, she looked really angry. She looked like she was raging. She looked like thunder. Her features relaxed the minute she spotted him in the distance. She put her hands on her hips and stood there, filling up the doorway. He knew he'd have a hard time getting past her. When he got closer she pulled a sheaf of papers from her back pocket. The topmost document came into focus as he drew nearer. Divorce papers, filled in, in black and white, and needing nothing but a signature.

She made a face as he approached. It seemed as if she were looking at him out of the corner of her eye. Maybe she recognized him ... or maybe she didn't ... Or then again ... She screamed.

"Who are you or where are you from or who are your people, or what hole did you crawl out of this early in the morning?" she demanded abruptly as he came up to the door.

"Your faithful husband of more than twenty years," he replied in a hurt tone, his voice trembling.

"Why don't I recognize you then?"

"Because my body left me last night."

"Well, maybe there's not much wrong with your body, but to me you're a complete stranger."

"You're calling your bed-mate a stranger, is it?"

"Prove to me so who you are, my good man. Prove to me that you are who you say you are."

She reached out behind her and took hold of the door bar and a kettle of boiling water, both of which were conveniently at hand, just inside the door.

"Pr ... ove ... to me ... so ..." he stammered. "Outside my front door ... right here in front of the whole village?"

"Right here now ... right here in front of the dogs in the street!"

He thought for a second.

Then, all of a sudden, he undid his fly and pulled himself out with his right hand, with his left hiding, as best he could, the spare that he'd got from the dead man.

"Look at that there now," he said. "Have a good look there now and you'll see the birthmark that's down underneath there, the same one you've seen often enough before," he said, lifting it up. "And there, see, the mark of your false teeth, from the other night."

She crouched down for a moment to look more closely. Looking. Examining. Scrutinizing.

Then she burst into tears, great fat drops rolling down her cheeks. Devastated, she fell to her knees, and she washed and cleaned both tools with her salty tears.

Then she dried them with her long gray hair.

TRANSLATED FROM IRISH
BY LOCHLAINN Ó TUAIRISG

BALŠA BRKOVIĆ

The Eyes of Entropija Plamenac[*]

A FRIEND OF MINE, WERTHER SULTANOVIĆ, went in for a career in one of the so-called new professions: he's a "Creature Creator."

That sounds so pretentious, we agreed as much many times, and it's definitely best to look on the humorous side of things—despite the compelling pathos of Genesis.

Werther's job is to make *simbies*: disposable, simulated beings used mainly in commercials, child care, pageants, and a wide variety of celebrations and events, from middle-school balls to the bizarre, orgiastic feasts of transvestites and cutting-edge bohemians.

These globular beings are the size of a strong man's fist and have a life span of up to twelve hours—the maximum every skilled and self-respecting Creator allows; for this is how they avoid getting emotionally attached to their products (and also how they increase sales, of course).

A *simbie* is programmed to constantly repeat a recorded message, no longer than about fifty words, and in a rhythm of the owner's choice. These can range from a mother's instructions to her child alone at home in the apartment to the feel-good jingles a party host uses to make it a special night for their guests. The recorded messages are mostly quotes—our world is an ecstasy of quotes, is it not?—all the way from the pre-Socratics to the current prophets of the energy of the End and the post-technobaroque illusionists.

While speaking their message, the *simbies* can hop, dart about, and make an intimidating, cheerful, or melancholy impression; the

---

[*] This surname, pronounced [plaʾme:nats], is based on the noun *plamen* meaning flame. A *plamenac* is also a flamingo.

options are almost unlimited and you can mix and combine them to your heart's content. They can be made to look entirely like cute, furry animals, beloved pets that have passed away, but with a trait that some would find bizarre—they just love to quote Philip K. Dick or Heidegger, for example, in the crisply articulated voice of a newscaster.

Their appearance is left to the imagination of the creator, albeit more or less in line with the standard expectations of the market.

Simbies are simply an undeniable part of today's event culture.

I remember a debate, perhaps fifteen years ago, as to whether this toy would dehumanize our world, and so on. Sociologists, urbanologists, philosophers, and imageologists all had their say on the issue.

Sometimes I felt this "millennium fever" was ridiculous; along with all the stories I heard and all the texts I read on the topic, it was one big, naive hullabaloo. But today, just thirty years on, it seems to me as if a whole millennium more has passed.

My friend Werther is well known in the profession as an aficionado of mucousy, organically visualized, but simple forms. He has always been successful at it. Above all, I believe, because Creature Creator Werther Sultanović is a rather atypical creation himself . . .

As usual at that time of day, I found him in the Double Moon bar in Podgorica, his favorite early-afternoon and late-evening hangout. The wall is painted with an old reproduction from a once-popular comic strip: a cartoon of a man looking into the sky above a picturesque neighborhood where there are two clearly visible moons. Werther's brother, Bodo, trades in memorabilia like that. He took on his mother's surname—Tatar—as a gesture of protest against their father's leading position in the conservative and arrogant GEA, the Global Ecological Association.

Oh, it's a long story . . . Today's world is ruled by ecological inspectors. And ecology has become a dangerously broad concept—it's the ideology of our age. They say that everything, absolutely everything, can be "polluted"—not only the soil, the rivers, and the air, but also language, art, and science. If they label you a "polluter" today, you're as good as snuffed out: no one will talk with you, no one can give you a job, and you even lose all welfare entitlements and civil rights. But that's common knowledge. Bodo is one of the few, ever rarer people who believe it's possible to lead a different life; they live in communes out in the wilds and do their own thing ... But the masses are convinced they're effectively avoiding history. Decades of turmoil have convinced people that total control is justified, as I'm sure you know.

Werther was not alone that day: sitting with him was the enchanting Entropija Plamenac. My friend makes *simbies* for this captivating lady, and she pays him well. The *motherly-message simbies* are for her five-year-old son, who seems to spend part of each day at home alone.

Put very briefly, she is an affluent and "well-married" woman. Her husband is one of those ecological inspectors with unlimited powers — the KGB generals of the new world — and as a result she is divinely bored. She enjoys her own laziness and the contemplative environment of the ultimate refuge. From time to time she does performances, some of which have caught on.

"Oh, Werther, I fear things aren't half that simple ... We're so insignificant, you know, like a fungal growth on this blue planet. Something like that. So at times I feel that concern is like arrogance ..."

I said hello, and my friend Werther immediately started explaining to me why their conversation was so lively. It must really be a gripping topic after all, I thought, because it hadn't struck me as I was walking up to them that they were having a particularly animated exchange. But what Werther now told me certainly sounded promising.

Entropija had been telling him about her problem: she had become one of the "Extraordinary." That is a blanket term for all the inexplicable and absurd new disorders that befall people.

"My eyes produce order. Fantastic, you'll say — at least I'm free of the need to clear away after lunch. I don't have to stack the glasses and plates, and I don't even have to do anything in the garden any more ... Which I do miss a little, I must admit."

"Hang on, hang on," I immediately had to butt in, in my hot-headed way. "Do you mean to say your eyes also have an effect on nature — not just on the world of human-made objects?"

"Exactly. However many shoots and branches need pruning, however much the plants need watering and so on, it's enough for me just to turn up at the garden door, and within a few seconds it's all done, everything is in its place ... A bit perplexing, don't you think?"

"That's the understatement of the year!" Werther added, as soon as Entropija had finished.

"But, Entropija, then you are a blessing for this world!" I exclaimed, spreading my arms. If anyone had happened to be watching us just then, I certainly would have looked ludicrous.

"It only works in a space that's mine: in the house, the garden, the car, our little boat ..."

"Otherwise known as a seventy-foot yacht!" said Werther, who will never overcome his habit of speaking his mind to people's faces.

"You know I'm incorrigibly romantic," she said with a flutter of her beautiful eyes, which had suddenly become the focal point of her whole being. They took on that inimitable expression of fatal naivety, like that of a little girl. Oh, that eternal charm—one of the three most dangerous female strategies!

Entropija, Entropija, you're stupendous ... My fascination for this woman will only change form but will never fade. Does she sense that? How do women sense that?

"What particularly intrigues me is that this force, whatever it is, respects the logic of private property," she continued. "Most unusual, don't you think? I'd always thought that superlogical things like this were somehow enthralling and limitless, but in my case, at least, it seems these inexplicable forces respect laws that are quite human and earthly. Who could have imagined?"

"Yes, that really is unusual. You'd expect higher powers to have a definite degree of anarchy to them." I wanted her to know I believed every word she said so she could rely on my support ... Too long a fascination for one and the same woman makes a man an idiot, at least judging by my experience.

But everything that is happening to Entropija today is not so strange anymore. Fifty years ago they would have laughed at you; or clapped you in a military institution, claimed you had gone missing, and used you as a guinea-pig for research. Today it's so arduously different ...

In a nutshell, incredibly often, in recent years, the media have been reporting the craziest of things. All the time people are levitating. It never lasts terribly long, and they don't do it at any great height—just a few inches off the ground, ten at most. Then, what I find strangest, there's no longer any public or individual doubt about these sorts of things. Everyone believes them; it's as if they've become almost normal. One of the most widely accepted interpretations of the phenomenon is that people are becoming perfect beings and in time will be more and more godlike. *Return to paradise* is without doubt the main catchphrase of the whole world today, with the exception of small, scattered groups of unhappy Arabs in the mountains of the Democratic Muslim Union, although no one knows for certain if they still exist or are just a myth—a bogey employed to keep today's pro-American Arabs in submission and constantly kowtowing to democracy. All these things are interpreted as a sure sign that we, this fucked-up human race, are on the way back to the Garden of Eden. Today it would probably be called Eco-Eden. And since the media have been flogging this without one ounce of doubt, things have actually begun to happen increasingly often. I'll be damned if they're not putting something in the water ... Before he left for the commune, Bodo was always saying that's what it's about—that they're tampering with the water supply.

Recently, a farmer from Andrijevica, up near the Albanian border, started speaking faultless Japanese. He spoke it for seven hours to the members of his household, who understood him perfectly, as did the birds and beasts. They called the local TV studio straight away. Two hours later the Japanese ambassador arrived from Podgorica with presents (valuable fans for the women of the family) and had a good chat with the man. The media, of course, started broadcasting live just three hours into the feat. It's madness ... When the program was almost over, just ten minutes or so before the miraculous skill left this fine fellow from the beautiful, pristine slopes of Mount Ekomova, Japanese state TV took over. The honorable man from Andrijevica was invited to spend a year in Tokyo. Then his skill abruptly disappeared and everyone went away again. Take another example: about ten days ago, a man from the small town of Tuzi turned ordinary glass into a mirror with just a touch of his middle finger. That really did look good on the television news, I must say: the guy walks down a corridor in one of those chrome-and-glass commercial blocks with hundreds of windows and touches each of the panes, and everywhere endless mirrors appear—the space suddenly begins to change and be consumed, as everything is reflected in itself hundredfold, as far as the eye can see. Everyone finds out about all this straight away, and there are channels that follow such events exclusively (Wonder TV, Miracle TV, TV Revelation, T-Vision, TV AlphaOmega, and others,) but, as a rule, each individual miracle doesn't last long.

"Hang on, hang on," Werther said and returned me to the conversation. "Do you mean your eyes won't react to chaos here at this table, but if we were sitting in your garden drinking the best Norwegian ecognac, everything would be in perfect order?"

"Exactly," she said, hyper-enunciating like a talk-show host. "But that's just one of the bizarre things. Today there's more of this than ever before in human ... Existence."

Entropija avoided uttering the nonecological word "history" and decided at the last instant to say "Existence," which is the more desirable term today. The capital E is a must. Recently hospitals have stopped referring to a patient's "case history," due to the allegedly negative connotations of the word, and have introduced the expression "genesis of the case." The ecological fundamentalists resemble all other former fundamentalists, except that they're completely cynical. And, on top of that, they screw this world more radically than the zealots of the past: they've found a way of destroying language, and that's the worst. Today you can be subversive by even just pronouncing the old words. So, to take a positive view of things, which the immature, like me, always do, this is a nice opportunity for some stirring. And we should do it on a daily basis. If words survive, the hypnotic tyranny will one day fall, and there we'll have it—freedom. Without ecology this time, I hope.

Curiously enough, they haven't banned the word "freedom." They've given it a new meaning instead. Today it relates exclusively to free time, in the sense of the time you spend outside your corporation. Once a year you have to answer a questionnaire with three hundred questions about how you spend your free time. It's enough to drive you round the bend ... But hardly anyone thinks that way—I mean, fewer and fewer people are bothered by it.

Entropija and Werther ordered another mountain-spring water, and she continued: "There's something else that disturbs me greatly, and I've got to know it better than anyone else: order in itself. The absence of chaos ..."

"And?"

"It's such a strenuous world. It looks sick to me, so sick."

"Ah, you mean sanitized—that it looks sterile like in a hospital?" That's Werther's legendary trait of wanting to clarify insubstantial details in the middle of a person's exciting tale.

"No, I know perfectly damn well what I'm saying. It looks sterile, yes, but I really did want to say 'sick.' As if reality itself is sick, and I alone can see it ..."

Entropija talked to us about her "problem" for another half an hour. She said she hoped it would pass soon. None of those bolt-from-the-blue "extraordinarinesses" last for long, to be sure.

Despite my fascination for that woman, I couldn't stand it any longer. I just had to leave. Even today I still refuse to believe all that baloney about perfection and the collective return to paradise. I refuse because I know it ultimately serves to make us slaves. Someone is doing it as a parody of reality, making it look like a goofy cartoon. After this, people will probably believe anything. I'm too cynical to go off and join Bodo's commune, but I'll never, ever go along with the games that turn people into dismal slaves.

I don't know how they managed to get Entropija hooked on that craze—who knows, perhaps they poke around in people's heads. But I refuse, refuse, refuse ... I don't want to believe.

But things aren't quite so simple. Despite the "blessed extraordinariness" of their owner, the eyes of Entropija Plamenac wreak havoc inside me. Wonderful, heart-warming chaos.

To be sure, only chaos will save the world.

TRANSLATED FROM MONTENEGRIN
BY WILL FIRTH

MATJAŽ BRULC

Diary Notes*

21 April 1994

WHAT IS IT THAT WE FIND MOST REPULSIVE about being in
contact with our own feces? The odor? Its shape and appearance? Is
the relation between its odor and form merely a transition of the relation between content and form? Is the smell the one and only content of shit? If I develop the thought further, I end with the following
tautology—the content of shit is the shit itself. And I must say that
this tautology does not please me.

These questions never cease to baffle me. They have embedded
themselves into my thoughts with unparalleled force; and now they
do not want to budge. It is as if I were possessed by an evil spirit—
but I merely laugh mockingly at this thought. I have felt good for the
past few weeks.

23 April 1994

Shit links us to nature; it makes us earthly, impure. Once I was done
with my morning toilet business I flushed the water with a simple

---

* These notes were discovered on top of a pile of faded paper and newspapers in the
basement of a flat that we recently acquired. Alma has not seen the text yet, nor has
anybody else for that matter. The diary ends on 11 June 1994, was written by hand,
and the author is unknown. I think it belonged to the previous flat owner who died
unexpectedly two years ago. While I was looking at the flat, A.M.—who inherited the flat—told me in her harsh tone that unfortunately his unhappy end did not
come as a surprise to her. I will certainly have to research the story of this person in
greater detail.

When I read the diary a couple of times, "a sort of light, mercy, some sort of
new strength that I had not known until then, entered me." I am secretly planning a
new "liberation" plan, but with other means. The possibilities are still open.

move of the hand. My feces, caught in a water whirl, disappeared into the unknown. I realized that, whatever the norms of civilization might dictate, once we lost contact with our own crap we lost contact with earth, nature. Not only was I shocked to discover this link, I was also startled by its simplicity.

24 April 1994
Everything that we were taught about shit is a lie.

27 April 1994
Resistance Day. Uttering this word gives me a pleasant feeling. Resistance. This is the only holiday that celebrates disagreement, the termination of order, upright posture, and also, implicitly, operation, action, even violence. Of course, the question arises as to the possibilities of resistance that are available to us in a contemporary world in which we are caught in a tight cocoon of futility. I am afraid that these possibilities are close to nought; however, this does not mean that they are non-existent. In an uncertain way I feel that the harder and more monolithic the outer form, the more megalomaniac and rapturous are the forms adopted by the individual who wants to resist it. I will have to think about this a tad more.

2 May 1994
Yesterday was another holiday: Labor Day. A large celebration, with singers and speakers, took place in the main town square. As I stood outside I imagined all of these people taking a dump together: it would be a truly festive occasion, dedicated to an essential biological chore performed by our bodies. Why do we have to be ashamed of our own feces? Why do we deny ourselves and, at the same time, pompously glorify the work that holds us in its grip, turns us into slaves and thus destroys the best in us?

I have started to notice that I love the odor of my shit. In the morning, as I was leaning over the toilet, taking pleasure in the invigorating odor, a sort of light, mercy, some sort of new strength that I had not known until then, entered me. I was bathed in elation similar to that experienced by early Christian hermits. I can safely state that I like everybody's shit and that I would wish for them to like my shit.

6 May 1994

I have been reading newspapers for the last few days. It is obvious that the world is heading into an abyss. Wars are devastating the south. The conditions in our country are disastrous. Shit is everywhere. The stench is spreading, but everybody is pretending that nothing is wrong. I have noticed a number of adverts for cleaning products in the newspapers. It is obvious that people want cleanliness, hygiene and order; however, their methods for achieving this are all wrong. I have a hunch that purification can be achieved only by plummeting into the biggest shit, but so far I have not managed to develop the logic that would provide a firm base for this idea. On an intuitive level I am strongly convinced of this; the light that I wrote about days ago has not weakened yet.

I have been told that I'm to be promoted at work. I was in the department chief's office today; of course my salary will also be slightly higher from now on.

7 May 1994

In the afternoon I was leaning against the window and watching a woman who lives in our building. She was walking her dog. When the animal shat on the green, the woman took a plastic bag from her pocket and cleared up its feces. There was something extremely sensual in this scene; I was touched deeply by her soft and motherly care. The pattern always remains the same: the dirt has to be carefully removed. The ideology of purity hovers above us, and yet we are in a world that has never been so dirty and ugly. In this I recognize a certain paradox of our times.

Of course, I am aware that truth can always be found stretched out on the surface, right in front of our eyes. Or even better, right in front of our noses.

10 May 1994

Dirt is dangerous. Shit is subversive. This is the origin of the immense strength it has over people. Maybe it would be possible to shake the world with decisive resistance against one of civilisation's key purposes: cleanliness. Suddenly it dawned on me: shit is rebellion. This is why it is wrong for us to hide when we are relieving ourselves—it is wrong to take a dump all alone between the four walls of our bathrooms.

The time has come for me to end these ridiculous illusions. At the beginning I am certain that I will encounter rejection, I have no doubt about that; all prophets and clairvoyants experience hostility from those around them. I still dare to state that I am well acquainted with history and human nature.

11 May 1994

A world in which shit would not need to be hidden would become more natural: I am certain that this is the only way for society to regain a feeling for reality and thus recognize the evil of true dirt, which is not personified by shit, but by mankind with its greed, selfishness, and stupidity. I believe with all my soul in the great emancipating potential of this great idea.

I am bathing in zeal; I am obviously taking the path of a revolutionary. My thoughts are as clear and penetrating as the sparkle of a diamond.

15 May 1994

The joy, the bliss! I came up with a plan and I carried it out tonight. My heart beats with the rhythm of untamed pride. I feel as if my body were pierced by thousands of spears. I am finding it extremely hard to write these lines; my hands are still trembling, and I can still feel the joy that I experienced when I held my feces in them.

I was outdoors. I sneaked in front of the building and defecated on the path that leads to the entrance. I felt a thrill, an embrace of pleasure covered me as I felt the thick, black mass, flexible as dough, warm as the safety of the bed in which I am currently lying, erupt from my taut body.

And how I trembled at the thought that I could be caught while crouching! I am aware that fear is a remnant of the old thought process with which I will have to deal as soon as possible. This will not be an easy task. Every revolutionary action demands a sacrifice, the old needs to die in order for the new to be born.

*

It is dawning outside and I still cannot sleep. I am over-excited; too many thoughts are rushing through my head. I have to show my shit—its smell, form and structure—to the people. In the traditional meaning of the word, purity is a dead notion; my task is to open people's eyes. Make them dirty with their own feces. Only if we return to the earthly elements and the natural will we re-establish the prime order and the elementary natural ethics as they were known to our distant ancestors. The world needs our shit, we all need our shit, I am sure of this.

16 May 1994

When I returned from work, my feces in front of the entrance were gone. Somebody had cleared them meticulously. Only a dark narrow mark remained in their place; at that moment I understood that this was the only proof of my existence and activity. I felt pride and unimaginable satisfaction. I finally had a goal in my life, my life had a meaning. I will tackle more ambitious plans; at some stage people are bound to notice how true and redemptive my path is!

20 May 1994

Last night I crapped in front of the entrance to the bank in our street.

"Shit is the only currency of our future."

This thought occurred to me today as I was visiting the department chief again. He took me to an expensive restaurant for lunch. After a hearty meal my intestines started to rumble; I stood up and proudly went to relieve myself on the toilet seat.

I was told by the chief that I should join the party. The time is now. The party needs people like me. I agreed after a short, feigned hesitation. One has to operate within the system and not outside of it; my shit needs to be institutionalized, it has to function from top to bottom.

24 May 1994

I eat strong, heavy food, full of proteins and carbohydrates. I shit every other day—outdoors of course. The fat, chestnut-brown sausages that come from my body are firm and nicely formed. I had an excellent idea: I cut out a narrow strip of fabric from the back of my trousers, so I would not lose any time undressing and dressing on my hikes. I use a kitchen cloth to make a special nappy that I place in my crotch after the task is completed. I would not want for the blessed scent of my interior to betray me. Then I tie a pullover around my waist. This makes my outfit perfect and my mission noble.

I live in ecstasy, the heart of which is represented by my shit, with which I will soil the world. My dreams are fulfilled every second day: due to my filth the world is becoming more compact, the consciousness clearer. I wonder whether people are aware of this. I am in humble anticipation of the ceremonious moment when I will notice the first changes amongst my fellow men.

26 May 1994

While I was at work, heavy, pressing doubts crossed my mind. A shadow of defeatism trailed behind me, and at home it only turned darker. Do my actions have any meaning whatsoever? Have I jumped the gun? Am I sane? Does shit represent the right way of saving a world full of shit? Is there anything worse than a disappointed revolutionary, a bitter idealist? Am I merely a new Martin Kačur, full of healthy and hard shit?

I purchased a bottle of spirits and started drinking from it a few minutes ago. I will get drunk like a large, dark animal, destined to fail miserably.

27 May 1994

While I was drunk yesterday night I shat in a bag. I went out carrying the shit in my hands. I was full of desperation. I scooped up my runny shit, which smelt of saffron, with my fingers, and used it to write on the dark buildings in the center of our small town. My defeatism was beaten; I felt like a flower enjoying the sunrays after a long black night.

This turned out to be a topic of discussion at work today. Our courier knew quite a bit about these writings. As he explained to my co-workers—the numb, self-centered ignoramuses—what he had seen, they giggled, and this really hurt me.

28 May 1994

I have heard that the matter is being investigated by the police. I decided to lie low for a few days.

2 June 1994

The matter has still not settled. Last night I struck again, this time in front of a shop on Stari Trg. I managed to create a large pile that glistened under the streetlights; it was a pile worth admiring.

8 June 1994

I am expecting results, a change, I am as restless as a child. However, I should not be sucked in by my naivety, beginner's zeal, impatience. The path ahead of me is long and hard, but this should by no means lessen my firm belief in feces. I have to sharpen my thoughts, form a firm, anthropologic and philosophic frame for my actions. There is plenty of work ahead of me, but I believe in myself; I will persist with my optimism, I will persist with my shit.

11 June 1994

The time for people like me will undoubtedly arrive. I am convinced that our shit will free ourselves, transform us, return us to the arms of the mother, who is always carefully looking over us but to whom we have turned our backs.

Disrespecting filth implies liberating, almost purifying oneself: I firmly believe that this brings opportunities for the appearance of new ideological and behavioral schemes in political, cultural, social, and private life.

There is still hope; the world stretches in front of my anal hole, in front of this hidden flower of endless pleasure.

One day I will live to see everything change. Just like my shit, hope can never disappoint me.

TRANSLATED FROM SLOVENIAN
BY SUNČAN PATRICK STONE

TUOMAS KYRÖ

Griped

MINUTES ON THE MEASURING STICK

IT SURELY DID GRIPE ME when I fell on the sauna steps. I spent three days lying on my side, waiting for someone to come out to the place and find me. I started getting hungry and wondering whether I should call out or something. Fortunately it rained, so I was able to get some water inside me, but the bad thing was this pneumonia and the hip replacement. The chimney sweep found me.

On the bed ward down at the health clinic I had a bag of salt to sprinkle on the food they gave me and a Phillips screwdriver for other emergencies. You can do just about anything with a Phillips screwdriver. But not go to the toilet. Grown man doing his business in the cold neck of a bed pan, not my favorite thing, but I tried not to think about it.

We had a TV, too, Koskinen wanted to watch the ice hockey and wouldn't change the channel, though I made it pretty clear that I don't like team sports. I wanted to watch skiing, and if they didn't have it live, why not watch it on video? They had the box there. We coulda ordered cassettes from the Ski Federation—don't the health clinic lab and the Ski Federation have some kinda mutual assistance pact or whatnot? Watching Marja-Liisa Kirvesniemi or Kari Härkönen win a race woulda cheered me right up.

The boy brought one of his daughters to visit me. The girl who's not in school yet. First she was a little shy, the place didn't smell like no roses, I guess, and then Koskinen got one of his bloody coughing fits. I let the girl play with the bed hydraulics and the radio buttons and had her go ask the nice ladies for a pitcher of juice. Kids ain't pissing and moaning if you let them do stuff on their own.

One thing felt good, namely the bags under the boy's eyes. He finally had to get off his butt and do something other than sit around in the library reading all those papers that he never graduates from. He said he's home with the kids—they decided, him and his wife—and that's cut into his sleep time.

I asked how a fella could be home with the kids, when it's hard enough being there just with yourself. What do they do, start some project, like papering the walls or building a playhouse? But he said no, they mostly just lie around drawing and watching kids' shows on TV.

Why everybody makes such a big fuss over who's with the kids and where, I don't know. First the women had something to say about that, then it was the men, as if they was the first generation had to raise kids. Everybody's counting minutes on a measuring stick, who did this and who did that: namely, filled some machine that washes, dries, or warms things, and generally does the work for people.

And all that means is, folks got too much time on their hands—if they got time to count how much time they got on their hands. If me and the wife had time to count, it was to make sure we had six kids in their beds, evenings. The boy asked what I was getting worked up about, nothing to get worked up about, says he. Every generation does things different.

Yeah, but some generations does it wrong.

The nurse came in to tell us visiting hours was over in fifteen minutes. The girl brought the juice and poured some for Koskinen too. They were going to my place for the night and promised to come see me again in the morning. The boy asked whether I needed anything from home. Don't need nothing but the home itself. I plan to skedaddle outta here just as soon as my legs'll carry me.

PS. At night they had sumo wrestling on the TV. I surely don't like to see folks let themselves get that fat.

POTATOES IN THE GARAGE

It surely did gripe me when they gave me rice and gravy for dinner. I got enough potatoes stored up my own self, I could feed this whole health clinic for a year, I betcha. Not to mention the carrots, rutabagas, and turnips, and a few boxes of red and black currants for the freezer, so's we could have a pie for Independence Day or a fruit soup for Sunday.

But now they're shipping rice from places where folks is starving up here to Finland and putting it on a plate in front of me—me, who's got potatoes at home in the cellar. Rice tastes like cardboard, if you ask me, though I never ate no cardboard. You can bet I demanded that the head doctor come have a little chat, so's we could get this food business straightened right out. He didn't come. So I've been writing this up for myself.

Your basic staples is spuds and brown gravy, with whatever's to hand added to it, depending on the season. Eggs is available locally and they're cheap. You buy rye crisp in bulk, it's filling and it never spoils. Fill up them little holes with butter and mm-mm. Delicious. Sundays and for special celebrations, like a Finnish win in the skiing, a slice of rye bread with a slice of cheese on top. Edam, Eurohopper brand, big chunk at the S Market, four ninety a kilo.

Ground meat, the neck and rib cuts, browned properly, preferably in the oven in a cast iron pot. Fish from the lake, or maybe from Päijänne at a pinch. It's close by, and a big clean lake. A big NO to trout and frozen tilapia. Let them sell that stuff to our neighbors, like the Norwegians.

Yesterday they put pineapple in the chicken gravy. What a abomination that is. Dessert is one thing, main courses another. You make them separate and you eat them separate. Maybe some macaroni on the side, and if you got sick kids in the ward you can squirt some ketchup on it, that much I can bend to.

Thing you gotta understand is where we come from. Spuds, that's where. I done studied my genealogy back to the eighteenth century, and ever since a tanner named Kaapo Sottinginpoika our family done growed the same variety of potato in the same ground. Blight won't touch it, and it can take the cold. Just the right amount of starch. When we finally come to our senses and stop shipping food halfway around the world, that's gonna be our salvation. Or, you know, if you got to ship food, why not ship my potatoes to India and China and make patients in their health clinics eat them.

The problem here is storage and logistics. But that ain't no problem, not really. Hospitals got underground garages. Get the cars out of there, they're ancient history anyway, or will be soon. Fill them garages up with potatoes and other tubers. Raise pigs and cows on the health clinic grounds, and poof, you're self-subsistent. No need to scrimp and save and buy cheap food from other countries, if you got everything free right here. You could rotate the farmhand chores among the doctor and nurse residents. Young folks would learn about the food they're putting in their mouths. The better you care for the animals, the better the meat tastes, and the richer the soil the tastier the spuds. I bet any hospital would have the instruments and the knowhow for slaughtering animals — folks would see how you stick a pig, 'stead of just poking four holes in the foil on a microwave dinner with a fork.

PS. I read my draft to Koskinen. He claimed rice is better than spuds. It don't fill you up as much, so you feel lighter after. He's been here longer than me. Probably you gradually get brainwashed, staying in here.

WHAT DAY, WHAT YEAR

It surely did gripe me when the boy told me he threw out all the spoiled food in his fridge. He figures out what's spoiled by reading the dates on the package; me, I smell and taste. Mold I scoop off the top of juice and jam with a spoon. Folks these days are a bunch of nervous Nellies. They have to wear a helmet to ride a bike and have to buy private health insurance even though they already pay for health insurance in their taxes. There's a epidemic of stupid in the land. I think it has something to do with heated floors.

I asked the boy to call around and make arrangements for those skiing videos, with the head doctor if that's what it takes. Otherwise I stop paying my taxes. I reminded him of what I read in the *Reader's Digest* they got here in the health clinic, that in America some man had died of discontent, or was it a woman? He suggested that Koskinen and I take turns watching whatever we want. Koskinen said he'd come to the hospital to be sick, not to negotiate. I asked him whether he was looking for a fat lip. The boy broke it up before it turned into a real scuffle. Folks are so afraid of a little fisticuffs nowadays. You can get sued for going upside a fella's head.

The boy wanted to push me down to the downstairs café in a wheelchair. I don't remember when I was so mortified. I grabbed my granddaughter and pulled her into my lap as cover. I've been walking on my own two feet and pulling my own pants on and choosing which direction to go since I was one year old. Now I'm being pushed around in hospital pajamas wherever other folks want me to go.

The boy brought us two cups of coffee. He doesn't use sugar so he didn't bring me none either. The girl went for it, wanted to rip open the paper, drop the cube in the coffee, and stir it with a spoon about a hundred times.

I asked the boy whether he was going to take me home today, or tomorrow at the latest. He said that he wanted to talk to me about that. He said that he was afraid to let me live alone any more, that we should be looking for an apartment in town or maybe a old folks' home. Nobody talks to me that way. I'm gonna live in my own house and nowhere else. I'm gonna get carried out of my yard with my boots on and a axe in my hand, or, if someday I don't wake up from my nap, with a *Reader's Digest* on my chest. Instead of the inscriptions on the funeral wreaths, they can read "Laughter Is the Best Medicine" at the memorial service.

The boy said he talked to the doc. He claimed he had all kindsa insider info about my health that I didn't have. My leg won't hold up, he said, and my blood pressure, and the plastic joints, and my memory, and my eyesight, and blah blah blobbety blah. The boy said I had to accept reality. My age and the challenges of living in a detached house. I asked him what TV show he got that phrase off of. He said I'm a danger to myself.

Let's think about that for a moment. Let's think about it with my brain, my eyesight, and my memory.

Who does it hurt, if I'm a danger to myself? Me. Right? If they take me to a old folks' home, it hurts the staff—who'll take bets on whether I'm gonna be snapping at the cleaning ladies, the lady who measures out the pills, the shower lady, the walker lady. I ain't no child, or a dog, or a idiot neither. I'm a man. Leave it alone.

I stood up from my wheelchair and walked on my own two legs into the yard. Grabbed a taxi and told the driver to take me home.

PS. The boy drove the girl home, but then came back hisself. He's sleeping in the hall and in the morning he'll be watching to see whether I can remember what year it is and what day it is. For Christ's sake I even remember whose name day it is. Caleb's.

UGLY PEOPLE

It surely did gripe the boy when I wouldn't leave my home but sent him back to his. But the little prig wouldn't go quietly. We had to make a deal first. Every Wednesday I have to let a person come measure out my pills, check the fridge, make sure I know how to use the toilet and know what it means when the big hand is on the whatever and the little hand is on the whatever, and don't kill myself by forgetting to open the flue on the stove. What am I, a science experiment?

But she's a good woman. I don't bitch about it, I let her do the work, the county pays, and at least I got somebody to gripe to. She's got the air about her of a old-time work horse, just gets the work done and don't ask, lifts the heavy things as if they was light. Besides, she understands me better than my own boy does. She got it right away when I explained the different kinds of safety.

For instance, what would happen if I moved to the city to some house where I didn't know what edge and what door comes after what corner? Here in my own home I can walk from attic to cellar with my eyes closed. The distances ain't in my eyes, they're in my senses and memory. And why even turn the lights on? That just runs up the electricity bill, and you're always having to change the bulbs.

Besides, out here in the country we ain't got no criminals burglarizing whole neighborhoods, and a fella ain't getting sucked into all-night poker games and drinking. Once you start getting helped, the danger is that you let them keep on helping you after you don't need it no more. There's no telling how I might get used to easy street, elevators, streets getting swept by somebody else. Before you know it I might be eating out every day, going around with women born in the forties, selling the inheritance that's meant for my kids and grandkids, using the forest as collateral.

This person who comes to see me every week is a spinster but she's ugly. I been watching how she works. Better than anybody. She even chops firewood, which ain't in the contract. Ugly's a good thing. I ain't no Leif Water myself.

And another thing. There's less chance I'll start lusting after a ugly girl than a pretty one. You can read in the papers how that happens all the time.

A ugly woman's life is more like a man's life. She has to suffer and work hard to make a living. She can't just go out dancing and pick the most suitable husband to support her. Ugly folks don't never get nothing for free, or ready made. They got to earn it themselves. Ugly folks get laughed at, get ugly things said to them, get things demanded of them. Ugly folks only get jobs if they're qualified for them, and they have to learn to be mean enough to them as are mean to them. And, above all, ugly folks learn how to boil potatoes just right and don't go enthusing over rice or olive oil. And that's 'cause it's no good to a ugly person if she's skinny. She's still ugly.

Yesterday that ugly person washed me in the sauna. And since I won't use them crutches the health clinic sent home with me, I couldn't get up the steps. Only solution was for her to carry me. I was ashamed, but also felt safe. Last person who carried me was my mama. Or maybe my papa, eighty years ago.

PS. The ugly person's name is Raisa. The more times she comes here, the less I think of her as ugly. Actually she ain't ugly Raisa, she's pretty

Raisa. I never dream, but one night I dreamed three times about Raisa. I don't understand what I'm feeling here.

BERRY PICKERS

It surely did gripe me when Kolehmainen got his nose out of joint. We been neighbors going on fifty years and I never yet learned to like Kolehmainen.

Now he's got this idea that there's this yellow peril in the woods between us, namely Thai berry pickers. You can bet Kolehmainen never picked a single berry out of those woods. He never does one blame thing to those woods 'cept sell a piece of it every ten years and buy a bigger car.

Kolehmainen don't even consider lingonberries berries. Only mushrooms he knows are the death cap and the package of champignons at the grocery store. Man like that, you gotta tell him what a berry is and what picking it is like.

Picking berries is the devil's own work. Me and the wife musta went berry picking hundreds of times, didn't matter if it was raining or we was at war. We had a clear destination, rubber boots, and color-coded buckets. And no berry picking machines, neither. A honest man makes do with his own fingers.

The rule is, the woods has to be so full of mosquitoes that you feel like running away, cursing. The sun has to heat up your windbreaker, and your water bottle has to get left in the trunk of the car. A successful berry picking trip has to fray your nerves to the point where the next step is divorce.

But, oh my goodness, how wonderful it is to see the red and blue buckets on the table loaded to the brim with nature's free sweeteners. We didn't have no sugar when I was a boy. Forest berries was our marmalade.

And if you find a raspberry bush or a cloudberry bog, you don't tell nobody, not even Cousin Veijo, no matter how tempted you are to brag. You go there in the dead of night and pick them berries with a miner's light on your head, and then you make jam out of those berries in secret, and eat it once a year, on top of Lappish cheese.

You have to pick at least dozens of liters of berries, preferably hundreds. Grownups get to eat six berries out of what they pick, children eight. When you get home you clean and freeze the berries. Then later you make jam, fruit soup, juice, and pie filling. Especially tasty are frozen lingonberries on top of a liver steak.

It ain't the Thais' fault is they're the only ones who understand all this these days, I mean besides me. I have the firm belief that the Thais know how to stir berries into porridge, and don't have sugar pops cereal for breakfast and eat cocoa with a spoon straight out of the bag like Finns these days.

According to Kolehmainen, every man's rights should only apply to Finns. Where I agree with him is that we should get rid of this idea of every man's rights. But in place of them rights we should have every man's responsibilities. Whoever has land where berries or mushrooms grow, let him pick them, store them, eat them, or sell them locally. If he don't want the money for hisself, let him give it to charity, for instance in Thailand, where I bet you could find somebody that's lacking something.

PS. I put up a notice at the Community Hall. I said I'd let ten Thais sleep at my place and buy anything they picked on Kolehmainen's land. I'll make those berries into jam and sell it to him as fancy-shmancy Swedish plum marmalade. The old man will never know he's buying his own berries back. Only one person will know that, and he'll be laughing on the inside.

DEPRESSING SCENERY

It surely did gripe me to see the sun shining through my windows today. Problem was, the rays could hardly get through. Downstairs, anyway, the windows ain't been washed since the wife stopped being able to do it. I haven't washed a window since I was a boy. Me and the wife had this division of labor: I wash the car and myself, she washes all the inside surfaces. The only exception was the freezer chest. We defrosted it once every ten years and the wife couldn't reach down to the bottom with a rag.

When you're young you don't realize that a time will come when all the jobs you once divvied up will fall to one person or the other. You especially don't realize that that person will be you. All of a sudden you have to learn how to do twice as much stuff, when you're twice as old as when you coulda learned it. Now it feels like it would be easier to learn French than to learn to make a brown gravy without lumps.

I found a bucket, a bottle of dishwashing soap, a squeegee, and a rag, and set to work. I scrubbed hard at the spots and the splashes, picked at the toughest spots with a fingernail, and then did the whole window with a clean rag before running the squeegee over it. But it surely is hard to avoid leaving lines with that squeegee.

Right away I was steamed. I took a break, then checked to see whether I was still steamed.

I was. Plenty steamed.

It must be the world's most pointless labor, washing windows. I just can't figure why they need to be washed any more often than a house's drain plumbing needs to be replaced, say every sixty years.

Sure, in the summer it's nice to be able to look out through a window. But when it's sunny out it's even nicer to be outdoors. And when a body can't see through a window, that's the time to go outside and see what things look like out there. Is it raining? Is it sunny? And in the fall and the springtime the weather outside is depressing anyway, why make it easier to look out at it. Don't be greedy.

A few days later my home helper came, this ugly and pretty woman who I've told if I was fifty years younger and not already married I'd make her happy. Seemed to me she felt the same way, though truth be told, what have I ever learned about women? She cleans, folds my sheets, loads the food packages into the cupboard. And does it all well, too, though a little differently than the wife did it, maybe a tad sloppier. I'm not criticizing; I'm just saying.

Her and me got into a little tiff when I said she couldn't wash the windows. I've explained my reasons here, no need to go into it with her, so I just said it's easier for both of us to forget about the windows and concentrate on the build-up on the kitchen counters.

She said I'd run out of light in the house if I didn't wash the windows. I told her I could carry light into the house in a sack, but this ugly pretty woman didn't get it. I guess they don't tell moron jokes in Lietua where she's from.

PS. Up in the attic, in the far back corner of the storeroom, I found a window that the wife herself never noticed. It had our middle boy's handprint on it. I know, 'cause it was missing his ring finger.

A HUNDRED AND THIRTY ON A MOPED

It surely did gripe me when the doc had to make a hard decision today. I could see on Kivinkinen's face that he didn't like to do what he had to do. It wasn't 'cause of my vision, which I woulda understood and accepted. It was my reflexes. Kivinkinen whacked me on the knee with his hammer: nothing. I thought, excellent, that means I can take the pain. But Kivinkinen said it meant data ain't moving fast enough inside of me.

He said my driver's license wouldn't be renewed, and my current one was no longer valid. Put me on permanent driving ban, like I was some kinda old drunk. He said I could no longer handle cars coming the other way, and traffic signs and stuff.

What I want to know is, how have I managed so far? On my drive to the store there's just the one traffic sign: STOP. I know its location so well that I could stop at it without looking or even moving. I can close my eyes right now and know that it's at the Kirstula intersection. Back in the eighties we had a long string of fights with the road co-op and the authorities over whether a plain old yield triangle would have been enough. I know perfectly well who's gonna be coming the other way and at what time, the school taxi at four and Kolehmainen coming from work around six.

Kivinkinen nodded. Meaning my explanations didn't help one iota.

Can't I just drive to the library bus? Kivinkinen said that even if he wanted to give me some kind of special conditions, they weren't allowed by law. I asked how I'd get back to the home I'd never again be able to leave. How would I get to my next check-up with him? Kivinkinen promised to handle the paperwork so I'd be able to ride the school taxi starting tomorrow. And today he'd drive me home hisself.

Kivinkinen put on his coat and helped me get mine on, then we walked out through the downstairs lobby to the parking lot, and there I left it, the Ford Escort I bought with cash and have taken such good care of, the nineteen seventy-two model.

I was so steamed I said I'd ski home. I'd buy a pair of Peltonen skis at Komulainen's Sport and Engine and head out through the woods and over the lake. We didn't have no car when I was a kid and got by just fine, which is to say, badly, but we got by. Only folks rode in taxis back in the day was top government officials and that one pop singer.

My car never left me anywhere and now I had to leave it. Had it serviced religiously at Nuronen's garage and you can do plenty yourself with wire and cable ties.

Kivinkinen's always been a good doctor, ever since the 1980s Olympics when he arrived in town with his soft face and exaggerated smile. Now I didn't feel like saying anything at all to him. I was thinking that just as soon as I got somebody to bring my car home, nobody's gonna stop me driving. I'll hire one of the boys on a moped over by the S Market to bring it on out. I ain't riding no school taxi, that's for sure. I ain't no schoolboy.

I'll buy a moped. I'll soup it up and drive my souped-up moped a hundred and thirty downhill. That what you want? I guess I musta said it out loud, cause Kivinkinen said no. A moped has lots more moving parts than a car, he said, and I'd never learn to use a helmet. Who cares, I'll ride it with a ski cap and swim goggles on.

PS. I'm so griped I ain't gonna write no PS.

TRANSLATED FROM FINNISH
BY DOUGLAS ROBINSON

IBAN ZALDUA

Three Stories

FUTURE

"MOM, WHERE DO THEY TAKE DEAD PEOPLE?"

The mother pretends she hasn't heard, hoping that her daughter won't ask again.

"Mom! I asked you a question!"

"What question, honey? Sorry, I didn't hear you. Anyway, aren't you eating your snack awfully slowly? Come on, eat up! If you finish your sandwich, I'll make you an orange juice."

"I asked you where they take dead people, Mom."

"Dead people? Well, some are buried. That's what cemeteries are for. You know, that garden on the way to the North Park ... We go past it often."

"They're buried?"

"Yes, buried, put underground."

"Underground? Naked?"

"No, no. With clothes on. First they put them in a wooden box, which is what they put in the hole in the ground. That's what they call a grave. Then they cover it with earth and leave it there."

"You said some are buried. What about the others?"

"Others are cremated."

"Cremated?"

"Yes, burned, turned to ashes. In special ovens."

"And what do they do with the ashes?"

"Well ... sometimes they scatter them in the wind, in a place the dead person would have liked. Otherwise, though, they keep them in a special urn."

"Oh ..."

"But tell me, Ixiar, who's been telling you about dead people?"

"Iñaki."

"Iñaki?"

"Yes, Iñaki in my class at school."

"But why was he talking about dead people?"

"Because his father told him he'll die some day."

"He'll die? But ... how ..."

"Yes, he'll die. And his father too."

"And he was telling you about what happens to dead people, after they die?"

"Iñaki's dad told him they go up into the sky and turn into stars. That's why there are so many. Is that true?"

"Well, that's what some people think."

"So, the ones that are buried, they leave their graves and fly up to the sky?"

"Well ... I don't know."

"But what about the ones that are cremated, Mom? How do they get up into the sky and turn into stars?"

"I told you, that's just what some people think, Ixiar."

"What about you, Mom? What do you think?"

"Well ... that there's nothing. After death, there's nothing. Dead people just disappear, like animals."

"What about me, Mom? Will I die?"

"No, not you, honey, don't worry."

"What about you, Mom?"

"Me neither. And now, eat up, or we'll never finish. If you want to go down to the park with your friends, don't leave a single crumb, okay?"

Later, after putting Ixiar to bed, while eating the *sole meunière* served by the home android, the woman tells her husband about it.

"Your daughter asked me about death this afternoon."

"Is that so?"

"'Is that so': is that all you can say?"

"Come on, woman, it's not that big a deal."

"A friend of hers from school told her about it. A kid named Iñaki. Do you know him? Do you know who his parents are?"

"Iñaki, Iñaki ... Is that that little blond kid from the stratobus stop? I think his last name is Argandoña ... They live in one of those domes next to the square."

"Do you think they could be ... mortal?"

"I never stopped to think about it, but ... yeah, I suppose."

"I thought by sending Ixiar to the Academy she wouldn't ever meet those sort of people."

"It's one of the most expensive schools in the city, that's why we chose it. Anyway, I don't think there are very many mortals enrolled. But the Academy can't make distinctions, at least not as long as the tuition is paid, and certainly not between mortals and immortals. They'd lose their government funding if they did."

"Well, I don't like it, Imanol. What if our little girl makes friends with this Iñaki? It would be a very unequal relationship. Iñaki will die some day, it's inevitable, and that would be terrible for Ixiar. I thought we already talked about this, that our little girl should associate only with immortals."

"They're only five years old, Maite! Don't worry ..."

"Even so ... Anyway, I don't understand. If they have the money for the Academy, why couldn't his parents buy him a genetic immortality program? It just seems cruel."

"We don't know why they didn't do it. Maybe they weren't as rich when the boy was born. And, don't forget, there are still people who are against immortality, even if they're rich."

"I'll never understand it, I really won't."

NOTHING TO BE DONE

My life. My life is a complete disaster. I've known it for a long time. A disaster. There's no other word for it. A complete and total failure. It has been like this forever, as far back as I can remember: an infinite string of failures. It started in high school—which I never finished— and then just went on and on and on. Until today.

These thoughts, which I confess are none too profound, turn over in my mind in a miserable rented room as I coax the last drops from a bottle of Gordon's. I'm lying on the bed, fully dressed. Around me, a carpet covered with old magazines and Pizza Hut boxes, a moth-eaten armchair, a television that stopped working a couple of months ago, a suitcase under the bed, and not much else; more would be impossible since the room is only about twenty square feet. The bathroom, which I share with other neighbors, is separate, at the end of a long hall. They don't charge me much, and that's exactly why I rented this dump. But soon I won't have enough to pay even that amount and I will have to leave. To tell the truth, even if I had more money, I might still have to go. Soon they will find this hideout, and when that time comes, it will be better if I am not here. My last "business," the one that was going to save me from this misery once and for all, has failed. Like all the ones before it, let's not deceive ourselves. And like those yet to come, no doubt. If there are any, of course. There's nothing to be done.

I know it sounds silly, but over time I have come to see clearly when it all started, when my life started to go wrong. The exact instant, the exact place. Until then—I didn't quite tell the truth before, I might have exaggerated: things didn't *always* go badly for me—up to that point, my life may well have taken another direction, or at least that's the way it seems to me.

The day was November 6, 1981. I was sixteen years old. The time: five past one in the afternoon. The place: my school playground. As school was letting out. We had agreed to meet by the fountain, and Arantxa got there before I did. It seemed like a good omen to me, even though, to tell the truth, I'm always late for appointments; that's just the way I am. In any case, I was very wrong. She said no.

It's impossible for me to forget that moment. And, anyway, I remember the day well because that morning there was a funeral in front of the school, in the courtyard of the central government offices, and because we saw President Calvo-Sotelo. Two days before, three civil guards had been killed—we had heard the explosion, which was very loud, from the school playground—and the Spanish president, the minister of the interior, and many other officials had come to their funeral. Services were not held right at the central government offices, but at the Parish of the Sacred Family next door. The coffins and procession usually departed from the courtyard, and that was where all those officials had gathered, surrounded by civil guards and the national police. There was a good view of that courtyard from our school windows, and on such occasions the teachers couldn't keep us in our seats. As soon as the procession set off, we all jumped up and ran to the windows, to see with our own eyes all those people that we saw day after day in the newspapers and on television.

"Look, that's Rosón!"

"And look over there, that's Garaikoetxea!"

"What do you mean, stupid, that's not Garaikoetxea, it's Marcelino Oreja!"

And so on. We got to see all the presidents of the transition up close: Adolfo Suárez, Leopoldo Calvo-Sotelo, Felipe González. I saw González on only one occasion: a couple of months later I was expelled, and since then, I have never again seen any president of Spain up close.

In any case, the crucial event of that day was not the funeral procession, but Arantxa's rejection. Our conversation was brief. She told me she was going out with someone else, though she refused to tell me who. I later found out it was our classmate, Páez, a hateful fellow, of course. But that didn't matter. What did matter was that they had started going out the day before. One thing Arantxa told me pierced my heart: "If you had told me the day before yesterday ..."

"If you had told me the day before yesterday ..." A conciliatory statement, as hollow and clichéd as the overused formula, "I hope we can still be friends." But that thought didn't cross my mind. I believed it was the truth, an absolute truth, and that if I had declared myself only two days earlier, Arantxa and I would have started dating. I thought she turned me down *because* I hadn't dared to ask two days before. Time has taught me that love is like that, fickle, and that you have to seize it in that unique and fleeting instant if you don't want it to slip away. "If you had told me the day before yesterday ..." I believed what Arantxa told me then and I still believe it today. But there was nothing to be done about it. At that time, at least.

And ever since that moment, as I said before, the direction of my life has been ever downward. It's not that I was particularly depressed then. I was sad for a time, of course, because I was truly in love with Arantxa, but it wasn't the first time I had been turned down, nor would it be the last, and so my wounds healed, as wounds do. That wasn't the problem. The problem was that things started to go wrong at that exact instant, and that, no matter how hard I tried, there was nothing I could do about it. And I knew that everything was somehow connected with what had happened that day. Not with Eli's rejection, or Aintzane's, or Josune's, but specifically with Arantxa's and her declaration, "If you had told me the day before yesterday ..." That was when I lost all the possibilities that remained to me. That was when I lost myself.

I have lived with that certainty since then. Anyone would write me off as a fatalist and it may well be true, but that does not mean that I gave up fighting against destiny, not for a single moment of my life.

In vain, of course.

It would be easy to say that I'm crazy, of course, that that stupid episode in my adolescence had nothing to do with the ups and downs of my miserable life, but in fact it has everything to do with it. A witch said as much to me the other day. Madame Marguerite, one of those women who read the future and the past in the lines of your hand. I don't know why I went into her shop — maybe I was just bored that morning. I won't record here what she told me about my future, I prefer to keep that much to myself. The worst was what she told me about my past. "And here," the witch dug her fingernail into the center of my left palm, "here your life took a dramatic turn. You would have been sixteen or seventeen years old. I see a river, or the ocean, maybe a fountain ..." "Yes, a fountain," I confirmed. "That's it, a fountain," continued Madame Marguerite, "a fountain and a girl, just like in Arthurian legend. The girl's name was ... Ane ... Teresa ..." "Arantxa," I prompted. "Arantxa, yes, that's it." And then Madame Marguerite described in detail, or pretty closely, what had happened on that distant day in 1981, as well as many other incidents from my past. "Is there any solution?" I asked when our session was over and I was paying her. Madame Marguerite told me there wasn't, but I heard something in her voice, a certain hesitation, as if behind that firm "no" she was trying to hide something. Nevertheless, I was so flustered that I didn't ask again and simply left.

But I have decided that I will go again today and wrest the secret from Madame Marguerite. I have nothing to lose. I have nothing to lose and, besides, I have in my possession an Astra, well loaded with six nine-millimeter bullets. A powerful argument, surely, for the witch.

Intuition does not fail me. I show the pistol only once and that's enough. "There is a way, yes," Madame Marguerite stammers, "but I don't recommend it. Not even I can see what will happen. Nevertheless, since you're determined to go ahead, I won't stop you." The witch takes my left hand again. "As you recall, I associated the change in the direction of this line on your palm with that profound change in your past," and the old woman pinches me right there, leaving a red mark on my skin. "I can correct this direction to some extent by making a parallel incision with this awl," and she shows me a small, pointed tool, decorated with geometric designs, that she has taken from a small ivory box. "It comes from ancient Assyria and was used by those who worshiped Baal. I won't tell you by what tortuous paths through the centuries it came into my hands; I will just say that it has not been used often, because the magic it holds is too powerful and dark."

I begged her to go ahead, of course.

The woman burns incense and holds the Assyrian awl in the smoke for a minute or so. Then, without further ceremony, she grips my left hand and, with a quick and sure motion, cuts my palm. I shout.

The world changes immediately. Even the colors all around me change. I am back at school, in those long, dusty corridors. I go into our classroom, my old book bag on my shoulder. I am still a little dizzy, but I haven't forgotten which desk is mine, and I sit at it. I am surprised to recognize my classmates' faces, one by one, and I become aware of the metamorphosis that my body has undergone: I am sixteen years old again. In the upper left corner of the blackboard, the date is written in chalk: November 4, Wednesday. I am in 1981. Two days until November 6. I still have a chance.

Recess is at eleven. I rip a page from my notebook and quickly write a note to Arantxa: "11:15 in the park, by the wall next to the highway." I get up and, even though the teacher has entered the room, walk up to the front row, where Arantxa sits. She is even more beautiful than I remembered. I leave the note on her Latin book. The teacher shouts at me. "Zumalde! What are you doing up? Get back to your desk right now!"

At that time no better place, no prettier place, had occurred to me for our meeting. Subconsciously, I'm sure I meant for it to be as far away as possible from that damned fountain on the playground where everything would happen the first time, two days from now. I remembered the ivy that covers—covered—the park wall. I like the dark-green color of ivy.

The two hours until recess seem to last forever and I don't pay much attention to the teachers. I don't need to. Soon Arantxa will give me her answer. A yes. The recess bell rings and my eyes follow the path that Arantxa takes: first she goes over to her friends and says something I can't hear, then she goes down the stairs and out of the school building, and finally she turns left at the corner, toward the park.

I let a few minutes pass. I want to arrive a little later than Arantxa. To enjoy the moment. The moment that will change my history. I sit down at the entrance to the school and light a Lucky. When I exhale the first puff, I remember.

I start to run, but the explosion sounds before I get to the corner. It's much louder than I remembered. The explosion that destroyed the civil guards' Land Rover. The explosion that killed three civil guards. Two kilos of explosives hidden in a car left next to the park wall.

In this 1981, however, the dead number four, not three. There's nothing to be done at this point, and I stop running. In any case, the occupants of the Land Rover behind the one that suffered the attack, and the national police that come running from the central government offices, will cordon off the area immediately. Even if I wanted to, I wouldn't be able to see Arantxa's body. That was what happened in the 1981 I remember. Those who went from the playground to gawk weren't allowed to see the remains. Won't be allowed.

I sit down again at the entrance to the school and light another cigarette. I don't cry and I feel strange. I start to think. Tomorrow, there will surely be a demonstration here to protest Arantxa's death. The day after tomorrow, without the slightest doubt, we'll see Calvo-Sotelo in the courtyard of the government building, surrounded by ministers and policemen.

But I don't know for sure what will happen with my life. Perhaps it will be like before, a complete disaster, and everything that has happened will have been for naught. I'll end up in a miserable rented room, surrounded by old magazines and Pizza Hut boxes, sprawled in a moth-eaten armchair in front of a television that doesn't work. But that's not the feeling I get. Somehow I feel something different: my life will lift and soar, and it will be perfect. I steal a glance at the palm of my left hand and there's the new line, covering the old one, completely healed over. There's no trace of any abrupt change in its direction.

If that is true—and, while I finish my cigarette, while I hear the sirens blaring closer and closer, I am more and more certain that it will be—will I go, twenty years from now, to meet Madame Marguerite again and ask her for a spell to return me to 1981 to save Arantxa? I would like to think I would, that it would be the right thing to do, that it will be what I will do.

But I'm not entirely sure.

THE SOFA
For Itziar

Why yes, thank you, I will have a little more. That's plenty, thank you. I don't want to get drunk. Or not today, anyway.

It's funny. Do you know when we realized that we had entered a new stage in our lives? When we decided to get a new sofa for the living room. Until then, I hadn't even realized. I hadn't, I mean. Maybe Elena had. I'm almost certain she had. She's smarter than I am about things like that. I bet the idea of changing the sofa was hers at first, but I don't really remember. You know what Elena is like, how she can make her own ideas become plans for everyone. It worked the same way in our group of friends, don't you think? Well, it's the same at home.

No, the music isn't bothering me. Don't turn it off on my account. It's Jeff Buckley, isn't it? I have the CD, it's quite good. Not as good as they say, but it's good. Yeah, I have it. Or had it. It must be at home, with all the others. With almost all the others. I put the discman in my bag with five or six CDs. Which ones? I'd rather not say. It's a bit embarrassing. They're not exactly the ones I'd take to a desert island. I grabbed them without looking. I didn't have much time. No, I haven't gotten into the MP3 thing. Yeah, I know it's really easy and all, and you can put hundreds of songs on it, but it was too late for me, you know what I'm saying? I'm still a fan of records. I might get used to it, like with the cellphone, I'm not saying I won't. But for now ...

So anyway, we went to IKEA to look for a new sofa. Yes, to Madrid. They hadn't opened the one in Barakaldo yet, but the one in Madrid had been open for a few months. It was my crazy idea. Elena wanted to look in Zalla or Valmaseda, around that area you know, like always, but I convinced her to go to Madrid. A guy from work loaned me his van. No, I still haven't been in the one in Barakaldo, but the one in Madrid is enormous, you could get lost in there. Of course, once we were there we came away with seven or eight more little things, as well as the sofa. Yes, that's right, we got that shower curtain there. You have a good memory. We threw it away ages ago — you know what happens to those shower curtains, they get covered with mold immediately. It had nice colors though.

No, I don't need any dinner, I'm not hungry. Thank you though. I figured you would have eaten already. That's okay, no need to apologize. Yes, okay, I know where the fridge is.

Anyway, after we looked around the IKEA a bit, we went to see the sofas. We spent a couple hours in that section. You know how it is: you try one out, look at another, compare the upholstery ... And then I realized, or we realized, that none of the two or three models we were thinking about was a sofa-bed. Until then, we had had a sofa-bed in the living room. I don't know if you remember, that brown one with the leaf design on it. It was incredibly uncomfortable. No, no, that one was much more uncomfortable than this one, to be sure, at least for sitting on. My back fairly ached every time I sat there for a couple hours, watching television. We got that sofa-bed as soon as we moved into the apartment. An aunt of Elena's left it to us in her will, if I'm not mistaken. But at that time we thought it was essential because we had a lot of visitors.

Someone was always turning up. If it wasn't someone we had met on a foreign exchange program who had come to see the country as a tourist, it was a new arrival to the city staying with us until he found his own place ... sometimes for months. Do you remember that Galician guy, Nuño? No, I haven't seen him for years. Elena's head of department sent him to us, we hardly knew him. The head said he wasn't adapting well, he was depressed, he wanted to go back to Galicia, and would we look after him for a night because he couldn't, and didn't want to lose a teacher like that, right at the beginning of the semester. That guy stayed at our house for two months, until he got involved with one of his students and then he got over his depression fast enough. Those were two long months.

And there were more, but never mind. Bedlam, that's what my mother said every time she heard about a new visitor: "Your house is bedlam." By the time we went to IKEA, however, things had changed quite a bit. We were taking in fewer and fewer people. The change was slow in coming. We didn't even notice it, which is how all fundamental changes come about. And suddenly people weren't looking to us for asylum any more.

No, you're wrong: it was nothing to do with Ixiar. By the time we had the baby, we had hardly any visitors. The girl was the final straw, I think, but it had been coming for a long time.

Yes, okay, age could have been a factor. Most people of our generation have their nest, they've put down roots. I agree. But I think there was more to it than that. The atmosphere in our house was changing. Between Elena and me, for example. For example, or especially. These things are noticeable. Vibrations or something. Perhaps we were no longer so hospitable. Toward people. Us or our house. Who knows.

And we bought ourselves that sofa, you know the one, the red Klippan. Without a bed. Cheap and elegant. From IKEA.

Yes, of course, you have to go to work tomorrow. I don't. Yes, I remember about the fridge, don't worry. Clean towels in the bathroom, great. No, no, no, really, I'm sure I can do it myself. After all, it looks a lot like our old sofa-bed. Just leave the sheets there and I'll figure it out.

It won't be more than a few days, just until I find a new place. A week at the most. I'll start looking tomorrow, right after breakfast. Don't worry, I won't be any trouble. I promise.

Yes, good night.

TRANSLATED FROM BASQUE

BY KRISTIN ADDIS

SOFIA ANDRUKHOVYCH

Out-of-Tune Piano, Accordion

WHEN THE AIR BECOMES THICK TO THE TOUCH, when the celandine comes through, wet and yellow in the dappled, rotten undergrowth, when the rubbish among the naked, sucked-naked trunks of the pines becomes white and shimmers like the giant flowers of some cosmic apricot tree, then you can be sure: the wandering ghost-camp is already here, nearby, in our forest.

You don't have to believe in it, you can make your familiar, pretty-skeptical expression: pouting lower lip, like a moist cherry, a horizontal furrow across your brows, wrinkled little nose with its little, semi-transparent nostril wings—you'll shake the morning dew off them, spread them sleepily—and you'll fly into the air, into the blue soup of the sky, daubed with homemade sour cream and Boeings.

The night breathes—the first mosquito swarms—gapes wide, its mouth full of warm rot. Like a vulgar old woman with a feeble, gelatinous body; what's more, almost blind, and hopelessly imbecilic—it's enough simply to behold her drunken smile, that cloudless joy.

With a dry rustle the blossom falls from the pear tree; a caterpillar contentedly and lazily chews on some rocket leaves, and the irises—those ritual crystal daggers—fold themselves like origami, like Japanese ships or lanterns, and glow from the inside with a weak, cold light.

At that moment it's unmistakable—the wandering ghost-camp has arrived. A vague, blurred melody is dispersed above the trees, amplified by its own echo—like a song from a gramophone or an old cassette player that constantly chews the tape. A girl's laughter rings out in the midst of teenage howling and yelling, and piercing, playful shrieks. An artificial female voice gives an elevated, solemn speech into a microphone—you can make out rhymes, pre-prepared jokes and the mechanical sound of someone reading from a piece of paper, yet you can't make out any of the words. Every night, and through into the early hours of the morning, the dachas become still and do not breathe, and the massive bodies of the dacha dwellers, baked in the sun until they've become like pink meat, snuggle up to one another; but in the deep darkness the atmosphere of feverish activity seeps eerily through cracks in the windows and walls, and even through the panes of glass. From the thick undergrowth of the forest, glistening with dimly shimmering sparks of light that dance among the branches, now disappearing, now suddenly reappearing in a different place, a barely perceptible and sinister smell, an acrid, otherworldly smoke, billows, flows and swells.

You can never tell exactly where they are—on Krasna Poliana, or near Poroskotnia or at Babka—the signs of their presence are everywhere and undefined, the music rings out from their speakers, as though from the very hollows in the trees and the badgers' dens, they peer at us from the blackcurrant bushes, rustle in the grasses by the cesspool, their elongated, greenish faces are reflected in the glass of the greenhouse walls as though in still water.

Everything is quiet only at dawn, when the outlines of the trees become visible, the birds shake their wings and clear their throats, and the air is filled with nano-droplets of moisture, the invisible strings of a necklace, which refresh and bring relief. The shroud of numbness and fear is shed, and your eyes become brighter.

Viola sits on the cold, wet veranda, her head thrown back, her mouth open wide. Her eyes, flung open, do not blink, but stare fixedly at a single point. She is tired, exhausted, worn out. Her big, softened body spills over the bed like melted butter. Her wet dress clings to her all over, feeling unpleasant on her skin. Renat comes over to her, dragging his left leg behind him, and covers her with a Yak's-wool blanket they brought from the Himalayas.

Renat is eighty. His left leg doesn't obey him and his left eye is glass. It has a matte gleam to it and his pupil is always aimed right at you, no matter where you go, no matter how you try to escape its gaze, just as icons—especially those old, cracked, woodworm-eaten, rotten ones—never avert their gaze from mortal sinners. Renat's right eye, narrowed and cunning, flits back and forth, and then looks behind the lining: what's hiding there? Renat has crooked, blackened teeth (he refuses to have false teeth on principle, saying that bodies already don't decompose in the earth), a wide mouth—open and frightening—a face composed of hundreds of wrinkles, like a sort of puzzle, and the husky, cunning voice of an old animal that used to be strong but now just lies and warms itself in the sun.

Renat always knew how to live. The package of his life consisted of starched white shirts with wide cuffs and gold-plated cufflinks, fragrant cigars, deck chairs, bricks off the back of a lorry, the smiles of stewardesses, banquets in hotel restaurants, flats, dachas, antiques, freshly laundered underwear, offices with lacquered furniture, cars with stereo systems, yachts, Cuban women, diving, lightly salted pink salmon, no queue to see the doctor, deals, jewellery, massage, yachts, do they really eat such stinky cheese, how much did you say it costs? You're kidding!

Even now, beaten and worn out by life, one-eyed, crooked, crumpled and threadbare, Renat hasn't lost his shine. He is like an ancient Steinway with a cracked front panel. Like a 1954 Rolls Royce Phantom with a broken headlight and an ungainly body, with doors that don't close quite right, and in which the scent of Princess Elizabeth can still be detected: lavender water, clary sage, vetiver, melissa and patchouli; and whose luxurious leather seats creak solemnly, like bald men coughing after the interval at the opera.

His first wife was his age. They lived together peacefully for thirty years, producing a couple of children, until the moment when Renat met Viola. Viola was forty and had managed to remain not only striking, but, in a certain sense, attractive: round, fair, and languorous; ripe, juicy, and soft, like a plum (you bite the dark purple, almost black skin, and underneath find moist, scarlet insides). Renat understood the situation perfectly (I'm sixty, she's forty, I've got two children and six grandchildren, property and savings, she has a passion for alcohol, is infertile, lives in a hostel and has complicated intimate relationships), and for that very reason, he unquestioningly opened his arms to her. He loved to watch as she raised her face to the breeze as they sailed on his yacht, loved how she tried to extricate an oyster from its shell in the correct fashion, how she tried to make herself look like a socialite, washing down strawberries with chilled champagne. Her honeyed voice and affected manner of speaking charmed him, in the way that the silly babbling of a child can charm. She would laugh raucously and vulgarly, opening her bright, lipstick-smeared mouth wide and throwing her head back, and he, settled comfortably beside her, would benevolently wink his only eye, smiling to himself and mumbling something, and paying no attention to the confusion and disapprobation around them.

He, a kind, sixty-year-old daddy, was showing her the world. At the dacha, which Renat had eventually managed to wrest from the grip of his first wife, they made a stone cairn, where they would pile stones brought from all around the world. Around the cairn they placed plaster gnomes, at one time bright and jolly, with drunkenly rosy cheeks and noses—which, in fact, was what had endeared them to Viola—after decades of rain, snow, and scouring winds, they had become pale and worn, their paint had peeled, and several had lost their noses.

In springtime, Viola, dressed in tight pink breeches and a revealing blouse, crawled around the sizeable plot with a tin of paint and a brush, reinvigorating the collection of plaster animals and fairy-tale characters. The carefully maintained lawn lay like a silk carpet. The decorative bushes were plastered with flowers.

As soon as she married Renat, Viola tried to turn herself into a good housewife. She studied books for amateur gardeners, bought seedlings and planted tomatoes—Aurora, Hussar, Turandot, and Halifa. She looked after them attentively and with dedication: that year Viola felt particularly sharply her hopelessly unsatisfied motherly instinct. And the tomatoes reciprocated: their bodies grew fat, red and flushed, and bent their elastic stems with their weight.

And then she wept loudly and wholeheartedly, choking on her tears, and wailed and moaned over her sixty buckets of sweet fruit.

"What can I do with them, Renat, darling?" she cried in a voice that was not her own, "Who can I give them to? We can't eat all this! I won't go to the market! I can't give them away to strangers! No way! They'll rot!"

The next day, in the afternoon, Viola could barely open her swollen, painful eyes. Her head was splitting, her throat burning, and her neck hurt from lying on a bottle of Greek Centenari.

When she finally managed to focus her eyes she saw Renat standing in front of her. He was holding a kitten—black, with a white triangle on his chest. This was Methodius.

How the old, sly wolf loved them, his children! He gripped the edges of the table with his short fingers until the tips went white, such was his desire to remain here with them. Narrowing his eye, he caressed with his gaze that plump, overripe woman in the bright dress with her generous cleavage, her formless, white shoulders, covered in reddish freckles, her plump hands with their sharp claws, covered in glittering nail varnish, her puffy face, covered in a pimply, reddish-violet network of blood vessels, her swollen nose, her little, faded eyes, which had been so surprised and blue twenty years ago, now hidden behind big, butterfly sunglasses. Methodius, as always, lay stretched across her lap, showing his pink, castrated belly and purring like a little motor. Just like the granulators, agglomerators, and shredders made by the Japanese company, Berlingtong, which Renat represented (one capsulator sold—holiday to Sri Lanka guaranteed!).

"He's sooo clever, gentlemen, you can't even imagine it!" Like a giant toddler, Viola clapped her hands, "He goes for a pee-pee—excuse me—in the bidet, opens the door with his paws, grabs the handle like this, just imagine!" And Viola tried to demonstrate how Methodius opened the door. "Our little baby, oh, how I cried when he came home all injured!"

Methodius, as an intrepid tomcat, got everywhere. No foreign territory, no disgruntled neighbors, no guard dogs could deter him. He went in to strangers' kitchens and ate soup off the cooker, nibbled parsley and spring onions in strange gardens, leaving stinking presents in his wake.

That morning Renat found him by the fence. Methodius lay on his stomach, spread-eagled, his rear legs unnaturally twisted outwards, and looked up with his right eye at his owner. His left eye was shut and something black trickled from it. The cat was hurt, badly injured. Renat gasped, knelt down in front of the cat, just as he did when he picked dandelions from the lawn, and carefully placed his forehead against the cat's little skull.

"You're a strong lad, you're not going to leave us!" Renat whispered.

Methodius was thinking the same thing. He survived, and he recovered, although they never gave him a glass eye.

"Only a human being could do that," said Viola, gesticulating dramatically, "An animal or a car couldn't inflict wounds like those. I don't know where such cruelty comes from, gentlemen. But someone from around here, one of our lot . . ."

Viola waited for the oppressive silence to thicken, scratching Methodius behind the ears, and then coquettishly continued:

"This little lad's been with us for eight years. He's the second man in my life. He'll never let anyone offend my honor, my knight in shining armor," she raised the cat's flat head with her bright-clawed hand, and puckering her lips and making a loud smooching noise, kissed him on the nose. Her voice was sweet, sugary, flies floated in it. "Just like my darling Renat, isn't that right my kitten? Remember, sweetheart, when they tried to kidnap me in Istanbul? In broad daylight, at the market, in a crowd of people. My darling Renat went ahead, and I was left just a step behind, I was looking at some amazing, beautiful coral necklaces, and suddenly some man, a little guy, shorter than average, grabbed my hand and pulled me. He was small, but he held me so firmly that I couldn't tear myself free. He pushed me down some stairs towards some kind of basement and opened the door, and only then my darling Renat turned around, saw me, and was beside me in a flash, my dears he was right there next to me — and the man just disappeared into thin air . . . Isn't that right Renat, darling? I'm not going to leave your side for even a moment from now on . . ."

Darling Renat was losing his strength. With each day, he felt he was dissolving into the air, becoming transparent, like the smoke from burning grass. Sitting in the cool room, he listened as Viola continued to play at having a social life, cheerfully welcoming, sweet as always:

"I'm just so happy to see you! How is everything? Why don't you drop by for a glass of wine?"

Thankfully, nobody dropped by. Viola wept by his side, sobbing like a little girl, and at first he calmed her, stroking her hair and promising never to die, but then he became irritated and sent her out, because she wouldn't calm down, she just whimpered softly, like a little bird with a great, worn out body.

Feeling hurt and neglected, Viola wandered from dark room to dark room for half the night, shifting cushions and rattling dishes, smoking on the sofa, drinking from the bottle. And then, picking up a jagged shard of a broken mirror, she thickly applied her lipstick, wiped away the streams of mascara from her cheeks, and swiftly and resolutely left the house, crunched along the gravel path and disappeared into the forest among the creaking, melancholy pines, which swayed gently, like pendulums.

Soon, little blue flames began to glimmer all around her. Viola passed the little summerhouse, filled with motionless and cowering shadows. A paved path wandered off among the prickly growth of wild roses. Somewhere nearby a cherry tree gave off a musty and suffocating scent, and Viola's head began to spin.

The benches under the switched-off lanterns were empty, and plaster children, whose eyes had no eyelids and never blinked, towered on pedestals. The space in front of the camp's main building also seemed empty, and from some unknown source a muffled, familiar melody could be heard: dum-dum-dum-da-da-dum-dum—an out-of-tune piano and an accordion.

Viola stopped in front of the broken fountain, which was full of dried leaves, and picked off a flake of paint with her fingernail. The wide-open front doors lured her into their black depths.

The empty corridors, strewn with broken bricks, exuded a suffocating dampness. Plants had poked their way into the rooms through cracks in the walls and floor: small, twisted pines, ferns; lichen in pools of stinking brown water. Iron beds with springs that sagged heavily like tired udders. Moldy bedclothes soaked in the stench of decay.

The melody was sometimes faint, and sometimes hissed at full volume and increased its tempo. Somewhere a window frame banged nervously, although Viola also thought at one point that someone was bouncing a ball on the floor above. In one of the rooms Viola heard a hoarse rasp or cough in the corner, and she stared into the room until her eyes hurt, but the darkness just became thicker, sucking itself closed and hiding everything completely.

Viola decided to follow the melody. She wandered through the building for a long time, passing several times through the same hole in the wall, until she finally found herself in a hall with a rotten parquet floor that was full of holes.

The accordion stood on a low sports bench in front of a gymnastics ladder. Viola looked at the motionless accordion and yet could hear the melody. A woman with curly hair sat hunched at the piano, with her back to the guest. Her dark, formless clothing merged with the surrounding darkness, and only two pale hands, like the empty sleeves of a white shirt, fluttered above the keys.

Viola closed her eyes and took the first step. Her body was light, weightless, she no longer felt her own heaviness, she forgot about her weakness and fatigue. The floor seemed to disappear beneath her feet, and Viola felt that she was floating in the thick, gentle air, which carefully embraced her, caressing her skin. Viola began to spin around, she felt a pleasant buzzing in her head—she made no effort, and yet span like a top, and she felt so happy, so joyful and carefree, that she couldn't hold back, she laughed loudly and resonantly, drinking in her own laughter, which scattered away all around her.

Those around joined in with Viola's glee. Only their laughter was muted, more like a rustle. As though plastic bags were rushing from all directions towards the woman in the colorful dress who was spinning just beneath the ceiling, her feet lifted off the ground.

Viola opened her eyes, feeling a dull pain in her neck. The boy, tall, terribly thin, with an elongated face, with eyelids that hung heavy over his eyes, seemed somehow familiar. He embraced her and led her in the dance, looking intently into her eyes. His colorless lips were painfully twisted into a tearful grimace. He held Viola so firmly in his bloodless, bony arms, that she could not have broken free, she could barely even breathe; he held her far more firmly than that little Turk had once held her by the elbow, and the spinning became so quick that a whirlpool formed around Viola, an icy whirlwind that was impossible to resist.

And then, when Viola's pulse had begun to race so quickly that she felt that at any moment it would stop all together—just at that moment there was a frenzied, piercing, wild screech, and somebody small and vicious threw himself at Viola's partner, and convulsively tore at the stranger's yawning emptiness with his nails and teeth, until the melody broke off with the twang of a broken piano string, while the accordion heaved convulsively a few more times, and then drooped towards the floor.

Renat woke up in the middle of the night to an empty bed, coughed heavily and got to his feet. Viola was nowhere to be seen. He went from room to room, his heart thumped frantically, the air forced its way through his alveoli as though through a blocked-up, dirty filter, and his leg hurt as though it were being cut by hot knives. Empty bottles, cigarette packets, and used tissues littered the floor. But his little darling was nowhere to be seen, neither in the garden nor on the path beyond the fence. So Renat, the old, sickly hunter, dragged his aching body into the deep darkness of the forest.

He walked, feeling his way with his stick, touching the trunks of the pines with his hand. He looked up: the tops of the trees were silhouetted mysteriously against the sky, creating a strange pattern.

Viola was sitting on a pile of dry leaves, staring straight ahead. Next to her, bloodied and exhausted, in an unnatural pose, lay Methodius. A stifled rasp came from his throat.

"What's all this my little ones, what have you been up to again?" said Renat, getting down on his knees in front of them, sinking deep into the pine needles. "'Let's go home."

. . . Viola, a cabbage-butterfly, drinks sherry on the terrace. On the table rests an open Reverte-Perez. Viola thinks: the heather will bloom on the heath soon, it'll be September, and that's something you should remember. Viola, the cabbage-lady. God, when will you stop being crazy? When will you come down to earth?—it seems that you've risen from death. Viola's looking for miracles at the bottom of a little green bottle. Her tired thighs quiver, olives pierced by plastic swords, seems you've come to grief: Viola's a woman-daisy, Viola's a woman-wheat-sheaf.

"' . . . And we'll never be parted again," said Renat, covering Viola with a blanket. The cat lay by her side, his pink belly peacefully rising and falling as he breathed. "Not long now little ones."

TRANSLATED FROM UKRAINIAN

BY UILLEAM BLACKER

MIKHAIL TARKOVSKY

Ice Flow

1

AUNT NADIA'S FIRST HUSBAND LOST HIS LIFE in the war. Her daughter died young. Her village was torn apart during a period of consolidation: they wanted the entire community to resettle in neighboring Bakhta, but nobody agreed, and they all dispersed and went their separate ways. In spite of everything, Aunt Nadia stayed put. Her second husband was killed by lightning in his boat on the way home from haymaking.

A zoological expedition set up their summer base camp in her village, which was otherwise in ruins and overgrown with burdock and nettles. The director and his family settled there permanently, which meant Aunt Nadia wasn't spending the winter alone anymore.

This little eyebrowless old lady, with the face of a bird, for some reason called everything big and dangerous an "opportunity." When a tugboat towing a raft was drawing near—"that thing better not drag off my fish traps. How about that—such an opportunity!" "The pikes were really jumpin' in the net—such an opportunity! The net was weak as a namby-pamby, they tore it to shreds." She fished all her life: as a girl, when her father was ill; during the war winters, when she worked her fingers to the bone; during her time in the ladies' work brigade; and even in her old age, although fish traps were a thing of the past, she still set her net beneath a ridge of rocks and paddled out to check it every morning. She made her way there right along the shoreline, never in a hurry, coasting on the current with measured strokes. She also had some very peculiar notions about fishing. Someone asked her how to properly weight a drift net, to which she gave this puzzling reply: "Make it a little lighter, then the sand will fill it up and it'll be just the right weight." In matters of fishing,

Aunt Nadia valued tenacity and courage—she was able to take pleasure in the success of others, and didn't care for lazy, listless, and cowardly people ("Kolka's a great worker. But that Lenka's a good-for-nothin', not a man of the North").

In the winter, Aunt Nadia still set her father's trapline and went out in the taiga to check the traps with her knapsack and pistol, a staff in her hand, on little wooden skis with fur skins on their bottoms, in toylike, almost round, winter boots, warm pants, a *fufaika* coat, and huge mittens.

Aunt Nadia and her village's visitors established a relationship. The students came to see the "colorful" old lady who served them preserves and pancakes, marveling at her vitality as she dictated letters to her sister, Praskova, in Yalutorovsk, and in the winter they sent her parcels and postcards. Aunt Nadia found this quite touching, and she replied: "Here I sit, alone as a stone, writin' you this letter," and sent them bags of cedar nuts, smoked sterlet, or jars of jam. The girls appealed to her for advice in delicate matters. Aunt Nadia always taught them: "Don't pin your hopes on a fella. Fellas are outside dogs."

The male students happily drank her homebrew, bit into her fried fish, which wasn't so bad compared to their standard-issue macaroni and the occasional canned meat, and giggled secretly to each other about the old gal who couldn't pronounce the letter "sha" and on holidays penciled in her eyebrows with charcoal.

Aunt Nadia had many acquaintances, but she was visited all the time by Petya Petrov and her cousin, Mitrofan Akimich. Mitrofan was a robust and stately old man with a whining voice, always tooling around with a brand-new outboard motor on his boat. When she spied her incoming guest, Aunt Nadia would run out of her house and holler at him from the top of the hill, and he would holler back at her, and thus they would holler at each other with him still in his boat, then after a while they would hug and go inside her cottage. When he got drunk, Mitrofan became impossibly frisky, running around hollering, greeting one person after another, shaking their hands with both of his, asking about everyone's health and how their babies were doing, pointing and hollering at the old gal, "And this here is my cousin, born beneath the arms of a cedar tree ..." He would shed a few tears as he stood there gesturing with his arms and laughing, and when he was leaving, would ask somebody to bring him his outboard motor. Once they did, he would climb in his boat, grab the tiller, put it in reverse, and zip away at a frightful speed, boldly whirling around with his index finger pressed to his lips, as if to say: not a word about our little shindig here!

Petya Petrov was an excellent, albeit thoroughly alcoholic fellow. He brought his wife, a woman of the Selkup people, from the North. They worked at the post office as a duo, and also drank together, and folks in Bakhta sometimes joked about them: "That there's the good life! They're both drunks, they're both content. They're lucky to have each other!" Petya loved conversation and spoke with passion, telling tales from a history he seemed to invent on the spot. His favorite expressions were all about "a boatload"—"The fish have arrived, believe it or not, a boooatload!" Once Petya and I went to see Aunt Nadia, and before too long Petya got loaded, at which point, and at his request, we began to put him back in the boat, but it turned out we weren't holding him very well. He slid headfirst into the water by the shore, his bald spot coming to rest in the pebbles. We picked him up right away, but for my whole life I will always remember his gray eyes staring through Yenisei's clear waters, and the slow stirring of his thin strands of hair.

Every now and then Aunt Nadia had Granny Tanya as a guest, an ancient denizen of the Sumarovskovo village. The only things she brought with her were a long fishing rod and a jar of worms. She spoke in a hoarse voice and spent her whole visit at the bottom of the hill, lugging along her catch of small dace, which Aunt Nadia fed to her cat. Besides the cat, Aunt Nadia also kept a rooster and two chickens, a dog, and a horse named Belka.

All that was left of the old buildings in Selivanikh were holes overgrown with nettles, and rotted frames, but Aunt Nadia stubbornly called them all by their former titles: the boarding school, the fur farm, the Budanov's house, the grocery shop, the bakery ...

Aunt Nadia loved entertaining guests. Whenever you walked past her house, she hopped out on the porch with plates of food in her hands and hollered:

"Miiisa! Stop by, I'll treat you to some *blini*!" She took holidays seriously, preparing for several days, cooking, putting everything in order in her cottage, fixing herself up. When guests arrived, she hopped out on her porch in a black skirt, red blouse, large beads, and a bright, flower-patterned head scarf, and called out in an unusually high voice: "Welcome, my dear guests, everything is ready!" She made everyone sit down at the table, served them food, kept her eye on everyone's plates to make sure they were all filled, fussed over the appetizers, brought someone a towel, someone else some water, and if anyone even thought to get up from his chair, she was filled with indignation: "Go on with you! I'm the hostess!" Later, when, according to her plan, it was time, she abruptly led the group in a folk ditty, such as:

> The priest fell off the stove
> With everything he was worth
> His teeth were cracked
> His willy got whacked
> His shirt torn at the girth!

When it came to songs, she knew them by the boatload.

Over time Aunt Nadia's house fell into disrepair, then partially collapsed, resembling a drowning ship, and at that point became dangerous to live in. After several long discussions, the director of the science station offered to build a new log house, funded by the expedition, on the condition that ownership would be transferred to the station, and Aunt Nadia would be able to live in it until the end of her days. Aunt Nadia thought for a long time, made a decision, then had some doubts, then finally agreed because she had nowhere else to go. The house was built by Borya, the scourge. Aunt Nadia made sure of one thing: that everything in the new house was exactly as it was in the old one. The partition had to be right in its place, and the stove had to be just so. When everything was almost ready, she popped out with a jar of blue paint and painted the door and window frames, then decorated them with white flowers and leaves: "Looky how I prettied up the windows!" Then she arranged her furniture in its previous order—buffet, bed, table, chairs—spread out the floor mat, hung everything on the wall that had hung on the wall in the old house: a rug with deer on it, a calendar, posters, photographs, the fanned tail of a wood grouse, the hide of a flying squirrel, ribbons, bellflowers, gifts in the bags they had come in. When I went to visit Aunt Nadia, I almost had the sense that it was her old house, she had managed so well to transfer everything from her previous set-up: it was just the way it had looked — with the photographs of Maksim Pylich, the one who was killed by lightning; just the way it had smelled, from the burnt fish fat on the stove; and just the way it had been, with the cat's tail hanging down from the shelf.

It's always good to visit Aunt Nadia on the way home from a hunt. You're tearing through, then you turn into her yard, cutting the engine on your Blizzard by the porch, and she's already yelling from the cottage: "Come in, come in, I'm home!" And even if she isn't expecting you at all, she starts chirping anyway: "I felt you were coming! I felt it. And Petyonka, that old Petyonka, he's been crowing like a potty-mouth since morning! Here, kitty kitty! Company's here, don't be so snitty! Take your coat off, take your coat off, look at that frost on you! Lay it on the stove. I just made some fresh bread. Well then, have a seat and talk to me. How's life over yonder, how's the hunting, your line of work? Well, praise God, praise God. And I've been a-huntin', too. Take a look at the varmint I got in my trap — just a rat, but it's all in one piece. It's a beauty! I'm skinnin' it now, and next summer the tourists will take it as a muskrat hide. Oooh, don't know if I should laugh or cry about that … And it's my birthday soon, Yura promised to come. He's bringin' Tolik. Out in the taiga, were you? Ahh. Well, what can you do? You have to do what you have to do."

Yura worked as a buoy keeper. On his route, as he checked on all the buoys and navigational markers, he often dropped in on Aunt Nadia and sat at her table, looking off to the side, telling her about how "the fishing inspectors implicated Wooden Vanyushka" over in Bakhta, or how a bear had pulled up the markers by the Sosnova stream again, and she would exclaim, "You don't say! That stinker!" and pour him some of her strong homebrew infused with burnt sugar.

It was finally her birthday — Aunt Nadia had made it to seventy-five. She got up before the crack of dawn, lit the stove, swept the floor spotless, prepared the table, ran to invite Kolya, the director of the science station, and his wife over to celebrate, came back home, bustled about some more, trying to guess whether Yura would be coming alone, or with his daughter, pricking her ears at every audible sound outside. Dogs start barking, a plane flies over, and she runs out on the porch with her binoculars, looking out over the Yenisei: what's that spot there, that couldn't possibly be Yura, no, that looks like it's an ice hummock, or maybe a bush. Alright, he must be coming for dinner. But the day passed, and evening came. No Yura. There were plates of appetizers on the table: mountain cranberries, mushrooms, pickled wild garlic, baked burbot caviar, smoked herring, *blini,* fresh bread, compote in a jar.

Kolya and his wife arrived, carrying a present: "What, no Yura?"

"Still waitin', still waitin'. Wearin' out my eyes, watchin' for him. Saw it in my dream, I did—he must be comin'. Petyonka, since this morning! What'sa matter with you! All you are is loud! Here, kitty! Well then, come in, come in."

It was already dark, and it was clear that Yura wasn't coming. Aunt Nadia said:

"Well, musta been work, he musta had work to do. I just laid out my cards—they said he's just now leavin' the courthouse. Or maybe his Blizzard broke down. We'll just hafta wait for him in the mornin'."

And so for three days Aunt Nadia kept her table cloth on and ran out to the hill with her binoculars, but Yura never showed up to see her. He was too busy drinking with his neighbor.

2

At the bottom of the hill beneath Aunt Nadia's house stood an old leather bench by a little cutter boat, and by her porch lay a doormat made from old, thrashed Blizzard tracks. In the summer, Aunt Nadia put an iron stove for cooking beside the bench.

On sweltering July days, when there was a blue haze over the flat Yenisei, the old gal wore pants so the bugs wouldn't eat her alive, something was always boiling on the stove, and by the cloud of smoke stood a gray mare, twitching her skin and fanning herself with her tail. ("Look at that—they're really snarfing on Belka.")

Aunt Nadia had a special love for Belka. She was an old horse but still healthy, left without work when the science station's Blizzard arrived in Selivanikh. Aunt Nadia kept stubbornly stacking hay. She took any suggestion about selling Belka as an insult, and became very animated about how the Blizzard would break down and they would need to come harness Belka to bring in supplies from Bakhta the next year. Belka somehow managed to get lost one summer, and Aunt Nadia cried:

"Called her and called her, I did. She's just not anywhere. A bear got her, most likely."

But Belka turned up. Years passed. Aunt Nadia grew older. It became more and more difficult to groom Belka, to stack hay for her. "It's all the same if I let Belka go to Bakhta,"—the old gal was growing accustomed to this idea—"she'll get to work there, she's been standin' around here at my place for too, too long." In Bakhta, horses hauled hay from the Sarchikh river and Banna Island, bread from the baker to the shop, and water for the houses. Finally Aunt Nadia made her decision. Some folks came for Belka in the evening, on a wooden boat outfitted with a corral made of poles, and early the next morning they pushed the boat into the water and brought her to Bakhta. I crossed paths with them as I was going fishing and glanced back a few times. The fog was lifting, its strata outlining the shore, blending together and shifting form, the boat was no longer visible, and it looked as though the horse was floating in the air over the Yenisei.

One day we were turning in our fish at the fur farm. We had to lower our wet, heavy bags down to the ice house. It was dark and cold inside the ice house, water was squelching under my feet. Suddenly my foot ran into something big and slippery. It was Belka's head. I never told Aunt Nadia, and to this day she thinks that her Belka is here in Bakhta, hauling water.

3

We have a custom: when the Yenisei moves, take a handful of its water. Everyone waits for the river's ice flow, like it's a holiday. Aunt Nadia keeps a watchful eye on every step of spring. She notes when "the wagtails have arrived," that "some geese were honkin' on the other side of the island, and my heart skipped a beat," and that "it looks like

Annisei's gone up some more, it'll go for sure by dinner tomorrow." But things happen slowly. There's an increase in melt water, the shore ice grows, cracks begin to intersect the ice, yet nothing will budge from where it's frozen. But finally, one marvelous day, a loud crash resonates like a shot, a team of ducks sweeps past—and now the enormous Yenisei creeps along through its murky, much despised ice, with its increasingly defined winter paths, and sticks jammed through its old icefishing holes, then a long stretch appears full of shining water, the ice rumbles up on the shore, and here comes Aunt Nadia, calling out something in a resounding voice, crossing herself, and running down the hill with a bucket, and bowing at the waist before Father "Annisei." She's been waiting so long for new life.

TRANSLATED FROM RUSSIAN
BY ANDREA GREGOVICH

SIMON DECKERT

A Dog's Fate or *The Diversion of Armin P.*

I

MANY THOUGHTS ARE LIKE A CUL-DE-SAC with a roundabout at the end. When you're done with them, you can either think back over them until you're back at the beginning, or you can go round and round the endpoint in order to convince yourself that it's a progressive thought that you're having, effectively circling around in the illusion of forward movement.

When Armin P. lay awake at night with a roundabout-thought in his head, he almost always chose the second variation. Nothing at all came of thinking over a thought again, neither satisfaction nor tiredness, and circling always ended in the latter. If he went round the result of a reflection for long enough (the results were unalterable, cold and unmoving, like heavy steel sculptures, as though they had nothing to do with him and his reflections), signs popped up at the edge of the roundabout showing exits where there were none, alternatives, attempts at solutions, precursors to a clarity that only exists in dreams.

One of these exits was the front door. With each lap of the roundabout he passed the sign that indicated the exit: Door. And once he looked at it, there was no way past it—with each lap it shone more brightly from the twilight that was his half-sleep. If the woman was in the house, the responsibility could sometimes be passed on to her: the idea was that she could have locked the door—if he had forgotten, and if she too had forgotten, no one could say, in the event of a break-in, who out of the two of them was guilty of leaving the door open. Comforted enough that the signpost for that exit could now be cut down without any further effort, he could give in to sleep. But most of the time he was alone, and then the sign shone so brightly that he couldn't think of sleep before he had gotten out of bed and gone down the stairs to the hall, felt the cold plastic curls of the doormat between his warm toes, and secured the lock on his being locked in. When he was lying in bed again, it normally took less than two minutes until all cul-de-sacs, roundabouts, and doors had disappeared from his mind.

The night, during which he breaks his own record and ends up in the cul-de-sac a whole five times, is, by the fifth time, almost not really a night at all any more. Rays of a July dawn cut through the blinds like a freshly sharpened knife, and as he finally opens his eyes, after a few more laps around the roundabout, he knows that this time the path to the door will be of no use. From the stairs, he can already make out the dresser drawers and the pattern of the carpet in the gray morning light, the key bow between his fingers is cool and feels like day and being awake. A bird chirps in front of the door. He turns the key all the way and pauses for a moment, then he turns it in the opposite direction, until the lock clicks, then back again. As he turns it back, he is wide-awake. He waits another moment and then turns it in the opposite direction, this time past the clicking of the lock, all the way.

II

In the neighboring house—behind a slit in the curtains—Mrs. Priska Eberle draws her breath through her teeth with a hiss as she sees Armin P.'s door handle moving from her first-floor bedroom window. She quickly turns around to her husband to see whether he has heard, but the husband presents the same picture as all the previous times that she has turned towards him, lying on his back, his arms tight to his body so that the floral summer quilt stretches somewhat over the curve of a beer belly in its seventh year of retirement. It is much too early, of that she is certain; it can't be much later than a quarter to five. Mrs. Eberle has, over the years, developed a sense of time that only an insomniac could have, but it was the emergence of Armin P. that first gave purpose to her sleeplessness. Invariably, at around half six, he steps outside his front door, in trainers and that sports coat from some foreign ski club. He has gray, mid-length hair, never more than a two-day-old beard, pronounced calves and broad shoulders, or what retirement has left of a pair of broad shoulders. The first few steps are always somewhat unsure, but when he rounds the corner at the end of the street, he has normally found his pace and leaves an image of a young athlete in her mind.

Right at that moment, as the latch moves, she notices the shards on the doorstep. Green glass, probably a beer bottle, and under it a dark stain on the stone. But as the door is now opening and a naked foot is stepping forward, it would already be too late to throw open the window and call out to him, even if she dared.

The scream that echoes through that part of the village a moment later negates, on this morning, the need for the first crowing of the cock.

III

The woman often seemed to him a natural phenomenon. He couldn't observe any regularity in her coming and going, and he certainly couldn't influence it in any way. When she came, she stayed for a few days or a week, and when she was gone again, two weeks sometimes passed before her next visit, sometimes a month or more. Sometimes she came alone, sometimes she had her children with her: the two sisters, seven and twelve—two charming little blond girls, even if the older was quite rebellious for her age—and the brother, ten years old, a quiet child with his mother's thick, dark-brown hair. That he dealt with them like the grandfather that he might well have been at his age, and their mother like a father, didn't seem to faze the little ones.

Once, when she had been alone at his place, he had cooked for her on the last day of her visit, fresh potato salad and microwave meatballs. On the table there was a bottle of Riesling and two glasses; he had just tidied the plates into the dishwasher and was in the process of making coffee when she asked him if he liked her hair color. Although he knew what was behind the question and how he would answer it, he took a moment to think through all the dimensions of the situation in which he believed himself to be. (Perhaps she would have called it a test.) A simple "yes" would have been considered disinterest, a more lengthy comment dangerous, had he not made clear at the same time that he was, of course, aware of the fact that brown wasn't her natural hair color. But the exhibition of this knowledge couldn't just be abandoned, without also telling her something about how well that brown suited her.

"I like how it makes your skin look paler. That suits you."

"You're a diplomat."

Why had she had it colored?

She took a sip of wine.

What did he think then?

"About the little one?"

"I don't know." She looked out the kitchen window. "When they came to me after the divorce, he was the only boy and the only one without blond hair. Somehow that seemed unfair to me."

Obviously her status as a newly divorced woman was so clear that neither of them had felt the need to mention it. This occurred to them both for the first time in that moment, judging by the silence that lingered between them after it.

IV

Before a blue four-by-four rolls up onto the tarmac in the narrow yard in front of Armin P.'s house and the woman gets out who has given the same sense of purpose to his retirement as he has to his neighbor's insomnia, first an ambulance, and three hours later, a taxi roll on to the same tarmac, and one July day comes to an end and another July day begins.

The absurd sum that the taxi driver had charged had been the final reason he had needed to retrieve a bottle of Schilcher from one of the dusty wine cases under the work bench in the cellar at half eight in the morning. Keep the foot up, the doctor had said, for at least three days. By the time the bottle had cooled and he could no longer take the state broadcaster, which, outside of the ski season, he dismissed as the "Austrian Windbag," it was after ten anyway. Other people in his financial situation went to wine tastings at this time, and so he twisted the cap and, for good measure, placed on the TV stand a bowl of chips, which would cleanse his palate after every sip of wine and facilitate a new taste sensation. In order to put the least amount of strain on the foot, the doctor had also said he was to walk as little as possible, and, if at all, then only with crutches. The crutches leaned against the saddle of the exercise bike beside the sofa, white and heavy and clunky, like a mockery of his past, and made him want to be honest with himself about his life. Over the course of the rest of the day the freezer lost a packet of smoked meat dumplings and the fridge two cans of Gösser, and, as he dozed off at around half four, the open second bottle of Schilcher sat beside his recliner, its apparently salmon-colored glass reflecting the images of some afternoon talk show, reflecting them in a room in which there were no longer any living beings that would have had sufficiently developed sensory organs or would have been in the position to adequately perceive such a relatively complex phenomenon as a reflection. A heavy, dark sleep began to suppress these thoughts and to fill his head with the perfection of liquid in a vacuum-sealed plastic bag, like a cool, damp cloth that exerted a comfortable pressure against his forehead, under which all thoughts fragmented.

When he wakes up, the alcohol is still there but also a very clear, clean thought, which he follows with the blind trust of a drunk: he gets up, goes over to the dresser in the hall, reaches for his phone, and begins to scroll though his address book. At the entry "Ludesch, Monika" he pauses briefly. Perhaps, he thinks, the human heart can take on every rhythm that it comes into contact with. The rhythm of the slalom, the clicking of the poles, red and blue and red and blue. His heart would now beat to the rhythm of the dialing tone.

"Armin?"

"I am an invalid."

Before her answer there is a brief silence.

"I know."

V

"I've had an idea for a special kind of cinema. A small room, classically decorated, but behind the screen no wall; instead a big window." She looks at him out of a pair of wood-brown eyes that look like dark stones in her long, white face. "The material for the screen would be the type that you can see through when nothing is being projected onto it, so that when there are no screenings you have a good view of the neighboring houses, and of a square, perhaps, where trams rattle by and people greet one another hurriedly." She turns her head a little and he feels the weight of her chin on his thigh. "Only when the film begins and pictures flicker on the screen can you no longer see the city properly from the window. Shapes and movements you can recognize, perhaps, but the flickering of the projected images veils everything. Who wouldn't get a headache from that?" She barks and lifts her head from his lap, then she runs into the kitchen where the woman is putting away the groceries.

VI

They hadn't given the animal a name yet, but had arranged to decide on one when they were leaving on Monday evening. As they drove to Balzers on the highway, midmorning, the radio on the lowest volume level, in order to be able to hear the panting of the bitch from the trunk, the animal seemed to her like an unwanted child—the product of an unplanned pregnancy that you had decided to keep. She gave her a good feeling, the bitch in the trunk, a warm satisfaction in her belly like you only get from the knowledge of having made a good decision. The radio presenter was talking about speeders, or drunk drivers, who had been seen on Friday night in Vaduz and Balzers. It shot through her mind that one of them was probably the idiot who had thrown a beer bottle in front of Armin's front door. Then the radio presenter played a song and she listened again to the panting from the trunk. She had neither thought of getting a dog, nor had she ever discussed it with Armin. Then she had been coming home from work on Friday afternoon, for the hundredth time driving past the dog pound that was on the way, for the hundredth time she had slowed down in front of the cracked speed bump and for the first time had seen how a dog was trying to nose its way through the wire mesh of the fence around a fire-hydrant, which was on the grass a few centimeters from the enclosure. She had gotten out of the car, and she had, on impulse, barely held out her hand to the animal, when it abandoned the hydrant and began to lick her fingers.

Since she was sixteen or seventeen she had had this habit: of seeing meaning in everything that happened around her — everything that occurred in her presence, perceiving it as a chapter of a story whose plot had something to do with her. Sometimes they scared her, the meanings that lurked around every corner or in every recess of her mind, on quiet evenings in the kitchen in which a mighty lake of terracotta seemed to lie between the broom cupboard and the fridge, in the house that the husband who no longer lived there had handed over to her. And sometimes a great happiness came over her when she felt that she saw things that others couldn't see. When, on that same evening, her phone had rung and Armin's name had appeared on the screen, any doubt that she had found the right gift for him had disappeared.

VII

Only a small lamp burns in the bedroom, a round wooden base with a white plastic switch on it, and over the bulb a stained lampshade. On the other side of the bed is a large window — looking out onto the night — in which dimly lit things are reflected, a wardrobe, a desk lamp, a blouse on the carpet, a carefully folded pair of trousers on the arm of the chair, a sock on the radiator. And on the bed in the window are a man and a woman, a man who is lying on his back and a woman who is sitting on him; and her hips are moving back and forth, and her hands are on his shoulders.

The woman pauses for a moment and tries to appreciate how it feels to not use a condom for the first time since her marriage ended. She closes her eyes and thinks she smells cooking vegetables, the smell of an old tea towel in the wash basket, and the aroma of fresh soap.

"What are you thinking about?" asks the man.

She looks at him and doesn't answer.

"Do you know what I did before I came here?"

She puts a finger to his lips and shakes her head, and her hips begin to move again.

VIII

If only she hadn't forbidden him the words; those comforting sounds with which people talked to one another and which gave his thoughts a reality that wasn't just his. If only she hadn't trapped the words with the finger on his lips, so that they were now jammed behind his forehead, composed into sentences like cumbersome metal rods that could no longer be dismantled, just thought, again and again. The woman's back was naked and lay turned towards him, and her side rose and sank like smooth, radiant, rolling hills in which, in his old age, he wanted to build himself a little lodge, if he could get planning permission. And if he succeeded in crossing the twenty-two-year-deep ravine that lay between him and that landscape. Maybe she really had never seen a ski race in the seventies and eighties, never turned on a sports program or looked at a tabloid in the nineties. But her ignorance, or her denial, or her pretense, whatever it was, didn't take the reality away from his life. A life didn't just shatter like a hip joint on a cordoned off mogul slope. And a man whose whole career was movement couldn't just separate himself from it after fifty-eight years. Movement was a force that could take from the mind as much as it did from the body (the two parts of which a person is composed), and if the body no longer fulfilled its demands, then it seized the mind. Giant slalom in the mind. Endurance race in the mind. Like an outward-turning wheel. From the stairs, he can already make out the dresser drawers and the pattern of the carpet in the gray morning light. He goes into the kitchen and is frightened for a moment when he sees the dog, who is standing in her basket, looking at him as though she had been waiting for him. You need to get out for a run, he thinks. The hands on the clock above the sink show twenty to five. Okay, why not. After he has drunk a glass of water, he takes the sports coat from the armchair in the hall, pulls on his jogging shorts over his underwear, and slips on his trainers, first with the left foot, then carefully with the bandaged right one. Two or three days this time, he whispers, and clips the lead onto the dog's collar, then he reaches with his free hand for the key in the lock and turns it past the clicking sound that on this morning seems to him in some way final.

The village is still in the dawn. A car can be heard here and there, the wind carries the perpetual drone of the industrial district and the autobahn from the direction of the Rhine, and in the narrow side streets his steps echo against the houses. He stops at a small crossing, crouches down, and takes a few deep breaths. Suddenly, a dull silence takes over his left ear and disappears again, then a weak whistling sound starts up. Great, he thinks. What next? As he straightens himself up and begins to run again in the same motion, it goes black in front of his eyes for a moment. He has time to wonder why the dog is trying to pull him back onto the pavement with the lead before the bumper rams against his thigh and sends him on a flight that ends a few meters further on with the thump of his skull on the asphalt.

A moment later, all thoughts leak out of Armin P.'s mind and disperse like a sandcastle in the wind, never to be thought again.

TRANSLATED FROM GERMAN
BY REBECCA MCMULLAN

Manuel Jorge Marmelo

The Silence of a Man Alone

A MAN SITTING ON A BENCH of thick wooden planks screwed to a cast-iron base.

A wooden bench in a square with few trees and barely any shade to speak of, late one summer's morning, hot, midday nearly, and the sun is high and scorches everything, parching the branches of the two plane trees that stand guard over the square, which, in spring, has little flowers in its grassy beds, green then, now the color of dry straw; and a round, muddy lake with goldfish in and, in the middle, a weak fountain, pumping a slow, tired spout into the air.

A square in a small town of impeccably whitewashed, single-story houses, huddled one against the other as though in this way they might protect themselves from the dry summer heat.

A small town in the middle of a plain of stubble fields, dotted with twisted, withered olive trees, the odd fig tree, skinny, black cows scraping their tongues over what little grazing is left. And, beyond, a small, sad country, opening out first into rolling fields of fertile yet uncultivated land, then hills and vineyards, woods and pine forests, cities enveloped in toxic fumes, parades of famished eucalyptus lined up like armies, drawing the nation down to the sea and merging into the foam of the tiny, warm waves that break on the shore in small, inoffensive, white folds.

Up above, a hazy, blue sky.

And, beneath it, a man seated on a bench of red planks that appear thicker than they really are due to the successive layers of acrylic paint which the sun dries out and fills with fine cracks, like wrinkles, which soon crumble and demand a fresh coat.

The man is not alone. At a safe distance, in the scant shade of one of the plane trees which stand guard over the square, are three old men, who look at the man, then at one another, as if each seeks in the others an answer to the most paradoxical of mysteries—that which decides upon life and death. A few paces away stands a cart, the reins of the mules held in the right hand of a fifth man, also old, and who, perhaps for that reason, holds a stick in his free hand. The two animals are still and docile, shuffling their hooves only to keep their balance on the cobbled ground and swishing their tails to keep off the flies. Further behind, in the middle of the gently sloping street, lies a crude coffin, split open like a watermelon that has burst on the ground. No man is in the splintered coffin; he who was in it now sits on the red bench in the square, leaning forward slightly, his hands on his knees and his eyes seeing beyond the dusty ground before him.

He is a man alone, despite the three friends who turned out to accompany him on his final journey and who now watch him. There is nothing new or extraordinary about his solitude. But it is this that has been on his mind since he crossed, with slow steps, the short distance between the splintered coffin and the bench in the square. This is the certainty that weighs on his breast as others begin to approach, noiselessly, the shade of the plane trees, halting at a cautious distance and eyeing the seated man; gradually forming a ring of motionless bodies, like a wall of mute astonishment: all have come to see a man who was already dead, over whose body a vigil had been held and the sacraments performed, and that was on its way to the town cemetery; yet here he now is, alive and seated, albeit motionless, on the bench in the square, though no one appears to see in this a demonstration of the Lord's unfathomable designs, but rather a cheap trick, a cruel flourish of the devil's wiles.

Luís Maria, according to those who knew him in life, that is, in the life before his first death, was a man thin and knobbly like a young olive tree, but dark and wrinkled like any man accustomed to working under that sun, gathering olives or harvesting wheat, mending fences or staking vines. There was no one who was not on speaking terms with him and did not seek his help whenever two hands and a man's strength were needed to accomplish some task or other. He was honest, and respected for it, good, yet taciturn, and little given to chit-chat, a characteristic which had become accentuated in recent years, since the death of *tia* Lurdes, his wife and only companion over many years—devoted and sterile, tiny and gaunt, a seamstress like no other in the town, not because she had extraordinary talents, but simply because there was no one else who practised the art of sewing button-holes and mending worn-out old trousers, stitching hems or replac-ing threadbare pockets. She would sit for hours on end on a minus-cule painted wooden chair with a wicker seat, stooped over her knees, laboring away with needle and thread. She would stop only to get the dinner—which would also be Luís Maria's lunch for the next day, re-heated and packed up in an old, blackened pot—and so that was where she died, bent double on the minute chair, her body not even tumbling to the floor. She was buried in a coffin which looked as if it were intended for a small child, only slightly higher to accommodate her bent knees, seeing as she had passed away in her working position and no one had been able to straighten her legs.

Luís Maria, who, up till then, had been reserved and quiet, be-came gloomy and gradually began to fade, speaking less and less, just the bare minimum to get himself a day's work and to keep up his old habit of playing five rounds of dominoes at the end of the after-noon—which was really a pretext to drink cherry liqueur and spend some time with his fellows. If they questioned his silence, he would say only, "Better to keep quiet than talk rubbish to pass the time. Time passes for the living and ends for those that die. There's nothing more to it. It can't be made to pass more quickly."

"But we've got to say something, old chap! Otherwise, we would be like sunflowers."

"That's a good one, Alberto! Sunflowers that play dominoes!"

"And drink *ginja*!" added Mário. "Talking of which: another round? Another round!"

And with this, the other three old men's tongues were loosened. But Luís Maria had already said all he had to say and did no more than play his domino pieces when it was his turn, and look out of the door of the *taberna* as if he was waiting for something or someone, even though he knew he was not waiting for anyone or anything and, for that reason, did not show the slightest sign of anxiety each time he turned his gaze to that bright patch of world which invaded the cool shade of the bar.

After the third round of *ginjas* or the fifth game of dominoes, whichever came first, the old man would stand up from the wooden bench, put on his black felt hat, and make his way unhurriedly home, walking as though time did not exist. Before he left, it was his habit to say simply, "Be seeing you tomorrow, then," with no further explanations or remarks, for the prolonged companionship of men at least has the advantage of dispensing with unnecessary explanations or formalities. Luís Maria left the table because his hour had come and the other three men stayed on because theirs came later, there being no need to go elsewhere when they could perfectly well remain where they were and continue to do as they fancied. It was tacitly agreed that it should be so, and no one thought to press he who was leaving to stay a bit longer or have another drink, nor they who went on playing to get up and follow their companion out. In short: they asked each other no questions, if only because they expected no answers. And, perhaps for that reason, the proximity of the tragedy occurred to no one on the sultry afternoon when, after the fifth game of dominoes and the third round of *ginjas*, Luís Maria remained seated on the hard bench of the *taberna,* wiping away with his middle finger the wet rings made on the table top by the bottoms of the little glasses. The game went on, while outside the sun faded, and the day cooled, round after round of *ginjas* were ordered, and it all happened as though it had ever been so.

When, at last, the time came for the men to return to their homes, where their respective wives and suppers awaited them, Luís Maria also rose, paid for the *ginjas* and tilted his hat in farewell to those that remained, then followed the other three out with his slow, shuffling step. He did not do so for long, however, for soon, without warning, his thin, bony body toppled helplessly to the ground, where it lay lifeless, yet with eyes wide open, as though, at the last moment, he was attempting to see all that had previously escaped him.

Having no known relatives in the town, the old man's body was deposited at the hospital, where it was hurriedly shoved in a simple, pine coffin, with no one to keep vigil over it, except for the three domino partners, who that evening would not even go off for supper, catering for the weakness of their bellies with two bottles of wine and a plate of salt-cod pastries which one of them picked up from the *taberna* while the other two dealt with the formalities of the death. When the new day dawned, bright and already threatening the heat that was to come, the three men still stood in a circle around the crudely fashioned coffin, their eyes red, holding their old black felt hats in their hands, only abandoning their wake after the priest had appeared to perform the last sacraments and hurriedly entrust Luís Maria's soul to God. And it was the same three who, with the aid of the carter hired to transport the coffin to the cemetery, carried Luís Maria's body to the cart, then accompanied on foot the trot of the mules along the cobbled streets of the town.

Whether it was the pitiless late-morning heat or because no one had been moved by the news of the death, no others joined the procession, so that it seemed almost as though the man lying in the coffin was already long dead in the memory of the townspeople. At most, one or two women appeared at their windows to watch the procession go by, shielding their eyes from the sun, which by then was beating down on the cobbles and on the white of the houses in a way that seemed capable of blinding anyone who challenged its merciless brightness. If to anyone watching from afar it seemed astonishing that the passage of the cart did not leave a trail of putrefaction in its wake, for at that hour and under that blazing sun Luís Maria was surely already being devoured by the worms that had taken refuge in his body, surprise gave way to fear when, on the way down the gentle slope of the road leading to the edge of the town and, just before it, the municipal cemetery, the coffin slipped from the cart and was smashed to pieces as it hit the ground, leaving the thin, dead man lying in the road. And the surprise was quickly succeeded by the paralysis of terror, for Luís Maria, awoken by the fall, got up from the ground, patted down his trousers, looked around him as if wondering what on earth he was doing lying in the middle of the road, and then walked slowly over to sit on the red wooden bench in the gardens which ran along the eastern side of the road.

What good is a man alone? What use is he? What nameless sin did he commit to receive the punishment of going on living? It may be that

Luís Maria formulated none of these questions as he sat motionless on the bench in the square—not because he preferred to avoid them, but because he was not equipped for cogitations and metaphysics, accustomed as he was to living without reflecting on what he did. But the fact that such ideas did not occur to him did not mean he did not feel them swelling in his breast like a fat bulb expanding around his throat until it nearly suffocated him. He lacked the words to express the weight he felt in his head, and it was perhaps this that he sought with his eyes as he stared fixedly at the dusty ground.

He had grasped, with one look around him, the reason for that implausible awakening in the middle of the road and, as he walked the few steps separating him from the bench on which he sat, he lamented the fact that the crude coffin should have fallen from the cart, resuscitating him. Better to have been buried once and for all, forevermore, cutting short his pointless existence and extending his silence into eternity, in the grave which was to be no more than a mound of dry earth denoting the volume of his body. When, at last, he mustered the willpower to get up from the bench and make his way home—where else?—he did so with his gaze still cast low so as not to face the shame of the eyes he felt glued to his back or feel in his flesh the questioning, the astonishment, perhaps the fear he would have found in their stares. He paused only when the three friends placed their hands on his shoulders, more out of camaraderie than to transmit any affection, but was not even capable of saying "I'm sorry."

He took the usual route to his front door, to the kitchen table where he always sits when he arrives home, with his feet together and the palms of his hands placed on the table top, gazing in front of him at the blackened wall, turning over the leaden emptiness above his eyes until it is time to sleep and await the coming of a new day.

On this day, however, when Luís Maria senses the house firmly closed in by the night, his steps will not lead him to his bed. He will come to the window to gaze at the stars, will open the door—which will remain wide open—after grabbing the rope which hangs from a nail inside, and will step slowly out onto the pavement, beginning to walk unhurriedly between the little houses that will look pale in the moonlight. He will have forgotten his hat. In the distance, a dog will be howling. He will cross the town in the direction of the cemetery, ignoring the bandstand, will settle the roll of rope on his shoulder and breathe in vigorously to smell the earth and the heat that emanates from it on summer nights. His feet will feel heavy, as though the old roots which had always pulled him towards the earth were stronger now. He will feel tired and will stop to drink water from a spring, before reaching the olive grove whose wall he had built, one day, with his own hands. He will force the iron gate, merge with the shadows of the wizened trunks and toss the rope up to a high branch, beside the ruins of a pressing house. Acting as though he has hanged himself a thousand times before, he will tie a knot at one end of the rope, fasten the other end, making sure the loop is at a fatal height, climb the olive tree, fit the noose around his neck, and let himself fall as if he were flying, without sadness, without distress, and will feel the rope tightening around his throat, the crunch of the vertebrae, his feet swinging more and more slowly—until the tree ceases creaking under his weight and the world goes back to being just silence and stars.

TRANSLATED FROM PORTUGUESE
BY DOMINIC GOURD

OLGA MARTYNOVA

Hospital Room Nr. 13.54

1

PROFESSOR BACH SITS HIGH OFF THE GROUND on his hospital bed, cross-legged, reading a book. Above his head hangs an IV bag: empty. The IV pole just stands there; the patient needs no more infusions. Probably never needed any. His therapist, Professor Bach recalls, thinks just once a week. "No, no," the therapist says, "everyday would be too much. Then the unusual would become routine."

Well then.

While Professor Bach thinks, the book continues:

there, well into the 19th century, a sickly girl, a teen from a family of Petersburg Germans (the book is a Russian novel) is standing in front of a bookshelf. Around her upper lip a little worm of a vein twitches under fine skin, a sign of her nervous alertness. While the girl is standing in front of the bookshelf,

Professor Bach thinks he is still reading the book.

When Professor Bach was still a student, he read everything that was on the list of recommended reading, even though practically every instructor would point out a few titles that were essential, or sufficient. Precisely that, this thoroughness, is his problem, his therapist says. His heart trouble is of a psychosomatic nature, he says. His nerves are being overtaxed. He needs to grant them some rest, trick them with some distraction:

Autogenic training;
Music;
Field trips out into nature;
Bubble baths;

A glass of wine in the evening;

Swimming;

Dancing, some people take dance courses, tango or something similar. People find it extremely satisfying;

Cooking wouldn't be bad if it weren't generally associated with a lot of eating;

Gardening, a very contemplative activity.

Yoga, Marina says. *And we'll take a trip to China. Ask your doctor. He'll say it wouldn't be a bad idea.*

"That wouldn't be a bad idea," his therapist says. "But," the therapist says, "one more thing: once a week, completely switch off. Fence yourself off from the world you've grown accustomed to. Restart. Do something you've never done before, or planned. But try to do it," his therapist says, "without trying too hard."

So what exactly would that be? Remarkable how few opportunities you have to do something that does not figure in the course of your life without causing what does figure in the course of your life to derail.

Professor Bach thinks of a sentence he overheard the day before in the hospital courtyard. Besides himself, waiting there for his wife, there had only been a couple, sitting at the window table: both young, well dressed, less suited to the dusty plush ambience of the glassed-in rooftop seating area than to the gray-white line drawing of the snow-covered branches outside. The whir of the coffee machine, the radio, the waitress's cellphone conversation, made them into characters in a silent film that ran until suddenly their coffee was ready, the radio announcer inserted a pause to increase tension, and the talking waitress shut her phone. The room would tolerate no silence; the silent film became a talkie, and a male voice said: "I can clean windows in trains and sell pretzels, no, seriously ..." The reawakened hissing, reporting, laughing, swallowed the woman's voice, and the couple transformed into two fish that opened their mouths noiselessly. Only now, a day later, does it occur to Professor Bach how strange this sentence was, spoken with a hard-to-pinpoint, presumably Eastern European, accent. No wonder, then, that the two of them swam out the window, opened only briefly to air the room. "Well, that's rude!" the waitress told her cellphone, but then found the money on the table and calmed down. The two fish, having swum away, out of the café aquarium, became smaller and smaller between the snowflakes—growing bigger and bigger until their hexagonal form became recognizable—and disappeared. Professor Bach grows a little envious, closes the book and raises his eyes to the hospital room window:

(in the closed book the girl with the twitching little worm above her upper lip is celebrating her sixteenth birthday and is buried in love and presents. A fashionable artist from among the family's acquaintances even gives her a picture of water nymphs, which does not please the narrator for some reason. Unsettles him)

Rose garden in the snow. A few flowers that did not let their petals fall at the proper time now let the snow powder their noses as they hallucinate summer. The remaining dust from the enlivened sky. The midday sun falls on a fifty euro note his neighbor in the room has left lying out, for tomorrow: he is (like Professor Bach) being let out the next day, and the money is for the nurses, as a tip. His neighbor's wife, a distinguished, energetic lady around seventy, thought he ought to put it in his wallet until then. He agreed but then forgot.

That's what I'm looking for! thinks Professor Bach.

In the blank winter light he sees a border between two worlds otherwise invisible: the world of the bourgeois and that of those free as birds (his professor's discernment protested against the generality of the two terms, while his unfettered doppelgänger did not give a damn). He steps into another dimension. He feels an elementary contempt for those who live in their apartments and houses *earning* money, arranging their lives around the money earned, traveling, practicing autogenic training, taking field trips out into nature, indulging in a glass of wine at night, taking cooking lessons, dedicating themselves to contemplative gardening. He takes the money and, by touching the hard paper (wing of a bug, Bach the elementary school student waves from a summer forest, sticking a bug he does not yet recognize in a matchbox), returns to *his* side of the world, where a thief is an asshole, hated and despised, who breaks into the lives of people already plagued by fears and worries.

He imagines the thief (presumably under-aged and Eastern European: according to the police, a gang of such had been at large in the city) who had cleaned out his apartment a few years before: how he had opened the door without a sound; how he had stepped from the dark hallway into the living room shot through with sunlight; how he had stood there as though he were not some miserable thief but an emperor in a newly conquered land—expectant. How anger had seized him when he found hardly anything but books. How he relished his rage as he trampled the old laptop and threw everything from the desk onto the floor, tossing the vase with the roses Marina had set on the table for who knows what reason at the already damaged laptop, from which later the computer man could not salvage any data. Professor Bach, who, as a result, had to rewrite the first chapter of his book on the Germans in nineteenth-century Russia (Marina thought it got even better), was not only inconsequential to the bastard, he was not real. Unreal. And now, for a second, Professor Bach was at once on both sides of the border between the two worlds—raptor and fowl in one. Once this second passed, only the shame remained. And—only a little, because improbable—the fear that someone would unmask him.

Enough, enough, thinks Professor Bach, *I can just put the money back now. I got everything there was to get from it.*

The doors slide open silently, and a nurse pushes in his neighbor in a wheelchair. The old man can walk well but is too slow for the impatient routine of hospital activity. So they roll him when he needs to be examined elsewhere.

Fortunately Professor Bach has stepped away from the bedstand and is standing at the window again. He cringes, but—no shortness of breath, no dizziness, no trembling; none of those things of which he was constantly afraid. Did it work? Not bad for the first time! But now he has a problem: the money has to be returned. Before anyone notices it is missing.

It has snowed again overnight (too early, really, it is still only fall and a few more warm weeks were expected). That means it will repeat again today: the dry, not yet crusty white will crunch beneath their soles.

Like starched laundry, he thought the day before and now thinks again. The fresh snow from the dresser. His mother had attached a great deal of importance to the linen being properly bleached, starched, and ironed. He still recalls how the cool material of the pillowcase felt on his cheek. She had done something with the laundry that no one could anymore. Only in very expensive hotels perhaps. But did it crunch? He cannot recall. Laundry has become different, softer. As if the snow were beginning to thaw. And no longer white, but colorful, which allows for a certain carelessness in washing and starching and ironing, of course. Maybe he has simply read all that about the snow and the laundry somewhere. Still, he has heard this crackling before, and not so long ago. He understands in a rush how exceptionally important it is to recall again which other crackling was stirred by this crackling. This recollection is almost there, almost visible, as if behind tracing paper, almost . . .

2

"Hey there, Andreas," Marina said, bringing into the room:

    1. his first name, finally;

    2. the cold from outside: plenty for the whole hospital room, plus some, compressed briefly, from her lips on his;

    3. two cappuccinos in paper cups.

Plus a great deal of freckles and wavy bright-red hair over the black-and-white herringbone pattern of her straight, slender coat. He almost missed that, however — the way one does not notice the outer appearance of those one is close to. He had gotten used to her: to her alert, elongated eyes; her mouth, currently unmade up, that always looked like it was about to say something:

"Drink your cappuccino and get dressed. Let's go to the garden," she said, hanging her coat on the hook next to the door.

It was always like that: when he was drinking his coffee, they had to be outside as quickly as possible. When they were outside, they had to find a café. When they stayed at home, they had to invite guests. And best of all would be to be constantly traveling, Andreas thought, but said nothing. In another train of thought the snow was still crunching. More and more depended on whether he would remember when he had heard that other crackling. *I will never again have this shortness of breath when I recall what that was*, he said to himself, and was immediately afraid that shortness of breath, breaking out in a sweat, dizziness, shaking hands, and panic would return any moment to every limb if he did not solve the puzzle.

"It's better we go out into the garden while there's still sun," Marina said.

Was it perhaps her restive nature that meant that, when, twenty years before, she had left him in a tacit and inexplicable manner, he could do nothing except accept the situation for what it was? Or: he did not *want* to do anything out of fear of her restiveness. *She* certainly believed that he did not *want* to do anything. When, after twenty years, she felt like being with him again, he wondered whether it was worth getting used to her, whether she would stick to that plan awhile. For her it would be no problem, once a week, or even more often, to come up with some ridiculous thing no one would even have thought of doing.

"Are you done? Shall we go?" Marina asked.

It was fine with him anyway. He needed to hear the snow underneath his soles again to be able to remember that other crackling.

He was already in his coat and on his way when she opened the book by Nikolai Leskov he had closed and read aloud:

> "Everyone knows: if you don't place value on whether or not the arms and legs are of a slight build and do not expect every face to have a particular expression, then you will hardly find as many fresh faces, white shoulders, and well-formed chests anywhere in St. Petersburg than if you are on the Vasilyevsky Island among its virtuous residents of German extraction."

Andreas wanted to say that the book told the story of a German girl with a twitchy worm of a vein and a very particular facial expression, which contradicted the ironic sentence that Marina had selected. He kept silent, however; all he needed was for Marina to laugh at him for being insulted by this description of Germans. He considered whether he should take his coat back off, so he could tell her the news while still in the room:

"The research semester is going to work out. So we'll drive to your place in St. Petersburg. I'll finally have enough time, and peace and quiet for my book."

Sitting in the libraries and archives from morning to night would not exactly be in line with his therapist's recommendations, but he would find something for himself to do there. More than here at any rate.

"What am I supposed to do in St. Petersburg?" Marina said. "I've only just found something I like to do. Finally!"

That was true. What was unclear was how she had been able to bear the academic life so long. The position she had occupied in a culture fund for a year suited her much better: a great deal of travel, of people—restlessness as an assignment.

"But you can live at my place. And I'll visit you. I have to go there often for a few projects anyway. Oh, you know what, I'll rent something for myself in Frankfurt for now, so I won't have to commute all the time. What would I be doing in Berlin without you?"

Good for her, he thought, but why did he always have to be surrounded by emptiness? He who liked to have someone speaking in the background, breathing, laughing, eating, talking on the phone, even if it bothered him while he worked. When he and Sabine had separated, he had even considered renting an apartment with a few single colleagues.

3

"You're in great shape for ninety," the nurse, a short Russian with hair of black cotton candy, tells his neighbor in the hospital room.

While his neighbor slowly opened his mouth to answer, Andreas's viscera were momentarily scalded by hot steam and then chilled by black ice. He did not look at his neighbor's bedside table, but he knew what was there (a plastic cup, a bottle of mineral water, butter cookies, boxes of pills, a bible, and an uncertain number of nerveless deadly sins eased by confession: yesterday, when Andreas was about to leave the hospital room to meet Marina in the café, a hospital priest had come, having been ordered before breakfast. Andreas's neighbor had wanted to confess. "Let us begin with the sixth commandment," he had heard the old man say, before he had hurried away. Now, though, he would be very interested in what the old man had to say about the seventh commandment or whether he had anything to say).

He also knew what was not there (a fifty euro note). Would the old man, his mouth now open to speak, report the theft?

"You're such a nice nurse," the neighbor said with a voice made of paper matching the crumpled tracing paper of his skin. "What's your name?" *Tracing paper*, Andreas thought, *what was that just now about tracing paper?*

"Liuba Rappoport;" the nurse gathered the empty boxes of tablets from the table.

"Strange," the neighbor said. "In my youth, before the war, I knew so many Rappoports. And then no more. Interesting."

The two women exchanged glances and laughed. The neighbor nodded in agreement, pleased at being someone who has successfully made a joke.

What was there to laugh about though, Andreas wanted to know, as Marina and he were finally walking between the squarely cut and white-covered rose hedges. The old man had not had the faintest idea what he was saying.

"What an innocent rascal," Marina said, distracted. She had to concentrate intensely to walk in her high-heels across the layer of snow, already compacted but still fresh.

"Why did you put those shoes on in this weather?" Andreas asked, no longer interested in defending the old man.

"I know, I know," Marina said. "You're right." What did she mean he was right about, when she always thought she was right: the old man or the shoes? "But you know what. Besides the fact that I'm so short, you have to put in the work, I don't know, take care of yourself. My grandma always had a tube of lipstick on the night table, a habit from the wartime. If she was surprised by the air-raid sirens while sleeping, she could put on lipstick on the way to the bomb cellar, in order to *look proper*, or, as her cleaning lady used to say, not to look like *an old Sarah*. Just imagine, she always had a cleaning lady. Even while she was starving, in the 30s, after my grandfather's death, when she had to trade jewelry and the silver for bread, she had a maid. She was proud of that. When I was a kid I was put off by it, maybe even outraged. I thought you ought rather to be proud you could do things yourself. I'm the same way now. I almost feel uncomfortable when that Polish girl of yours comes, ashamed she's doing the dirty work while I read a book. Whatever. Reading the book *is* my work. If, say, my socks had slipped down, my grandmother's cleaning woman would tell me: 'Well, don't you have socks like an old Sarah.' For me it was just another saying. Once I told Lisa: 'Well, don't you have socks like an old Sarah.' Her reaction first made it clear to me, not *what* I was saying to *whom*, but what the phrase even meant. That is, I understood *what* I was saying only because of *who* I was saying it to." So that covered both the shoes and the room neighbor. But what was he right about? Well, whatever.

"My grandmother also had one—a lipstick tube also at the ready. I think for the same reason: air-raid sirens," Andreas said, not telling, however, what all *he* had picked up on as a child. In order not to leave Sarah's socks just hanging there, he said, in his capacity as Marina's host, in the German language: "It's the same as when the Bavarians say '*Kruzitürken*,' that is 'crosses and Turks,' without even thinking about Turks."

"Hey, so why don't you want to pay a little more and ask for a single?" asked Marina, who, frivolous as she was, had opted for fancy private hospital insurance and did not want to admit that a double hospital room was all the luxury she could afford. He ought to just tell her that he had a frivolous wife, namely her; that his mother was in an expensive nursing home (though she could still pay for it herself, how long would that last?); that he had two children; that he had private matters that also cost money. No, he should not tell her that last point under any circumstances. Or, ultimately, that he did not like being alone in a room.

By the way. The crackling meant Laura. He knew it now as if a curtain had noiselessly lifted. It was last fall. Marina was in St. Petersburg. He invited Laura to spend a weekend with him in the countryside. In the morning the autumn sun smelled of frost. The blades of grass listened for the approaching winter. In the middle of the field stood a barn that only had lengthwise walls. The lack of widthwise walls transformed it into a tunnel. Dead ladybugs collected on the ground. Some were an orange-red with black dots. The others had red dots on black. A crunching carpet that crackled beneath the soles: red-black, black-red.

"I read that ladybugs copulate for up to nineteen hours, the females sometimes die from exhaustion, but the males don't notice and keep going," Laura said: "Imagine if those were all females under our boots: literally loved to death by the males and then left." The snow under their soles = the crackling of the dead female ladybugs.

(A child waves hurriedly from the late-summer-like Baltic coast, running after Uncle Peter who hums:

> Little ladybug, ladybug
> Fly to little Marienbrunn, Marienbrunn
> Bring us a bunch of rain soon
> and then a bunch of sun

—or something like that)

She loved somebody else, who didn't love her, the famous writer, Caspar Waidegger, she said as they ate breakfast for the first time in her small student apartment, coffee pot in her hand, strands of hair on her lowered face. *Me too*, he had almost said, because, back then, he still did not know how things would go with Marina (did he know now?) and, besides, could have used some sympathy. But a man can't say something like that to a woman, he thought, and kept quiet, hurt. How did it feel for her: skin on skin with the slowly dwindling existence of an aging body. He always wanted to ask her. But dared not.

What if he seemed as foreign and fossilized to her as his room neighbor did to him? He raised his eyes to the second floor. On the windowsill stockpiles had accumulated that his neighbor had lovingly arranged and that the man's wife had not yet cleaned up: rectangles and cylinders of various colors and sizes.

4

"I'm going now," said Marina.

"No," said Andreas.

"Yes," said Marina.

"No," said Andreas.

"Yes, I am," said Marina. "I promised your children I'd meet them at the pastry shop."

"Oh, alright," Andreas said, "but why a pastry shop?"

And Marina replied: "In family sagas the new partner is always taking the children to a pastry shop. Didn't you know that?"

They walked, and the snowflakes grew increasingly large and clear, until their hexagonalness was recognizable. Suddenly he could not breathe again. He sat down on a garden bench. He could just as well have sat down in a pile of snow. And maybe it was a pile of snow that he mistook for a garden bench. He trembled as if the blood in his veins was flowing in a zigzag. He lifted his hands and looked at them: the fingers remained still, even the trembling was only his imagination.

Get up. Otherwise you will turn into a pile of snow in the shape of a Professor Bach.

Aha, that would do — becoming a pile of snow. That would be what he had never done and never planned to do before. Become a pile of snow — no one will find you; no one will have to bury you. Then children will come and make a snow man out of you. Then spring will come and make a puddle out of the snowman. Then the sun will come and make vapor out of the puddle. Then the fall will come and make a cloud of the vapor. Then winter will come and make snow out of the cloud. Then the children will come. But you will no longer be.

Get up.

Would a visit to a brothel work? That would be something new, anyway. Stepping into the foreign realm that exists just outside your life. Thus not real for you. Unreal. Not knowing who said what to whom, or how much of a tip should be on the counter (the table?). Looking for a woman who performs services that are at once much more personal than a normal service, but much less personal than the service of, say, a waitress (*you've read too much Russian literature*, Professor Bach tells himself and thinks about his American friend, Professor Perlman who had told him how aging prostitutes are retrained as nurses in the US, which they are well suited to, being accustomed of course to attending to old, unattractive bodies, to accomplishing everything quickly and in a friendly manner).

Get up.

What else would work? What would his therapist approve of?

Why did his ideas of the unusual tend this way? Why not do something good? Something unusually good.

"One of my patients spent a few hours begging," the therapist said. "His feeling of relief was powerful. He could not stop talking about it. But he's a younger man, an actor at that, and, I suspect, someone whose primary purpose is to live an artistic life. Naturally I would not recommend that to you, Professor. Try skydiving first."

What is that supposed to mean? Why not? Am I already so old that people don't think I could go begging? Would the others, the real beggars, chase me off?

Marina told him there was a teacher in India who sent his students begging—and these were young men of aristocratic and wealthy families. They were to become experienced in the unpleasant. "I went hitchhiking with a friend once, and we did it. It's unbelievable. You're no longer you. You're someone, sure, but not you. It's another dimension. I wouldn't want to have missed the experience, but I wouldn't want to repeat it either."

Get up. Otherwise you'll turn into a pile of snow, into a snowman, into a puddle, to vapor, to a cloud.

5

When Professor Bach arrived in front of his hospital room, the doors separated noiselessly, and two nurses rolled out the bed containing the abandoned cocoon of crumpled tracing paper. What was he supposed to do with the fifty euro note now?

Maybe Marina was right about the additional insurance, thought Professor Bach, wanting suddenly to see Marina, to speak with her, to touch her. Touching a living body, the skin under which blood still flows. But he was alone in his spacious hospital room, thinking that everyone he knew was in a position to get along just fine without him, that they were continuing to live their mysterious lives while he stood there alone in his spacious hospital room. *Marina*, he thought, *come back. Come now.*

The doors separated again. They rolled in a new, still empty bed: a rose hedge from the garden, cut into a rectangle and covered with snow.

TRANSLATED FROM GERMAN
BY DUSTIN LOVETT

JOHN TOOMEY

What the Dying Heart Says

…These months have been forever. Please, Tommy. I endorse you as executioner. I assign you the duty of mercy…Please…

ONE

I SKETCH THEM IN MY MIND, and so I have it that they are young. For starters. But the broad and depthless caricatures don't end there; they are conceited too. My contempt demands this. I imagine how ambition and complacency are kneaded onto their collective countenance, and how lazy patterns of thought begot their arrogant dreams. These novices, whose belief in medicine's black arts is so profound that they neglect life's dumb tragedy.

But they *are* young, I remind myself, aware their futures reside in the laps of the surgical oligarchs. Which is how it happens, I suppose, that the unashamedly arrogant are reduced to shuffling in and out of the room in fearful reverence, each middle morning, behind this man they call Carson. Professor Carson, in person, but simply Carson in his absence.

I imagine Carson too: a stout, chubby-fingered man. Thickly haired, graying, the last player in a disappearing generation; cream slacks, boxy shoes, and curt manners. Glasses, almost certainly. A veiny red nose, and tremor-prone hands. One of these young clones probably gets talked through surgeries these days; endowing his high-stakes experience with the precision and stamina of youthful eyes and fingers. But this Carson, I tell you, he's formidable. The atmosphere he carries with him into a room is something to behold.

I had a moment, only yesterday, when I almost believed I wasn't dead myself. He keeps telling people that, you see. Carson talks at them all the time. Lectures them, but not in medicine and promethean vanity—which is what they long for from him—but in humanity. He tells them that the human capacity for hope is virtually bulletproof. It's what makes us stubbornly resistant to finality, he says. And he keeps telling them that I could well be hearing everything that's said. But I don't think anyone really believes it. Which is a pity, because it's the only thing he's right about. He's dog-wrong about everything else. Just goes to show, doesn't it.

I believe that, with a little conviction, I could force my eyelids open. I'm certain of it. But what's to see? That's the question. So I don't. To do so would be to infuse these strangers with renewed compassion.

And that would only cloud the issue further, of course. Months it has taken, you realize, to break their faith in a medically orchestrated recovery. Even though I've given them nothing, still only now do they circle the bed with submission in the mix.

TWO

My brother, Tommy, has been telling Carson all along, but he won't listen. Tommy's told Carson I'd want to go. But Tommy lacks conviction when it comes to things that aren't wholly factual. He's unable to convince himself of the wisdom of intuition. What hope, then, these strident demigods?

And you should hear the interns around the bed, talking about Tommy, after he and Carson are gone. They think he's one cold bastard. Most of them.

But one voice has begun to dissent. A woman. She sometimes speaks up for him. She, his anonymous defender, comes accented. European. Croatian, perhaps. That's the smell I get from her. A blend of something distinctly rugged and sensuous. I catch the whiff and touch of her Slavic skin each time her fingers undo my buttons, and when she leans over to put the cool stethoscope to my chest, I feel her breath dance across my neck. The first time, I was almost moved to open my eyes.

She tells the others that Tommy is my brother, and that families know each other better than doctors. Better even than Carson. She says to them, "What man would want to live? Now?" She knows what I'm not.

It is with an utterly unsentimental alchemy of sympathy and disgust that she defends us, my brother and me. It's that Dalmatian spirit of hers. She understands that I simply cannot be allowed to recover. The imaginative range of her clinical assessment has them all rattled.

There is a precocious empathy in her, as though she feels more than she could yet have learned. I consider her my ally. As Tommy is. And once they began to talk, I knew I had a chance. Tommy wanted to know how he could ever be sure. Understandable from his perspective. Infuriating from mine. But that was how it began. They spoke. They speculated.

THREE

Shed no tears for me, Tommy. That much I'm telling you. No tears for me, brother. We've not been close but we've been strong. And I love you, Tommy. As Sarah did. And the kids. I love you for having loved them and because they loved you. And because you've always just been there. To my end, it seems.

But what about your end? Who will be there for you? Perhaps this anomalous Croatian will coerce you into something approaching intimacy. That's always been your problem, Tommy. It will be why you will end up alone—you allow yourself to be loved, and you can love in return, but only remotely. You can't trust. Those tiny betrayals of youth still hang over you. They gather in the dark shadows of your heart, in the recesses of your over-serious mind.

Give in to this intrepid little doctor, Tommy. I'm telling you. Something happens to her when you walk in the room. She becomes more earnest. She smells differently, like the quickened heartbeat of adolescent sex. She could be everything or just something. Either way, you shouldn't let opportunities pass.

You should run away together! You would be vilified, of course, but solace could be taken in the sheer bliss of each other. The romance of it! Just imagine; how your single act of rebellion would come to define your life.

Abandon me! For your own sake. But do what's needed first. That's all I ask.

Try not to be angered by the tone of this, Tommy. I know how my words have always made you want to thump me. But this trumps a thumping, brother. By a long shot. You get to be the one that kills me.

I don't want to be revived ...

Can they hear it if I think it like that?

And I'm as lucid as could be, believe me. Don't let there be any question over the fitness of my mind. I'm one hundred percent lucid. I am bitterly aware, I assure you. My body performs like an aged cock: limp, flaccid, useless. Fucked, I am! But without the glory of the fuck.

My only remaining trace of muscularity is cerebral. I have vision, and a potent fucking memory, but no legs to run from it: shattered glass; blood oozing thickly from my earlobe, running across my cheekbone and pooling shallowly about my temple; Sarah, folded on the roof of the jeep like a string-puppet flung head-first across time; Alex, sprawled across Lily; and the mechanical twitching of her small foot, suspended in the air, above the carnage, with only my living eye to see it. To watch her life ending, ebbing away through a prism of involuntary spasm — unheld, frightened, alone. And I — her father — looked on but did nothing ...

If excuses are intended to alleviate men of responsibility, then paralysis just isn't one, Tommy. Don't waste your breath.

So, to decoding brainwaves it is then; frequencies, phases, and amplitudes. A brain-computer interface? Sounds far-fetched. And, of course, then there's Carson. Bar my sitting up and pulling the plug myself, I think we're up against it with him. No matter.

FOUR

I opened my eyes last night, Tommy. Nobody saw. It was late. The corridors were quiet. I knew I could take a chance.

And I saw her. By Jesus, you're a lucky bastard! Just as I imagined. Slightly smaller, perhaps. You have no choice, brother. I entrust you with the two customary wishes of a dying man.

Customary? There are a million cultures out there, Tommy, I'm invoking the tradition of whichever one grants a dying man two wishes. Can we get on with it now?

Convince these bastards to let me go. And take this girl home with you.

These are my two wishes. If I could, I'd undertake both tasks myself. But we are reliant on you, unfortunately, my Prince. Dillydallying. Humming and hawing.

Did she not hold your hand at the bedside? Did she not pull your weeping head to her bony shoulder? The neon light is on, and it's flashing, Tommy. Follow the arrows. She feels more than sympathy for the brother of the vegetative patient, I assure you. She yearns for you in places that are strictly unprofessional.

FIVE

I hope this works, Tommy. So that I can give you the imprimatur. You or whoever needs it: the Croat or Carson.

Holy fuck, Tommy, this has to work!

I'm stuck. Hanging upside down, emptied of consequence and influence. Useless in the most significant way. The head-splitting silence. That fucking foot! And her toes, the creases of her heel. Her soft calf, clean and pale, wreaking of imminent dislocation. Her soul squirming from her toe like a tadpole.

SIX

The Croat says this technology will deliver. I hear her assuring everybody that it is slow but operational, and that she has convinced our nemesis, Carson. Should I be oddly disappointed by that?

So what now then? Must I continue to remember? Must I recall all this again each time those electrodes touch my scalp? To convince you all? Or is it done already? Am I recorded now? Should I recite this daily, just to be sure? To allow no ambiguity? Or should I be more direct, maybe?

I wish to die! I wish to die! I wish to die!

I am already dead with grief.

Was that enough? Will that do it?

SEVEN

These months have been forever. Please, Tommy. I endorse you as executioner. I assign you the duty of mercy ... Please ...

*

I sketch them in my mind, and so I have it that they are young. For starters. But the broad and depthless caricatures don't end there; they are conceited too. My contempt demands this ...

CHRISTOPHER MEREDITH

Somavox

1

... during which time he has the most vivid confidence, that he could not have composed less than from two to three hundred lines of poetry; if that indeed can be called composition in which all the images rose up before him as things, *with a parallel production of the correspondent expressions, without any sensation of consciousness or effort.* —S.T. Coleridge

The linguistic/physical barrier has been crossed with our new interactive system. —G. Pallander, MD Somavox Corp.

AFTER THE EQUIPMENT WAS INSTALLED and they'd taught her how to switch it on, she called him. She said, *Meet me by the fence between the trees and the moor.* They talked.

*

The fence was straight and went to the horizon. On one side of it there were tall trees and on the other side there were none. A woman came through the trees and stood by the fence, waiting. The sky was overcast and the grass on the treeless side was frosted white like a blank page. At last a man in a dark coat appeared. His body semaphored angular dark shapes as he picked his way along. He was out of breath. His face was fresh with the cold and he was quite young. She looked straight into his face and knew every part of it.

She greeted him and suddenly he saw her. Her face was nested in the vee of the upturned collar of her gray coat and the wings of her hair were closed on it. She was unclear against the downstrokes of the trees. Then he could see her eyes and the corner of her mouth smiling, and through a shift of hair the flash of a small earring.

"I like your earrings" he said.

Her hand went up and touched the lobe. "I didn't know I was wearing them" she said. The hand dropped. "Come on, you can cross by the stile."

He saw the stile nearby. It looked black against the whitened ground. He climbed over its A frame and she reached to steady him, but they didn't quite touch hands as he stepped down among the trees. His joints were stiff with cold.

"Let me look at you" she said, and she lifted her face close to his and panned her nose close to his upper lip. Her electricity would thaw him.

He stretched his nostrils to smell her, but the air was still very cold. It hurt his throat a little, and his eyes.

"You're young" she said.

"Well—"

She pushed a finger against his chest. "Arguing doesn't work."

"No. Then so are you." He touched her face. Some of the numbness melted from his fingers. "So. Where to?"

"Through the trees. Where else?" She turned from him suddenly, catching his hand and dragging him with her as she walked.

Her coat, he saw, had a fine herringbone pattern. The thin black ribs leant together in rows like indecipherable script.

The blank moorland fell away behind them as they walked and the trees closed in. No branches were so low as to get in their way. Some were lopped so the dark trunks were pothooked and seriffed.

"To my cabin!" She hammered up the words to hide a little embarrassment.

It was as she knew it would be. Dark timber, one door, one window, a chimney.

"Here" she said. She turned to look at him. "One door, one window, a chimney."

He looked past her as she spoke and the detail emerged from the quiet gloom. An earring flashed as she turned again and the door was opening. He felt the chill drop from the air as he reached the jamb. He looked at the tongue of hair on her shoulders.

She felt his arms come under hers and his hands close loosely on her breasts. Even through all the layers of clothes she could feel this. He pressed against her back and she turned her head so that his cold mouth brushed her cheek, found the edge of her mouth. She was laughing and he laughed too as they stumbled through the door. He tried to kiss her properly but their teeth collided as she tried to speak.

"Oh, I remember you."

And they laughed as they tumbled to sit on the threshold and he lay on her and they were still laughing. She put her hand on the back of his neck and tasted his mouth. His lips warmed and filled, and she wanted to hug him into the same space as her body, though she didn't say this, and they were struggling to get their clothes out of the way, like that, lying across the threshold, their legs outside on the frosty crunch of dead leaves, and her shoulders inside on the floorboards. The lower parts of their coats were parted and she could feel him hard against her as he lay between her legs and frotted at her skirt.

She pushed at the jambs with either hand so that they slid into the room.

"Do you feel how it's warmer?" she said.

"Yes. It's warm on my face and there's a fire in the hearth. Feel it on your face."

And she could. She turned her head to see the yellow flames. "Is it coal or wood?"

"Coal?" he said.

"Yes." And it was. She could see the welded architecture of the black lumps. "Like when I was a girl."

"I shut the door" he said, and he shut the door. "And I take off your shoes. Are they shoes or boots?"

"Oh—" she stretched out her arms, "—one of each."

He slid the squaretoed, sensible, brown shoe off her left foot. Then he unzipped the black boot on her right and slid it the length of her calf and off, held her leg and told her how he kissed it as he kissed it.

"Touch yourself" he said. He whispered it and drew back her

skirt and pulled her hand onto her knickers and while her fingertips kneaded there he kissed the length of her leg and then kissed her
moving knuckles.

She drew her hand away to open her coat and put her palm on
the crown of his head as he sucked at the material until it was wet
and he could feel the shape of her through it. She could feel his jaw
move as his tongue worked on her. She articulated her hips so that she
rolled against his mouth. He looked up along her body and saw her
head lying to one side, her eyes shut.

And he sat up and they fumbled at one another's clothes, sliding
the zeroes of buttons loose, unhooking clasps and buckles and slipping limbs free of sleeves. She slid his trousers away and saw and felt
how ready he was.

The bed was one she could just remember. Her family got rid
of it when she was five or six. Highframed and solid, with a foot-
board, manyblanketed. She drew him to it and sat. It was so high her
feet were off the ground. He kissed her and she could taste herself in
his mouth. Standing, he slid into her and she lay back and lifted her
knees.

He looked at the delta of dark hair, the white page of her skin.
She slid back and he climbed onto the bed, a bit awkwardly for all he
was so young, but kept inside her, and felt her clench and loosen on
him with the pulsing of his hips. He turned her so that he could press
his feet against the board.

She felt the thicket of his young hair against her face, pressed
her hands against his working back, wrapped her calves at the back of
his knees and felt herself open completely. As her eyes rolled up she
saw the windowpanes still hieroglyphed with frost.

A little later he said, "Let's have some wine." There were a bottle and
two glasses on a table by the bed. He laughed. "We'll leave the tea and
jigsaws till much later. Red or white?"

"Red."

He poured her a glass and she tasted it and it was warm as
blood.

"I'll have white" he said, and he poured it from the same bottle.

He kissed her and she could taste the crispness of it against the softness of the red. He dipped his fingertips into his glass and sprinkled droplets on her nipples so that they rose and then he tongued them clean. They put their glasses down and she let him touch her while he kissed her breasts. She knelt on the bed and took some droplets of red, and unpacking his head she scattered some wine there and closed her mouth over it. She smiled up at him and moved away, held him as if he were a microphone.

"Hello?" she said. "Am I receiving you? Come in."

She laughed and climbed onto him and watched their pubic hair meet and part as he slid into her and away and felt her breasts and hair hang against him. He turned her over and lay on her and he was tight inside her. She started to lose her sense of where she ended and he began, or the bed, or the cabin. The hieroglyphs on the windowpane had melted and streaked into exclamation marks.

"!" they said. "!!. !!!. !!!!"

2

The fact that there is no single-participant version gets rid of the nerd-factor. The system is purely collaborative. Disagreements are literally impossible. —G. Pallander, MD Somavox Corp.

Energy is eternal delight —William Blake

In the morning they put him in a chair by the window. He was dry and comfortable and still able to speak. When he had managed to operate the earpiece, he called her. He said, *Wake up, darling. Let's go to the sea.* They talked.

*

She felt him naked and wrapped to the curve of her back so that they made a double-ess. Under the heavy blankets he slid a hand around her hip and found her clitoris.

"Wake up, darling" he said.

She could feel him hardening against her buttocks and wanted to be full with him.

"Come in" she said, and she helped him and they lay cupped together on their sides. His fingertips on her at the front rubbed against him where he entered her.

The cabin was flooded with sunlight. It lit the ceiling as if it were reflected off mirrors, or water. He looked at how it described her shoulder and the long dune of her back.

"Tell me what's outside" he said.

She eased away from him and stood at the window. The frost was gone and the trees were rippling with leaves. There was birdsong.

"I think it's late spring" she said.

"So do I." He watched her as she leant against the sill and the spring light told him how she looked.

As he spoke she saw the sunlit clearings pulse a more intense green. On the pothook of a sawn branch a swallow hung like a comma.

He was out of bed and pressing lightly against her back. She rubbed her shoulders against his chest and turned to nuzzle his cheek.

"Well, I'm not cold anymore" he said.

She arched her back and leant forward and he crouched a little and entered her again. He watched as he closed on her and ran a hand up the knuckles of her back. It was veiled with fresh sweat and her hair clung to it.

"Too warm in fact."

She moved from him and turned and pressed to him. They saw that the grate was empty and clean.

"Let's go to the sea" he said.

They opened the door and stepped out and, after walking a few yards through the trees, were among the dunes.

He remembered the beach at the end of the headland. It clamped a disc of ocean in a sweeping C-shape. At the northern end were the mud cliffs and to the south the rocks where the snorkelling was good. He'd swum there years and years ago. The eastward sea beyond the bay was an immensity of liquefied light. The sun and the moon hung close together in the sky.

As they stood at the edge of this she pressed to him and saw how their shadows overlapped on the hatchwork of coarse grass. Again she wanted to press their bodies through one another into the same space, as she had on the threshold of the cabin, but she couldn't say this. Not quite.

"Today" she said, "today, I want to be you. Just for today."

He paused and looked at her and said, "Yes. Then I do too. Come on."

As they ran across a little stream and down onto the beach she felt her shoulders thicken and her muscles grow heavier. The water was tepid round her feet after the hot sand. She looked at her new, broad feet, felt the heavy purse of her testicles. She saw that he was running his hands over his new hips and breasts.

He looked up at her and laughed. His eyesight was stronger. The sea glittered in tiny sharp points. Her face was long and masculine. He touched it. She was tall. He pressed against her and heard her breathing. He wanted her inside him but couldn't say it yet.

They walked out into the sea and swam. His shorter legs were better for kicking, and he floated so well. He watched her dive among turtles and shoals of neon fish around the southern rocks. They flew over the strange landscape until the seabed fell away and there was nothing but depth under them, and then they let the rhythmic swell carry them back and northward to the mud cliffs.

They stood in the shallows there and he showed her what he'd done as a boy.

"Here" he said. He took a handful of the mud and smeared it on her chest, knelt and worked it round her penis and thighs. "This keeps the sun off."

"Is *that* what it's for?" she said, and she took some of it and smoothed it over his breasts, wrote her initials on his belly. She held him to her and palmed it across his buttocks. She felt herself harden against him, felt the weight and the tightening of it. She worked the muscle that moved it a little, as she'd felt men do to her.

He knew he was wet. He led her to the edge of the water and pulled her down onto the sand. He dug to make a hollow for his hips and, opening himself, drew her onto him. She felt the skin pull back along the shaft as she went in, and the way he clenched her. She dug her feet down into the sand and pushed.

"It's very clever how you do that" she said.

"You too" he said. "I don't know which of us is which." He put his hands on her buttocks as she tightened and relaxed.

She spread her arms across the sand so that their overlapping bodies made an ex and over her shoulder he watched the wheel of the sky. The color deepened and the stars came out. With his new eyes he saw them sharper than in childhood. Cassiopeia swung above the mud cliffs first as a double-you and then, as it revolved around the Pole star, an em.

"Why don't we get tired?" he said.

The stars flared and faded in time with their movement. Then the light held its intensity and he braced himself against her. The lights strengthened and grew, swelling and joining so that the whole sky whitened, blank as a sheet. He held his breath.

She felt how close he was and thought that she would burst inside him. Her toes clenched in the sand.

The whiteness spread until the cliffs and the headland and the rocks and the sea and they themselves were annihilated by it. Then she burst and emptied into him. The world refilled with colors, and the filmy thread of the Milky Way and an alphabet of constellations threw themselves across the sky.

Her weight slackened on him and she laughed. She moved away and touched him for a long time because she knew that he would be slower in coming down.

The sky over the sea was turning pale. Lying next to her, he touched his breast and ran the other hand through his pubic hair to rest a finger lightly on his clitoris and between his lips. As the sun was about to rise he felt the breast withering and hardening into muscle, the nipple retracting. The arm across his abdomen got heavier, the pudendum under his fingers swelling back into a penis and testicles. He felt his legs lengthening and coarse hair growing on them. While this happened he watched her breasts and hips swell, her flesh soften and her hair thicken. She put a hand to his face and stroked it.

He shivered. "Somebody's treading on my grave" he said. "I think we should go back."

And, though the sun was coming up, the air had chilled a little.

3

*This is more than a plaything. As it has no harmful effects, and partici-
pants need only be lucid, able to think and speak, even if only in a mur-
mur, it can have many beneficial functions. Gerontologists are currently
trialling its potential in palliative care.*

—G. Pallander, MD Somavox Corp.

Language is the incarnation of thought.   —Wordsworth

As soon as the assistants left her alone she pushed the jigsaw and her
cup aside. She didn't like them to hear her muttering. She switched
on the earpiece and called him. He was asleep at first, but eventually he woke and answered. After a while he remembered who she was.
He was slurring a little, but she could understand him. *Let's walk*, she
said. *Meet me in the trees.* They talked.

*

She was leaning against a tree, waiting. He had walked down off the
autumn-yellowed mountain into her forest and he was still a little
numb. She smiled.

"Hello, you" she said.

She was wearing a dark coat, its front open, and under it a yellow frock patterned with a fine black print. Pale patches of sunlight
washed across her.

"I like that yellow frock" he said. He was a little out of breath.
"I haven't seen you wear it in years."

She looked down at herself. "I didn't even realize I'd put this
one on" she said.

He kissed her. Her breathing was shallow and a little anxious.

"Are you all right?" she said.

"Yes. It's not so cold down here. Are you?"

"I'm always nervous at first when we meet. Let's walk."

He put his arm round her as they went. He could smell her hair,
her skin. "It's a funny thing" he said. "I felt half dead up there, but,
god, talking to you brings me to life." He felt his limbs loosen, the
old urgency.

"Do you remember this place?" she said.

They'd come to a stream. He stepped onto a large stone in the middle of it and pulled her on after him. They stood front to front in the middle of the stream.

"Yes" he said. He slid his arms under her coat, round her back and downwards over the flare of her buttocks. He thought of her, firm and packed away and waiting for him. "Alph. The sacred river. *L'origine du monde.*"

"Show-off" she said. She squeezed herself to his dark jacket. She wanted their trunks to fuse.

He stepped to the other bank and she followed.

Nearby was a place among the trees, full of dried dead leaves. Their chiselled shapes were effs and ees and curly jays. She pulled him down among them. His hand under her dress was cold, but it didn't matter.

"We lay here together once" he said. "Years ago when we were young."

"Yes." She undid his trousers and brought him to life. She straddled him with her face towards his feet and sucked him and rubbed herself against his face. He gathered her skirts away and pulled aside her pants so that he could tongue her and they rolled onto their sides and made an endless loop.

"I want to be in you" he said.

She slid her knickers off and sat astride him. "Let me do it" she said, and she worked on him with her dress spread across his lap.

He could feel her lips kneading round his thickness. "Yes, I remember" he said. "It's the same dress. I remember it."

She watched his face and touched herself where he went in. His hands were on her hips, tightening and relaxing in time with her. She smiled but he didn't smile back.

Above her the sky had clouded. He felt cold where she ground him against the leaves. Tiny flecks of ice were falling on him. He tried to sit up, to pull her trunk to his. They rolled onto their sides and hugged.

She felt him shivering a little. She was wound around him and he was still inside her. She held him tighter.

"We can go back into the cabin" she said. "'It's just here.'"

He looked, and the door was a few yards away. They got up and moved to the threshold. The door was stiff. He hugged her again.

"Do you know" she said, "do you know what I want sometimes when I'm holding you like this?"

He smiled. The door had opened a little and they were standing in the jamb, but the flecks of snow were blowing on his jacket. He rubbed his lips against the fine print on her yellow collar. "Oh, I can read you like a book."

"I want" she said, "I want to occupy the same space as you."

"Yes" he said. "I've felt that too. Yes."

They lay down on the threshold of the cabin and she squeezed against him. Their brows, noses, chins, slid through one another. He felt his torso ease through hers. It seemed to her that they were like two huge buildings, or cities, with their complications of floors and passageways, stairwells and liftshafts, the lacework of girders and fills of brick and concrete, and then the surges of electricity and fluids, the traffic and commerce of every day. Imagine all that thinning and becoming porous, and then these two universes interpenetrating, the stairwells from different buildings intertwining and joining, the skeletal architectures permeating one another and interlocking. The mechanical inhabitings of sex, the crude transformations on the beach were nothing to this, where the different-same energies whispered in the different-same channels. And he felt this too. All the space that matter is made of suddenly understood itself, and was generous, and let the other in. Their different grammars and lexicons didn't just blend into a creole. They atomized as they crossed and reconfigured. And once this had happened there could be no images, nothing to observe, only this new building, with nothing outside its own self-awareness and an apprehension of the marvellous.

And immediately some part of this new place started to fail. Images started to return of lights going out and pipework cooling, a sense of some shrivelled, hard thing disconnecting itself back into being.

She lay against him on the threshold. He didn't move. The snow fell in tiny pieces on his dark jacket. Eventually it would white him out. But for now it was a scattering, and it wasn't true, what they said about the flakes. They weren't all unique. Each was a word and they were identical.

"Yes" they said. "Yes. Yes."

DIEGO MARANI

The Man Who Missed Trains

AT THAT TIME, I WAS WORKING IN THE COFFEE BAR at the Ferrara train station. I ground coffee and poured grappa for people who left in clean jackets, tickets still fresh in their hands, and for people who'd just arrived, lost, frightened, still smelling of iron from the trains. I'd stare out the bar window at the hours going by on the station clock, and every hour had its trains, every train its faces, every face its coffee waiting on the zinc counter. There were empty hours, too, the saddest hours. That's when I noticed the humming refrigerator; and the cashier's smelly feet when he took off his shoes, with an expression like someone taking off his underwear; and the two tired flies sitting on the same salami sandwich. I've always felt intimidated by train stations but drawn to them as well, to that aura they have of provisional eternity. And when I left, I'd try to transform myself, to change my skin like a lizard, but I always knew I was camouflaging myself for the wrong place. I suffered in train stations, but I reveled in them, too, in their gratifying confusion. Maybe it's my fate to always take the train when I'm in love. When I'm lost in the memory of someone's face or I don't even know I'm in love yet—it's just a feeling. This is why I gladly accepted my position in the snack bar overlooking Track One: to see this miraculous, enchanting world close up and fool myself into thinking I could understand it, and so avoid it.

On hot summer afternoons, when the city swarmed to the beaches, I always took it as a point of pride to wander around by myself downtown, on the hot tar, along with the crazies and the drunks. I couldn't really tell them apart, and I found myself thinking that maybe drunkenness corrected for madness. So maybe more than one crazy person could regain his sanity for a short while with a couple of liters of Malvasia. He could choose the amount and type of wine according to the amount and type of mental illness. A slight neurosis might take a big bottle of Lambrusco. The guy digging around in the garbage cans, who smiled when I walked past, might easily clear his head with two bottles of Passito a day, taken before meals. The inverse was more complicated: correcting the impulses of the mentally healthy with neurasthenia therapy. So: a light dose of schizophrenia for someone too full of himself; or a little melancholia for pushy people. A great advance in psychiatry. Something to explore, and in my solitary days, I had all the time in the world. Now and then a motorcycle rumbled past and rattled the dazzling silence of the piazza. The trains slipped under the platform roof like enormous fish forced to rise from deep water. Crying, they ground to a halt with a screeching of brakes.

All train stations are women, you know, so it means something that we're always leaving one for the other. There are haughty, scornful stations, like the one in Trieste, accustomed to eccentric, international trains, or troop trains burdened with tragedy. They rarely give in, but when they do, it's for a regiment. And then there are matronly, big-breasted stations, like the one in Bologna, with the sensual, dirty embrace of an old whore. They'll give themselves to anyone, they're tried and true, but they never enjoy it. The Milan station's a plumed *signora* accustomed to every known perversion. You can do her with your clothes on, against a wall, grimacing slightly with disgust or pleasure—who can tell? The Florence station has long legs, and you'll need to court her a while before you can have her. She likes tilting trains: all flash and no substance. She knows she's beautiful, which spoils her charm. After you've had her, you say it wasn't all that great and you only remember the wrinkles. Vulgar, dirty-mouthed— the Ferrara station's a naive little bitch. It's easy enough to slip your hand between her thighs, but then she gives you that reproving stare. She's used to diesel trains, is scared of those high-speed, hard-snouted electric trains that pull onto Track Four late in the day. But she's still willing to do it with them out in the grass. It's beautiful leaving from some stations, arriving in others. Leaving Trieste is beautiful, the eastern light on your face. And arriving in Ferrara's beautiful, under the red summer sun, when it's too late to go any place else.

*

One June day, the direct train to Bologna had just left, the platform was empty, and I was putting glasses away out of the next-to-last dishwasher. The blue shadow of late day had already fallen over the station, though there was still a brief reflection of gold. Like every other evening at that time, the usual group lounged around near the end of Track One. Scattered figures sat against the baggage-storage wall, upper bodies in shadow, a row of legs in the sun, shifting slightly, like reeds waving alongside a canal. A pair of old-age pensioners, a worker laid off from Montedison, an education student who never made it through, and two of our bums-in-training. What I'm saying is that these guys were still one step away from being irredeemably out of luck. They weren't sleeping under cardboard yet, they didn't beg for a living, didn't keep to themselves, drunk, slung against some wall. They'd find some kind of shelter, a hot meal at a church or union soup kitchen, a pair of shoes when necessary, and some oddball to keep them company through the long hours of the day. But that afternoon there was a new shadow added to the mix. Someone distinguished, almost aristocratic. An imposing man of about fifty, in a Panama hat that he kept tapping as if to reassure himself it was still there. He wore an impeccable white linen suit and very shiny English shoes. Maybe he was traveling and had left his luggage somewhere while he asked for information. But there weren't any suitcases in the waiting room and the platform was empty, too, except for the trickle of water spilled from the geranium vases sitting on the ticket-office window ledge. Besides, no train had come in, and the next one wasn't due for almost an hour. I was curious, so I stood in the bar doorway and spied on the group. The man was listening to the veterans, laughing warmly with the others. When he spoke up, his voice was so polite, the rest of them grew silent. I didn't catch a word. But I could tell his companions deferred to him. From his manner, the way he moved his hands and his extreme politeness, he had to be a foreigner. The cashier was totally involved in gnawing his fingernails and staring at his heel, so I took the opportunity to go and sit on the low wall by the underpass to get a better look at this new arrival. The tracks shone in the sun. The shadow of a freight train licked the pavement. Insects filled the air, wheeling in the distance, over the dry brush along the canal. Soon my wait grew pointless. The group of men walked off, still chattering, toward the water tank. The men seemed almost invisible; they went unnoticed by the railroad police agent, the porter, and the street cleaner. They were already wandering in that secret orbit the evening saves for madmen, when she sweeps them away from this arid world for a moment's comfort. I couldn't follow them along that path, and so I regretfully abandoned my spot. I went back behind the counter. The cashier had dozed off. Head on his chest, roosting on his chair.

I filled the sugar bowl, put an empty bottle away, wiped the counter with a sponge. My mind wandered. I felt agitated, like I'd missed a date. Out the window, the piazza was empty, scorching hot. The hotel's rolling shutters were down. The last, forgotten bicycles, leaning against a post, sent long shadows across the asphalt. By the sidewalk, an orange bus was burning, still in full sun. The traffic lights were wasting their colors on an empty street. As I was taking in all this desolation, suddenly, there, in the first green grass by the highrise, a white silhouette glowed in the setting sun. He was alone, hands clasped in his lap, and he seemed lost in prayer, but once in a while, he'd look toward the station and wipe his forehead with the handkerchief under his hat. I went back behind the espresso machine, almost hiding from his gaze. The loudspeaker crackled loudly, the shadow from a train blocked the large station windows so you could just make out the faces of those dazzling forms beneath the columns. And right then, I glimpsed the man in white dart from the grass—his agility was startling—onto the gravel by the bike racks, and up the marble stairs. He emerged from the lobby and raced to the underpass tunnel just as the stationmaster sounded the final whistle on Track Four. The Venice express was leaving. The last doors slammed shut, and the few people saying goodbye pulled back to avoid the lime dust whirling up from the track pit. The train whistle blew, the switch joints banged against the rails with the soft thud of hot iron. A flash of light through dirty glass skipped across the bar walls as the man in white reemerged and was now running alongside the elusive train. He reached for a door handle, just brushed it with his finger, before it slipped away. His coattails flapped behind him like a cloak and filled with sunlight as he ran from column to column. He reached his highest speed, then his legs slowed, his heels clicking like hooves as he pulled to a halt. The last car swept away the one remaining shadow under the platform roof, and in a flash of red, it disappeared into the rusty scrap metal along the horizon. The man stopped at last, panting, and he turned around, smiled, doffed his hat, and took a deep bow. Out from the tunnel the group of bums emerged, silent at first, then clapping and shouting for joy.

Missing trains: this was the man in white's special skill. His business card to his new group of friends. Taking a train is automatic; anyone can do it. Nothing's required, you just show up on time, buy your ticket, and drink your coffee while you wait for the train to roll in. After you've found your seat in a car, every minute's exactly like the next. The departure's over before it begins. But missing a train is just one precise moment. Arrive a moment too soon or a moment too late, you've missed the point. A moment too soon, you haven't missed the train at all; a moment too late, the train's already gone. And you can't miss a train if it's already gone. Missing a train also means renouncing everything that could come with that train; it means sidestepping one life and choosing another. Every train's a journey, and every journey's a place, and we're never the same from one moment to the next. By letting the door handle slip away from his sincerely reaching fingers, the man in white became a juggler of possibilities: every train, like every pin, was different. What mattered was the gesture, the acrobatic move. Of course, not all trains were equal. Missing the local for Codigoro wasn't the same as missing the intercity for Udine. But the man in white missed each and every train with the same flair, the same love.

He went by the name of Zlatko and said he was Croatian. But he spoke Italian with a Hispanic accent, and that slight bravado in his eyes made you think of a sharp South American. His proud step, the way he carried himself, reminded me of someone astride a horse. Something had caused him to dismount; someone had driven him from the saddle. Maybe this was the reason he ran after trains. During his few months at the Ferrara station, he gave those of us who knew him the useless courage not to hesitate, to go ahead and chase after everything we wanted. In the night hours, when the bar was closed, instead of going home, I stayed with the bums to watch Zlatko miss the best trains. Like the night express to Lecce, which arrived with gaping windows, loaded with sleep and sweat. Zlatko missed that one with a delicate run almost on tip-toe. It was an aching scene on sheer, moon-lit nights, all our own, a scene that always moved us to tears. Crowded together in the dark, against the freight-yard wall. Someone would light a cigarette, and the orange embers were lanterns in the night, stars that, instead of guiding us, made us feel ever more lost. For Zlatko, the hardest thing of all was missing late trains, those enormous, dusty trains returning from the south, ripped apart, then put back together again, in depot after depot, with detached cars from dead-end tracks: flat-beds, tank wagons, other kinds of freight cars. Impossible to figure out when they arrived. And the announcements over the loudspeaker didn't help at all. The minutes kept ticking off like liters of gas into a bottomless tank. Those trains drew special-event crowds. Bums came all the way from Bologna to see Zlatko, off in the distance, walking like a gunslinger along the paths by the high-rise. He was listening, waiting. To the bums, pondering that wait was crucial — a demon had to be spurring him on. And then, at the exact right moment, Zlatko flung himself at the station and popped onto the track with the first shifting of rods. His white form was puffed-up with wind, and even the train, humiliated at being late, took some pride in the chase. It whistled in the night, iron screaming, tracks writhing, straining to be missed, to escape that blackmailing time-table forever.

No doubt about it: the most fascinating train that went through the Ferrara station was the weekly 4:32 Bratislava express. It wreaked havoc with every schedule, could even arrive in the early afternoon. The train's dusty form slipped in alongside the locals, full of students, and the brown diesel going to Suzarra-Mantua, as if to say, "What do *you* know about travel?" In order to miss that train, Zlatko started preparing the day before, right when the train left Bratislava. I watched him walking down the tracks, toward Pontelagoscuro, watched him stretch out on a scrap heap and study the sky. Up there in his white clothes, surrounded by filth, he looked like an angel just taking a breather. He sniffed the air; he could even make predictions on the wind. The color of the horizon, the rising dust, the drifting noise, it all spoke of his train, of the forces working against him, or in his favor. Zlatko could feel it in his gut, the exact moment among thousands when that train would pull away from the platform and plunge into the vortex of moving things. Once he'd made his calculations, he'd walk back toward the station, climb over the wire fence behind the bike racks, and fall asleep on a park bench in the gardens by the high-rise. Seeing him lying there like a corpse, it was hard to believe he'd ever rise again. Certainly his spirit wasn't there: it had gone someplace else for shelter, some other body, closer to warm, pulsing life. Zlatko woke when it was time, and he approached the station, studying the enormous hands of the clock over the entranceway. Then he went back to the gardens, to prepare himself for a running start. The perfect, controlled running start that always gave us the shivers.

By the end of August, his white suit was a rag. But he still wore it with the same elegance, paid no attention to the missing elbows, the frayed knees. His jacket, stiff and dirty, hung on him more like armor than clothing. His heels had worn through the hem of his trousers so his pant legs dragged along the ground in fringy clumps, like muddy feathers. But, every time, Zlatko still bowed with dignity, his crushed Panama hat turned to the joyful crowd.

No one knew where he went when he left the station. Not that he was trying to hide or slip off. He'd just put one foot in front of the other, and walk away. And, though he never bothered explaining, it was clear some hours weren't important, weren't worth worrying over. Someone figured he had to have a secret life, maybe there was even some woman downtown putting him up in her luxury apartment. But I had a hard time seeing him sprawled out on a horsehair couch, surrounded by crinoline and china, entertaining shriveled former beauties just for a place to stay. Zlatko would never be satisfied with so little. He'd have to get more from a strange torture like that. It was just by accident that I discovered his refuge. On Sundays, though the landscape was dismal, I often walked along the Ferrara canal, toward the Pontelagoscuro factories. By the dark warehouses and the corrugated-metal sheds, next to some hidden vegetable plots, I'd found a field full of wrecked cars, and I enjoyed going out there and taking a look around. That's where I saw Zlatko—stepping out of a car half-sunk in dried mud. I was sitting on the bank, tossing stones into the water. When we saw each other, I got to my feet, almost apologizing for the intrusion. Like always, he tapped his hat in salute, and then he jumped down and walked off, white as a seagull against the abandoned cars. And that gloomy place suddenly felt cozy. I went back again, but avoided the cars. I pretended to be out for a walk, and I stayed close to the canal. Zlatko understood this was my way of paying my respects, and maybe he was doing the same when we saw each other and he tipped his hat and gave me one of his little bows. That man in rags, surrounded by rusty cars, sparked a sadness in me that was frightening, but he remained unblemished, clean. He was in this world without touching it, without dirtying himself, because he didn't really live here; he lived someplace else, in the time to come, when he'd plunge into the game.

And maybe that's where he returned to when he disappeared down the tracks in the liquid light of a September afternoon. But these days no one wants to recall the eerie mystery of the 754 Crotone express that arrived in Ferrara twenty years too late.

By midmorning, we knew something had happened. The stationmaster was shut up in the control room with two plainclothes officers in dark glasses. All the railroad workers were waiting outside. They paced in front of the door, hands in their pockets, caps pulled down low. Then we heard a siren. A blue car squealed to a halt on Via San Giacomo, by the freight yard, and two men in dark glasses popped out, faces stiff as their collars. Next came the *carabinieri*. With submachine guns and bulletproof vests. They quietly assembled by the newspaper kiosk. The NCOs smoked and whispered together. When the stationmaster threw open the control-room door, he had big sweat stains under his arms. He shouted a name, and a worker came running. The two guys in dark glasses ordered some beer and *panini*, then went back inside. At one o'clock, still nothing. The *carabinieri* took off their helmets and lowered their guns. They kept staring at the clock. The first commuters came into the station on the old, wooden locals, climbed down, sweaty and tired, saw all the khaki uniforms and scurried off. They were cautious as they crossed the piazza and plucked their bikes one by one from the tangle at the bike racks. Finally, the word was out. The 754 Crotone express, due at 12:02 AM, had disappeared.

"Vanished without a trace," said the railroad worker who'd leaked the news, and then he shrugged. "At first they thought it was terrorists," he said, popping up at the window. "But terrorists can't just make a train disappear—the most they can do is blow it to smithereens!"

The cashier, feeling very emotional, put his shoes back on. With that crowd, the bar quickly ran out of supplies. *Panini, biscotti, gelato,* drinks—all gone—the only thing left was the liquor. We even sold the ancient, dried chocolates in the window, which had melted then hardened a thousand times; with the window shelves completely empty, the light was different in the room. Long hours passed, and no one spoke. By midafternoon, we heard a helicopter roaring overhead.

The same railroad worker ran into the bar and pointed at the ceiling with his cap: "They're even searching from the sky! But there's nothing. Christ! Four guys I work with are on that train!" He shook his head. In that voice, you could hear the relief of someone who'd escaped disaster, but there was guilty fear as well; the fear of falling victim to something even worse. He slammed one grappa after another. We couldn't pour them fast enough. He leaned on the bar, staring blankly, waiting with us to see what had happened. The *carabinieri* began inspecting the tracks. They wandered around, calling to one another under the burning sun. The door to the control room opened again, and all the railroad workers turned to see. The stationmaster was making his way through, hands raised. He stared straight ahead while he followed the two men in dark glasses. They crossed the lobby and entered the bar. They were looking for me. I could see it in the faces of the railroad workers in the window.

"You know where to find that man?" the stationmaster asked in a strangled voice. I didn't relish the idea of revealing Zlatko's hideout to that bullying crowd. But I didn't seem to have a choice.

"I can find him," I said.

"Okay. Hurry—come with me!"

The stationmaster grabbed my arm and walked me to a blue car. All the railroad workers followed. They crowded around the car as the doors slammed shut. Others noticed: soldiers, and children I'd never seen before out gathering cigarette butts and bottle caps. I saw their bland faces reflected in my escorts' dark glasses. The *carabinieri* pushed the crowd away. We sped off, siren screaming, toward Viale Po. When we reached the field of wrecked cars, we got out and walked down to the canal. I went to the car on my own.

"They need you," I shouted into the wreckage, my hand over my eyes to block the sun. A few seconds later, Zlatko poked his head out and stared at me. Then he disappeared. He came out the other side: he'd gone for his hat. I set off, and he followed.

There was chaos at the station. The *carabinieri* were straining to hold back the crowd that wanted to know about the train. "Indefinitely late" was up on the arrival board. At the ticket windows, the clerks held up their hands and told people to ask at the control center. But the door to that office was bolted shut, with *carabinieri* standing guard. The stationmaster had us come inside. Behind his desk, the little man waved his hands around as he gave out orders and answered the constantly ringing phones. He hung up and marched over to us, took Zlatko by the arm and walked him to the window. I stayed off to the side, with the men in dark glasses. They could look anywhere they pleased behind their black lenses. I didn't know where to look, so I concentrated on the fan that covered the room in three swings. Its final movement raised a few hairs on the back of the stationmaster's neck. They stayed that way, half up, rigid, like grass sprayed with insecticide. The sun through the poplar leaves sent a watery reflection up the wall. It almost felt like the sea was outside; I could almost hear it. Zlatko listened very seriously to what the stationmaster told him. He straightened his filthy jacket, pulled his cuffs out, smoothed his sweaty hair beneath his Panama hat, then left the office without a word and slowly lowered himself onto the tracks. Hands on his hips, he looked into the distance, as if he'd spotted something. The worried stationmaster was right behind him. For the first time, I studied the stationmaster. He wasn't fat, but his individual body parts seemed swollen. Some kind of liquid seemed to be festering under his skin.

As soon as he wiped his face with his handkerchief, it was shining wet again. He breathed through his mouth in short, wet bursts, from his belly instead of his chest. Zlatko stood straddling a railroad tie.

"You see, physics teaches us that time varies everywhere. There's our time, but there are also many others. And these times can be a lot faster or a lot slower. The proof is in the universe's varying stages of evolution. There are galaxies far ahead of us in the flow of time and others far behind us. Every part of the universe has its own rhythm as it moves toward the end of all time, toward (if you believe in God) what's called eternity. Sometimes, as they're traveling, two times will collide, like two bodies in space. A direct hit can cause real catastrophe. If they just graze each other, then there might be a switch, something might be pushed from its own time into another. That's probably what happened to your train."

The stationmaster stood there listening and rubbing his neck with his handkerchief. His eyes flashed with annoyance. He frowned, and stuck his nose in the air like he had a sudden, unreachable itch. Zlatko watched him in silence. He had the expression of someone who was used to others not believing him; he hadn't really wanted to talk, wasn't interested in persuading anyone else. Sweat beaded slowly down his face, and I tried to see where it landed.

"So—what now?" the stationmaster snapped, even more annoyed.

Zlatko slowly spread his arms wide, his shadow a dark puddle in the burning gravel.

"Time is like a flame. You stand too close, you get burned. If I were you, I'd let it go."

The stationmaster started turning purple and wheezing like he had asthma; then he broke out coughing. He almost seemed to be laughing. "I don't want to hear it!" he sputtered. "I didn't send for you to hear this nonsense—you have to help me!"

"I can try to get to the time where your train wound up. I just hope it's not a super-fast time."

"Why? What could happen?" The stationmaster's voice was insistent.

"In a faster time, our years might be days, or maybe hours, or even minutes. If that happened, then hardly anyone on that train would survive the return trip. As soon as they stepped off the train, stepped into our time, they'd be hit by old age. The minutes and hours of that other time would turn to what they are here: years, decades."

"How can you be so sure?" the stationmaster asked, still unwilling to accept Zlatko's theories, which seemed like lies.

"Nothing's sure. I don't even know if I can get back. You see, it's like jumping between two boats. If the boats are too far apart, you fall right in the water."

"But there's still some hope, some chance!" the stationmaster insisted. He was wadding his handkerchief into a ball.

"Let's just hope the 754 express wound up in a slower time. Then the people getting off the train won't realize anything's happened, and they won't believe us even if we tell them." Zlatko gave the stationmaster a look that the official didn't seem to understand. Without another word, Zlatko started down the tracks.

"What are you doing? Where are you going?" the stationmaster shouted, waving his handkerchief like a red signal.

"If you must know," Zlatko answered patiently, raising his hand, "I'm going to look for that train."

"And when will you bring it back?"

Zlatko turned, started walking backward. "That depends on where the train wound up. It might take me an hour, it might take me twenty years. Times might meet, but they don't mix, and if your train's in a faster time that's equivalent to a year in our time, it'll be in limbo a year, where time has stopped, before it can get back here. The only thing I can do is try and get it going again." He said this without emotion. Suddenly, he seemed exhausted. He looked up at the sky, nodded briefly, and pulled his hat down on his head. Then he held his hands out, imploring, tired. "But why are you so insistent, anyway? Those people are lost. If they come back alive, they'll just go insane."

"You bring that train back!" the stationmaster shouted, standing on tiptoe. "No matter what—you hear me!"

Zlatko stood there. He drew his hand across his mouth, as if trying to gather his courage. His eyes rolled back in his head. Without another word, he walked off in long strides, and the air grew electric around him. The sky, the rocks, his clothing: everything was blinding white. That was the last time I ever saw him. A light dust started to fall. Not rain, not moisture. Then I knew: it was that other time whisking by. A chasm we couldn't see had opened beneath our feet. We felt its cold presence. A buzzing filled my head. I squinted. The stationmaster was shielding his eyes. Lightning struck, a smoky flash. But it was hard to tell where. There was no one left on the tracks. We fled, stumbled, ran into each other. We shouted his name. The only answer came from the silent warehouse windows, the blowing field stubble, the old rusty water tank. The stationmaster gave me a stunned look. He dug for his handkerchief in the wrong pocket, spun all around, muttering: "Impossible! You saw it—impossible!"

A low, heavy wind rolled in from the countryside and rose up to our hips, like stagnant water. The September sun grew dark, seemed almost on the verge of disintegrating. My head reeled. The stationmaster, arms wide, whirled faster and faster before my eyes, a spinning shaft of light. I was surprised he didn't scream. A *carabiniere* lifted me up by the armpits. The stationmaster was now sitting on the platform, head drooping over his belly. He didn't dare look back toward the track, at that dark wall of a crowd that stood there waiting.

In the days that followed, the *carabinieri* and the soldiers scoured the tracks and every meter of the countryside up to Poggiorenatico, and even along the banks of the Reno River. But all in vain. There was no sign of Zlatko anywhere. Police jeeps, surrounded by sandbags, were positioned on the piazza in front of the station. A small military camp grew up along the canal fence and eventually became a permanent fixture. At the end of the summer, new soldiers arrived. They moved the jeeps to cut the grass that had sprouted up all around them. Metal sheds replaced the tents. On winter nights, the sheet metal hummed with a slashing wind we'd never heard before. It was an evil howl, like a faraway scream from the river.

No one heard anything more about the 754 express. The city didn't want to remember and stopped talking about it. As to the rest, who can say for sure what really happened? The stationmaster was transferred to a different city, the soldiers and *carabinieri* went back to their barracks, and their sheds were just a rusty stain on the gravel.

But those of us who were Zlatko's friends, we couldn't forget. In the afternoons at the end of summer, drawn by a secret memory, we met at the end of the platform and scanned the horizon. We could feel it, Zlatko's presence, just a few meters away, in the place he'd disappeared that September afternoon. We could feel him walking past, and we thought we could see his white form in the shadow, chasing an invisible train.

Today, it's been twenty years; today, Zlatko's predictions came true. Once again, sirens were heard throughout the city. The *carabinieri* and ambulances came, and more blue cars and men in dark glasses. But there was no point. There's nothing left to do now. It was a terrible sight. I saw it for myself: the passengers stepped off the 754 express, which appeared in the station like a dream. The oldest crumpled and crackled like leaves in a fire, leaving only a pile of dust on the platform. Others were suddenly covered in wrinkles, like cracked plaster. Their flesh melted off them, and they stared in horror at hands that were no longer their own. Right before our eyes, the children were growing, exploding out of their tiny clothes suddenly turned to rags. Arms and legs swelled like monstrous flowers. Faces were clay masks that an invisible hand endlessly molded until they froze into stunned grimaces. People were crying, giving their last death rattle, or writhing as if swallowed up in invisible flames. Then the soldiers came. They pushed us out of the way, their shouting mixed with the horrible cries of the passengers. And they couldn't take another step; they stood paralyzed on the platform, hardly able to believe what they were seeing. Then the soldiers pushed the passengers into ambulances. Someone, gripping his submachine gun, went back and collected all the clothing on the ground; then he kicked the greasy dust away with his boots.

I hid between the tracks, waiting until the sirens grew faint. I was the only one left. Zlatko's terrified friends had all run off. My heart pounding in my head, I climbed on the train. I wanted to call out, but my voice was gone. I looked in every compartment, at all the abandoned luggage, the drinks no longer for sale, the old-fashioned shoes, the twenty-year-old papers. With a knot in my stomach, I even dug around in some piles of dusty clothes, hoping—terrified—I'd find a white linen suit, an old, beat-up Panama hat.

I haven't worked at the bar in the station for a long time. The cashier owns it now, and he sneers when he sees me stretched out under the freight-yard roof. During the day, I slip behind the grain cars to sleep. But at night I lie on the platform and watch the trains roll by. I see the light, then wait for the whistle, and I figure the time it takes the train to arrive by my heartbeat. Sometimes I used to chase them, like Zlatko. I'd stretch out in the grass, sniff the air for the right moment, and study the old clock on the station wall like a star in the desert. But these days, trains don't have door handles, they're sleek as torpedoes, the windows don't open, and no one looks out anymore, laughing or crying. They're convoys of washing machines with blind windows, and they don't go anywhere at all. And so I sit and wait for the day to come when I'll be swallowed up in that chasm like Zlatko, and I'll escape somewhere far away from this time without poetry.

TRANSLATED FROM ITALIAN
BY ELIZABETH HARRIS

EDY POPPY

Dungeness

HARDLY ANYONE USED TO NOTICE HIM; it was as if he didn't exist. The few people who did speak to him quickly forgot about him, forgot his name and failed to invite him to parties. Neither did he draw much attention to himself. When he went to his café, he usually sat in a corner or behind things. Hidden amongst the sounds of others, he listened to his own thoughts, to his pulse, to his heart, to the slow rhythms of life. He pinched his arm without feeling anything. The chairs were soft, so he often remained seated, submerged. The stuffiness of the air, the dimness of the lighting, the flowered curtains, which were drawn even in the middle of the day—all of this was like a warm duvet that he could pull over himself. And when the light from outdoors penetrated through a gap in the curtains, he took hold of his chair, moved it back and forth, like a dancer almost, to secure his place in the shadow.

But one day the corners are filled up with others. He stands in the doorway, looks around in despair, meets a gaze that blinds him. Coincidence, he thinks, because he can't believe that anyone could look at him on purpose. He wants to leave. He stands there, wavering. Hesitates. Still, it feels as if the wind pushes him inside. He sits down at a table in the middle of the room. Looks inward, closes his eyes. Waits. Until his hair grows out, long and shaggy, and covers them up.

With this long, somewhat greasy hair he no longer seems so anonymous. When he opens his eyes again, there are many people seated around the table with him. He pinches his arm. It hurts. He acquires an expression, an impression, of being someone. It gives him courage. He pinches his arm again. The bruises form pretty patterns on his pale upper arms.

Summer, in a park:

He notices her because she noticed him. He observes that she is observing him. Backlit. He squints so that his eyes are almost completely hidden behind his eyelids, then he stands in the shade of a tree. She approaches him in an indiscreet, obvious, and insistent manner that he is not used to but that he likes. He says his name many times, says it to her and hopes that she won't leave without remembering it. She nods in recognition, as if supposedly she had heard it before. She comes closer; she is also in the shade now. He can feel the hair standing up on her arms, her breath on his cheek. When he looks at her, it's as if he is blinded by snow, his eyes large and vacant, like winter.

Then he tries to relax, to avert his eyes. Thinks that she is beautiful, that she emanates something bordering on depressiveness, in spite of her blonde, almost white hair and skin. She looks albino. He wants to say something to her, but doesn't know what, or how. He is not used to being listened to, but her insecurity makes him feel more secure. She wants to know more about him. Instead, he tries to describe her.

"You are thin in a way that doesn't make you look skinny," he whispers into her ear. His voice has an unusual quality to it, as if he's ashamed of himself.

She listens. She doesn't want to miss anything. About herself.

"Your cheekbones are very prominent and form a crooked line running down to your mouth," he continues.

She smiles. She looks as if she is crying when she smiles, he thinks: beautiful, bemused, bewildering. He takes her in his arms and holds her tightly. They both have thin skin, almost transparent, so the blood vessels are visible. He doesn't feel comfortable with so much contact, so quickly. He wants to crush every single bone in her body. It's a disgusting thought that doesn't sit well with him. He immediately releases his grasp.

She opens her mouth to say something. He holds his breath.

"What do eyes look like that have been blinded by snow?"

"White."

"What does a person look like who has been blinded by love?"

"Lonesome."

"How does it feel to be blind?"

"Black."

"Is it dangerous to stare at the sun for too long?"

"It makes your eyes hurt."

"Is it dangerous to lie in the sun for too long?"

"It damages the skin, making it age more quickly. But for everything else the sun is a life-giving blessing that makes things grow."

They look at each other in astonishment. He summons up his courage and kisses her. She retreats into herself. He follows. She tells him that she is too weak to have her own opinions. That she goes from relationship to relationship and stays with the person who desires her most. For the moment, that's him, she says. He nods. She gives him her hand, or is it he who takes hers? They are a bit unsure about that. They stand there with sweaty palms and squeeze each other so hard that their blood almost stops circulating. It's as if they each want to keep the other from slipping away.

He doesn't know exactly where they are going, but all the same he is the one leading the way. He takes her into a narrow and twisted street. Several times he stumbles a bit, as if the cobblestones had set out to trip him. She smiles a vague smile. With her eyes. And he laughs back guardedly with his own.

Instinctively, without really meaning to, he brings her directly to his local café. He stands outside and wonders whether they should enter. A cat runs past them, hisses, and disappears into an alleyway. He loses focus for a moment; his knees buckle, as does his courage. He releases the door knob. Doubtfully, he leads her along, onward, past empty benches, deserted cemeteries, down traffic-congested streets. Searching, yearning for a hiding place, an alley. He wants this walk to last. He almost forgets where they are. She isn't paying attention to where they are going; instead she stares at the sun without blinking, as if she had eyes of glass.

She asks: "What does a person look like after love-making?"

"Red," he answers, pushes her up against a wall and penetrates her.

When a tomcat fucks a she-cat, his member cuts her open like a knife. It is a painful experience which ends in a violent battle. Cats howling like infants in the night is an example of this: of lust that has soured.

The city:

As soon as she opens the window, the pollution and the noise over-whelm her—cars honking, braking, crashing sometimes. She squints before this artifice: neon lights, car lights, street lights. It's not prop-erly dark outside, even though it's late. She misses the inky darkness that is found only outside of densely populated places, where the cit-ies cease to be cities. Another kind of loneliness, perhaps. Outside the window people cross the street without looking, go home together without a second thought, rush away. That's also how she sees him: every morning and every night, he comes and goes, as if he were im-prisoned by time. And in a strange way, she feels imprisoned by him.

She is home alone in his flat. It's on the third floor of an old, yellow block. She doesn't listen to music, reads no books, doesn't turn on the television.

She closes the window. His flat is full of antiquated things. In the living room there are candlesticks on all the tables, on the chests of drawers, the windowsills, with hardened candle wax dripping all the way down to the floor. The walls in the hallway are decorated with sun-bleached photographs from the childhoods of strangers. She walks by several times without stopping, looking up cautiously. Then she tears them all down, picks off tape, blu-tack and thumbtacks. She gathers the photographs together in a pile and shuffles them. Lays them out on the carpet, one by one. Studies them. A photo of a young boy on a swing catches her attention. The boy has been col-ored in with auburn hair and blue knickerbockers, but the landscape behind him remains black and white. Mud and ocean. A flat, endless landscape. She goes to get a pair of scissors. Cuts the boy out. Gets a magnifying glass. Studies the skyline. She is unable to find a single knoll or mound. The placename is on the back of the photograph. She takes the atlas down from the bookshelf and looks under D, for Dungeness.

Then she throws herself down into the cracked leather chair with a back resembling a beetle. Her skin sticks to it. It gives her goose bumps. Sometimes she thinks that his things are more alive than she is; they give her an uncomfortable sense of being superflu-ous. Every once in a while she has the feeling that the rooms are about to contract, enfold and suffocate her. She gets up from the chair, hurries into the kitchen and knocks back a glass of water. On the tiny shelf above the kitchen sink sit two porcelain dolls, naked; their blue eyes, white socks and black shoes have been painted on. He found them at the same flea market where he found the photographs and the atlas—where he found the cracked leather chair, where he found almost everything in this flat—and brought them home with him. She was the one who discovered the teeny-tiny swastikas afterwards, hidden beneath their synthetic blond hair. It's as if the dolls stare out into the emptiness without noticing her, as if she didn't exist.

It happens that she also stares through him, past him. Perhaps she's in the process of forgetting it: two people who must have felt something for each other, how they experienced the first day and many days after that. Perhaps she's in the process of forgetting that she knew about him before they met, noticed him before they made eye contact, spoke about him before she spoke with him. When he'd told her his name, she pretended that she'd never heard it before.

The city:
One day she isn't there. One of his photographs is lying on the kitchen table, with a hole in the middle. Only the dismal, flat surrounding landscape remains. And this note from her:

I have gone to Dungeness. Back soon to get you.

He walks around in the flat. Naked. Confused. Thinks about this word: Dungeness. The photographs in the hallway have been re-arranged, shuffled. He catches sight of himself in the mirror. An old, baroque mirror that distorts his appearance.

With his hair in his face he doesn't seem to be quite awake. He rolls his eyes back until they almost disappear into his skull and only the whites are visible. Walks around the flat as if he were blind, bumps into things that he usually avoids, rehearsing a route.

It's been a long time since he was alone in the flat. He doesn't really know how to handle so many feelings without having her nearby. He collects objects that he believes could make her smile, wants to make things nice for her. Hangs up a painting of an elk over the bed. Finds a knife, begins scraping the dried candle wax off the floor, off the tables and the windowsills. He plans to wash the windows, the bathroom, clean up the kitchen. But then suddenly he stops before her green knee socks, thrown into a corner. He picks them up and discovers other things, such as her polka-dotted skirt on the cracked leather chair. Wherever he goes he finds traces of her: a bowl of blueberries on the nightstand, a dirty pair of knickers in the bathroom, soiled sanitary napkins in the dustbin, white hair in the sink. It's not much, but it makes him happy.

He puts down the knife. He wants the flat to be the same as it was when she left it, so that when she returns, it will look as if she's never been away. He goes into the bedroom, takes down the elk painting and puts it in the closet. He opens the refrigerator door and closes it again. His feet are cold. He takes a hot shower, but forgets to dry himself off. Then he gets dressed, in clothing that's a bit too tight, a bit too short, but which suits his state of mind. He has been alone in the flat for long enough now.

The city:
When she comes back, she opens all the windows. The exhaust fumes and the noise of the city don't bother her as much anymore, she says. It's worse in the flat. It feels claustrophobic. She complains about the dust in all the nooks and crannies. Asks why he hasn't cleaned things up a little while she was away. He replies that he could have, but he was busy with other, more important things. She doesn't ask what, looks out of the window instead, absorbed by her own thoughts. It is overcast and the sky is without stars. As always. Dismal.

She attempts to describe the place where she has been.

"It was beautiful in an unconventional, almost unappetizing way," she explains.

He feels that the shadows outside affect her, that she has been a bit extinguished, internally. But he doesn't complain. He likes her way of being. A little dark, like the sky in polluted cities. He tries to get her attention. Stands in front of the window and asks her to continue.

"The ocean was far away because of the low tide," she explains. "I had to walk through the mud forever before reaching the water. I liked the way my feet sank down into the mud, soiling me. Everything seemed silvery in the piercing light, making my eyes sensitive and attentive, making me appreciate things that I usually ignore."

She laughs without being aware of it. Continues.

"There were boats stranded in the gardens and the houses slanted sideways from the wind. In some of them there were so many holes that you could see right through the walls, to the flat and endless landscape that continued on the other side. A tiny little train ran across this countryside, making a lot of noise and pumping thick smoke out of the smokestack. A nuclear power plant loomed large in the background."

She tells him that this is the place where she wants to live. That she likes the impact the surroundings have on her. Emotionally. That if he still desires her, then he must go there with her.

He closes the window, draws the curtains. She is about to say something else, but he holds a finger up in front of her lips. They remain standing like this for a while, in silence. She waits for an answer from him that doesn't come. Instead he tears her clothes off. They remain lying in a heap on the floor. Then he lifts her up, carries her into the bathroom and puts her down on the porcelain sink with yellowish-brown edges and white hairs in the drain. He doesn't wait for her to spread her legs, but penetrates her immediately. They are released now. The words. He whispers some of them into her ear.

The next day they eat breakfast together for the first time in ages. He boils eggs and makes coffee. She sits in the kitchen wrapped up in a quilt, white hair dishevelled. It seems as if she is already looking forward to it, he thinks, and feels a mild sense of dread. He pours coffee into their cups. Then he slices off the top of his egg. It is so hard-boiled that it's almost green. He looks at the clock many times. Puts his half-empty coffee cup down in the basin, puts on his shoes in the hallway and runs out. He must do it. He must do it. He must quit his job.

The city:

He hurries home. As he is taking off his shoes in the hallway, he hears a strange laughter. She is sitting in the living room with another man. On the table is a half-eaten cheesecake and tea. The candles are also lit. She goes to get another plate and cuts him a piece of cake. A few blueberries fall off the top. She picks them up from his plate and puts them in her mouth. Then she tells him that the stranger is an old friend. He notices a tenderness in her voice and in the gestures of the stranger. He immediately thinks that the stranger is, instead, an old lover. His palms start sweating. He gets to his feet to greet him. The man's hand is so large and powerful that his own virtually disappears within it. They exchange names, but he is too nervous to remember it afterwards. The stranger says that he likes it here. He is sitting, comfortably submerged in the cracked leather chair, lighting cigarette after cigarette. He says if everyone agrees, he would like to move in after they have moved out.

Interlude:

They pack. When she is going through the things in the closet, she finds the elk painting. She wonders why he hasn't hung it up. She rolls it up in silk paper, but leaves it behind. Then she goes into the living room and gets the antique candlesticks, ties them together with stockings and t-shirts and places them among their things. She asks him to help with the cracked leather chair. He looks at her as if she is mad, but she nods resolutely.

But apart from this, they take almost nothing with them. She says that they're not meant to stay together for very long, that she will leave him the minute his desire has waned. She decided this a long time ago. He looks at her in astonishment. Shocked, almost. Because he both loves her and desires her. He has proven this. But he says nothing.

She draws a breath, listens to the sounds outside, cars; to the sounds inside of her, forlorn. Then she closes the windows. Says that she is looking forward to opening them again, somewhere else. That she can hardly wait. He thinks that sounds nice. Goes and gets the gramophone and all of the vinyl records that he bought at the flea market. She claims that they won't need music by the sea, that they can listen to the waves instead, to the ebbs and flows of nature. He packs them all the same.

She checks the rooms one last time. Thinks about all of the

hours, days, months. A blurry image. Because all this time she has been longing for something else with him. She looks at the pair of dolls on the little kitchen shelf. Puts them in her handbag. They leave.

Displacement:

There are almost no places available on the train. They have squeezed their baggage into their reserved seats. They stand outside, in the gangway. In the compartment, through a tiny gap in the curtains, he notices a couple. The man has one hand down the Asian woman's beige Bermuda shorts and is moving it violently between her thighs. She leans her head back in pleasure and catches sight of him. Her slanted eyes are shameless, he thinks, for her gaze does not waver. He, on the other hand, turns away, looks instead into the light, round, wide-open eyes that he knows so well. Together they look out of the train window and admire the stark landscape.

They get off the train. She carries the suitcases and the rucksack while he takes the cracked leather chair and the gramophone. Finally they find the bus stop. He stands there at the edge of the road, waiting, while she sits crossed-legged on the leather chair.

When the bus finally comes, they squeeze all of their things into the luggage compartment. She hurries up to the upper deck, runs almost. He follows her.

Leaving the city feels strange to him. He doesn't quite dare to let go. He sits down beside her but keeps turning around all the time. The road twists and turns. She holds his hand. Hers is cold, he notices, not the least bit sweaty, the way it usually is. He asks if she can tell him about the place again, describe the mud and the nuclear power plant. After a while he stops looking back, and looks ahead instead, until the bumps in the road rock him to sleep.

Without realizing that they have been closed, he opens his eyes, eager to experience the same things as her. She is still holding his hand. He can feel a prickling sensation in it. He pulls it away, shaking his bluish-white fingers. The bus is no longer moving. The driver is reading an old newspaper, mumbling the television listings out loud to himself and drinking coffee from a child's thermos, the colors of which have almost completely faded away. She hurries off the bus, impatient now, and he follows behind her, as usual.

Autumn, in Dungeness:
The first night in the boathouse they sleep on the floor, on top of their clothes. He is unable to get comfortable, lies on his side, on his stomach, on his back, restless. Nudges up against her many times. He can't bear to look at her sleeping with her eyes open, can't bear that she looks at him without noticing him. He wants to take off his jacket and cover her face. Instead he closes her eyelids as if she were a corpse.

When he finally falls asleep, he is awakened immediately by her shaking him, eagerly. Sunlight is filtering into the room; it penetrates through his eyelids and forces him to open them. He is confused, doesn't know where he is. He sees her get to her feet. She has bruises all over her body, her cheeks are red and his jacket has made funny stripes on her skin. Barefoot, she steps on some fish bones, dry as tinder, opens all the windows. The sound of the ocean, of seagulls, natural sounds that he can't find words for, overwhelm him. He asks if she must absolutely have the windows open. She is trying to air out the moldy and abandoned atmosphere, she explains, and gives him her hand. She says that she wants to make the place their own, that the odors they are carrying have to permeate the walls. He feels weary and dull. A little afraid. But she pulls him up.

They walk out into the mud by the ocean that she has told him so much about. It is warm for this time of year. His ears are like snail shells, absorbing everything left unsaid. And she, with drops of salt water in her hair, is blissfully withdrawn.

They go their separate ways, without noticing it. Many hours later they meet up again, by chance, down by the shore: two silhouettes in the darkness. The only light is from the beam of the old lighthouse, sweeping across the flat landscape from time to time. They fumble after each other's hands. Find them finally. He tells her that he has bought a mattress, a duvet, pillows and bedding. That it's all at home waiting for them. She smiles so the crooked line down to her mouth almost curls. He cannot remember having seen her smile like that before. They frighten him a little, all these new things. She finds some broken rushes on the ground, picks them up, braids them together and hands it to him. Perhaps they can hang it on the front door, she suggests. He holds tightly onto the rush braid so it won't blow away. The wind teases around their heads. Her white hair almost covers her entire face. He likes her this way, a little wild, a little crazy. And he feels dizzy from so much fresh air.

They walk on in the twilight. Away from the ocean. On the side of the road there is a pyramid made of children's shoes. He stops. Looks around, nervous for a moment. The lights are out in the few houses that can be seen along the narrow road.

"It's very quiet here," he says. "It's quiet everywhere."

She takes hold of his hand again and pulls him along. Explains that she needs external calm in order to cultivate her internal disorders. Asks whether he has seen any people today, apart from in the store.

He thinks about it, then he points toward an almost completely overgrown path.

"At the start of the path there were two young girls sitting on the ground and playing with a rusty rifle. A middle-aged man was walking behind them, bent over and looking for earthworms. The sisters were both beautiful red-heads and undoubtedly resembled their ugly father, except that his repulsive genes had been carried to their extreme in them and made attractive."

He thinks some more but nothing else comes out.

She draws him with her down towards the ocean again. There she takes off her shoes. He does as she does: lets his toes sink into the mud. The sky is full of stars. She shows him Orion: blinded in punishment for love, his sight was restored by staring into the whites of the Sun's eyes. He asks if they shouldn't go home and go to bed.

The mattress is placed in the middle of the room. The bedding is black, like a hole that sucks you in, he thinks, and likes that it's a little disturbing, sinister almost. She, on the other hand, says that this blackness, this darkness, illuminates her skin, her thoughts. She says that she loves the feeling of lying down in new bedding, on a new mattress, under a new duvet. Like the day before, she falls asleep almost immediately, while he lies awake. He looks at the white back of her head. She turns over and hits him unintentionally. He strikes back at her, but she pays him no heed. Then he finally relaxes, lets go. Sleeps. He dreams that her old friend rings from the flat in the city and asks if they've had sex in the boathouse yet. He creeps closer to her. Imagines taking her in every way possible, that she rides him until he cramps. But she doesn't touch him; her body, bleeding and moody, has no patience for him tonight. Instead he kisses her and, the taste of menstruation on his tongue, masturbates. She doesn't wake up. She sleeps like a rock on this night and for many of the following nights. Deeply.

It takes him a while to get used to her here. For a long time he wakes up unsure of where he is, with the city still in his gut.

Nonetheless, slowly, he settles in, puts down roots. The sounds from the window in the morning, in the evening: birds singing, wind, rain, the sound of the ocean, of the weather, and once in a great while, people, footsteps; and even more seldom, conversations, words. All of this, he learns to like.

Dungeness:
She has forgotten why they are there.

"Why isn't important," he says. "As long as you are with somebody like me."

He feels as if he has never had such an important role in his own life as he does now.

She eats blueberries that stain her teeth, lips and hands. She reminds him of a young child, or of somebody dying. He doesn't know which is more suitable. All the same, he enjoys watching her lick her fingers, sucking them, one by one, with her blueberry-blue tongue.

She says that her teeth were the first thing that started growing on her, then her legs, before her hair and, finally, her breasts. But never at the same time. He observes her eyes while she is talking. And he discovers now, for the first time, that her eyelashes go all the way around her eyes, even in the tiny corners reserved for tears. They remind him of the work of a spider, or of a spider itself. He fears that if he looks at them for too long, he will be caught and eaten like an insect. A fly, maybe. So he never looks for too long, only on the sly, when she has forgotten that he is there.

He remembers how much his body had been in pain during puberty. His genitals ached for almost a year; his shoulders, legs, torso. But the pain was the most intense where his awareness was. Where it still is.

Dungeness:

A car comes driving up. It reminds her of the city, of people who come creeping, like insects. The car is a tiny dot that she watches, following its progress until it grows large and familiar.

A yellow car. A Volkswagen Beetle.

Often, when she has a new man, her mother comes to call, that's just how it is. She's almost a little hurt that her mother hasn't come before. She recognizes it now; she has been waiting for this encounter. She asks him to make her feel welcome, doesn't explain why, puts on her rubber boots and goes out the back door, out in the mud.

Her mother jumps out of the car. She seems happy to see him, even though they don't know each other. He looks at this strange woman with familiar facial features. Her grayish-white hair is pulled back tightly, and she has wrinkles at the corners of her mouth and around her eyes. He looks at these eyes. They are light, almost translucent, like a blind person's. And with eyelashes all the way round, just like her daughter's. He tries to look away, to disengage, but is unable to keep from staring.

Her mother doesn't seem surprised that her daughter isn't there. That astonishes him. He tells her his name. Many times. Her mother laughs. She promises not to forget. He shows her around. There's not much to show. They left most of their things behind in the city. And the few things that he insisted on bringing, like the vinyl records, he doesn't listen to anymore, just as she had predicted. He hadn't understood it then; that the ocean foaming, the insects, yes, even some odors; that these were the things that would set the tone for their existence. And in a strange way he likes this material emptiness, the feeling of having just moved in. He likes it because it was her choice. Because she's so beautiful when she gets her way.

He explains, makes excuses, mostly to himself. It's chilly in the boathouse. They sit down in front of the front door. The sun is shining, uninhibited. Her mother looks at it. He notices that her armpits are sweating. There are two dark stains on the fabric of her synthetic top. He doesn't know what to say, so he talks a steady stream.

He says: "On one single day you can experience many different kinds of light, many colors."

He claims that it's because the place is so flat, because the sky covers it like a lid. Beneath the lid, behind windows, behind masks, are the Dungeness people. Many of them resemble one another just a bit too much.

He shows her mother a garden made of broken tools, fishing gear, seashells, snail shells, stones, driftwood, local plants, shrubbery and all manner of available rubbish. He can see that her mother is not paying attention. That her thoughts are elsewhere. With her daughter, perhaps. He wonders where she is, until he catches sight of her in the ocean. She is wading further and further out.

Suicide: The best way to take one's own life is to cut along an artery with something sharp, then lie down in a bathtub full of hot water and wait for the blood, thoughts, and time to run out, for the body to fill up with something other than fear.

He goes inside. He doesn't feel like saying anything more today, his throat is dry. Her mother follows behind. He makes coffee for her, even though she says she prefers tea.

She looks at him for a long time.

She says: "You're trapped, aren't you?"

He looks down, takes a large gulp of coffee, burns his tongue, keeps the words inside of him, swallows. Her mother also takes a sip, then she calmly holds out her cup. He has to keep refilling it all the time. She has a lot to say that he doesn't want to hear. He wants to ask her to stop, but instead he asks her to continue. He goes to stand by the window. Sees her daughter in the ocean, still. She is going to get sick, he thinks, he hopes, and takes yet another sip of his coffee. He is unable to follow what her mother is saying. Like talking over a faulty telephone connection, his replies are always a little delayed. She doesn't appear to be concerned about it. Instead she takes a stack of cards out of her handbag and puts them on the floor in front of her. From the corner of his eye he sees that she draws a card, then another. Her hands are shaking. The place darkens. He closes his eyes.

Finally her mother leaves. Without having seen her daughter. And when she comes back from the ocean, she doesn't ask any questions about her mother either.

Dungeness:

She is sitting in the cracked leather chair in front of the window. At first he almost thinks that she's asleep: were it not for the fact that her eyes were so different, wide open, almost frighteningly so, were it not for the fact that her mouth was moving, making sounds, telling him things. He puts his hand on her forehead. She has a fever, is sweating. He likes how it affects her. The lethargy in her eyes.

"I saw a dog here the other day," she whispers. "About a week ago. A beautiful dog with a gray, almost green coat. But when I looked at its pecker, I discovered that it had no balls. Just some stitches from surgery."

He watches her while she speaks, eyes shiny, red. He wants to stick a needle in them so that all the liquid can seep out.

"Go on," he says.

"The dog, Takashi was its name, nuzzled the stitches, licked them. It seemed content. The dog's owner told me that he had it castrated to give it a longer life. It seemed as if he loved him, and the dog appeared satisfied, so I guess there was nothing wrong with what he'd done. The dog's owner said that when Takashi reached puberty, he became so obsessed with licking bitches that he didn't want to play anymore. That when he discovered his sexuality, he became boring. The dog's owner believed that the dog, in being castrated, would rediscover life, small pleasures, things that had nothing to do with sex. He told me that he personally also liked to lick pussy, that sometimes he'd been jealous of Takashi, of his lack of inhibitions."

"Go on," he repeats.

She closes her eyes to try and remember better.

"We went to the dog owner's house together. An old, wind-blown fishing hut. The half-rotten beams were painted copper red, but the paint had begun to flake off, like sunburned skin peeling. Inside, on a chair in the hallway, a woman sat reading a book. He said hello to her, then he went into the kitchen to make some tea. I followed him. While he was making the tea and chatting with the dog, he suddenly pulled me to him and started kissing me like a madman. Then he asked me to go into the living room, take off my knickers, lie down on the table and spread my legs. He said that he would come and join me in a few minutes."

She stops, uncertain of whether or not she should continue.

"Go on," he insists, without looking at her.

"I did what he said," she admits. "Obeyed him, like a dog would obey its master. I took off my knickers, lay down on the cold coffee table, on the white, slightly soiled tablecloth, with my bare ass. There were bread crumbs all around me and there was a half-empty bottle of wine. I waited. Heard him talking with the woman. He asked her if she liked the book. She said no, but that she would keep reading it all the same, since they had no other books in the house. Then he came in to join me, put his head between my thighs and started licking me."

Suddenly, she stops talking.

"Go on!"

"At one point the telephone rang. The dog's owner answered it, opened his fly and had a short conversation while I was sucking on his dick. Then we went back to the kitchen and drank Japanese smoked tea with the woman, who was still reading."

After this she doesn't say anything more for a while. She has already said more than she thinks he can handle.

The days pass but he is unable to get the story out of his head. One evening, when he is lying close to her in bed, he asks her to tell it again. Asks her to help him get a clearer picture. He wants to focus on the table, on how she was lying, her sensations. She pretends to be asleep, but in the morning she decides to talk. He slides his hand down into his shorts while she tells him what she saw from the coffee table, describes the huge windows with a view of the nuclear power plant, the stranded boats, everything he has come to love. And that Takashi, the dog, was watching them the whole time. She believes that the dog is now living out his sexuality through the owner. Because he had the most beautiful dick she has ever seen, almost purple. When she left, he promised to think about her for a while.

She admits: "For many days I could feel the tickling of his tongue."

She doesn't say any more, waits for a response from him.

There is almost no reaction whatsoever.

He takes his hand out of his shorts, lightly clears his throat and drinks a glass of water. It gets stuck in his throat. Tastes bitter.

"Thinking of something beautiful makes me sad," he says then, almost apologetically, and tries to kiss her, but it's as if his tongue is numb.

He then says that it's not what she thinks. What she has predicted. That despite what she might be imagining, he desires her, still.

Interlude:

He looks at her from the side and thinks that there is something he really likes about her, he's sure about that, but he can't remember what it is. Now it seems as if he has lost it. He has seen a man look at her, smiling. He thinks again that he has lost it, but that someone else has found it. Only when this someone loses it as well can she be his again.

Winter:

They hardly touch each other at all. The cold has settled in like a wall between them. Outside it's foggy. Fishing boats can be sensed in the distance. The wind howls. Indoors, she makes up short, erotic stories in an attempt to satisfy him. His hand moving in a steady and recognizable rhythm beneath his fly both excites and saddens her. She can feel his breath on the back of her neck while she is talking. She knows that he no longer feels any shame. That he is capable of imagining anything. She notices that he is tense, keyed up. That he likes what she says in a way that is painful. He tries to smile, but his lips are sore, especially the corners of his mouth. He takes out a jar of Vaseline and spreads it first on his mouth and then all over his face. Ever since he was a little boy he has used Vaseline to keep his skin soft. He spreads on a thick layer every night before going to bed. When he cries he spreads Vaseline under his eyes. She has often thought that must be why he doesn't have any wrinkles. She finds it ugly, almost frightening. She wants to see the marks from the joys and sorrows that life has given him. But his face is empty.

"I'm in an in-between stage," he explains, "where I should have been happy, but in fact I'm depressed. I can't really explain why I make myself so sick."

He asks whether she has seen the man with the dog again.

"No," she says.

But she admits that she has called a former lover and told him about the incident. It aroused him and he asked her to call him more often. When her desire for the dog owner becomes intolerable she does so.

He asks if she can tell him the story again, once more. She doesn't want to.

"Thinking about something sad makes me happy," he says then. "I know it's difficult to understand but that's the way I am."

Dungeness:
Far from the city. She can no longer remember how they met or why. Often she is out, elsewhere. She says she is going to the cinema, but there is no cinema in Dungeness. She travels far on the tiny little train to watch the big screen. She says that she feels comfortable in the dark. He never asks her about what she has seen. Instead he tries to get her attention, asks whether she likes his long hair. She doesn't.

So he picks up the scissors and walks down to the ocean. Outside it's cold and unpleasant, not the least bit beautiful. It's raining, it's sleeting, soon it will also be hailing. The wind sings in a faint voice. It sounds like a foreign language that he can't understand. All the buildings and boathouses are dark, with the exception of theirs. He closes his eyes, doesn't want to know how he's going to look after the shearing. His hair falls in large clumps into the ocean. His hands are frozen. He is sloppy, careless.

He returns to the boathouse. Running, almost. Finds her sitting in the cracked leather chair, her face towards the window. He whispers her name many times, but she doesn't turn around. He moves closer, stands in front of the window so that she can look at him with her wide-open eyes that he loves so dearly. But she is asleep. He closes her eyelids, takes firm hold of her sleep-laden body and carries her to bed. He takes off her clothes. His own as well. Then he lies down beside her.

When she wakes up the next day, she looks at him, looks at his short haircut, and starts missing his long hair.

Forgetting is a gradual process by which a memory is misplaced.

She forgets him as he is looking at her, every day a little more. He tries to tidy up her thoughts. He irons. All kinds of things. Folds edges into her knickers, stacks the newspapers in alphabetical order, rearranges the music by number of instruments, the feelings by date. But instead of clarifying things, he almost disappears, seated there in the cracked leather chair, straight legged with his ramrod back, freshly bathed body, neatly trimmed hair and cleansed skin. Forgotten.

Dungeness:
He takes her hand, holds her tightly, forces her to touch him: nose, cheekbones, nipples, dick.

She opens the door and goes outside. He follows her. He is filled with a sensation of heaviness, as if he were standing underwater with his pockets full of stones. He doesn't hear what she says, because she says nothing. He tugs at her white hair in despair. She puts up no resistance. Not even when he pushes her head down into the almost solid mud does she resist. He looks at her dirty face, full of scratches, unappetizing. He sees that she has streaks of mud on her lips. Sees a tiny insect crawl down under her sweater.

It is a cold winter. The chill penetrates the bones, into the brain. The tip of his nose is red, his earlobes too. When he opens his mouth, frost steams out of it, but not a sound. He wants to apologize, but is unable to. He thinks: bad things happen only when one tries to hide them. He slides his fingers under her clothes and down into the warm crack in her backside. Pushes them in so far that she closes her eyes. Only then does he pull them out, sniff them, stuff them into her mouth. He still has no reaction, erection, and this makes him lose his nerve. He tears off her skirt, long johns and knickers. Lets his own trousers drop to his knees, but can't get it up. Ashamed, he releases her. She picks her clothing up from the ground and disappears into the boathouse. He puts his trousers back on. Remains standing there, motionless, as she runs from one window to the next.

After a while she runs out again, dressed, wearing a woolly hat, a warm jacket, and a small, gray rucksack on her back. He wants to say something to her, but the only sounds that can be heard are from the birds in the sky, the waves of the ocean. She runs out across the beach, until he can no longer see her. The lighthouse illuminates the road, but she is gone.

His shame chases him into the boathouse. He observes that she has made a terrible mess. One of the dolls is gone. The closet doors are wide open and clothes have been strewn across the floor. He picks them up patiently, folds them and puts them back into the closet. He wants things to be nice and neat when she comes back. A cut-out picture of a little boy falls out of the back pocket of a pair of her trousers. He puts it in his breast pocket. Then he goes into the bathroom, removes the dirty toothbrush glass, replaces it with a clean one and puts two new toothbrushes in it. He wonders what else he can do to please her. He opens the refrigerator, takes out fish, butter, cheese, and milk. Then he takes flour, salt, and pepper out of the cupboard. He starts by cleaning the fish. While it is cooking, he crumbles the butter into the flour. He follows an old English recipe. When he is finished with his preparations, he puts the fish pie in the oven, at a very low heat. Waits. He sets the table for two. Opens a bottle of wine. Pours two glasses. Knocks back his, then hers.

He takes the fish pie out of the oven and eats his share. The rest he puts in the refrigerator for her. Eventually the wine bottle is empty, and outside it's just getting darker and darker. He looks at the stars, searches for Orion, and is unable to find it. An uneasiness fills him but he tries not to give in.

When he finally goes to bed, he leaves all of the lights on, so it will be easier for her to find her way back. All night long he lies squeezed up in the corner on his side of the mattress. While her side remains empty, cold.

A flat, barren landscape:
The next day he gets up bright and early. He looks at the thermometer, feels the temperature in his entire body. Wonders where she could have sought refuge in this cold. In a panic he runs out in the direction where he last saw her: along the beach, towards the nuclear power plant. He looks at all the fishing huts. Then he stops suddenly. Goes to stand in front of one that looks like all of the others, but that nonetheless stands out. It has been recently renovated, repainted. There is a ladder and a paint bucket by one of the walls. He wants to move closer to the window, but is afraid of what he will see: her, in there, somewhere, lying on the table maybe, wearing the green knee socks and her polka-dotted skirt. He imagines her splayed legs, the pink labia and white pubic hair. Suddenly he catches himself fantasising about a huge, hairy spider coming out of her pussy. He can imagine how it creeps out from between her labia, down onto the table, across the tablecloth, down the table leg, all the way to the floor. That the dog owner steps on it without even noticing; he has his head between her thighs.

He puts his cold fingers down his trousers, until he can no longer feel his body, his thoughts. He sees his reflection in the window. He walks to the front door, tries it. It's locked. Not a sound to be heard.

He walks home with head bowed. When he is almost at the boathouse, he glances up and sees that all the lights are on inside. He runs over, tears open the door, calls out enthusiastically. But everything is just as he left it.

He turns off the light, sits down in the cracked leather chair and stares vacantly out the window. It is only now that he is starting to realize that she may not come back. He is suddenly gripped by a terrible rage. He retrieves the rest of her things. Packs them in a suitcase.

Then he picks up the telephone and rings her mother. He asks what he should do. She doesn't say much, except that she warned him, told him that all of this was going to happen. Then she gives him a few telephone numbers. Says that her daughter is perhaps with one of these men. He thanks her, hangs up. Picks up the receiver again right away and starts dialing. Different male voices greet him. Nobody knows who he is, where she is. Finally he hears a voice that he recognizes. He asks her old friend if she is there, almost screams it. Imagines his large, powerful hands on her fragile body.

Before the friend can answer, he hangs up.

He goes out onto the front doorstep with her suitcase. Remains standing there for a while, staring, without knowing what he should do or where he should go.

A solar eclipse is when the moon passes in front of the sun and everything falls silent. There are no dogs barking, birds singing, leaves rustling, water rippling. Silence.

"We look the same in the dark," he mumbles gripping the handle of the suitcase tightly.

He hopes that she is somewhere nearby and can hear him.

He waits a little while. Then a little while longer. Before he goes inside. Puts her suitcase into the hall closet, goes into the bedroom, drags the mattress into a corner, lies down and pulls the duvet snugly up over his ears. When he was a little boy he could lie like this for days. As if he didn't exist.

Invisibility depends on the eye of the beholder. An object or a person can thus seem invisible without actually being so. But in the laws of physics, invisibility is defined as an object that does not reflect or absorb light. Accordingly, an invisible person must, of necessity, also be blind.

Interlude:

When he finally pulls the duvet down from his eyes again, he no longer knows what day it is. His back hurts, he is hungry and thirsty. He wraps himself up in the damp duvet, patters out into the kitchen, opens the refrigerator and drinks a glass of spoiled milk. Then he takes out the bread and makes himself a banana sandwich. Dry and brown. He eats standing up, looking out at the flat winter landscape: faded, as if there were almost no colors to be found at this time of year.

He wanders along the beach, looks up towards the buildings and the boathouses. Many of them are unoccupied at this time of year. Most people only come to Dungeness in the summertime, he has heard. But even then, apparently not very many come.

At home again, he goes into the kitchen, takes the moldy fish pie out of the refrigerator and tosses it into the dustbin. Then he moves the mattress from the corner of the bedroom back into the middle. As he is doing this, he catches sight of a spider web: the dust has attached itself to the sticky silk threads, dangling like streamers. He is about to wipe it away, but then decides to leave it. When the sun shines on it, it looks like a snow crystal.

He doesn't know what he is going to do with himself, so he starts taking an interest in the lives of others. He pokes around in the empty summer houses first. He usually finds the key under the doormat or a flowerpot. He loves this sensation of strangeness: the invasion of other people's privacy. The first thing he does is to remove the sheets from all the chairs and tables, pull back the curtains, open the windows wide, air out the abandoned and dusty atmosphere. In this way he makes himself at home — looks at their pictures, reads diaries and letters, writes short greetings in guest books, walks around in the slippers of strangers.

Once he spends the night in a strange bed. For the entire night he lies there with his heart pounding.

He just grows bolder and bolder. Soon he doesn't care whether the houses are empty or not. He has become his old self. Someone who hides in corners. Someone who goes unnoticed. It is the way he carries himself and lowers his gaze that enables him to get away with things.

The loneliness of Dungeness didn't bother him so much before. But now that it can no longer be shared with her, it feels intolerable. Nonetheless, he doesn't return to the city; he fears the loneliness among others even more.

He wades slowly in the ocean, collecting tiny, round stones that he puts in his pockets. He gets wet; the water seeps into his boots, his cold toes. He grows numb, turns back to the boathouse. Empty. Only a stray dog runs past. The stones rankle in his pockets. He pulls one out and looks at it. It's gray, with a hole in the middle that you can see right through. He holds it up to his eye. Feels how slippery it is. Squeezes it so hard that his hand almost stiffens.

He walks and walks. Up until he reaches the recently renovated fishing hut on the beach. He stops there. A flock of birds flies over the house. He looks at the formations they create. He would have liked to have been able to tell her how beautiful he thinks it is. He looks towards the boats as well, stranded, stuck in the frozen ground.

He is still holding the stone. Then he loosens his grip and throws it at the largest window. It makes only a hollow sound, before the stone drops to the ground. He waits. It's chilly out, but comfortably so. Soon it will be spring, he thinks, and with foreboding: the flowers that will grow out of the soil, the leaves on the trees sprouting and turning green, the birds of passage returning, everything that's nice. He thinks: then certainly the people will come too. He walks closer to the fishing hut. Tries to look in the windows, but the sunlight blinds him. He tries the door. It is still locked. He looks under the doormat, in all of the flowerpots, but finds no key.

Finally he goes home. Empties his pockets and lays the stones beside the porcelain doll. It stares at him. These doll's eyes that never release him make him feel ill. As if they want to blame him for the fact that the one doll was separated from the other.

He takes out the gramophone and blows the dust off the needle. Flips through his old vinyl records. Sinks down into the cracked leather chair as muted classical music plays in the background. He is waiting for his shamefully shorn hair to grow out again. He looks down at his balls.

Dungeness:
After she disappeared her mother started coming to call. He likes sitting by the window, waiting for the yellow Volkswagen Beetle to come driving up. He prepares coffee or tea. Slices a cheesecake; he

bakes it according to her recipe, which calls for a thick layer of blue-berries on top. He combs out his short hair.

He likes looking at her mother. Her skin is full of wrinkles, as if it had been carved with a knife. In the wrinkles he searches for marks that could have been caused by her daughter.

She looks at him, smiles a brittle, yearning smile.

She says: "You have begun to resemble her, too."

He looks away. She pulls him along into the bathroom. She shows him in the mirror how his eyelashes also go all the way around, even in the tiny corners reserved for tears. His cheekbones as well seem more prominent than before, and he now has a crooked line running down to his mouth.

He thinks that her mother is visiting him so frequently now be-cause he is the closest she can get to her daughter. For her mother has not heard anything either. They are united in this loss. This anger. This lack, this longing, perhaps.

Spring:

One day her mother opens the suitcase and puts on her daughter's clothes: the green knee socks, the polka-dotted skirt. He stands there passively, watching as she walks out the door, down to the sea, in her stocking feet.

He goes into the bedroom and looks at the spider's web. This is something that he does often. Now a fly is entangled in it. He studies it: how the tiny, transparent wings are beating, how it is struggling. The silk threads are dusty and almost not sticky at all any longer. Af-ter a while it succeeds in disentangling itself and flies away.

He looks out the window at her mother. She is walking along the beach in the green knee socks. From a distance there is almost no difference between mother and daughter. He feels something tug in-side him. The loss. That he grows hard, between his legs. Erect. How easily he is duped. He decides to succumb.

He pulls down his fly and lets his trousers fall to his knees. Her mother approaches. She looks at him, asks him to put his trousers back on, asks if there is anything that she can do. He shakes his head, thinking sadly that she looks old.

Her mother walks up towards the boathouse. Finds a hoe and works a bit in the garden. He trots behind her, like a dog, perches on the doorstep and gives her some of the round stones with a hole in the middle. She decorates with them.

After a while she sits down on the front doorstep with him. They look at the flat landscape, endless and threatening, like a memory. They look at the ocean. Empty without her. The sound of wind, of weather, of fishermen. They look at the nuclear power plant, at the lighthouse, at everything she was fond of.

Her mother says: "It was meant to be that you would only have a short period of time together. You loved her also because you were going to lose her. I am certain of that."

TRANSLATED FROM NORWEGIAN
BY DIANE OATLEY

AUTHOR BIOGRAPHIES

SOFIA ANDRUKHOVYCH, born in 1982 in Ivano-Frankivsk, Ukraine, is a writer, translator and publicist. Her prose works include *Milena's summer* (2002), *Old people* (2003), *Their men's women* (2005), *Siomga* (2007), and *Felix Austria* (2014). She has been awarded the prestigious Smoloskyp magazine award and was co-editor of *Czetwer* magazine. She has translated from Polish and English.

NICOLAS ANCION was born in 1971 in Liège, and studied Roman Philology at the University of Liège. He has written fiction for readers of all ages, as well as drama and poetry. He won the Prix Rossel des Jeunes for his novel, *The 35 Billion Euro Man*. Ancion has used the Internet as a medium for public writing for performance, writing two novels publicly online, first in 2010, and again in 2013, both within 24 hours. Having previously lived in Montreal, Brussels and Madrid, he is now based in France, near Carcassonne.

ARMEN OF ARMENIA (Armen Ohanyan) was born in 1979. He launched his literary career at 30, creating innovative-experimental works of Armenian, Interactive Prose. His short stories "The Return of Kikos" and "Superstar Mario" have won local literary prizes, while his first collection of short stories, published in 2013 under the title *The Return of Kikos*, brought the author wide recognition in his country.

BALŠA BRKOVIĆ, novelist, short-story writer, poet, and book and theater critic, was born in Podgorica in 1966, and studied General Literature and Theory of Literature at Belgrade University. He has been the editor of the influential Montenegrin daily, *Vijesti*, since its foundation in 1997. Brkovic has published five books of poetry— *Horses Eat Peaches, Silvery Filip, Saint Mary's Cape, Contrapposto*, and *Parting*—and a book of short stories, *Berlin's Circle*. With his novels *Private Gallery, Paranoia in Podgorica* and *Imelda Marcos Beach*, he gained popularity with a wider audience and with critics, with *Private Gallery* winning the state award Book Of Miroslav.

MATJAŽ BRULC was born in Novo Mesto, Slovenia in 1976. In 2002 he graduated in art history at the University of Ljubljana. Since the late nineties he has worked as a freelance journalist and art critic for various media, writing mostly about contemporary visual arts and culture. He's also active as an art curator, producer and event manager. He has published two books of short prose: *Diznilend* and *Kakor da se ne bi zgodilo nič*, as well as a book of poems entitled *Balade za psa in prhljaj*. His short prose has been published in various magazines, has received awards in Slovenia and has been translated into German, English and Croat. He lives and works between Novo Mesto and Ljubljana, Slovenia.

AIXA DE LA CRUZ (born in Bilbao, Basque Country, in 1988) is author of the novels *Cuando fuimos los mejores* and *De música ligera*. Her work has also been included in the anthologies, *Mi madre es un pez, Última Temporada, Bajo Treinta*, and *Presencia Humana #2*. As a playwright, her dramatic text *I Don't Like Mondays* was shortlisted for the Madrid Sur and Margarita Xirgú awards and premiered in Mexico in 2012 in the context of the International Week of Young Playwrights in Monterrey. At present, she is a researcher at Universidad del País Vasco, where she studies the representation of torture in television fiction after 9/11.

SIMON DECKERT was born in Austria and brought up in Liechtenstein. He studied English literature and philosophy at the University of Zurich, and Literary Writing at the Swiss Literature Institute in Biel. He has worked for the International Book and Literary Book Festival of Basel and was part of the Artist-in-Residence Program of KulturKontakt Austria and the Austrian Federal Ministry for Education, Arts and Culture. Since March 2014, he has lived in Bern, working as a writer, tutor and freelance journalist.

ADDA DJØRUP (born 1972) is one of Denmark's foremost new voices. Her first book was the collection of poetry *Monsieurs monologer*, followed in 2007 by the collection *Hvis man begyndte at spørge sig selv*, in which her BEF 2015 story 'Birds' appears. Her third book, the novel *Den mindste modstand* received the European Union Prize for Literature 2010. Adda Djørup's most recent work is the collection of poems *37 postkort*, which was published in 2011.

ZDRAVKA EVTIMOVA was born in Bulgaria, where she lives and works as a literary translator from English, French and German. Her short stories have appeared in thirty-one countries worldwide. Her short-story collections published in English include *Bitter Sky, Somebody Else, Miss Daniella, Pale and Other Postmodern Bulgarian Stories, Carts and Other Stories, Impossibly Blue*, and *Endless July*. She has published two novels: *God of Traitors* and *Sinfonia Bulgarica*.

BIRUTĖ JONUŠKAITĖ is a novelist, poet and journalist. She has published five short-story collections, five novels, two books of essays, a book of poetry, and one novella for children. She has also translated a number of Polish authors, such as Czeslaw Milosz and Jacek Dehnel, into Lithuanian. Her awards include the Antanas Jonynas Award for the best prose work of the year, and the Petras Cvirka Award for best short-story collection, and the Witold Hulewicz Prize for her work in bringing Polish and Lithuanian literature closer together. Translations of her work include a German version of the short-story cycle *Jahreszeiten*, her book for young adults, *The Curious Story of Levukas*, (Belarusian), and a collection of her short stories, *Tylus žydėjimas* (Georgian). Since 2003 she has held the post of vice-president of the Lithuanian Writers' Union.

TUOMAS KYRÖ (born 1974) is one of the most versatile, prolific, and acclaimed Finnish authors of his generation. He has written novels, columns and plays, and drawn comics and cartoons. His recent works include *Long Live the King, The Beggar and the Hare, Griped,*

Parts 1 and 2 and the children's book *Santa's Bad Day.* He is also a regular panelist on the Finnish version of the internationally famed television panel show *Have I Got News for You.*

PEDRO LENZ (born in 1965 in Langenthal) is highly regarded both for his spoken-word performances and his writing in dialect. His best known work *Der Goalie bin ig* was the first (and to date, only) novel written in dialect to be shortlisted for the Swiss Book Prize — and has been translated into standard German, French, Italian, Lithuanian and the vernacular of Glasgow (where Pedro spent a six-month residency in 2005 which was to impact greatly on his work). Donal McLaughlin's translation, *naw much of a talker* appeared in September 2013. Arabic and Hungarian translations are forthcoming, and an award-winning film adaptation was released in December 2013. Pedro's eight books to date include *Liebesgschichte,* written — as the spelling of the title reflects — in dialect; a collection of poems; and a spoof guide to provincial literature (*Das Kleine Lexikon der Provinzliteratur*).

KAJA MALANOWSKA is a writer, columnist, geneticist, and teacher. She has published two novels: *Little follies of everyday life* and *Look at me, Klara!* and a book of short stories *Immigrations.* Her debut was nominated for the Gwarancje kultury award, and her latest book was shortlisted for the Nike, which is the most prestigious Polish literary award. She also writes a bi-weekly column for the Internet magazine *Daily Opinion,* and works as a teacher with refugee children. She holds a PhD in bacterial genetics from the University of Illinois at Urbana-Champaign.

DIEGO MARANI was born in Ferrara, Italy in 1959. He has worked as a translator at the EU Council of Ministers and as policy officer at the EC Direction General for Culture. He now works for the EC Direction General for Interpretation, where he is in charge of international cooperation, training and support for universities. He has published many novels and essays, including *New Finnish Grammar,* which received the Grinzane-Cavour prize in Italy, and *The last of the Vostyaks,* which received the Campiello prize in Italy. His books have been translated into several languages. He is also the inventor of the mock language, Europanto, in which he has written newspaper columns and the collection of short stories *Las adventuras des inspector Cabillot*. He is also a columnist, blogger and commentator.

MANUEL JORGE MARMELO was born in Porto in 1971. He started his career as a journalist in 1989, working for the daily national newspaper *Publico*, and in 1996 achieved an honorable mention at the Prémios Gazeta de Jornalismo of the Clube de Jornalismo. His first book *O Homem que Julgou Morrer de Amor* launched the series *Campo de Estreia*. His novel *Uma Mentira Mil Vezes Repetida* won the prestigious Correntes d'Escritas Prize in 2014.

OLGA MARTYNOVA was born in 1962 in Dudinka, Krasnoyarsk Krai, Russia. She is a Russian-German writer, writing poems in Russian, and poems, prose and essays in German, and has received numerous awards and prizes. Her poetry collections in Russian include: *Postup 'yanvarskikh sadov, Sumas`shedshiy kuznechik, Chetyre vremeni nochi, Frantsuzskaia biblioteka*, and *O Vvedenskom. O Chvirike i Chvirke/Issledovaniya v stikhakh*. In German she has published poetry, essays, book reviews and the novels *Sogar Papageien überleben uns* and *Mörikes Schlüsselbein*.

CHRISTOPHER MEREDITH is a novelist, poet and translator, born in Tredegar, Wales. He works mainly in English, though he has written a short book for children in Welsh, as well as some poetry. His first, novel *Shifts*, won the Welsh Arts Council fiction prize and was recently nominated for the title of greatest-ever Welsh novel by the Wales Arts Review. *Griffri*, the "autobiography" of a 12th-century poet, was shortlisted for the Book of the Year. His most recent novel is *The Book of Idiots*, and his most recent poetry collection is *Air Histories*.

MICHEÁL Ó CONGHAILE was born in Co. Galway, Ireland in 1962. He has published poetry, short stories, a novel, plays, a novella and translations. Among his awards are the Butler Literary Award, the Stewart Parker/BBC Ulster Award, multiple Oireachtas awards and a Writers Week/Listowel Award. His books include *An Fear a Phléasc, Sna Fir, An Fear nach nDéanann Gáire, Cúigear Chonamara, The Connemara Five* and *The Colours of Man*. His works have been translated into various languages, and An Taibhdhearc has produced three of his plays. He is a member of Aosdána, was writer in Residence at Queen's University Belfast and at the University of Ulster at Coleraine, and received an honorary degree from NUI Galway in 2013. His novella, *Rambling Jack*, will be published by Dalkey Archive Press in 2015.

RĂZVAN PETRESCU was born in 1956. His first book of short stories, *The Summer Garden,* appeared in 1989. Since 1990, he has worked as an editor for a number of Romanian literary periodicals and publishing houses. His second collection, *Eclipse,* was published in 1993, followed by two plays, *The Joke* and *Springtime at the Bar,* and a third book of short stories, *On Friday Afternoon*. He currently works for the Bucharest publishers Curtea Veche, and is a frequent contributor to the Romanian literary and cultural press. *Foxtrot XX*, a collection of mainly non-fiction prose, was published in 2008, and his latest book, *Variations On A Theme By Vater-Puccini*, a collection of interviews-in-prose, appeared in 2013.

EDY POPPY was born in 1975 in Norway. In 2005 she published her first novel *Anatomy. Monotony.*, which was translated into Italian, Finnish, German and Polish. It won the contest for best love story by Gyldendal, Norway's oldest and most renowned publishing house. In 2011 the short-story collection *Coming.Apart* was published, with *Dungeness* as the opening story, the English translation of which appears in this anthology. Edy Poppy is currently based in Oslo, working on several theater plays and her next novel, *Dark.Room*.

ALEKSANDAR PROKOPIEV, born in 1953 in Skopje, is a Macedonian writer, essayist and a former rock-and-roll musician. His short stories, essays and poetry have been translated into English, French, Italian, Japanese, Russian, Polish, Hungarian, Czech, Slovak and other languages and include: *The Young Master of the Game, Sailing South, A Sermon on the Snake, Was Callimachus a Post-Modernist?, Fairytale on the Road*, *Ars amater-ia*, *Image Which Rolls*, the diary *Anti-instructions for Personal Uwwwwwse*, and the novel *Voayer.* His story collection *Homunkulus* won the Balkanica prize for best book of the year.

REIN RAUD was born in Tallinn, Estonia in 1961. He graduated from the Oriental Faculty of the St. Petersburg (then Leningrad) University in 1985, earned a PhD from the University of Helsinki in 1994, and has since worked in various academic capacities. He has published fourteen books of fiction and poetry in addition to numerous translations from various languages, and academic work, mainly on comparative philosophy and East Asian literatures. He has been awarded various Estonian literary prizes, including the Cultural Endowment Annual Best Book Award, which he has received twice, for *Hector and Bernard*, and for *The Reconstruction*. Raud's work has been translated into German, French, Russian, Finnish and Lithuanian.

VEDRANA RUDAN is a Croatian blogger and novelist, whose books have been widely translated and adapted for the stage. Her popular blog, *How to die stress-free*, covers issues ranging from politics and gender relations to personal stories from Vedrana's life.

MIKHAIL ALEXANDROVICH TARKOVSKY is a Russian poet and writer. After graduating from the Moscow Pedagogical Institute he left for Siberia, where he worked first as a field zoologist, and later as a hunter. He is the author of short stories, novels and essays, including *Poems*, *Five Years Before Happiness*, *Frozen Time*, *Yenisei, let me go!*, and *Favorites*. He has won several literary awards, including the Yasnaya Polyana Prize, named after Leo N. Tolstoy.

EKATERINA TOGONIDZE was born in 1981 in Tbilisi, Georgia, and is a writer and journalist. She has published short stoies in several collections, including 'Theft' and 'It's me,' the story that appears in English in this anthology. Her short novel, *The other w-a-y* (2013) won Best Story Of The Year in Georgia in 2012, and her short-story collection *Anestezia* won Best Debut award at the 2012 Saba Annual Literary Competition. *The other w-a-y* has been translated into German.

JOHN TOOMEY grew up in Dublin. He is the author of two published novels. *Sleepwalker* was published first by Somerville Press, then by Dalkey Archive. His second novel, *Huddleston Road,* was published by Dalkey Archive Press in 2012. He has recently completed his third novel, *Slipping.* Extracts from both of his published novels, as well as essays, short stories, and a very early draft of the opening to *Slipping,* can be found on his website: *www.johntoomeybooks.com.*

KRISTĪNE ULBERGA was born in 1979 in Riga, Latvia. Her first book was *I Don't Read Books,* and it was included in school reading programs and translated into English. Shortly after, she published two other books for young adults: *The Virtual Angel* and *I Don't Read Books 2.* Some of her short stories also have been included in various contemporary fiction collections. Her last book, *The Green Crow,* an excerpt of which appears here, received the Raimonds Gerkens' prize.

JOANNA WALSH's work has been published by Granta, Tate, Salt (*Best British Short Stories*), *The White Review, Gorse, The Guardian, The London Review of Books* (online) and others. *Fractals* (short stories) is published by 3:AM Press. She is currently working on *Hotel.* She also runs the campaign #readwomen2014.

IBAN ZALDUA was born in San Sebastian in 1966 and lives in Vitoria, where he teaches Economic History. He has published short-story collections in Basque, including *Gezurrak, gezurrak, gezurrak, Itzalak, Etorkizuna,* which won the Euskadi Literature Award 2006, and *Biodiskografiak.* He has also published short stories in Spanish, *La isla de los antropólogos y otros relatos*; a novel in Spanish, *Si Sabino viviría*; and another in Basque, *Euskaldun guztion aberria.* He has written ten essays about Basque literature, including *Ese idioma raro y poderoso,* which won the Euskadi Essay Award 2013, and a comic book script and children's literature.

TRANSLATOR BIOGRAPHIES

KRISTIN ADDIS holds a Master's degree in Basque Linguistics and a Doctorate in Spanish Linguistics from Cornell University. She has worked for 15 years as a copy editor, and for 25 years as a translator. She translates between Spanish and English, and specializes in direct translation from Basque to English and in translations of works about the Basque language and culture. She has spent many years in the Basque Country; but currently resides in Iowa with her family.

MARTIN AITKEN's many translations of Danish fiction include books by Peter Høeg, Dorthe Nors and Helle Helle. His translation of Kim Leine's acclaimed *The Prophets of Eternal Fjord* will be published in the USA by Norton in 2015. His work has also appeared in a host of journals and magazines, among them *The New Yorker, Harper's Magazine, A Public Space* and *AGNI*. A recipient of the American-Scandinavian Foundation's Nadia Christensen Translation Prize in 2012, he lives and works in rural Denmark.

UILLEAM BLACKER is a lecturer at the School of Slavonic and East European Studies, University College London. He has written widely on contemporary Ukrainian, Russian and Polish literature and culture, and has translated the work of several contemporary Ukrainian authors.

ALISTAIR IAN BLYTH was born in Sunderland, England, attended the universities of Cambridge and Durham, and has lived in Romania for fifteen years. He translates fiction, poetry and philosophy by authors from Romania and the Republic of Moldova.

NATALIA BUKIA-PETERS is a translator and teacher of Georgian and Russian. She is a translator for the Poetry Translation Centre in London and a member of the Chartered Institute of Linguists, and translates a variety of literature, poetry and magazine articles. Her published translations include *Sex for Fridge* by Zurab Lezhava and the poem *Giacomo Ponti* by Dato Magradze.

THOMAS BUNSTEAD was a British Centre for Literary Translation mentee in 2011-12, working under Margaret Jull Costa. Since then he has translated and co-translated several novels from the Spanish, including work by Eduardo Halfon, Yuri Herrera, Rodrigo Fresán and Enrique Vila-Matas. A guest editor for *Words Without Borders* (Mexico feature, January 2015), he also writes for *The Paris Review Blog*, the *TLS*, the *Independent on Sunday*, *3ammagazine*, *>kill author* and *The Quarterly Conversation*. @thom_bunn

ELLEN ELIAS-BURSAĆ has been translating novels and non-fiction by Bosnian, Croatian, and Serbian writers since the 1980s, including writing by David Albahari, Neda Miranda Blaževic, Daša Drndic, Antun Šoljan, Dubravka Ugrešic, and Karim Zaimovic. ALTA's National Translation Award was given to her translation of Albahari's novel *Götz and Meyer* in 2006.

VICTORIA FIELD is a writer and poetry therapist who lives in Canterbury, UK. She has been co-translating from the Georgian with Natalia Bukia-Peters for the past five years. Her new play *Benson* was show-cased at The Marlowe Theatre in 2014 and her most recent poetry collection is *The Lost Boys* (2013, Waterloo Press). Her fiction and poetry have been broadcast on BBC Radio. She has co-edited three books on therapeutic writing and is considered a pioneer in the field.

WILL FIRTH was born in 1965 in Newcastle, Australia. He studied German and Slavic languages in Canberra, Zagreb, and Moscow. Since 1991 he has been living in Berlin, Germany, where he works as a freelance translator of literature and the humanities. He translates from Russian, Macedonian, and all variants of Serbo-Croat.

MARGITA GAILTIS was born in Riga, Latvia, and grew up in Canada. In 1998 she returned to Latvia to work on a Canadian International Development Agency-sponsored project translating Latvian laws into English. Her poetry has been published in Canada and the US, and she is the recipient of Ontario Arts and Canada Council Awards. In 2011, she was awarded the Order of the Three Stars by the President of Latvia.

DOMINIC GOURD has a degree in Latin American Studies and a postgraduate diploma in translation. He has a keen interest in contemporary Portuguese and Brazilian fiction. He has lived in Brazil since 2006.

ANDREA GREGOVICH's translations have appeared in *Tin House, AGNI Review, Hayden's Ferry Review, 3:AM Magazine, BODY, Guernica, Café Irreal* and several anthologies. Her translation of Vladimir Kozlov's story "Politics" represented Belarus in Best European Fiction 2014. She lives in Anchorage, Alaska, where she is writing a book about her grandfather, an infamous Arizona cowboy who was one of the first pilots in history to experiment with cloud seeding.

ELIZABETH HARRIS has translated fiction by Italian authors such as Giulio Mozzi, Marco Candida, Domenico Starnone, Mario Rigoni Stern, Antonio Tabucchi, and others. Her translated books include Rigoni Stern's novel *Giacomo's Seasons* (Autumn Hill Books) and Mozzi's story collection *This Is the Garden* (Open Letter Books). For her translation of Tabucchi's *Tristano Dies* (forthcoming, Archipelago Books), she received a Banff Centre Translation Residency and a PEN/Heim Fund Grant. Her translations have also appeared in BEF 2010 and BEF 2011.

ALEXANDER HERTICH is an Associate Professor of French at Bradley University. His translation of René Belletto's *Dying*, which was a finalist for the French-American Foundation Annual Translation Prize, was published by Dalkey Archive Press in 2010. In addition to translating, he has written about Jean-Philippe Toussaint, Raymond Queneau, and other modern French novelists.

ANNA HYDE (Anna Blasiak) translates from English to Polish (mostly children's and young people's fiction) and from Polish to English (fiction, art exhibition catalogues, film subtitles). Her first book-length translation into English—Mariusz Czubaj's crime novel *21:37*—was published in 2013 by London-based Stork Press. The same year saw the publication of her translation of children's story *Pam-Pam-Pam* by Jerzy Szczudlik (Wydawnictwo ElSet). She has worked in museums and a radio station, ran magazines, written on art, film and theatre and published some poetry.

MATTHEW HYDE is a translator of fiction and non-fiction from Russian and Estonian. After studying Russian and politics, he worked for 15 years for the British Government, as a translator, research analyst, and diplomat, with postings in London, Moscow and Tallinn (as Deputy Head of Mission). He now lives in Tallinn, where he plays the double bass and translates.

MARLON JONES grew up in California, has lived in Lille and Montpellier, and currently lives in the UK with his wife and son. He has translated works by authors including Céline, François Cusset, and Marielle Macé. His translation of *The Dance of a Sham* by Paul Emond was published by Dalkey Archive Press in 2014.

DUSTIN LOVETT studied comparative literature and translation at the University of Illinois and the University of Vienna. In 2010 he was the recipient of a fellowship from the American Literary Translators' Association and a Fulbright grant to research translation methodology. His translations have appeared in BEF 2010, 2011, and 2012.

DONAL MCLAUGHLIN featured as an author and a translator in BEF 2012. In 2014, Dalkey published both his new collection of stories—*beheading the virgin mary & other stories*—and his translation of Arno Camenisch's *The Alp*.   donalmclaughlin.wordpress.com

REBECCA MCMULLAN lives in Dublin, Ireland. She is a freelance translator and editor, and a PhD student in the Department of Germanic Studies at Trinity College, Dublin. Her research interests are contemporary Swiss literature and identity studies, particularly the literature of Christian Kracht.

HAIK J. MOVSISIAN is a translator, editor, and educator. He was born in Yerevan, Armenia in 1977 and moved to the United States in 1994, where he has lived most of his life. He has two Master of Arts degrees, one in English Literature and the other in Applied Linguistics, from California State University, Los Angeles. He has also attended Cornell University and New York University. He has taught English in universities and colleges across the US, including Santa Monica College and California State University, Northridge. He is married and has a son.

DIANE OATLEY has an MA in comparative literature (Anglo-American and Scandinavian traditions of the novel) from the University of Oslo, with areas of specialization in gender issues and expressions of the body in language. She is an independent scholar, writer, and translator. Born and raised in the US, since 2005 she has divided her time between Oslo, Norway and Jerez de la Frontera in Andalucia, Spain, where she is studying Flamenco.

LOCHLAINN Ó TUAIRISG is from Cois Fharraige in Conamara. He works as an editor with Cló Iar-Chonnacht.

DOUG ROBINSON is Dean of the Arts Faculty at Hong Kong Baptist University. He is the author of numerous literary and dramatic translations from Finnish, a novel written in English and translated into Finnish by Kimmo Lilja (*Pentinpeijaiset, Avain,* Helsinki, 2007), scholarly books, textbooks, and a Finnish-English dictionary.

SUNČAN PATRICK STONE was born in 1971 in London, UK, and lives in Ljubljana, Slovenia. He started translating during his student years and has since translated a myriad of works, from scientific books and articles to poetry and children books. He is also a photographer and has held over 15 solo exhibitions and participated in almost 20 group exhibitions in Europe and Australia. Some also know him as a writer, performer, conceptual artist and DJ.

ADRIAN WEST is the translator of several books of poetry and fiction, including Pere Gimferrer's *Alma Venus* and Josef Winkler's *When the Time Comes*. His essays, stories, and shorter translations have appeared in numerous journals in print and online, including *McSweeney's*, *Words Without Borders*, and *3:AM*.

JAYDE WILL is a translator of Lithuanian, Latvian, Estonian and Russian literature. His most recent translations include short stories and excerpts for the *Dedalus Book of Lithuanian Literature*. He has also translated subtitles for Lithuanian films, including the award-winning *Vanishing Waves* and *The Age of Milosz*, and has been involved in several poetry installations as both a translator and performer. He is currently working on a translation of Ričardas Gavelis' *Memoirs of a Young Man*.

ACKNOWLEDGMENTS

ACKNOWLEDGMENTS

PUBLICATION OF BEST EUROPEAN FICTION 2015 was made possible by generous support from the following cultural agencies and embassies:

Armenian Literature Foundation

Books from Lithuania

Cultural Services of the French Embassy

DGLB — The General Directorate for Books and Libraries / Portugal

Elizabeth Kostova Foundation for Creative Writing

Embassy of Spain, Washington D.C.

Estonian Literature Centre

Etxepare Basque Institute

Fédération Wallonie-Bruxelles

FILI — Finnish Literature Exchange

Georgian National Book Centre and the Ministry of Culture
and Monument Protection of Georgia

Kulturstyrelsen — The Danish Agency for Culture

Latvian Literature Centre

Liechtensteinische Landesverwaltung

Macedonian Ministry of Culture

NORLA — Norwegian Literature Abroad, Fiction & Nonfiction

Polish Cultural Institute

Polish Book Institute

Pro Helvetia, Swiss Arts Council

Welsh Book Council

Armenian Literature Foundation
50a/1 Mashtots Ave, 0009
Yerevan, Armenia
info@literature.am
www.literature.am

**ARMENIAN
LITERATURE
FOUNDATION**

PURPOSE

❡ The establishment of the foundation ensures international recognition of and access to Armenian literature

MISSION

❡ Promote Armenian literature worldwide

❡ Disseminate information on Armenian literature locally and worldwide

❡ Give grants to international publishers for the translation of Armenian literature

❡ Organize book fairs, professional development training, seminars and other business meetings for writers, publishers, translators and other professionals

DGLAB – *promoting Portuguese literature abroad*

DIRECÇÃO-GERAL
DO LIVRO E DAS
BIBLIOTECAS

For more than 20 years, the DGLAB has funded the translation of over 1700 works of Portuguese literature into 56 languages around the world

The DGLAB – Directorate for Books, Archives and Libraries – is under the auspices of the Portuguese Secretary of State for Culture. It coordinates the Portuguese system of archives and runs the public libraries network. It also coordinates an integrated policy for books and reading promotion which includes the dissemination of Portuguese literature abroad.

For further information:
internacional@dglab.gov.pt http://livro.dglab.gov.pt

PROMOTING & FUNDING
POLISH LITERATURE
IN TRANSLATION

www.polishculture.org.uk

Supporting Vibrant Expression:
Liechtenstein's Office for Cultural Affairs

Liechtenstein's participation in this publication was made possible
through funding from Liechtenstein's Office for Cultural Affairs.
As part of the Ministry for Foreign Affairs, Education and Culture,
the Office for Cultural Affairs is, among other activities, in charge
of supporting Liechtenstein arts, including its dynamic literary
community. Cultural projects in and from Liechtenstein are a
vibrant expression of the freedom of spirit found in the country.

To learn more about Liechtenstein, please visit
www.liechtenstein.li

AMT FÜR KULTUR
FÜRSTENTUM LIECHTENSTEIN

Government of the Principality of Liechtenstein
Office for Cultural Affairs
Peter-Kaiser-Platz 2, P.O. Box 684
9490 Vaduz, Liechtenstein
T: +423 236 63 40 / info.aku@llv.li

RIGHTS AND PERMISSIONS

319

MICHAL AJVAZ, *The Golden Age.*
The Other City.

PIERRE ALBERT-BIROT, *Grabinoulor.*

YUZ ALESHKOVSKY, *Kangaroo.*

FELIPE ALFAU, *Chromos. Locos.*

IVAN ÂNGELO, *The Celebration.*
The Tower of Glass.

ANTÓNIO LOBO ANTUNES, *Knowledge of Hell.*
The Splendor of Portugal.

ALAIN ARIAS-MISSON, *Theater of Incest.*

JOHN ASHBERY & JAMES SCHUYLER,
A Nest of Ninnies.

ROBERT ASHLEY, *Perfect Lives.*

GABRIELA AVIGUR-ROTEM, *Heatwave and Crazy Birds.*

DJUNA BARNES, *Ladies Almanack.*
Ryder.

JOHN BARTH, *Letters. Sabbatical.*

DONALD BARTHELME, *The King.*
Paradise.

SVETISLAV BASARA, *Chinese Letter.*

MIQUEL BAUÇÀ, *The Siege in the Room.*

RENÉ BELLETTO, *Dying.*

MAREK BIENCZYK, *Transparency.*

ANDREI BITOV, *Pushkin House.*

ANDREJ BLATNIK, *You Do Understand.*

LOUIS PAUL BOON, *Chapel Road.*
My Little War.
Summer in Termuren.

ROGER BOYLAN, *Killoyle.*

IGNÁCIO DE LOYOLA BRANDÃO, *Zero.*
Anonymous Celebrity.

BONNIE BREMSER, *Troia: Mexican Memoirs.*

CHRISTINE BROOKE-ROSE,
Amalgamemnon.

BRIGID BROPHY, *In Transit.*

GERALD L. BRUNS, *Modern Poetry and the Idea of Language.*

GABRIELLE BURTON, *Heartbreak Hotel.*

MICHEL BUTOR, *Degrees. Mobile.*

G. CABRERA INFANTE, *Infante's Inferno.*
Three Trapped Tigers.

ARNO CAMENISCH, *The Alp.*

JULIETA CAMPOS, *The Fear of Losing Eurydice.*

ANNE CARSON, *Eros the Bittersweet.*

ORLY CASTEL-BLOOM, *Dolly City.*

LOUIS-FERDINAND CÉLINE, *North.*
Rigadoon.
Castle to Castle.
Conversations with Professor Y.
London Bridge.
Normance.

MARIE CHAIX, *The Laurels of Lake Constance.*

HUGO CHARTERIS, *The Tide Is Right.*

ERIC CHEVILLARD, *Demolishing Nisard.*
The Author and Me.

MARC CHOLODENKO, *Mordechai Schamz.*

JOSHUA COHEN, *Witz.*

EMILY HOLMES COLEMAN, *The Shutter of Snow.*

ROBERT COOVER, *A Night at the Movies.*

STANLEY CRAWFORD, *Log of the S.S. The Mrs Unguentine.*
Some Instructions to My Wife.

S.D. CHROSTOWSKA, *Permission.*

RENÉ CREVEL, *Putting My Foot in It.*

RALPH CUSACK, *Cadenza.*

NICHOLAS DELBANCO, *Sherbrookes.*
The Count of Concord.

NIGEL DENNIS, *Cards of Identity.*

PETER DIMOCK, *A Short Rhetoric for Leaving the Family.*
George Anderson.

ARIEL DORFMAN, *Konfidenz.*

COLEMAN DOWELL, *Island People.*
Too Much Flesh and Jabez.

ARKADII DRAGOMOSHCHENKO, *Dust.*

RIKKI DUCORNET, *Phosphor in Dreamland.*
The Complete Butcher's Tales.
The Jade Cabinet.
The Fountains of Neptune.

WILLIAM EASTLAKE, *The Bamboo Bed.*
Castle Keep.
Lyric of the Circle Heart.

JEAN ECHENOZ, *Chopin's Move.*

STANLEY ELKIN, *A Bad Man.*
Criers and Kibitzers, Kibitzers and Criers.
The Dick Gibson Show.
The Franchiser.

STANLEY ELKIN (cont.), *The Living End.*
Mrs. Ted Bliss.

FRANÇOIS EMMANUEL, *Invitation to a Voyage.*

SALVADOR ESPRIU, *Ariadne in the Grotesque Labyrinth.*

LESLIE A. FIEDLER, *Love and Death in the American Novel.*

JUAN FILLOY, *Op Oloop.*

ANDY FITCH, *Pop Poetics.*

GUSTAVE FLAUBERT, *Bouvard and Pécuchet.*

KASS FLEISHER, *Talking out of School.*

JON FOSSE, *Aliss at the Fire.*
Melancholy.
Melancholy II.

FORD MADOX FORD, *The March of Literature.*

MAX FRISCH, *I'm Not Stiller.*
Man in the Holocene.

CARLOS FUENTES, *Adam in Eden.*
Christopher Unborn.
Distant Relations.
Terra Nostra.
Where the Air Is Clear.

TAKEHIKO FUKUNAGA, *Flowers of Grass.*

WILLIAM GADDIS, JR., *The Recognitions.*

JANICE GALLOWAY, *Foreign Parts.*
The Trick Is to Keep Breathing.

WILLIAM H. GASS, *Cartesian Sonata and Other Novellas.*
The Tunnel.
Willie Masters' Lonesome Wife.

GÉRARD GAVARRY, *Hoppla! 1 2 3.*

ETIENNE GILSON, *The Arts of the Beautiful.*
Forms and Substances in the Arts.

C. S. GISCOMBE, *Giscome Road.*
Here.

DOUGLAS GLOVER, *Bad News of the Heart.*

WITOLD GOMBROWICZ, *A Kind of Testament.*

PAULO EMÍLIO SALES GOMES, *P's Three Women.*

GEORGI GOSPODINOV, *Natural Novel.*

JUAN GOYTISOLO, *Count Julian.*
Juan the Landless.
Makbara.

JUAN GOYTISOLO (cont.), *Marks of Identity.*

HENRY GREEN, *Back.*
Blindness.
Concluding.
Doting.
Nothing.

JACK GREEN, *Fire the Bastards!*

JIŘÍ GRUŠA, *The Questionnaire.*

MELA HARTWIG, *Am I a Redundant Human Being?*

JOHN HAWKES, *The Passion Artist.*
Whistlejacket.

ELIZABETH HEIGHWAY, ED., *Contemporary Georgian Fiction.*

ALEKSANDAR HEMON, ED., *Best European Fiction.*

AIDAN HIGGINS, *Balcony of Europe.*
Blind Man's Bluff.
Bornholm Night-Ferry.
Flotsam and Jetsam.
Langrishe, Go Down.
Scenes from a Receding Past.

KEIZO HINO, *Isle of Dreams.*

KAZUSHI HOSAKA, *Plainsong.*

ALDOUS HUXLEY, *Antic Hay.*
Crome Yellow.
Point Counter Point.
Those Barren Leaves.
Time Must Have a Stop.

NAOYUKI II, *The Shadow of a Blue Cat.*

GERT JONKE, *Awakening to the Great Sleep War.*
The Distant Sound.
Geometric Regional Novel.
Homage to Czerny.
The System of Vienna.

JACQUES JOUET, *Mountain R. Savage.*
Upstaged.

MIEKO KANAI, *The Word Book.*

YORAM KANIUK, *Life on Sandpaper.*

HUGH KENNER, *Flaubert.*
Joyce and Beckett: The Stoic Comedians.
Joyce's Voices.

DANILO KIŠ, *The Attic.*
Garden, Ashes.
The Lute and the Scars.
Psalm 44.
A Tomb for Boris Davidovich.

ANITA KONKKA, *A Fool's Paradise.*

GEORGE KONRÁD, *The City Builder.*

TADEUSZ KONWICKI, *A Minor Apocalypse.*
The Polish Complex.

MENIS KOUMANDAREAS, *Koula.*

ELAINE KRAF, *The Princess of 72nd Street.*

JIM KRUSOE, *Iceland.*

AYSE KULIN, *Farewell: A Mansion in Occupied Istanbul.*

EMILIO LASCANO TEGUI, *On Elegance While Sleeping.*

ERIC LAURRENT, *Do Not Touch.*

VIOLETTE LEDUC, *La Bâtarde.*

EDOUARD LEVÉ, *Autoportrait.*
Suicide.
Works.

MARIO LEVI, *Istanbul Was a Fairy Tale.*

DEBORAH LEVY, *Billy and Girl.*

JOSÉ LEZAMA LIMA, *Paradiso.*

ROSA LIKSOM, *Dark Paradise.*

OSMAN LINS, *Avalovara.*
The Queen of the Prisons of Greece.

ALF MAC LOCHLAINN, *Out of Focus.*
The Corpus in the Library.

RON LOEWINSOHN, *Magnetic Field(s).*

MINA LOY, *Stories and Essays of Mina Loy.*

J.M. MACHADO DE ASSIS, *Stories.*

MELISSA MALOUF, *More Than You Know.*

D. KEITH MANO, *Take Five.*

MICHELINE AHARONIAN MARCOM, *The Mirror in the Well.*
A Brief History of Yes.

BEN MARCUS, *The Age of Wire and String.*

WALLACE MARKFIELD, *Teitlebaum's Window.*
To an Early Grave.

DAVID MARKSON, *Reader's Block.*
Wittgenstein's Mistress.

CAROLE MASO, *AVA.*

LADISLAV MATEJKA & KRYSTYNA POMORSKA, EDS., *Readings in Russian Poetics: Formalist and Structuralist Views.*

HARRY MATHEWS, *Cigarettes.*
The Conversions.
The Human Country: New and Collected Stories.

HARRY MATHEWS (cont.), *The Journalist.*
My Life in CIA.
Singular Pleasures.
The Sinking of the Odradek.
Stadium.
Tlooth.

JOSEPH MCELROY, *Night Soul and Other Stories.*

DONAL MCLAUGHLIN, *beheading the virgin mary.*

ABDELWAHAB MEDDEB, *Talismano.*

GERHARD MEIER, *Isle of the Dead.*

HERMAN MELVILLE, *The Confidence-Man.*

AMANDA MICHALOPOULOU, *I'd Like.*

STEVEN MILLHAUSER, *The Barnum Museum.*
In the Penny Arcade.

RALPH J. MILLS, JR., *Essays on Poetry.*

MOMUS, *The Book of Jokes.*

CHRISTINE MONTALBETTI, *The Origin of Man.*
Western.

OLIVE MOORE, *Spleen.*

NICHOLAS MOSLEY, *Accident.*
Assassins.
Catastrophe Practice.
Experience and Religion.
A Garden of Trees.
Hopeful Monsters.
Imago Bird.
Impossible Object.
Inventing God.
Judith.
Look at the Dark.
Natalie Natalia.
Serpent.
Time at War.

WARREN MOTTE, *Fables of the Novel: French Fiction since 1990.*
Fiction Now: The French Novel in the 21st Century.
Oulipo: A Primer of Potential Literature.

GERALD MURNANE, *Barley Patch.*
Inland.

YVES NAVARRE, *Our Share of Time.*
Sweet Tooth.

DOROTHY NELSON, *In Night's City.*
Tar and Feathers.

ESHKOL NEVO, *Homesick.*

WILFRIDO D. NOLLEDO, *But for the Lovers.*

FLANN O'BRIEN, *At Swim-Two-Birds.*
The Best of Myles.
The Dalkey Archive.
The Hard Life.
The Poor Mouth.
The Third Policeman.

CLAUDE OLLIER, *The Mise-en-Scène.*
Wert and the Life Without End.

GIOVANNI ORELLI, *Walaschek's Dream.*

PATRIK OUŘEDNÍK, *Europeana.*
The Opportune Moment, 1855.

BORIS PAHOR, *Necropolis.*

FERNANDO DEL PASO, *News from the Empire.*
Palinuro of Mexico.

ROBERT PINGET, *The Inquisitory.*
Mahu or The Material.
Trio.

MANUEL PUIG, *Betrayed by Rita Hayworth.*
The Buenos Aires Affair.
Heartbreak Tango.

RAYMOND QUENEAU, *The Last Days.*
Odile.
Pierrot Mon Ami.
Saint Glinglin.

ANN QUIN, *Berg.*
Passages.
Three.
Tripticks.

ISHMAEL REED, *The Free-Lance Pallbearers.*
The Last Days of Louisiana Red.
Ishmael Reed: The Plays.
Juice!
Reckless Eyeballing.
The Terrible Threes.
The Terrible Twos.
Yellow Back Radio Broke-Down.

JASIA REICHARDT, *15 Journeys Warsaw to London.*

NOËLLE REVAZ, *With the Animals.*

JOÃO UBALDO RIBEIRO, *House of the Fortunate Buddhas.*

JEAN RICARDOU, *Place Names.*

RAINER MARIA RILKE, *The Notebooks of Malte Laurids Brigge.*

JULIÁN RÍOS, *The House of Ulysses.*
Larva: A Midsummer Night's Babel.
Poundemonium.
Procession of Shadows.

AUGUSTO ROA BASTOS, *I the Supreme.*

DANIËL ROBBERECHTS, *Arriving in Avignon.*

JEAN ROLIN, *The Explosion of the Radiator Hose.*

OLIVIER ROLIN, *Hotel Crystal.*

ALIX CLEO ROUBAUD, *Alix's Journal.*

JACQUES ROUBAUD, *The Form of a City Changes Faster, Alas, Than the Human Heart.*
The Great Fire of London.
Hortense in Exile.
Hortense is Abducted.
The Loop.
Mathematics: The Plurality of Worlds of Lewis.
The Princess Hoppy.
Some Thing Black.

RAYMOND ROUSSEL, *Impressions of Africa.*

VEDRANA RUDAN, *Night.*

STIG SÆTERBAKKEN, *Siamese.*
Self Control.
Through the Night.

LYDIE SALVAYRE, *The Company of Ghosts.*
The Lecture.
The Power of Flies.

LUIS RAFAEL SÁNCHEZ, *Macho Camacho's Beat.*

SEVERO SARDUY, *Cobra & Maitreya.*

NATHALIE SARRAUTE, *Do You Hear Them?*
Martereau.
The Planetarium.

ARNO SCHMIDT, *Collected Novellas.*
Collected Stories.
Nobodaddy's Children.
Two Novels.

ASAF SCHURR, *Motti.*

GAIL SCOTT, *My Paris.*

DAMION SEARLS, *What We Were Doing and Where We Were Going.*

JUNE AKERS SEESE, *Is This What Other Women Feel Too?*
What Waiting Really Means.

BERNARD SHARE, *Inish. Transit.*

VIKTOR SHKLOVSKY, *Bowstring.*
Knight's Move.
A Sentimental Journey: Memoirs
1917–1922.
Energy of Delusion: A Book on Plot.
Literature and Cinematography.
Theory of Prose.
Third Factory.
Zoo, or Letters Not about Love.

PIERRE SINIAC, *The Collaborators.*

KJERSTI A. SKOMSVOLD, *The Faster I*
Walk, the Smaller I am.

JOSEF ŠKVORECKÝ,
The Engineer of Human Souls.

GILBERT SORRENTINO, *Aberration*
of Starlight.
Blue Pastoral.
Crystal Vision.
Imaginative Qualities of Actual Things.
Mulligan Stew.
Pack of Lies.
Red the Fiend.
The Sky Changes.
Something Said.
Splendide-Hôtel.
Steelwork.
Under the Shadow.

W. M. SPACKMAN, *The Complete Fiction.*

ANDRZEJ STASIUK, *Dukla.*
Fado.

GERTRUDE STEIN, *The Making*
of Americans.
A Novel of Thank You.

GWEN LI SUI (ED.), *Telltale: 11 Stories.*

LARS SVENDSEN, *A Philosophy of Evil.*

PIOTR SZEWC, *Annihilation.*

GONÇALO M. TAVARES, *Jerusalem.*
Joseph Walser's Machine.
Learning to Pray in the Age of Technique.

LUCIAN DAN TEODOROVICI, *Our*
Circus Presents...

NIKANOR TERATOLOGEN, *Assisted*
Living.

STEFAN THEMERSON, *Hobson's Island.*
The Mystery of the Sardine.
Tom Harris.

TAEKO TOMIOKA, *Building Waves.*

JOHN TOOMEY, *Sleepwalker.*
Huddleston Road.

JEAN-PHILIPPE TOUSSAINT,
The Bathroom.
Monsieur.
Reticence.
Running Away.
Self-Portrait Abroad.
Television.
The Truth about Marie.

DUMITRU TSEPENEAG, *Hotel Europa.*
The Necessary Marriage.
Pigeon Post.
Vain Art of the Fugue.

ESTHER TUSQUETS, *Stranded.*

DUBRAVKA UGRESIC,
Lend Me Your Character.
Thank You for Not Reading.

TOR ULVEN, *Replacement.*

MATI UNT, *Brecht at Night.*
Diary of a Blood Donor.
Things in the Night.

ÁLVARO URIBE & OLIVIA SEARS, EDS.,
Best of Contemporary Mexican Fiction.

ELOY URROZ, *Friction.*
The Obstacles.

BUKET UZUNER, *I am Istanbul.*

LUISA VALENZUELA, *Dark Desires and*
the Others.
He Who Searches.

PAUL VERHAEGHEN, *Omega Minor.*

AGLAJA VETERANYI, *Why the Child is*
Cooking in the Polenta.

BORIS VIAN, *Heartsnatcher.*

LLORENÇ VILLALONGA, *The Dolls'*
Room.

TOOMAS VINT, *An Unending Landscape.*

IGOR VISHNEVETSKY, *Leningrad.*

ORNELA VORPSI, *The Country Where No*
One Ever Dies.

KEITH WALDROP, *Light While There Is*
Light

AUSTRYN WAINHOUSE, *Hedyphagetica.*

CURTIS WHITE, *America's Magic*
Mountain.
The Idea of Home.
Memories of My Father Watching TV.
Requiem.

DIANE WILLIAMS, *Excitability:*
Selected Stories.
Romancer Erector.

DOUGLAS WOOLF, *Wall to Wall*.
Ya! & John-Juan.
JAY WRIGHT, *Polynomials and Pollen*.
The Presentable Art of Reading Absence.
PHILIP WYLIE, *Generation of Vipers*.
MARGUERITE YOUNG, *Angel in
the Forest*.
Miss MacIntosh, My Darling.
REYOUNG, *Unbabbling*.
VLADO ŽABOT, *The Succubus*.
ZORAN ŽIVKOVIĆ , *Hidden Camera*.
LOUIS ZUKOFSKY, *Collected Fiction*.
VITOMIL ZUPAN, *Minuet for Guitar*.
SCOTT ZWIREN, *God Head*.

Praise for

BEST EUROPEAN FICTION 2015

"An appealingly diverse look at the Continent's fiction scene."
— *The New York Times*

"The work is vibrant, varied, sometimes downright odd. As [Zadie] Smith says [...]: 'I was educated in a largely Anglo-American library, and it is sometimes dull to stare at the same four walls all day.' Here's the antidote." — *Financial Times*

"With the new anthology *Best European Fiction* ... our literary world just got wider." — *Time Magazine*

"The collection's diverse range of styles includes more experimental works than a typical American anthology might."
— *Wall Street Journal*

"This is a precious opportunity to understand more deeply the obsessions, hopes and fears of each nation's literary psyche—a sort of international show-and-tell of the soul." — *The Guardian*

"Readers for whom the expression 'foreign literature' means the work of Canada's Alice Munro stand to have their eyes opened wide and their reading exposure exploded as they encounter works from places such as Croatia, Bulgaria, and Macedonia (and, yes, from more familiar terrain, such as Spain, the UK, and Russia)."
— *Booklist Starred Review*

"We can be thankful to have so many talented new voices to discover." — *Library Journal*

"There is sex, and there is history, and there is the uncanny." — *Gorse*

"[A] widely varied collection of stories by both emerging and established writers has been assembled." — *Irish Examiner*

"Has something for everyone." — *Irish Independent*

"A kaleidoscopic view of what is being written on the European continent today in a single anthology." — *The Millions*

"What the reader takes from them are not only the usual pleasures of fiction—the twists and turns of plot, chance to inhabit other lives, other ways of being—but new ways of thinking about how to tell a story." — Christopher Merrill, *PRI's "The World" Holiday Pick*

"The book tilts toward unconventional storytelling techniques. And while we've heard complaints about this before—why only translate the most difficult work coming out of Europe?—it makes sense here. The book isn't testing the boundaries, it's opening them up." — *Time Out Chicago*

"The English-language reading world, 'wherever it may be,' is grateful." — *The Believer*

"Does European literature exist? Of course it does, and this collection … proves it." — *The Independent*

BEST EUROPEAN FICTION 2015

Please see rights and permissions on page 319 for individual credits

ISBN 9781564789679
ISSN 2152 6672

Partially funded by the Illinois Arts Council, a state agency

Please see Acknowledgments on pages 313-317 for additional information
on the support received for this volume.

www.dalkeyarchive.com

Cover design by Gail Doobinin, composition by Mikhail Iliatov
Printed on permanent/durable acid-free paper

BEST

EUROPEAN

FICTION

2015

Preface by Enrique Vila-Matas

DALKEY ARCHIVE PRESS
Champaign / London / Dublin

Contents

CONTENTS